Keri Arthur, author of the *Ne~~~~~~~~~~~
Jenson Guardian series, has now ~~~~~~~~~~~
~~~~~ She'~ ~~~~~~~~~~~~~~~~~~~~~~~
~~~~~~~~~~~ Paranormal catego~~~~~~~~~
Reviewers Choice Awards and has w~~~~~~~~~~~ ~~~ievement
Award for urban fantasy. She lives with her daughter and two old
dogs in Melbourne, Australia.

Visit Keri Arthur online:
www.keriarthur.com
www.facebook.com/AuthorKeriArthur
www.twitter.com/kezarthur

By Keri Arthur

KERI ARTHUR

THE
BLACK
TIDE

piatkus

PIATKUS

First published in Great Britain in 2017 by Piatkus

1 3 5 7 9 10 8 6 4 2

A CIP catalogue record for this book
is available from the British Library.

ISBN 978-0-349-41826-1

Printed and bound in Great Britain by
CPI (UK) Ltd, Croydon, CR0 4YY

Papers used by Piatkus are from well-managed forests
and other responsible sources.

MIX
Paper from
responsible sources
FSC® C104740

Piatkus
An imprint of
Little, Brown Book Group
Carmelite House
50 Victoria Embankment
London EC4Y 0DZ

An Hachette UK Company
www.hachette.co.uk

www.littlebrown.co.uk

With thanks to the Miriam, The Lulus, The Central Vic Writers, and my gorgeous girl, Kasey.

CHAPTER ONE

SUNSHINE.

Bright, fierce sunshine.

It bathed my body, burned into my closed eyelids, and had sweat trickling down the side of my face. Only that sweat felt as warm as the sunlight and oddly sluggish.

I frowned and tried to open my eyes. Couldn't.

Panic stirred, along with an odd sense of urgency. I raised a hand, but the movement was not only as slow as that trickle, it hurt like hell.

I carefully touched my eyes; something sticky glued my lashes together. Further probing revealed a barely healed wound that slashed my forehead, and one I couldn't remember getting. In fact, the last thing I remembered was looking back at Jonas—a cat shifter who was, like me, a surviving relic from the war that had ended 103 years ago— as I'd stepped through the smaller of the two rifts we'd found at Winter Halo, a now-defunct Central City pharmaceutical company. It had played a key part in the mad scheme to give both vampires and the creatures we knew as wraiths immunity to light, and the scientists there had not only dissected the brains of women with latent psychic skills, but had been testing unapproved drugs and pathogens on children they'd stolen from Central City. We'd put a stop to the dissection, rescued seven of those children, and had now killed two of the three people behind the insidious plot. One of those had been Samuel Cohen—the man who'd assumed the identity of Rath Winter, the person in charge of Winter Halo, and whose death had, in my opinion, been far too quick given the pain he'd caused so many others. The other death was Sal's—a man who'd been a déchet like me, and someone I'd once considered my closest friend.

But two out of three was not good enough. We still had to stop Ciara Dream—the very elusive final member of that unholy trinity—before she managed to give either the vamps or wraiths full immunity.

Light—be it sunlight or the UV light that was cast from the huge towers that surrounded all cities, banishing both shadows and night—was currently the *only* thing protecting both human and shifter alike from the relentless attacks of either monster.

I scrubbed the muck away from my eyes and then opened them. The sky was an endless sea of blue. There were no clouds, no birds, no sign or sound of life.

I tried to sit upright, but pain surged and a hiss escaped through my clenched teeth. My entire body ached—even my damn hair felt like it was on fire.

Which I guess wasn't really surprising, given the rift I'd come through was one of the biggest I'd dared enter so far.

True rifts had come into being 103 years ago—after the shifters had unleashed the bombs that ended their five-year war against humanity. But such was the force of those bombs that they'd not only leveled entire cities, but had also torn drifting holes in the very fabric of our world. While a few of these were doorways between our world and another, most of them simply mauled the essence of anything and anyone unlucky enough to be caught in their path. For most, being ensnared in such a rift meant death. Those of us who survived were forever altered by the magic and the energy that were part and parcel of the rifts, though the consequences of Jonas's and my recent encounter with one had yet to be fully revealed.

But the two we'd found at Winter Halo weren't a result of the bombs. They were what we called false rifts, and had been created by the people behind the immunity scheme as a means of transportation from one point to another on *this* world.

It was my task to uncover where the damn things led to, simply because I—thanks to my rather unique DNA makeup—had the unfortunate luck of being the only other person outside those behind their creation able to both see *and* use them.

But doing so came at a cost—at least for someone like me, who wasn't "tuned" into them. The false rifts worked by breaking your body down to atoms before transporting you to the other end, where you were reformed and released. They did at least spit me out in one piece, but my state was very definitely bloody and worse for wear.

But why would this one dump me in the middle of nowhere? Every other false rift had at least led into a building of some kind; landing in the middle of a desert was definitely outside the norm.

I took a deep breath and rolled onto my stomach. Once again various bits of my body protested rather vigorously—something that wasn't helped by the grittiness that rubbed into the sorer spots. My clothes obviously hadn't come through the rift intact this time.

When the pain had eased again, I pushed up onto my hands and knees and studied my surroundings. There wasn't much to see—just a long flat plain of yellow sand. I had no idea where I was; as far as I knew, there were no deserts anywhere near Central City or its surrounds. But my knowledge of the world was somewhat limited to the areas I'd been assigned to during the war. I certainly hadn't traveled far after it. In fact, I'd basically spent the century since living in the remains of old military bunker outside Central, along with the ghosts of all those who'd been murdered there.

As a déchet—a lab-designed humanoid created by humans before the war as a means to combat the superior strength and speed of the shifters—I'd had little other choice. While the war might be a century past, the hatred and fear of déchet remained, even though I was now—at least as far as I knew—the sole survivor. Everyone else had been erased at the war's end.

I twisted around to check out what lay behind me. Twinges ran through my shoulders and torso, but it was nowhere near as bad as it had been only moments ago. My body seemed to be healing at a far faster rate than was normal for me, and I'd been genetically designed to recover quicker than either humans or shifters.

The false rift sat about forty feet away, a dark orb of oily energy that gently turned on its axis. There was no sign of the jagged strips of lightning that ran across its surface when active, but that really wasn't surprising. I wasn't close enough for it to recognize my presence, and I seriously doubted Dream would risk using it when Winter Halo's activities were currently under full investigation by both the corps and the council.

I pushed back onto my heels and took stock. The rift's whips had indeed shredded my uniform, but the two automatics and the spare magazines were still clipped to the remains of my pants. Both my backpack and the slender machine rifle—which I'd adapted to fire small, sharpened stakes rather than bullets—were missing. After another look around, I spotted the pack half buried in the sand about fifteen feet away. Relief stirred, and not just because that pack still had the rifle attached to it, but also because it held —amongst many other things—a small geo-locating device. Without it, I wouldn't be able to record my current location or where the base—or whatever else this rift had lead me to —was. Both were important, given my main mission here today was simply one of discovery. The task of dealing with the base—and whatever evils it might hold—would fall to Jonas, his mercenary partner and human witch Nuri, and whatever government forces they were working with. *Not* that they'd ever actually admitted to working with the government on this particular case.

Of course, I was also well equipped to deal with a worst-case scenario—such as the discovery that they were far further along the road of making wraith or vampire life forms immune to light than we'd hoped or feared.

I crawled over to the pack and pulled out the geo-locator. After inspecting it to ensure there was no damage, I pressed the switch to log my position and then grabbed the water bottle and quickly swished the metallic bitterness from my mouth.

A sound invaded the stillness. It was little more than a soft whine, but it was coming toward me at some speed. I turned around. A plume of dust was now visible on the horizon, though I couldn't yet see the vehicle causing it. Which was good, because if I couldn't see them, they more than likely wouldn't be able to see me.

And I needed to be sure it remained that way.

I stoppered the water bottle then raised my face and let the sunlight caress my skin. While the bits of vampire DNA in my makeup meant I was genetically adapted to night and shadows, there was still a part of me that needed the heat and life of the sun. It was *that* part that enabled me to disappear behind a shield of light. It wasn't magic, but rather a psychic talent, one that had been enhanced in the lab during my creation. And it wasn't the only talent they'd given me. Shifters might have hated and feared déchet soldiers, but we lures were far more deadly. Soldiers had strength and speed; we'd been built not only for seduction but with a veritable arsenal of both psychic and shifting skill sets at our command.

I took a deep breath then called to day's brightness, drawing it deep into my body in much the same manner as I could draw in darkness. Heat flowed into every muscle, every fiber until my entire being burned with the force of it. I imagined that force wrapping around me, forming a shield none would see past. Energy stirred as motes of light danced both through and around me, joining and growing until they'd formed the barrier I was imagining. To the outside world, I no longer existed. The light playing through me acted like a one-way mirror, reflecting all that was around me while hiding my presence.

I pushed to my feet and retreated as that plume of dust drew closer and the vehicle became visible. It was a hover, and military in design, but much older than anything I'd ever seen in Central City. For some reason, the blast shields at the front of the vehicle were up, which possibly meant they were relying on radar to guide them. If that was the case, then my light shield might be next to useless. I unlatched one of the automatics and held it at the ready.

The vehicle came to a halt twenty feet away, blasting me with dust and hot air as its skirts lost shape and it settled onto the sand.

There was no immediate indication that they'd seen me.

A door on the left side of the vehicle opened and a woman got out. She wore a combat uniform that was obviously designed for desert use, as the camouflage swirls were gray and gold rather than the black and gray of mine. A rather old-fashioned electro pulse rifle was strapped to her waist and an odd strip of thick black plastic wrapped around her head, completely covering her eyes.

My fingers twitched against the automatic, but I didn't move. I had no idea who these people were or how sensitive this woman's hearing might be. She smelled human, but that didn't mean anything when we were dealing with people who had the technology and the determination to alter DNA.

The woman took several steps away from the hover then stopped, one hand on the pulse rifle. Her banded gaze did a long sweep of the area, sliding past me without any indication she'd sensed my presence, and then returned to the rift.

Could she see it?

"Anything?" the man still inside the vehicle said.

"No." The woman's voice was curt. "If this is another false alarm, I'm going to be pissed."

The man snorted. "And? It's not like you'll say anything—not given how complaints are handled. Check the other side of the thing."

The woman grunted and obeyed. I quickly moved around the rift, making sure I kept enough distance between it and me to prevent activating the energy whips.

The woman reappeared and walked toward me. Her scent was unpleasant and acidic, but she nevertheless registered as human to my senses. If she *were* anything else, she surely would have smelled me by now. Or, at least, smelled the drying blood on my clothes.

But if she was human, then that also presented a problem. The scientists who'd designed us had made damn sure we could neither attack nor kill a human. I'd never actually tested *that* particular restriction before—it had never occurred to me to do so during the war, and there'd been no need in the 103 years after it.

She walked past me. I glanced at the rift; I couldn't see the hover, which meant that even if her partner had raised the blast shields, he wouldn't be able to see us. I flexed my fingers and then stepped up behind her. Though I'd been specifically designed to infiltrate shifter camps and seduce those in charge in order to gain and pass on all information relating to the war and their plans, I was no stranger to killing. Very few of the shifters I'd lain with had survived to tell the tale, but it was never something I'd done by choice—not until recently, at any rate.

But assuming this woman's identity was possibly the only way of uncovering what was going on in this desert with any sort of speed, and merely knocking her out wasn't really an option. I simply couldn't risk her coming to and raising the alarm.

I guess I was about to discover if old programming still held sway.

In one smooth motion, I covered her mouth with one hand and forced her head up and back with the other, shattering her neck and taking her life between one heartbeat and another.

And felt neither restriction nor remorse at doing so.

How could I, after what had been done to the children and the horrendous dissections that had happened at Winter Halo? Everyone involved in the mad scheme to provide light immunity to the vamps and the wraiths deserved nothing more than death.

Everyone.

I lowered her body to the ground then released the light

shield and quickly stripped her. Once I'd exchanged clothes, I shoved my two guns, the tracker, and the ammo into the backpack, and then strapped on her pulse rifle.

With that done, I bent down and studied the woman's face, fixing her sharp, thin features, lank yellow hair, and pale brown eyes in my mind. Her body shape was close enough to mine that I didn't have to do a full shift, but her features were so different that a facial change was necessary.

Once I had a firm grasp of the look I needed to attain, I reached for the part of my soul that made shifting possible. The force of the change swept through me like a gale, making my muscles tremble as my face restructured, and my skin, hair, and eyes changed. It was a process that was usually very painful, but this time, there was barely a flicker of protest from the nerve endings and bone structures being rerouted in the process.

"Banks?" the driver said. "Everything all right back there?"

"Yeah." Even though my vocal chords had been altered and I now sounded like the woman, I hadn't heard her speak enough to catch the rhythm of her words, and that meant keeping my replies short.

After a quick check to ensure there were no comm devices attached to the woman, I dug the Radio Frequency Identity chip out of her right arm and wiped it clean on the discarded remnants of my shirt. It was law these days that everyone, be they human or shifter, have RFIDs inserted into their arms at birth. They held everything from medical records, work history, and credit information, but could also be programmed for use as a key in areas that required secure access. I currently had two of them—one inserted into each arm—thanks to Nuri and the fact I'd assumed two very different identities in Central.

I grabbed the small tin of false skin out of the pack, positioned the chip over the one in my right arm, and then sprayed it into place. Jonas had assured me it would be undetectable and, after a few seconds, it was indeed hard to tell where my skin ended and the false skin began.

Finally, I unlatched her eye device and put it on. The world became nothing but a strange blur. I fiddled with the dial on the right side of the visor; turning it one way sharpened focus, allowing me to see the terrain but not the rift. Turning it the other made the rift jump into focus but threw everything else into an odd sort of darkness.

That was the reason she'd seen the rift, but not me.

"Banks, stop fucking about and get back here," the driver said. "That sandstorm we spotted is getting far too close for comfort. We need to get out of here."

"Give me a minute—I've got to dig the thing out."

I set the eye device to normal vision, quickly shoved enough sand over the woman's body to cover her, and then grabbed the pack and headed for the hover.

"Is that it?" The driver—a thin, wiry looking man with dark skin and a shock of coarse yellow-white hair—pointed with his chin at the backpack. "That hardly seems worth the time and effort to retrieve it."

"Yeah." I dumped the pack into the foot well then climbed into the vehicle.

"Did you open it?"

"You can. I'm not."

He grunted and returned his attention to the craft. "Better hand it to Martin. He's paid to deal with the shit that comes through that rift, not us."

Meaning if I wanted to find out exactly what they were using this rift for, Martin needed to be my next target.

The hover's engines kicked into gear and her skirts began to fill and lift. I grabbed the seat belt and pulled it across my body, brushing my fingers against the driver's arm as I did so. Seeking was a psychic skill all lures had, and one that had made us very successful at uncovering information during the war. It wasn't exactly telepathy—shifters tended to be sensitive to that sort of mental intrusion—but rather the ability to see various memories as images. And while my seeking skills had been honed for use during sex, I could still snatch information from a brief touch if I went in with a simple question that needed answering.

Although in this particular case, I not only needed to know who Martin was but where we were going.

Pictures snapped into my mind, providing a glimpse of a thickset man with a flat nose and oddly shaped eyes, and what looked to be an intersecting series of round metal and sand tunnels. If the latter was part of an old military bunker, then it was one I'd never seen before.

"Are we going to beat the storm?" I asked.

He glanced at the radar and screwed his nose up. "It'll be nipping at our heels before we reach the compound, I think."

The hover slowly spun around, and then the big engines

kicked in and we rumbled forward. Thankfully, it was too damn loud in the cabin to allow much talking, so I looked through the door's small portal, trying to find something remotely familiar. But even the few stunted trees we passed bore no resemblance to anything I'd seen before.

The wind picked up, buffeting the big craft and sending it sliding sideways. The stabilizers kept us upright but from the little I knew of these types of hovers, they weren't designed for use in any sort of dust storm—a fact borne out a few seconds later when an amber light began to blink on the console. The intake valves were losing efficiency.

The driver responded by increasing our speed. Maybe he thought he could outrun the problem, even though the storm was a huge red mass that now dominated half the radar screen.

As a red light joined the amber one, the comms unit on the console crackled to life, and a harsh voice said, "Identify."

The driver hit a switch. "Pickup three, Lyle and Banks."

"Code?"

"Two-five-three-zero."

"Access granted, guidance on. Open in five."

Lyle punched another button on the console, switching to auto mode, and then leaned back. "It's going to be a bitch of a night to be on surface duty."

Which suggested we were headed underground, and that meant we might indeed be dealing with another old military base. The three bases in which we déchet had been created had certainly used the earth as protection and, though I hadn't seen any of them, I knew other human military installations had also buried their main centers deep.

The hover swung left and slowed. Up ahead, an odd sort of turret emerged from the ground. Sand poured off its domed top and slithered down its metal sides. As it rose higher, I realized it was some sort of elevator. Two guards wearing breathing apparatus stood on either side of the open doorway, but there didn't appear to be any cameras or scanners in the shadows beyond them—which didn't mean anything given my companion's comment. I might not be able to see any other security measures, but they were obviously around here somewhere.

The hover came to a halt and settled onto its skirts. The driver rolled the neck of his uniform up over his mouth and nose, then opened the doors and got out. I recorded my position then grabbed the pack and followed. The wind hit me immediately, throwing me several paces sideways before I could catch my balance. Sand stung my face and hands and felt like stones as it pounded my body. The air was so thick that I could barely see the hover, let alone the driver or the elevator. Then I remembered the eye visor and quickly flicked the switch. The world sprung into focus again.

I slung the pack over my shoulder and followed Lyle into the elevator. One guard stepped out into the storm and headed toward the vehicle. The other placed a rather gnarled-looking hand against the control panel; his prints were scanned and the elevator began to descend.

I returned the visor to normal vision and looked around. There definitely weren't any security measures aside from the guard, which was odd—just as there was something decidedly odd about the guard. While the breathing mask covered his entire face, his domed head was almost reptilian, and the stray tufts of pale yellow that poked out from the top looked more like the strands found on a wire brush than any sort of hair. His uniform was bulky and loose, giving little indication of his body shape, but his spine was so badly curved the top part of his body angled sharply away from his lower. His scent rather reminded me of meat left too long out in the sun, but the undertones were once again human in origin, even as his reptilian dome suggested otherwise.

Of course, smelling human didn't mean he was. We lures had been designed with the ability to alter our base scent, and if either Dream or Cohen were a surviving déchet scientist or a handler—as we now suspected at least one of them was—then they'd be aware of that skill.

The one thing this man couldn't be, however, was a surviving déchet—not when he was so deformed. The scientists involved in the Humanoid Development Program had been merciless; if a déchet had been imperfect in *any* way, they were killed and their DNA carefully studied to see what had gone wrong.

Which meant he was either a life form I'd never come across before—and surely nature could not be that cruel—or the trio had been playing around with DNA and pathogens far longer than we'd presumed.

And *that* was a scary thought.

The elevator continued to drop. I had no idea how deep we were going, as there were no level indicators. Maybe this base only had the one, although that would be rather unusual if it was another repurposed military base. Most did have several levels, if only for security reasons.

The elevator finally came to a bouncy stop. The guard pulled his hand away from the console and the doors opened, revealing a small landing and stairs that led down to a massive circular room with a domed ceiling supported by thick metal struts that arched across the space and met in the middle. There were five tunnels leading off it; the one directly opposite looked big enough to take large vehicles, but the other four were smaller in diameter. There was a multitude of wooden boxes and pallets of plastic-wrapped items stacked in haphazard piles, and rusty-looking forklifts were scooting about, some of them driving loads into the smaller tunnels and others returning from them. This area was obviously some sort of receiving bay.

What I didn't see were any sort of additional security measures. Did they believe the sand hid them so well nothing else was needed, or were the measures here, but simply very well disguised?

Instinct suggested the latter. And that presented a problem, given I couldn't get around what I couldn't see.

Lyle had paused at the bottom of the stairs to allow a forklift to pass, so I clattered down to catch up with him. "Where's Martin likely to be at this hour?"

"Where he always fucking is—in supplies." He made a vague motion toward the tunnels on the right then threw me a sour look. "And don't forget it's your shout at the bar tonight. No feigning illness again."

"Shout" wasn't a term I was familiar with but it obviously had something to do with drinking and alcohol. While shifters did drink, they didn't do it to excess, as the humans seemed to. Which was probably just as well given a drunken shifter could cause a whole lot more damage to flesh and furniture than a human ever could.

"Right," I said, and walked off.

Aside from the buzz of the forklifts, this place was strangely quiet. The yellowish lights dotting the dome high above lit some sections of the sandstone walls but cast others into shadow. The air was cool and somewhat stale, suggesting the purifiers weren't working at full capacity. Maybe that was why the guards had been wearing breathing apparatus—although it didn't explain why everyone else wasn't.

I reached the first of the two tunnels on this side of the room and paused. There was no guide to tell where it went, and the tunnel itself curved sharply away from the entrance, making it impossible to see what might lie up ahead. I moved on to check the other tunnel. It, too, was decidedly void of any useful information.

I pulled the small dart gun from the pack and then headed in. I couldn't afford to linger, given the woman I was impersonating would obviously know her way around this place. The last thing I needed was to attract unwanted attention.

Once again the ceiling lights were dull, creating smalls pools of yellow surrounded by shadows. There were no doors cut into the thick metal walls and no sound other than the soft echo of my steps.

Then, from somewhere up ahead, came a sound so soft human hearing wouldn't have caught it. It was nothing as clear as a footstep, but more a scrape, as if something had dragged briefly across the metal flooring. I frowned, my gaze sweeping the shadows, seeing nothing, sensing nothing.

The odd sound came again. Unease stirred, and my grip on the dart gun tightened as I continued on.

The noise echoed a third time. Tension wound through me, but I resisted the urge to stop. The tunnel began to curve to the right, and the shadows became thicker—so thick, in fact, that they chopped off the pool of light that puddled under-neath one of the overheads.

That darkness wasn't natural, I realized abruptly. It was someone hiding behind a shield of shadows. *That* was why this place was so oddly lit.

My fingers twitched against the dart's trigger, but I resisted the urge to fire and continued past that odd patch of dark-ness. Once I was sure there were no cameras or other guards hidden in the shadows further along the tunnel, I turned and fired. The drug on the dart's tip was fast acting. In little more than a couple of seconds, there was a soft clang as something—someone—hit the metal floor.

The shadows remained clustered around the guard, but a quick pat down revealed the presence of some sort of device connected to his chest plate by several wires. Once I broke that connection, the shadows evaporated, revealing him to be another of the masked guards. I pulled off his breathing apparatus; his features were a twisted mess that was half human and half reptilian, and his skin was brown with odd patches of scales that were almost fishlike.

Whatever else this man was, he *wasn't* a product of natural selection. He was either a rift survivor or a result of human engineering.

If the latter applied, then maybe the only reason Sal and his partners hadn't acted on their mad plans before now was the simple fact that they'd been unable to recreate the success of the déchet program. It also meant that these lizard men, however ill-formed, might not be the only ones successfully raised to adulthood.

He was beginning to wheeze, his body shuddering as he struggled to suck in enough air. Either his lungs were malformed or the weird mix of his DNA meant he simply couldn't survive on regular air. And while I had no desire to let him suffer any longer than necessary, I also needed information. I couldn't keep wandering around this place aimlessly. I hesitated, and then touched his face; his skin was cold, clammy, and unlike anything I'd ever felt before.

I shuddered, even as information began to flow. Within seconds I had a somewhat fractured mental map of the base; this tunnel led to the bunkhouse and the medical facilities, which was perhaps why my approach hadn't been challenged. The stock and supplies area was in the first tunnel, but it was the information on the largest tunnel that snagged my immediate attention. It apparently led to what the guard's memories simply knew as research and production.

I pushed a little deeper and caught various images of needles being injected into his arm. We knew the trio had been intent on developing a pathogen capable of altering a vampire's base physiology so that they no longer had to fear sunlight, but maybe they were also trying to find a shortcut to creating an army with the strength and speed of the déchet.

I could only hope that this poor man was an indication of how far they'd yet to go with the latter.

But maybe *that* was only because they were, unfortunately, a whole lot closer to achieving the former. The children they'd stolen—all of whom were either rift survivors or the children of survivors—had been their test subjects for such a pathogen. And at least one of those children—Jonas's niece, Penny—had recently developed vampire-like tendencies while showing no fear of light.

If they'd developed a pathogen capable of turning a shifter or a human into a vampire, how far off could they be from being able to do the reverse?

Not far at all, if the recent attack on Chaos—the ramshackle city that clung to Central's metal curtain wall—was any indication. Neither firelight nor regular light had affected the vampires who'd gone there to retrieve Penny, but at least the UVs had still turned them to ash.

I removed the spent dart from his arm then replaced his breathing apparatus and sat him upright against the wall. Hopefully, given his restless movements earlier, he'd put his collapse down to exhaustion and wouldn't report the incident. Even if he did, how likely was it that he'd connect his collapse to Banks, given it had happened after I'd walked past him?

I reattached the wires on his chest unit and, as the thick shadows wrapped around him again, thrust up and strode back down the tunnel. No one paid me any attention as I walked across the loading bay, but the minute I drew close to the entrance to the larger tunnel, a light flashed on, bathing the entire entrance in eye-watering brightness. A burly, pale-skinned man stepped forward and held out a small scanner.

"Present your chip, soldier."

I raised my right arm and watched as the screen flashed red.

"You haven't the clearance to proceed into this area," he growled.

"I know, but I've been ordered to take this bag to Martin."

The guard pointed with his chin at the tunnels behind me. "Martin is over in supplies, not here."

"And they told me I'd find him in research three."

My gaze swept the shadows hugging the other side of the entrance. There was a second guard standing watch, but the fierceness of the lights made it impossible to see what other security measures might be here. Which meant I *could* risk wrapping myself in light to sneak past them, but if there were bioscanners set into the walls of this entrance, I'd be in all sorts of trouble.

"If they said that, they're fucking idiots," he said.

"So, he really hasn't come through here?"

"No, but it wouldn't matter if he had, because your ass can go no further." The guard's tone was impatient. "So leave, before I decide to report you."

I didn't argue. I just spun on my heel and walked back to the tunnel that led to the supplies area, but stopped the minute the shadows wrapped around me again.

What in Rhea was I going to do now?

I crossed my arms and leaned against the wall, studying the loading bay and the movements of the various forklifts.

Rather interestingly, none of them went into the larger tunnel. In fact, right now they seemed to be doing nothing more than shifting the various pallets and boxes into a stack on one side of it. Given the tunnel was obviously designed to allow trucks passage, perhaps the intention was to transport it all at once rather than piecemeal.

But what was in those boxes, and where exactly were they being taken?

There was only one way to find the answer to either question. I pushed away from the wall and sucked in the energy of the shadows, just as I had the light earlier. It filtered swiftly through every inch of me until my whole body vibrated with the weight and power of it. The vampire within my DNA swiftly embraced that darkness, becoming one with it, until it stained my whole being and took over. It ripped away flesh, muscle, and bone, until I was nothing more than a cluster of matter. Even my clothes and the backpack became part of that energy.

Now that I was hidden from ordinary sight, I swept out of the tunnel but kept close to the wall and the shadows that hugged it. Light was the enemy of this form—while it would never harm me as it did the vampires, it could certainly tear away the shadows and revert me back to flesh and blood.

I slowed as I neared the stack of boxes. It wasn't exactly surprising to discover that most of them bore government and military IDs. Both Cohen and Dream had inherited the ability to body shift from Sal when the three of them *and* a wraith had been caught in a rift. While Cohen had taken over the identity of the man who'd owned and run Winter Halo, Dream had usurped the position of someone in Central's governing body. Unfortunately, we currently had no idea whether she merely worked in Government House, or if she was on the ruling council itself. I rather suspected the latter, if only because an audit would have surely picked up the amount of missing equipment and who knew what else lying in both these boxes and the ones I'd discovered at the other old military bases.

I detoured around a puddle of light to inspect the half dozen pallets stacked at the end of the boxes, and discovered the one thing I'd been hoping not to. Intrauterine pods. Six of them, in fact.

A deep sense of horror stirred. While I'd discovered similar pods in other bases, I'd thought—perhaps foolishly—that with the deaths of both Sal and Cohen, Dream would put aside that part of their plan and just concentrate on the immunity portion. But the transfer stamps on these pods held yesterday's date, which was two days *after* I'd exposed their machinations at Winter Halo.

Rhea help me, there could be *babies* in this place. Young-sters. Just as there'd been in my bunker when the shifters had unleashed the gas that had killed them all.

I took a deep, shuddering breath and tried to ignore the painful rush that always rose when I thought about that dreadful day. But the memories would not be ignored, and once again I witnessed the disintegrating features of the little ones who'd been in my charge, heard their screams as the Draccid gas that had been fed into our air systems ate at their tiny bodies. Could feel the weight of them in my arms as Cat, Bear, and I tried—and failed—to get them out of the nursery and save as many as we could.

We hadn't known it was useless, that there was no safety to

be found anywhere in the bunker. Not until the Draccid began eating at me, anyway, and Cat and Bear had crawled into my arms to die. I was the sole survivor that day, and only because lures had been designed to be immune to all known toxins and poisons. We had to be, because that's how we usually killed our targets once we'd bled them of information.

Tears stung my eyes, but it wasn't just the memories. It was the knowledge that if the déchet children who were being created in this place in *any* way contained wraith blood, then I would be forced to commit an act as unthinkable as what the shifters had done to the children in my bunker. It didn't matter if that death came to them now, while I was here, or later. Didn't matter if it was far kinder than the death the shifters had given to my little ones—the fact was, I'd be killing children when I'd sworn on that day so long ago to never, ever let harm befall a child if I could at all stop it.

I drew in another shuddering breath, then resolutely turned away from the pods and went back to the crates. To know for sure what I might be dealing with, I first had to get into the research area. My best chance of that was hitching a lift. While all the crates were well battened down, my energy form didn't actually need anything more than a small hole to squeeze through. After a quick search through the various stacks, I found a crate with a small knothole and slipped inside. It was jammed with smaller boxes, most of them seeming to contain various chemicals, none of which I was familiar with.

There was no room to regain flesh form, so I hovered in the

small, dark space and hoped I didn't have to wait too long before the crates were moved.

Eventually, the growing splutter of an old engine indicated a vehicle was finally approaching. Light speared through the small knothole and sent me scrambling backward, but it disappeared almost as quickly as it had appeared. Headlights, I realized. The truck must have been turning around. After another moment, gears ground and brakes squealed as the truck came to a halt. A door opened, and then a second engine started up, this one more a whine that spoke of an electrically powered vehicle.

One by one, the crates were loaded up, mine included. A quick check via the knothole revealed the pallets holding the pods were being placed into the truck. With that done, the tailgate was lifted into position, and a canvas curtain dropped back down, though not secured. I slipped out of the crate but didn't immediately regain flesh form, still worried about the possibility of biosensors hidden within the walls. There were some parts of my bunker—parts that had once only been accessible to our creators—that had certainly had them, as had the labs in the other old bunkers that Dream and her cohorts had been using.

The driver climbed back into the truck, and with the gears grinding in protest, the vehicle was soon rolling forward again. As we drove under the arch and into the tunnel, I peered past the curtain again. I'd guessed right—there were sensors. Given they hadn't gone off, they must have been tuned to flesh intrusion rather than matter.

The tunnel swept around to the right and darkness dominated for some time. I couldn't see any guards but I had no doubt there were. And if this tunnel *did* lead to the laboratories, there'd surely be other measures, too.

Gradually other sounds intruded over the rumble of the truck's engine, all of which suggested we were nearing a secondary loading dock.

Time to risk leaving the truck.

I slipped past the heavy canvas and moved to the thick shadows that lined the left wall. Up ahead, the tunnel gave way to a brightly lit circular receiving bay—although, just like the first one, there were still spots of darkness hugging the outer walls and the various exits. There were also people and forklifts everywhere, and plenty of visible guards. I stopped at the tunnel's mouth to get my bearings as the truck swung toward a small loading dock on the right. The information I'd taken from the guard's mind had been rather sketchy when it came to this area, but it didn't really matter. These tunnels were all signposted. The one I wanted—nursery and development—was the second tunnel on my left.

I flexed fingers that held no flesh and pushed away the trepidation that rose within me. It was no use fearing what I might yet have to do without first knowing if there was any reason for that fear.

I slipped around the corner and rose to the ceiling, where the shadows were thicker and there was less chance of guards—hidden or not—sensing my presence.

The entrance into the nursery tunnel was packed with sensors. Two guards stood on either side of the gateway, their expressions bored and stances relaxed. I hesitated, and then sped through the gate, pressing myself flat against the rooftop in an effort to avoid the biggest mass of sensors that lined either side of the tunnel.

No alarm sounded. Relief flowed through me, but it was a fleeting thing. The goddess Rhea might have favored my mission so far, but even *she* could only extend so much good fortune before the axe fell.

This tunnel, unlike the others, ran straight, and I sped along it, my fear and trepidation increasing the deeper I got.

In the distance, light flared. It wasn't the puddled yellow lighting that was everywhere else, but rather a bright light that held a bluish tinge. I knew that light. It was the same one they'd used in all the nurseries at my own bunker.

Please, please, don't let these nurseries be occupied....

The tunnel opened into a small antechamber. There were four metal doors leading off this, and above each was a simple number. There was no indication of what might lie beyond any of them, and all the windows were opaque. There were no cameras, either, and nothing to suggest this place was, in any way, being monitored.

Which was decidedly odd—and rather unnerving. Luck was a fickle thing at the best of times, and Jonas and I had certainly had our fair share of it over the last few days. I couldn't help feeling it was about to run out, and I could only hope that was born of fear and pessimism rather than instinct.

I halted in the shadows and listened for any indication that there was someone nearby. If they *were* breeding déchet, then there would have to be technicians and doctors here, at the very least, even if the place looked and felt empty.

After a moment, I heard a faint rasp—someone breathing a little too heavily. It came from the darkness hugging the right edge of the antechamber. I reformed my right hand then raised the dart gun and fired.

I waited, my gaze on the antechamber and the doors rather than the shadows. After a minute or so, there was a soft thump as the guard collapsed. Tension knotted my particles as I waited for some kind of reaction, but the silence stretched on, empty of both life and threat.

It shouldn't have been this easy to raid this place. Not after Sal's death and the loss of Winter Halo. Even Dream couldn't be so sure of this place's location and invisibility that she'd kept security at a minimum rather than ramp it up.

I released the shadows that hid me and regained form as I dropped to the ground. But as I stepped into the light and started to create a light shield, the door to my left slid open and a man stepped out. His gaze swept past me then abruptly returned. "What the hell are you doing here, soldier? This is a restricted area."

Though he was frowning, his expression was more annoyed than suspicious.

I quickly hid the dart gun behind my back. "I know, but I was ordered to bring this pack down to you. We retrieved it from the rift this morning."

"This is well outside usual protocol." His frown deepened as he motioned me forward. "Who gave you the order?"

"Martin."

"He hasn't the authority to issue such an order. Give me that pack immediately."

I stopped and held it out. As he took it, I surreptitiously fired. He must have felt it, because he immediately looked down, but thankfully the dart was hidden within the folds of his coat.

He opened the pack and pulled out the geo-locator. "Why the hell would Martin have sent this down here?"

I shrugged. "I'm just doing what I'm told. If you want answers, you'd best talk to him."

"And I will. You're dismissed, soldier."

He started walking back toward the room, but stumbled and would have fallen had not a second man—this one wearing a white medical coat—caught him as he exited the room.

"What the fuck?" he said. "Soldier, help me get him back into the lab, will you?"

I did. Once I was sure there was no one else in the room, I darted the second man. When he collapsed to the floor, I looked around.

There were no intrauterine devices and no cots in this lab, but my gut nevertheless twisted. It might not be a nursery, but I'd seen the equipment like this before and knew it to be a creations lab—the place where the DNA of tiny embryos was sliced and diced. I walked over to one of the many cryonic cylinders and unlatched the lid. Inside was a veritable test tube forest, all of them cells that could never be allowed to become anything more.

I closed my eyes for a second, the need to destroy the DNA within these tubes before they could become life warring with the knowledge that my main task here had to be uncovering how far along the creation scale these people were. The guards I'd ambushed certainly suggested they'd at least been partially successful in altering life, if not creating it, but lizard men who couldn't breathe without assistance weren't what Dream and her cohorts had been after. They wanted to erase the stain of humanity and shifter from this world. They wanted it to belong to the wraiths and vampires—the two races they now saw themselves as, thanks to rift intervention and at least one of them being a rare vampire survivor. And to do *that*, they needed a fighting force that could walk without fear in daylight.

But a creations lab generally *wasn't* a part of that process as far as I was aware. It was about life—or rather, the manipulation of it. I owed my existence to a lab such as this, but I'd been one of the lucky ones. I'd survived into adulthood, when hundreds, if not thousands, of others had not.

This place—and these cells—had to be destroyed. *Had* to be. But I had no doubt alarms would sound the minute I took any direct action to either destroy or otherwise interfere with the cylinders. I needed to uncover what other horrors might lie in the remaining laboratories before I decided what action—if any—I took next.

But not before I took some precautions. The feeling that my time was swiftly running out was growing, and I needed to ensure this place—and the other labs—was destroyed if the worst happened and I was either captured or killed.

I dug one of the RTX devices out of the pack and pressed it up into the bottom lip of the nearest table. Like all plastic explosives, this one was extremely pliable but had the advantage of the detonator being inbuilt. I linked it to the remote firing mechanism then called the light to me and walked out to the next lab. There was a security panel to the right of the door—one that was both a fingerprint *and* iris scanner. I swore and headed back to the first lab. While such security measures weren't surprising, it was neverthe-less frustrating. The longer I spent in this place, the more likely it was that my presence would be discovered.

I hauled the first man upright and half carried, half dragged him across the antechamber. I shoved one hand against the scanner then forced an eyelid open. The scanner did its work and the door opened.

The room beyond was large and bright, filled to the brim with medical equipment. There were also another two doors, one that led into an office and monitoring area, and another that led into a second lab. This room was also occu-pied. Not only were there three scientists and a guard, but also four rows of neonatal cribs and a final row of what could only be described as restraint cots. Any hope that they were all empty quickly died, not only because I could see small forms in the cots, but because the light screen monitors above each one were emitting the soft sound of heartbeats.

I let the scientist fall to the floor, half in and half out of the room, and then quickly stepped over him and moved to one side. My light shield shimmered slightly as it adjusted to the bluer light within the room, but none of the four people noticed—they were too busy looking at the unconscious scientist.

"Greg?" one of the other scientists said, then, when there was no response, swore and ran over. He bent and felt for a pulse, and then grunted. "Mark, help me get him into a chair. Betts, call the medics."

As the woman walked over to a comms unit and the two men picked up the drugged scientist, I walked across to the nearest crib.

What lay inside was everything I hadn't wanted to find.

It was a child. A physically perfect child.

A child with coffee-colored skin and the biggest smile I've ever seen.

But her almond-shaped eyes dominated her face and her nose was squashed so flat it was almost nonexistent. They were features I'd seen before. Features I feared.

This beautiful, happy little girl was born of wraith DNA.

CHAPTER TWO

Rhea help us....

I closed my eyes and tried to contain the pulsing horror of not only what they'd achieved, but also what would inevitably come next.

Death.

Of this child, and of all the other children in the remaining cribs. Not just because of what they were, but because none of them showed any discomfort from the lab's bright lights. My stomach churned at the thought, even if I understood the necessity of it.

And yet I couldn't help but think of my own little ones, who'd never been given the chance at life simply because of what they were and the way they'd been created.

If we killed these children without thought, without even pause, then we'd learned nothing from the horrors of the past.

No doubt Nuri and her crew would say it was the horrors of the future they were trying to prevent.

The small babe gurgled, the sound so soft and merry it just about broke my heart. She reached up with chubby little fingers, and it was at that moment I realized she could see me despite the light shield.

I hesitated, and then lowered my hand into the crib. Her fingers latched unerringly onto one of mine, and her warm touch had my seeking skills flaring to life. There was no anger in this child, no hate. She was warm, comfortable, and happy enough, but she was also desperate for human contact. She wanted to be held—to be loved.

They weren't unusual emotions for a child this young; even those of us born in the déchet program had wanted such things. Or, at least, those of us who remained capable of emotions had. Many déchet—but especially those designed to be soldiers—had been both chemically and physically neutered of any ability to think or feel.

But this little girl, with her big amber-green eyes that shone with intelligence, had *not* been mentally castrated—just as the little ones who haunted my bunker hadn't been. And, like them, her mental maturity seemed to be well advanced. She might be physically no more than five or six months old, but if what I was sensing through our connection was anything to go by, she was at least a couple of years older than that intellectually—if not more.

In fact, I'd go as far as saying there was a very old soul in this very young body.

Her grip tightened on mine, and I had this weird feeling she was trying to either tell or show me something. My seeking skills were dragged deeper into her mind, and what I discovered was a force as fierce as anything I'd ever encountered.

This child might have wraith blood, but she was also a seeker and a witch. While her power and abilities were at an embryonic stage, they were untainted and unrestrained, and promised to be a force every bit as strong as anything I'd seen Nuri produce.

But it wasn't *that* she wanted me to see, but rather the fact she'd known I was coming.

That she saw me as her friend—her savior.

Me, the woman who'd been sent here primarily to scout the location, but also to kill any such finds as these children.

What was I supposed to do now?

I pulled my finger from hers. Her little face immediately screwed up and big tears welled in her eyes. I closed mine, took a deep breath, and then touched her chest lightly. *I'll be back.*

Though I was empathic rather than telepathic, I had no doubt she'd understand me. The seeking skill we both possessed—the same skill that was in part the reason behind my ability to communicate with the ghosts in our bunker, be they young déchet or full-grown, fully trained soldiers —ensured it.

She made no further sound, but those tears remained in her eyes, a silver glimmer that threatened to tumble down her cheeks at any minute.

The door opened and two men—one of them guiding a powered medical stretcher—walked into the room. They quickly examined the man I'd drugged then placed him onto the stretcher and walked out. I hoped the medical facilities weren't close, because once they ran full blood work, they'd find the drug and the game would be up.

I quickly moved to the next set of cribs. Not only were this group of six older and sicklier looking, their features were decidedly more wraith in design. Their eyes were bigger— more almond shaped—than the little girl's, and their mouths far smaller. Wraiths had no mouths at all—how they actually fed was anyone's guess—and it once again suggested these four weren't full-bloods. I gently touched the nearest child, but there was no response from him, either physically or mentally. All I felt was pain. Terrible, terrible, pain.

I clamped down on the fury that rose and continued to the next row of pods. There were four in this group and, once again, they were a few months older and even further along the scale of becoming wraith. Were the different rows of cribs an indication of development lots? Not only was the little girl far younger than any of these other children, she was also the most "human" looking of any of them.

But why was she the only one in her row? Had the rest of her group died, or was something stranger happening here?

I didn't bother touching any of the children in the third group. There was no need to—not when the light screen readouts indicated that even with all the tubes inserted into their little bodies, they were barely alive.

As I moved across to the final row of cots, an alarm went off. The light screen above one of the restraint cribs—which held children who resembled full wraiths, right down to the gray, almost translucent skin, and who had no facial features other than their overly large eyes—was flashing red as the heartbeat monitor flatlined. The three scientists swore and immediately began instigating CPR and recovery procedures, but it was all for naught. His soul was already rising —it was almost as if he couldn't wait to get out of his own body.

As was typical for the newly dead, his form was real and solid looking. All ghosts tended to cling to the shape they'd worn in life initially, but most soon realized that doing so drained their energy far too quickly.

What was interesting about *this* young ghost, however, was not the fact his ghostly flesh looked real, but rather that it didn't, in any way, resemble the body that lay in the crib. Instead of wraith features, this ghost had black hair, blue eyes, and a smattering of freckles across his sharp little nose.

So why the change? It was something I'd never witnessed before and it had intuition stirring.

He continued to hover over the crib and the scientists trying to revive him for several more seconds, and then his gaze rose to mine. He could obviously see past the light screen, but then, ghosts generally saw the world as it actually was rather than whatever front or guise was being presented, be it via magic or psychic skill.

Like the others in the restraint cribs, he appeared to be about two years old, but—as with the little girl—there was a much older soul shining out of his blue eyes.

I half reached out, unsure how he'd react or if it was even wise to make an attempt to talk to him. But I needed to know what was going on within this lab and, if he were anything like my little ones, then he would at least be able to give me some idea even if he wasn't capable of anything too technical.

He continued to study me for several more seconds and then slowly drifted forward. His hand touched mine and energy tingled across my skin as a connection formed—and that meant he was either of shifter origin, or that my inability to use my seeking and psi skills against humans had faded right along with the inability to kill them.

Who are you? I asked softly.

I don't know.

His mental tone was somewhat harsh, as if communicating was something he was not used to. But then, those who'd raised déchet hadn't exactly encouraged conversation with their creations, either.

Are of you of this place?

This place is all that I can remember.

Which wasn't a surprising reply, and yet it was something else that tugged at my instincts. *What are they doing to you here?*

They test their drugs. It changes us. He paused, his gaze drifting back to his body. *It is painful. It is why they strap us down. It is why we are kept quiet.*

My fury deepened at his words. The mere fact that these kids were being used as guinea pigs suggested they weren't lab created but rather born of natural means. It also meant the fourteen kidnapped children we'd been trying to find weren't the only ones Dream and her cohorts had been experimenting on.

But the kids here weren't being used to test pathogens capable of altering the DNA of a human to make them vampire—which was a warped means of understanding the process so that they could reverse it—but rather to make wraiths.

Are those of you in this room the only ones they're testing on? I asked.

Yes. He paused, his gaze moving past me. *None of us will survive what they do to us. None of us want to survive.*

Even as he said that, another monitor went red. It was the crib next to his. Two of the scientists quickly repeated the recovery procedures, but the result was the same. Another soul rising.

You must end this madness, the first child said. *Please, you must help those of us for which there is no hope. Promise that you will.*

I hesitated. Making such a promise would go against the one I'd made to myself so long ago, and yet if I didn't accede to his wishes, I'd only be condemning these children to more pain.

You cannot save us. No one can, he said. *All of us will die; it is simply a matter of when, and in how much pain.*

His words stirred the memories of melting flesh, and tears stung my eyes. I rapidly blinked them away. *I promise.*

His form had begun to fade. At first I thought he could simply no longer maintain the fiction of his flesh, but then a smile twisted his lips, and his form began to glow with a warm, golden light.

The tears that had been threatening to tumble finally did; they came not from sadness, but rather relief and happiness.

His soul was being called on. He was being given the chance of rebirth.

It was a gift we déchet would never receive, although I had no idea why. Nuri *had* forced some of the déchet ghosts haunting a military bunker we'd been investigating onwards, but I very much suspected the place she'd sent them and the place these little souls were being drawn to were two completely different things.

As the second soul also moved on, I raised the dart gun and shot the guard and the two men. None of them registered the attack—the scientists were still trying to bring the second child back to life and the guard was too engrossed in the unfolding drama. I hooked the dart gun onto my utilities belt and waited for the drug to take effect. As the two scientists and the guard collapsed in quick succession, I lunged forward and grabbed the woman by the neck.

"Scream," I said, as I shed my light shield, "and I *will* kill you."

Her eyes went wide and the stink of her fear stained the clinically clean air of the lab, but all she did was nod.

"What are you doing to these children?"

She hesitated. I tightened my grip just a fraction, and she hastily said, "Testing a series of pathogens on them."

"Wraith pathogens?"

Her eyes went even wider and she all but stammered, "Yes."

"And the children here? Were they created in this place?"

"No. We bought them."

Bought them? Why in Rhea would any parent sell his or her own child? "And where exactly does one buy a child's life?"

"I don't know!" Her eyes darted desperately for the door, undoubtedly hoping for salvation. "I just work here."

"And your work involves testing pathogens created from the DNA of the Others on human and shifter babies!" My voice was no louder than hers, but it was filled with the deep anger that coursed through me. The stink of her fear sharpened. "Do you expect any of these children to live?"

She hesitated again. "We do have an extremely high fail rate—"

"Define high."

"One hundred percent so far."

Even though that was exactly what the child had said, part of me had hoped it wasn't the case—that the death toll here *wasn't* as bad as the déchet program had been at its worst.

What was she thinking? What were *any* of them thinking? In the name of Rhea... it was all I could do to not shake her, to *not* rant and rave at both her stupidity and her inhumanity. To not end her life here and now, just as she and her cohorts had ended the life of who knew how many children —slowly, and painfully.

But there were still things I needed to know. "So you expect all the children here to die?"

"Yes."

There was no remorse in her voice, not even the slightest

hint that she felt anything close to regret for either her actions or for what they were trying to achieve here. Something within me hardened—the same something that had killed the soldier whose uniform I now wore.

"But we do have great hopes for the latest bacterium batch," she continued. "Subject forty-five certainly hasn't shown any of the side effects we've witnessed previously."

Which meant forty-four other little ones—including all those within this room—had been forced to bear the unbearable before their deaths. "I gather you're talking about the little girl on her own?"

"Yes."

"And how long have you been here, doing this?"

"Me? A couple of years."

"And this site overall?"

"Ten years, at least."

"Does that mean the lizard men who guard this place are a result of your testing?"

"Yes." She licked her lips again. "It was one of our more successful development streams—just over fifty percent of the test subjects lived."

"Because you were using DNA from this world?"

"Yes. But those men were all volunteers, and well paid."

I couldn't imagine there'd be any amount of money that would ever make up for what had happened to their bodies. But then, as Nuri had noted, it wasn't like I was at all familiar with what it was truly like to live as one of the poor in a city such as Central.

"What was the end aim of that program?"

"To create supersoldiers," she said. "To create beings capable of battling the Others."

I snorted. Given Sal had told me their end game was to completely erase the stain of humanity from this place, I doubted they'd actually be creating a fighting force capable of matching blows with the Others. It was more likely they were aiming for a force capable of going where the Others could not.

"And the wraith pathogen? How long have you been testing that?" I asked. "And why aren't you testing it on adult volunteers rather than babies?"

"That particular pathogen has been in development for close to a year, and we did initially start with adults. All the test subjects died within hours of administration. We started using children after similar explorations in other labs —but with different drugs—proved they were better test subjects."

My fingers tightened, and there was absolutely nothing I could do to force them apart. *Nothing.* Her face mottled and her breathing became shuddering, shallow gasps, but I felt no sympathy for her. "Other labs?"

"In Central," she somehow said. "And in Longborne."

I had no idea where Longborne was, but the lab in Central was undoubtedly the now defunct Winter Halo. "How long have the children in this lab been here?"

"The ones in the restraining cots have been here the longest, the little girl at the end the shortest. She's only received two shots so far." The woman paused, her breath wheezing in and out of her lungs. I still couldn't ease my grip on her. I was barely resisting the urge to do the opposite. "Look, I only work here. I was just doing what I was told—"

"You were torturing goddamn *children*. You're trying to create a pathogen to allow wraiths full light immunity."

Her eyes widened further, and I hadn't thought that was possible. "No, I swear, we're trying to find a means to kill them!"

"By first turning human and shifter babies into wraiths? There's only one world in which something like that would be acceptable, and it's certainly not *this* one."

"You have to believe me—"

I didn't. Not one iota. There might be fear in her, but there was no guilt or doubt, and surely there should have been at least a fraction of either. How could anyone truly believe that testing alien-based pathogens on humans and shifters would lead to a means of killing wraiths? If that was truly their aim, why wouldn't they be testing any drug developed on wraiths? Granted, they were very deadly and extremely hard to capture alive, but that didn't mean it was impossible. The DNA they were using in their pathogens had to come from somewhere, after all. For all I knew, there *were* government approved lab facilities that had the Others in captivity, and that were currently researching various means of destroying them.

But this lab was *not* one of them.

Not given it was a false rift that had led me here.

"Is this lab the only one containing live subjects?"

She nodded. "We did have two other production labs in operation here, but babies have been hard to come by of late."

Before I could reply or respond in any way, the door into the lab from the antechamber opened and another scientist walked through. "Betts, I need you to—"

He stopped abruptly, his expression shifting from confusion to horror in quick succession. I snapped a gun from my belt and fired, but his reactions were just as fast as mine. He dove out the closing door, and the bullet pinged off the metal and went who knew where.

My time here had just moved into the red zone.

I shifted my aim to the scanner that controlled entry into the room and blasted it. Sparks and black smoke flew as the screen went dead. Though the door was now locked shut, I doubted it would keep anyone out for long.

As a siren began to sound, I killed the woman then stepped over her body and walked across to the chemicals cabinet. I'd made a promise to the soul of a dead child, and I intended to keep it. Had there been *any* sort of hope for the little ones within this room, I might have hesitated, but the scientist had basically confirmed what the child had told me. It was far better that they die a painless death now than spend who knew how many more weeks or months in unremitting agony.

I was all too familiar with such a death. I would rather break a vow than allow it to happen again.

If this lab was anything like the labs that had developed us, then there would be some means here of putting down unwanted test subjects. After a moment, I found what I was looking for—pentobarlazol—a newer, swifter-acting form of an eons-old drug. It was basically both a sedative and an anticonvulsant, and in higher doses it gently put the subject into a deep sleep even as it shut down heart and brain functions. I'd seen déchet injected with it, and knew it to be a quick and peaceful death.

I clipped the gun back onto the utilities belt and then grabbed the bottle and several syringes. It didn't take long to inject the pentobarlazol into the feed lines of all the children.

In all the lines but one.

I just couldn't do it to the happy little girl. She, out of all of them, had some hope of survival. She deserved a chance, and I was going to do everything in my power to give it to her.

I put the pentobarlazol back into the cabinet, dumped the syringes into the medical waste chute, and then primed two of my remaining four RTX devices. I stuck one under a bench near the cribs, and another on the wall behind one of the metal cabinets. As the sound of approaching steps began to echo in the antechamber, I pulled off my stolen jacket, detached the drip feeds from the little girl, and carefully constructed a sling so that I could carry her.

She made no sound. She merely placed one little hand on my chest, right above my heart, as if drawing comfort from the sound.

The footsteps stopped outside the door. I hurried across to

the guard I'd darted and quickly stripped off his body armor. I loosened the side straps, then carefully pulled it over my head. The guard was much taller than me, so not only did the heavy vest drop past my hips, it completely protected the little girl. Once I'd tightened the straps, I wrapped a light shield around the two of us and hurried over to the internal door. Fortunately, this one wasn't scanner locked, and it opened to reveal another laboratory —one that appeared to be at the epicenter of their pathogen development. I concealed another RTX and then drew a gun and walked over to the corner of the room near the door that led back out into the antechamber.

Even as I stopped, five soldiers quickly but silently entered the room. Three moved toward the other lab while two positioned themselves either side of the open door. My fingers tensed around the gun, but attacking either man really wasn't the best option right now. To have any hope of getting out of this place in one piece, I needed to slip past without being sensed.

I eased off my boots and hung them on the back of my belt. I was no master at walking silently, and the combination of the boots and these floors meant there would at least be some noise, no matter how quiet I tried to be. It might not have been obvious when everyone had been intent on helping the fallen scientist, but there was no such distraction now.

I drew two guns and then sucked in the light shield as tightly as I dared. It would shimmer if it touched either man and that would be enough to at least raise suspicion. They might not know what a light shield was, but they would undoubtedly suspect something odd was happening and react accordingly.

After crossing mental fingers and praying that the luck I'd been gifted with so far continued, I headed for the door. But just as I was going through it, a third soldier appeared and tried to do the same. I had little choice but to thrust him out of the way and run.

The two soldiers guarding the door immediately spun and opened fire. One bullet caught my leg and sent me stumbling, but I somehow retained balance and jagged sideways, running to the right and around the outer ring of the antechamber rather than directly across it. Bullets pinged off the walls, floors, and ceiling, deadly missiles that came very close but didn't hit. The noise of all the gunfire was deafening, but the soldiers themselves were quiet.

As was the child. She just gripped my shirt fiercely, as if intent on hanging on no matter what happened next.

A gruff order was barked, and the gunfire immediately ceased. I slid to a stop, trying to control both the sharp rasp of my breathing and my surging fear. The tunnel—and the safety it represented—was close. So damn close. If I could get into it, become nothing more than shadowed particles, I could avoid the worst of the gunfire by rising to the ceiling and moving swiftly out of this place.

But there were still soldiers piling out of the tunnel; some formed a line in front of it, blocking any hope of an easy exit, while others were beginning a methodical sweep of the antechamber. If I remained still, I'd be caught. Not just by those soldiers, but by a lack of strength that would surely happen sooner rather than later if the amount of blood now soaking my pants was any indication. Even if it wasn't currently dripping onto the floor, it soon would be. And that, in turn, would be a very easy path to follow, shield or no shield. At least there weren't any shifters amongst the soldiers—there couldn't be. They would have scented both the blood and me by now.

Not that it really mattered, because the soldiers were drawing closer and my options were fast running out.

I took a deep breath, raised my guns, and unleashed metal hell as I ran full pelt at the tunnel. Even as some went down, others returned fire. A bullet grazed my cheek, another my lower thigh. Others thudded into both the sides and back of the body armor, and it felt like someone was pounding me with a heavy wooden bat. But even though each successive bullet hurt like hell, and breathing was becoming more and more difficult, the armor was working. So far, there'd been no hits to my chest. The little girl remained safe and untouched in her cocoon.

But blood from my other wounds splattered beyond the boundary of my shield. It didn't matter—nothing did but getting us both safely into that tunnel.

Two soldiers ran at me. I shot one, dodged the other, and continued. But they knew where I was now and it would only be a matter of seconds before they took me down.

I had one chance, and one chance only.

I reached back, grabbed the remote, and pressed a button. The lab to my right exploded into a ball of fire, heat, and chaos. Such was the force of the explosion that it engulfed the men nearest it and sent others flying. I ran, with every ounce of speed and strength I could muster, at the two men who still blocked my way. They must have sensed my approach because their guns rose as one. Even as their fingers tightened on the triggers, I threw myself down onto my back, firing both guns as I skidded through the small gap between them.

The light shield disintegrated in the heavy darkness of the tunnel, and I immediately reached for the shadows. As the force of it surged through me, I touched the top of the little girl's head with a bloody hand and silently said, *Don't be afraid. What happens won't hurt you, but it is necessary to escape.*

Again, she seemed to understand, because she made no sound even though the switch to particle form was as fast and as brutal as anything I'd ever experienced.

The change had barely finished when the second of the bombs went off. As smoke and heat billowed into the tunnel and sprinklers dropped from the ceiling and began spraying the entire area with water, I pushed upright and kept going, keeping as high as possible.

Gunshots pinged around us, but, as I'd hoped, the main barrage was not aimed high. They didn't know what I was, didn't know what I was capable of. I could only pray it remained that way, at least until I managed to get out of this place. If anyone thought to contact Dream and tell her what was happening, I was in deep trouble.

Not only was she well aware just what I was capable of, but she'd also be desperate to stop a repeat of Winter Halo's destruction.

I continued to speed along the darkened tunnel but slowed as I neared its scanner-packed entrance. There was no movement in the receiving bay beyond, but it was far from empty. There were at least two squadrons within the room; while some were positioned in front of other tunnel entrances, the majority had their weapons aimed at this one. I paused and studied the bay's roofline. Thankfully, there were still enough shadows to hide within. As the final bombs erupted and a heavy rumble filled the air and shook the walls around me, I slipped past the scanners and moved to the tunnel that led to the main receiving dock.

The intensity of the ominous rumbling increased until the noise of it overran even the screech of the alarm. Cracks appeared in both the walls and the ceiling, fine lines that seemed intent on racing me through the darkness. Jonas had warned me that the RTXs packed a serious punch, so maybe using so many in a relatively small area had created enough force to compromise the integrity of at least *this* part of the base.

I couldn't help but hope so. It would make getting out a whole lot easier.

The end of this larger tunnel came into sight and, once again, I slowed. There were still guards on either side of the gateway, and both had their weapons raised and ready to use. But they were scanning the walls uneasily, probably wondering—just as I was—how far the destruction would go before those in charge of this place ordered something done.

I slipped through the gateway and made my way around the shadowed wall. An ominous crack appeared in the center of the loading bay's ceiling, and dirt and debris began to rain down. People were now bolting for the side tunnels, but I wasn't entirely sure that was wise. Given the noise and the multitude of fissures appearing absolutely everywhere, it really did seem possible the whole base was now in danger.

I dodged the debris as best I could and continued to make my way toward the elevator. As I drew near, the indicator light flashed on and the doors opened. Light poured out of it, and in an instant, the shadows were torn from me.

I dropped heavily to the ground and staggered forward several steps, fighting to keep my balance against the rush of people now racing for the elevator. If I went down, I might not get up.

Someone hit me side-on and threw me against the wall. My head smacked against the stone and stars danced as my legs threatened to buckle. I forced my knees to lock and wrapped my arms around the body armor, giving the little girl an additional layer of protection against the tide of hits and bumps as people continued to rush past.

Another siren went off, and then a metallic voice grimly gave the evacuation order. People pushed and shove even more fiercely in their desperation to get into the elevator. But, beyond it, a red light flashed and then a section of wall slid aside to reveal a stairwell.

The elevator doors began to close, even though people were still trying to get in. Others were racing up the stairs. The quake was now so fierce that the floor buckled and large parts of the ceiling started to drop. It surely wouldn't be too long before the whole lot came down.

I gathered my strength, and then forced my way into the thick throng of people running for the stairs. No one paid any attention to me, let alone the tightly wrapped bundle I carried. They were all too busy avoiding the debris and trying to escape.

Just as we reached the stairs, there was a huge crash behind us, and then a fierce blast of dusty air hit, knocking several people over. I stumbled as someone ran into my back, but somehow kept my balance and kept on moving. The screams of those who *had* fallen were quickly cut off.

We raced upwards, a human mass of fear and desperation. I could see neither the top end of the stairs nor daylight, but given the length of time the elevator had taken to get down to this level, that wasn't really surprising.

Though we were tightly packed, no one was pushing. Everyone was too intent on keeping their balance and their position. But those cracks were beginning to chase us upwards, and the stink of fear, of desperation, became so fierce it filled every breath.

A shudder ran through the metal stairs and then the lights went out. The man next to me hesitated, only to be sworn at and shoved forward by the people behind us. He stumbled, and I instinctively reached out to steady him. He thanked me and kept on going.

The earth's rumbling was now fierce. While the walls and stairs in emergency exit tunnels were generally built to withstand great force, they *could* be destroyed—something I now knew all too well, thanks to the bombs that had all but obliterated the two tunnels I'd used to get in and out of my bunker.

This place, like the loading bay and the laboratories below us, wasn't going to last.

I didn't even think about it. I simply sucked in the shadows and once again became one with them. And then, with every ounce of speed I could muster, I surged upwards.

I reached the exit in a matter of seconds but the storm still raged on the surface, and it almost tore me apart. Panic surged and I hastily regained human form, hunkering down on one side of the exit and shielding the babe with my body as I tried to see where we were.

The elevator appeared out of the ground, sand falling like water from its roof as people scrambled out. They all headed to the left and, after a moment, I saw why.

Transporters were waiting for them.

I kept as low as I could and ran toward them. There were over a hundred people trying to cram into each of the first five trucks—trucks that had been designed to carry an eighth of that. I ran past them. There were another three trucks parked beyond them, as well as a number of hovers and sand barges. I went to the very last vehicle in line and jumped into the main cabin.

"Sorry, love," the pilot said, without even looking at me. "We're not cleared for takeoff as yet. Hop into the back and wait."

I didn't bother replying. I simply hit him over the head with the butt of a gun, and then dragged his unconscious body out of the pilot's seat and dumped him into the storm.

Once I'd closed and locked the door, I stripped off the armor and used it to create a rough sort of pouch to hold the little girl secure in the passenger seat, and then slipped into the pilot seat. I'd never been at the controls of a barge before but they didn't look all that different to the truck I'd recently driven into Winter Halo. After a moment, I located the starter switch and kicked the engine into action, then pulled out the geo-locator and transferred the rift's coordinates into the GPS.

As the big machine rolled forward, I leaned back in the seat and finally allowed myself to relax.

The minute I did, a red tide of pain hit, threatening to overwhelm my senses and sweep me into unconsciousness.

I fought it with everything I had and, after a few minutes, the threat receded, allowing me to do a quick wound check. There was a large and painful lump on the side of my head, a graze on my cheek, several surface wounds on my left arm, and a deeper one on my right. Blood ran freely down my side and hip, and my left thigh burned. Though my pants were soaked in blood, it didn't feel as if the blood was still running. All in all, despite the pain, I'd been pretty lucky. I took a deep, somewhat quivery breath, and then checked the little girl. No hits at all. There wasn't even a speck of dust on her. Rhea really *had* been watching over her.

I secured her once again then glanced at the radar. The storm was a big black blob in the middle of it but there was no indication of pursuit. We'd gotten away, at least for the moment.

I dropped the backpack onto the floor and then settled into a more comfortable position. While my body might be healing at a far faster rate than was normal, I still had to do something about the wound on my side. I really couldn't afford to lose any more blood.

I closed my eyes and slipped into the healing trance. I had

no idea how much time passed before I woke, but the storm was no longer battering the barge and sunlight now glimmered through the cracks along the edges of the storm shields.

I hit the release button and, as the shields slowly retracted, the little girl made a sound that was part surprise, part laughter. I quickly glanced down at her. The sunshine pouring in through the thickened glass bathed her entire body, and though her eyes were little more than amber-green slits, there was a look of what could only be sheer joy on her face as she reached upwards with chubby little fingers.

She was trying to catch the sunbeams.

I smiled and touched her hand. Her fingers once again wrapped around mine and the link surged to life. What I sensed was belonging. Homecoming.

I might be comfortable in either daylight or night, but this little girl was very definitely a child born of the sun. Who knew how the drugs she'd been given would affect her in the future, but right now, she was bathing in her element and simply happy to be.

"Raela," I said softly. "It's a shifter word meaning little sunshine, and it's yours from here on out."

A smile touched her lips and found an echo on mine. I had no idea what was going to happen to her once I got back to my bunker, but one thing was certain. Neither Nuri nor Jonas nor anyone else was going to get near her until they could guarantee that she would be safe, that she would *not*, in any way, be placed into another military installation, to be monitored and watched like some unusual animal. She deserved more than that.

The barge rolled on, its progress slow and very tedious. After a while, I pulled out the small flask and carefully dribbled some water into Raela's mouth. She was too young for the protein bars I was carrying, and I didn't have anything else. I might not have had—or ever would have—children of my own, but I'd been around enough déchet nurseries both before and during the war to know hydration was the key in a situation such as this.

After what seemed an eternity, the GPS finally indicated we were approaching our destination. As the barge automatically slowed, I leaned forward and peered out the windows. Dust devils were lazily pulling at the sand, creating gently spinning funnels that clouded the immediate horizon. I couldn't see the rift, but the alarm that stirred was as sluggish as those devils.

The rift *couldn't* have gone anywhere, after all. The only person capable of either moving or destroying the things surely wouldn't risk doing either when Winter Halo was filled to the brim with officialdom and security forces, most of whom were intent on figuring out what had been going on in that place as much as who might have been responsible.

We hit the coords I'd fed in and the barge stopped. There was nothing but sand for as far as the eye could see. That stirring of fear grew stronger, but I clamped down on it. It was no use fearing something until I knew there was something to fear.

I hit the door release and jumped down onto the sand. The

air was warm but the wind that teased the back of my neck hinted at the coolness of the oncoming evening.

I walked to the front of the barge and then stopped, my hands on my hips. The rift had to be here somewhere. *Had* to be. But there was absolutely no sign of it. Nor could I feel the caress of its poisonous energy against my skin.

I pulled the geo-locator out of my pocket and double-checked we were at the right location.

We were.

It was the rift that wasn't.

CHAPTER THREE

I'D BEEN EXPECTING something to go wrong—things always did whenever I stepped through a false rift—but the possibility of it disappearing hadn't even occurred to me.

I walked around the barge, just to be sure I wasn't being blinded by the bright sunshine, but the result was the same.

No damn rift.

I thrust a hand through sweaty, blood-caked hair and squinted up at the sun. It might have begun its journey toward night, but I couldn't risk waiting for the stars to come out to see if any of them were familiar. Dream knew I could traverse the false rifts, and the minute she was informed of the attack, she'd order a search made of this area.

I needed to move. Trouble was, I had no idea where home was in relation to our current location. I hadn't thought to input Central's coords into the geo-locator when I'd left, and I didn't have any sort of comms unit with me—a totally stupid move I'd rectify the next time I went through a rift.

Or anywhere else, for that matter.

I climbed back into the barge, brought up the GPS, and scrolled through the screens until I found the tracklog. While the two rifts within Winter Halo had been large enough to cater to a barge this size, the sand base surely couldn't have been getting all of its supplies from them. There were simply too many people working and undoubtedly living at the base for someone in either Winter Halo or Central City not to notice the steady stream of trucks going in and out of the building.

The list of previous journeys that appeared on the screen was relatively short, which suggested the log was overwritten regularly. I scrolled down but didn't immediately recognize any of the names—until I got to the last two.

Longborne and Carleen. The latter had been one of Central's five satellite cities before the war, and the very last one to be destroyed at its end. These days it was little more than a broken wreck—a place filled not only with shadows, alien moss, and human ghosts, but also rifts, both real and false.

But it was only an hour's walk out of Central.

I'd just found my way home.

I imputed the saved route into the GPS and then pressed the start button. Lights flashed across the panel and, as the barge trundled forward once again, I went back into the log and bought up the Longborne record. While it made me none the wiser as to where it was actually located, I nevertheless manually entered its coordinates into the geolocater.

After that, with Raela asleep, there was nothing I could do but eat some protein bars and watch the landscape roll by. Somewhere along the line I must have fallen asleep, because the next thing I knew, it was not only night but there were red lights flashing across the control board, Raela was crying, and a proximity alarm was going off.

I muted the alarm, then picked up Raela to comfort her and peered out the front windows. The desert had given away to a thickly treed forest, and the vehicle was barely scraping through an increasingly narrow roadway. I glanced across at the GPS and realized we'd somehow gotten off course. I knew some of the more modern vehicles were programmed to detour around potential hazards, but the barge could never be described as modern. Besides, I doubted there'd be a hazard much worse than a forest this vehicle was ill equipped to traverse.

I hit the kill switch but the barge didn't stop. It just kept trundling deeper and deeper into the forest. I frowned and hit the switch again.

Still no response.

Foreboding stirred. I ran a full system check and soon realized what was going on—an external force had taken control of the vehicle. It didn't take much effort to guess who that might be.

I swore and bought up the terrain map. The reason for the proximity alarms immediately became obvious. It wasn't because we were bashing our way through a forest, but rather because we were drawing ever closer to what looked like a goddamn cliff.

I immediately swung around and hit the door open switch.

Once again, nothing happened. The bastards were remotely controlling *everything*.

Another light flashed up on the control screen. This time, it was warning of approaching vehicles. What it didn't tell me was who the vehicles belonged to. It was always possible that they weren't from the sand base, but I really couldn't afford to take that chance.

Besides, even if they *were* friendly, they were still a couple of miles behind us, and wouldn't reach us before we hit the cliff.

Which was now altogether *too* close.

I ignored the thick thrust of fear and looked around for another means of escape. The front windows were too thick to shoot out with any of the weapons I had on hand. There were no side windows in the barge's cab, but there *was* a rear-facing window, which I guessed was used to check whatever cargo was being hauled. It was little more than porthole barely bigger than my fist, but that was all my shadowed form needed.

Thankfully, the porthole's glass didn't appear to be as sturdy as the front windows. I glanced around, spotted a tool kit secured in a storage space to the left of the door, and pulled it out. Inside was the usual assortment of tools, including one rather large wrench.

I covered Raela's face to protect her from flying glass then grabbed the wrench and swung it, as hard as I could, at the small window. It took three blows before the glass shattered.

By that time, it wasn't just the flashing red lights telling me we were closing in on the cliff. I could actually see its edge.

I had to get out of here, and fast.

I dumped the spanner and then properly secured Raela's sling around my body. Once she was safely tucked close, I grabbed the body armor and the pack, and then called to the darkness. Even as the power of it tore through the two of us, the barge's treads rolled into emptiness and the vehicle's front end tilted alarmingly.

Once again panic surged, threatening to overwhelm my control and halt the change. I braced my body against the ever-increasing decline, then closed my eyes and concentrated on nothing but becoming shadow. The second I was, I surged through the shattered porthole.

Just as the rear of the barge went over the edge and began a tumbling descent down the cliff face.

I got out of its way and then hovered in midair for several seconds, watching it crash through the treetops and come to a sudden stop upside down on the rocky ground below. The barge's treads were still in motion and there was steam and smoke coming from the engine bay, but it didn't erupt into flame. Maybe it wouldn't—I guess it depended on whether the fuel tank had ruptured or not.

A light speared the darkness, almost catching me in its beam. I thrust away and glanced up. There were figures lining the cliff top, but the spotlights they were holding were so bright that they were little more than silhouettes behind it. It was impossible to tell whether they were friend or foe—although I seriously doubted they were the former. Even though I wouldn't exactly call some of Nuri's people friends, I doubted any of them would simply stand there if they'd thought I was in the vehicle.

And if Jonas had been up there, he certainly would have been scrambling down to check for survivors.

I surged upwards and discovered my instincts were right. They weren't friends—they were wearing the sand base's uniform. There was also at least thirty of them here—either Dream was overestimating my combat abilities or she was absolutely determined that I would *not* escape this time.

I rose higher to get above the cliff top's tree line and slowly turned around. Given I'd been traveling for some time before I'd woken off course and in the middle of this forest, there was a good chance I was a whole lot closer to Central than I had been. If that were the case, then her lights should be visible, even from a distance.

And they were.

Or, at least, the night sky was lit by a glowing sphere of light some distance away to my left. Even if it wasn't Central, I'd be able to find a means of contacting Nuri there, as well as a source of nourishment for Raela. Aside from the one bout of crying, she'd been amazingly quiet, but that wasn't likely to last once her belly started to rumble. Even déchet babes had made it thoroughly clear when they were hungry.

Between those lights and us was a wide, wooded valley that swept up the foothills of another mountain range. The only mountains I could think of anywhere near Central were the Broken Mountains, where the few remaining nomadic shifter clans lived, and where the other military base we'd invaded was located. That would certainly explain why this entire area—and the desert I'd woken up in—was unfamiliar. I'd never been stationed beyond the Broken Mountains during the war, and I certainly hadn't ventured very far from Central after it.

Movement caught my attention—the soldiers had begun to rappel down the cliff. It wouldn't be long before they realized I'd escaped. Time to get moving.

I dropped to treetop level and arrowed forward as fast as I was able, desperate to put distance between those soldiers and us. Time passed, but the spherical glow of the city didn't seem to be getting any closer. It was obviously a whole lot farther away than I'd initially thought.

Tiredness rippled through my particles, gently at first but gradually increasing in intensity, until it felt as if every part of me was afire. I might have rested and healed on the barge, but it had still been a very long day, and the protein bars I'd eaten weren't really enough to fuel me for long. Not after everything I'd been through. I glanced over my shoulder to check the distance I'd put between the cliff and us, and decided to drop to the ground and resume normal form. I could always shadow again if necessary, but right now, it was better to conserve some strength. I might not be able to move as swiftly in flesh form as I could when shadowed, but I did have tiger shifter blood in me and could run a whole lot faster than most humans. And at least it didn't tax my strength quite as much as maintaining particle form.

I dribbled some water into Raela's mouth to keep her hydrated, drank a little myself, then stoppered the bottle and moved on. Though the forest was dark, it was far from silent. There were night creatures in this place, rustling through the scrub and scrambling up trees as I ran past. That at least meant I didn't have to worry about a vampire attack. We appeared to be a long way out from any sort of human habitation, and those night creatures would have been the vampires' only means of sustenance had there been an infestation here. All the forests close to Central had been stripped of life for decades; in fact, I hadn't even seen any birds for a least twenty years, if not more.

The night rolled on and the moon rose ever higher in the starlit sky—something I could feel more than see, thanks to the thickness of the overhanging canopy.

My muscles—unused to running so fast for so long—were beginning to ache, but I didn't slow down and I certainly didn't rest. A niggling sense of danger was beginning to creep across my psychic senses and the need to be out of this forest was growing.

The ground started to slope upwards as we neared the foothills of the other mountain range, and my pace slowed. It didn't ease the muscle burn. Nothing short of a good massage and rest would.

Then, from behind, I finally heard what my senses had been picking up on for the last hour or so.

The whine of engines.

They were coming at me, and fast.

But how in Rhea had they known where we were? Aside from the fact this valley was vast and there had to be more than one path through these trees, I'd traveled in particle form for at least the first hour and had left no trail for even the most experienced hunter to follow.

And yet they were behind me.

I could understand them locating the barge, as it was easy

enough to trace a vehicle's location via its GPS signal. Of course, Dream was not only one of the evil trio, but a witch of some power. I didn't know a whole lot about witchcraft and the use of earth magic, but I did know that anyone who stepped on the earth could be traced by it. The minute I'd regained normal form, she could have pinned me.

But that thought was quickly chased away by another. I briefly closed my eyes and cursed my own stupidity. They didn't *need* a witch. Not when I still had Banks's RFID chip stuck over my own.

I slid to a stop, sending a spray of small stones and dirt scattering through the darkness, and pushed up my sleeve. The false skin covering the RFID chip was visible thanks to the grime now lining its edge. I slid a nail under one side and peeled the entire thing away from my arm. The RFID chip clung to the fake skin like a limpet, and gleamed brightly in the darkness, as if mocking me. I dropped it onto the ground and stomped on it, and then glanced down at Raela. While I'd blown up the labs, it was still possible they were aware that one of their test subjects was missing, especially if she'd been chipped. Most déchet had been implanted with a tracker or a control device—in some instances, both had been used. Their handlers had not only needed to know where they were at all times, but had also required a means of control if their charges flipped out or started attacking the wrong targets. Not that the chips had always worked—one of the reasons we lures had been installed into the nurseries as guards when not in service was because a déchet soldier had gone berserk and killed a number of déchet children before he could be stopped.

But could I afford to waste the time checking her?

Could I afford not to?

I glanced over my shoulder, trying to guess how much time we had left before they found us. The hum of the pursuit vehicles was definitely closer than it had been only minutes ago, but there was little point in running if Raela did have a tracker in her.

Besides, if she also had a control chip in her, they might well decide to take her out rather than risk her falling into the "wrong" hands.

I moved across to a fallen tree and carefully unwrapped her. She giggled lightly and waved her hands at the sudden freedom, making me smile even as I caught one of her arms and gently checked for implants.

It wasn't until I reached her feet that I found the chip—it had been embedded into the heel of her right foot.

And *that* meant I'd have to cut it out. There was no other choice—not if we wanted to escape. I took a deep breath to gather my courage and then lightly placed a hand on her chest. *I'm about to hurt you, little one, and I'm sorry. But bad men are chasing us, and there is a device in your foot that is leading them to us. It needs to come out.*

She should have been too young to understand either the words or their import, and yet her happy expression melted into one of solemnity, and the old soul I'd glimpsed before once again shone from her eyes.

She placed her hand over mine and the size difference oddly reminded me a grain of sand against a rock. And yet that grain was offering *me* both strength and courage.

She couldn't—*wouldn't*—go back to any sort of military or

governmental organization or lab. I might not have been able to save either her companions or even my own little ones, but I would do everything in my power to give her the one thing they'd never had: the chance of a *real* life.

I pulled my hand from under hers then swung the backpack around and pulled out both the small medikit and the knife. If I'd had anything smaller, I would have used it, but I didn't. The blade's tip was fine, but even so, against Raela's tiny foot, it looked like a carving knife.

There was no deadening spray in the kit, only a sealing antiseptic, so I simply located the chip in her heel and pressed the knife's point against her skin. Then, with another of those breaths that didn't do a lot to calm the turmoil inside, I pushed it deep.

She screamed. I closed my heart to the sound and sliced sideways until the edge of the chip was revealed. Then, using the tweezers from the kit, I carefully grabbed it. In the past, heel-inserted control chips had often been connected to small vials of quick-acting poison. They could be detonated from a distance, and killed the host quickly but not exactly painlessly. We lures had been designed to be immune to all sorts of poison, so they'd used a different system on us—a miniaturized but extremely powerful incendiary device buried under our ribcage. It was no longer in my body, of course, but I hadn't destroyed it, as tempting as it had been at the time. In those early years after the war, when I'd been so uncertain as to what was happening in the world above our bunker and whether another attack would come, I'd thought it prudent to keep hold of every weapon I could.

As I drew Raela's chip free, I saw the wires and swore. They were the same sort of wires that had been in me and meant this little girl was basically a flesh and blood bomb.

"I'm sorry, Raela," I said, my voice barely audible over the sound of her sobbing, "but I've got to get the rest of it out."

I dug the knife deeper, and again she screamed. The blade tip hit something solid, but the welling blood meant I couldn't tell if it was bone or whatever device had been placed in her.

I swabbed the blood away then used the tweezers against the edges of the wound to widen it. That's when I spotted it —a small silver tube.

Though it was microscopic in size, it nevertheless looked to be the same type of device that had been used in me. I carefully pulled it free from her body then threw the entire thing as hard and as far as I could. It eventually buried itself in the leaf matter that was banked around an old elm's feet, lost from sight but not from memory.

I quickly sprayed the sealer onto Raela's foot to stop the bleeding, then wiped away the rest of the blood and hugged her close. Even as I whispered words of comfort, I hurriedly reattached her sling and the body armor. Crying or not, we had to move. The pursuit was now close enough that I could hear the different engine notes of the various vehicles; if I delayed much longer, they'd be on us.

I snapped the water bottle, guns, and remaining ammo clips to my utilities belt and then slung the rifle over my shoulder. As Raela's sobs quietened to hiccups, I set the remaining RTX and walked back to place it at the base of the old elm. Between it and the incendiary device, they should not only bring the old tree down but also start a fire big enough to cause problems for those who chased us.

I wrapped my arms around Raela and once again called to the darkness. It surged through me, but its force was muted, a warning I was very close to reaching the limits of my strength.

It didn't matter. Nothing did, as long as we escaped.

I flowed on through the night, keeping very close to the ground just in case my strength went. The old road grew ever steeper and narrower, and the roots of the trees that lined either side crept across its surface like thick wooden fingers. I had no idea where this road had once led, but it very obviously was no longer in use. Even the old barge, with its thick caterpillar tracks, would have had some trouble traversing the ever-growing wildness.

On and up I went, but the tiredness was growing and my particles were once again beginning to burn. I'd never really pushed myself to the utter end of my strength in this form—I'd never dared, as I'd always feared doing so would simply mean a loss of coherence. That rather than reforming and becoming flesh—as I did whenever light hit my shadowed form—my particles would simply unravel and float away, leaving me without the possibility of even a ghostly form.

Then, from behind, came a *whoomp*, and an orange glow suddenly lit the night sky. The RTX had just exploded. I spun around but couldn't really see anything through the thick scrub surrounding us, so I pushed up past the treetops into the starlit night.

To discover a huge swath of forest was now on fire.

The combination of the two bombs had obviously created a force far greater than I could ever have hoped for, and it surely would have taken out at least a good portion of the pursuit.

Would it be enough?

The pessimistic part of me said no.

I dropped back down and became flesh again, but my leg muscles gave way and I dropped to my knees, grunting as pain rippled up my spine.

Rhea help me, *everything* hurt.

I sucked in air, trying to at least ease the burning in my lungs. One thing was becoming very obvious: I couldn't go on for much longer. I just couldn't. Not without help.

I closed my eyes and called, with everything I had, for Cat and Bear. I had no idea if my two little ghosts would hear me from this distance, but I had to try. Though it was highly unlikely they'd provide much of a front against whatever force was still pursuing us, they could at least contact Jonas and get him out here. Ever since he and I had gone through the rift together, he'd been able to hear, if not converse with, them.

Raela somehow wriggled a hand free from the confines of the sling and armor, and gently patted my face. Once again it felt like she was comforting me—telling me that everything was going to be all right.

I smiled down at her. Saw her answering smile.

And knew in that instant I would *not* release her into the care of anyone else. That it had, indeed, been a foregone conclusion from the moment her tiny fingers had grabbed mine.

Somehow, someway, I would raise her.

If we survived the current situation, that was.

And that didn't mean just *this* pursuit, but the whole matter of tracking down Ciara Dream and dealing with her mad scheme to give the wraiths and vamps light immunity. Until we found and destroyed both that final lab and *her*, her evil scheme was still very much in place and active.

I drew in another of those deep, somewhat shuddery breaths that did little to ease the pain or give me strength, and then pushed up and on. Progress was slow, though, and not just because of my weariness. The road was now so bad that I had to watch every step lest I stumble or fall.

The night rolled on. For a long time, there was little sound other than the chirruping of insects, the rustle of animals through the undergrowth, and the harsh rasp of my breathing. Raela was asleep, but she'd now gone quite a long time without any sustenance, and the fact she remained so quiet was beginning to worry me.

I trudged on, forcing one foot in front of another when all I wanted to do was stop and rest. But the stars were at least growing brighter and the scrub around me was beginning to thin, which meant that even though I couldn't see the mountain's ridge, it had to be getting closer.

Then, once again, came the sound I'd feared.

The hum of engines, closing in fast.

I cursed their persistence but didn't call to the darkness or even increase my speed. Given the incline and instability of the road, I didn't dare the latter, and I simply couldn't risk using the last of my strength on becoming shadow until it was absolutely necessary.

I trudged on, keeping my eyes on the ground but acutely aware of the rising rumble behind me. If that noise was anything to go by, they were no longer just coming directly along the road but had spread out, possibly to cut off any prospect of a double back.

I unclipped one of the guns and held it by my side. I doubted it would have the power to cause much damage to any of the vehicles I'd seen on the cliff top, but short of running me down, they couldn't actually harm me, as none of them had been armed.

A small oversight I was fervently grateful for.

Then the engine noise stopped. I paused, listening. There was no indication that anyone was coming after me—no bouncing rocks or crunch of leaf matter to indicate we were being chased on foot.

And yet they were coming.

Fast.

Shifters, an inner part of me whispered. I closed my eyes and hoped it wasn't true. Or that the shifters belonged to one of the groups who still lived in these mountains rather than from those who pursued us.

But it wasn't like I dared hang around and uncover the answer.

I called to the shadows, let them wrap around me, then

raced on upwards, taking the most direct route rather than following the tangled, meandering road.

Just as I hit the ridge, I felt the unraveling begin. I quickly called to flesh and fell, twisting as I did so that it was my back that took the force of it rather than Raela. Déchet were made with very strong bones but we were not unbreakable. And break I did—the snap was loud, and seemed to echo across the night.

But for several rather terrifying seconds, there was no pain —absolutely nothing—and the fear that I'd broken my back surged. I moved my neck, my arms, my right leg... but the moment I tried to move my left, the pain hit, and so fiercely I had to bite my lip against a scream.

I wrapped a hand around Raela to ensure I didn't squash her, and somehow found the strength to push upright. And discovered that I'd broken both my tibia *and* fibula—a nasty break at the best of times, and certainly not one I could recover from in a matter of minutes.

Which was all I had left.

I tried to ignore the throbbing, heated agony that threatened to consume me, and looked around. I'd been fairly lucky when I'd fallen—three feet in either direction and I would have landed on top of a range of wickedly pointed rocks. Those same rocks formed a semicircle-shaped cave behind me, and were probably my best—and really, only—place to make some sort of stand. If I could reach them, that was.

I unclipped my knife, cut a small section from a nearby tree root, and shoved it into my mouth. I needed something to bite down on—something that would smother the screams, if only a little.

And scream I did. Moving was agony itself. My body went hot, and then cold, and sweat slicked every bit of skin and made gripping the rocks and pulling myself backward even harder. The blackness of unconsciousness loomed large and it was tempting—so very tempting—to give in to the serenity it offered. But the minute I did, any hope of freedom—of a future for Raela—was gone.

Somehow, I reached that cave. But I was a quivering, sweating, stinking mess, with little strength to do anything more than lean back and close my eyes.

They were near.

I couldn't hear them, but I could feel them.

And I could do nothing. Nothing more than grip my weapons and hope I had both the strength and time to use them.

They were not going to take me alive.

They were not going to take Raela back to her prison.

If nothing else, I would ensure *that*.

I waited.

Closer and closer they came, a wave of determination and anger that burned my skin and made breathing even more difficult.

Sound scraped across the night—a rock, bouncing lightly across the ground only ten feet away from the entrance of my small cave.

I opened my eyes and raised the guns.

For several heartbeats, nothing happened. They were out there—I could smell them now. There was six of them, and they tainted the air with the thick need to kill.

But they didn't. Not immediately. Maybe they were waiting for someone, or maybe they were simply being cautious. After all, they had no idea what weapons I might yet have with me.

A tremor ran through my arms, but I locked them in place and kept my fingers pressed against the triggers.

A footstep. Just one, and then nothing.

The tension within me was becoming so bad I could barely breathe, and part of me just wanted to scream at them, to make them attack and get it all over with.

But I'd never been one to give up, and I wasn't about to now. I kept the guns raised and my mouth shut.

Stone scraped lightly against stone—not from in front, but rather above. Someone was crawling across the roof, making their way toward the entrance. I scanned the ceiling, but there were no breaks or fissures he could see through, and no way to appraise the situation other than dropping down into the cave's entrance.

More movement, this time from both the left and the right of the cave's entrance. They had me surrounded. Time had just run out.

I closed my eyes and contemplated doing the unthinkable. But until there was absolutely no other choice, I would not go down that path.

They didn't attack.

They didn't get the chance.

Energy spun around me, energy that was warm, familiar, and filled with a mix of both happiness to see me and concern at my state.

Against all the odds, Cat and Bear had not only heard my call but had brought help in the form of the Broken Mountain shifters.

Relief flooded through me, washing away the last of my resistance and strength.

As the sound of gunfire broke the silence, I asked my two little ghosts to protect Raela, and then finally slipped into the welcoming arms of unconsciousness.

CHAPTER FOUR

IT WAS the steady sound of beeping that broke through the layers of darkness and dragged me back to consciousness. I didn't immediately open my eyes; I wanted to assess the situation before I gave any indication I was awake.

Both the softness of the bed that all but enveloped me and that steady electronic beeping indicated I was lying in a medibed. All trace of pain had fled, but whether that was because I was heavily sedated or because all my wounds had healed, I couldn't say. IVs had certainly been inserted into my arm, but I didn't in any way feel hazy or languid. Not that *that* meant anything, as I'd discovered in Winter Halo that modern drugs could affect me, and they'd surely invented better drugs than the ones my old medibeds still used. I twitched my fingers and toes, and then shifted my leg slightly. No pain, full response. The relief that swept me was almost ridiculous given my body had healed wounds far worse than a shattered leg before. Hell, I'd survived the chemical meltdown of almost my entire being.

But this was the first time since then that healing actually mattered. Not just for me, not just for Raela and my little ghosts, but for our entire world.

What I couldn't hear was the beeping of a second medibed, and that suggested I was the lone patient in this room. I also couldn't sense the presence of my two ghosts, and concern instantly surged—until I remembered my last-minute request to protect Raela. They were obviously still with her.

We are, Bear said. *She is safe. So are you.*

And Jonas? But even as I asked that question, the familiar scent of cat, wind, and evening rain warmed the otherwise sterile air, and I couldn't help the smile that touched my lips.

He wasn't only here—wherever "here" actually was—but in the room, sitting beside the bed.

Despite my desperate request for my ghosts to send help, I hadn't been entirely sure he'd answer. The Broken Mountains were a good distance from Central City, and while he did have kin here—both children *and* grandchildren—I'd gotten the impression he tended to avoid the place these days.

Besides, he and I were in a rather strange situation. We were situational allies who'd stepped past old enmity to become something more. We weren't really friends, and certainly weren't lovers, but there was definitely a spark—an attraction I'd not felt with anyone else ever before—happening between us.

And it was far more than just the instinctive reaction of a lure who'd been bred to seduce shifters such as him. How much more was something we'd agreed to explore *after* we'd caught Dream and put an end to the trio's immunity madness.

And it was an exploration I was looking forward to.

He's been rather grouchy, Cat said. *We've avoided both him and his questions.*

Which probably made him even grouchier. He was well aware of my deep connection with both Cat and Bear, and I had no doubt his irritation would have stemmed from them thwarting his attempts to gain information. No matter what might be happening between us personally, Jonas was first and foremost a soldier—and in times past, had in fact been a general. And like most good leaders, he was of the belief that while the life of every scout did matter, information retrieval had to be the first and foremost priority.

It was rather odd, though, that he simply hadn't ferreted the information out of my mind himself. While neither of us was telepathic, the rift that had caught the two of us appeared to have mashed my talent to hear the ghosts with his rift-given ability to mind speak with Nuri, and created a somewhat fragile connection between the two of us. It was a connection that had oddly strengthened in the days after he'd saved my life at Winter Halo, and one that—rather frustratingly—seemed to be stronger on his side than mine. But then, I guess he did have an advantage—he'd been communicating with Nuri that way for decades.

I opened my eyes.

Jonas immediately lowered his feet from the edge of the medibed and leaned forward. "How are you feeling?"

My smile grew. "A lot better than I look, if your expression is anything to go by."

An answering smile tugged at his lips and it gave his weatherworn features a warmth that was decidedly attractive. He was a lean and powerful man with mottled black hair—the only sign of the panther he could become—and vivid green eyes. But the three scars that ran from his right temple to just behind his ear and signified his former rank as a ranger —a feared group of soldiers back in the war who were still formidable frontline peacekeepers—seemed to be more visible than usual, and there were shadows under his eyes.

"That's because you almost died, Tiger, even with the transfusion—"

"Transfusion?" I frowned. "Does that mean I'm back in Central rather than in the Broken Mountains?"

While the medical facilities in the room were certainly more modern than anything I had in my bunker, I wouldn't have said they were state of the art, which was what I'd have expected if we were back in Central.

He raised an eyebrow, his amusement increasing. "Just because the Broken Mountains shifters still lead a nomadic life doesn't mean they go without modern conveniences or trappings. And given your history with them, you should be well aware of that."

There was no rancor in his voice when he mentioned my past, which was so vastly different from our initial conversations that—despite our agreement to move past old prejudices and hatred—I still found it surprising. But then, I was just as guilty as he when it came to judging people based on history rather than current actions and words.

"How long have I been unconscious?"

"Two days, which is not long enough by half, according to Tala, the head medic here." He half shrugged. "I told her the same lie you told us initially—that you were half shifter and had inherited the ability to heal without having to attain cat form."

I frowned. "She would have known the lie the minute she did blood tests."

"Except that she didn't do them. I forbade it, as it would have been too much of a risk."

Because of what I was. Because there were still those in these mountains who remembered the war, and who held great hatred for déchet.

"Yes and no," Jonas said, obviously catching my thoughts. "I didn't fear either the blood or DNA tests in and of themselves, as they wouldn't have revealed anything specifically worrying—"

"But I've tiger and vampire—"

"Yes, but so have I, thanks to that rift mixing together our DNA," he said. "But that bastard at Winter Halo *did* take blood samples from you, and it's more than possible Dream now has them."

"But surely she can't have people up here. I mean, you trust your own kin, don't you?"

"Again, yes, but my kin are a minority amongst the clans here. There is no telling how far her canker might have spread."

And being cautious never hurt—I'd learned *that* long ago. "So where did the blood come from?"

"Me—I'm also O positive." The amusement touching his lips reached up to crease the corners of his bright eyes. "Chalk it up as returning a favor, given how many times you've pulled my butt out of the fire."

"I think *that* score is more than even." I paused. "What about Raela? Have any suspicions been raised over her presence?"

"Everyone's presumed she's yours, and I've not said otherwise." He motioned at the wall to my right. "She's in the next room, and under the very watchful eye of your two young ghosts. It was all I could do to convince them to let Tala give her sustenance."

"Have any tests been run on her?" Because if there had been, all sorts of red flags would have been raised.

"No, though it was certainly an order Tala fought." He paused, his gaze narrowing. "What happened to you in that place? And where did you find the child? Were they using her for drug experimental purposes?"

"Yes." I hesitated, and then told him the whole story. What I'd seen, and what I'd done. To the base, and to the rest of those children.

He reached out and placed his hand over mine. It was such a simple touch, and yet it was one that said he knew. That he understood.

"You couldn't have done anything else for them," he said softly.

"I know. Just as I know Raela was the only one who had a chance." I squeezed his fingers and then gently pulled my hand from his. "That doesn't help the bitterness of a promise broken."

"It should, given you were fulfilling a promise to that child's ghost." He frowned. "Raela is a shifter name, yet I sense no shifter in her."

My smile held little in the way of amusement "That's because she's human, not shifter. I gave her the name, not the scientists."

He studied me for several heartbeats, his expression giving little away. Eventually, he said, "You *cannot* raise her."

"I can and I will."

"She was given wraith blood. She has to be monitored—"

"She's a *child*, Jonas. A *baby*." I balled my fists into the light sheet that was covering me, fighting to remain calm. "I'll *not* allow her to be raised in a sterile environment, being prodded, poked, and examined every single day of her existence. I saw what it did to my little ones—"

"Your ghosts are remarkably well-adjusted for beings who were created and raised in such conditions. I don't—"

"They're well-adjusted because I was able to give them at least some affection and caring!" I exploded. "And because they've spent the last century with me."

"Yes, but—"

"There is no 'but' in this. There is no negotiation." I took a deep breath and tried to calm down. "She's both a seeker and a witch. I can help her control the former, and Nuri can help with the latter. But I can tell you now, the worst thing anyone could *ever* do is put that child into a military situation."

"Is that your psychic instinct speaking?" he asked, voice flat. "Or the maternal one that has driven your actions ever since your failure to save the children in your bunker?"

I opened my mouth to say it was my seeker self, and then saw the compassion in his eyes. If there was anyone who could understand, it would be him. Thanks to the fact he could now converse with my ghosts, he not only knew the full horror of how they'd been killed, but had also glimpsed the cold aloneness they'd felt whenever I'd been assigned another mission.

"To be honest, it's both." I paused and scraped a hand through my short hair. Someone must have washed it, because it felt decidedly clean. "Have you told Nuri about her?"

"She knows you came out of that place with a child, but that's it."

"Then don't tell her the rest of it—"

"The child has wraith *blood* in her," he cut in. "I know where you're coming from, and I *do* understand, but you cannot expect—"

"Your niece has vampire blood and Rhea only knows what other pathogens in her system," I cut in. "And yet you fought Nuri tooth and nail to keep her with you in Chaos because you believed it was the only way to save her."

"That is different—"

"*How* is different, Jonas? Because she's kin?" I waved a hand toward the wall that separated Raela and me. "There is a connection between that child and me that is every bit as strong as a blood."

He studied me for a second, his expression troubled. "I still don't think—"

"Bring her in here," I said flatly.

He blinked. "Why?"

"Because I want you to see—to understand—why I can't let anyone else raise her."

He frowned, but nevertheless pushed from the chair and walked out of the room. I listened to the soft echo of his footsteps and, after a few minutes, heard the soft hum of a motor kick into gear.

Cat and Bear rushed into the room and spun around me, their energy and happiness flooding my mind and making me smile.

I like the little one, Cat said. *She's funny.*

Though I had no idea why, the rift that had hit Jonas and me had not only given him the ability to hear my ghosts, but me the ability to converse with them directly rather than via touch. It not only made our conversations a lot easier but also a whole lot less taxing on their strength. I raised my eyebrows. *She can talk to you?*

Well no, Bear said. *She makes lots of funny sounds and tries to catch our energy.*

She tried to catch the sunshine too, I said with a smile.

She likes the light, Bear said. *She cried when they dimmed them.*

I wondered if that was due to a fear of darkness, or something else. I guess none of us would know that until she was able to speak.

Jonas reappeared, guiding the air-powered miniature medicot with one hand. I pushed up into a sitting position and tugged the sheet back over my breasts. I wasn't normally so modest, but for some weird reason, I was in Jonas's presence.

He stopped the cot next to my bed and locked the brakes. Raela giggled and reached one hand toward me. I smiled and caught her little fist, then held out my other hand to Jonas. Without comment, he wrapped his fingers around mine, his palm calloused and skin warm.

"Now what?" he said.

"Connect with my mind."

It was easier if he did it. I was still very much a novice when it came to that sort of thing, and was only randomly catching his thoughts unless I concentrated extremely hard.

An odd buzzing ran through my mind—a connection that was different and weaker than the one I had with my ghosts, and one that very much spoke of his skepticism.

I closed my eyes and reached with the seeker part of me for Raela. Heard her giggle and then felt the spark of warmth as her fledgling seeker skills merged with mine. I dove deeper into her being, deeper into her thoughts, showing Jonas all that she was, all that she could be. Showed him her knowledge that I would come for her, that I would save her.

And then I quickly retreated, not wanting to tax her strength too much. Her talent might be impressive, but she was still untrained and extremely young.

Jonas released my hand but for several minutes, didn't say anything. He simply studied the little girl, his expression remote and giving little away.

Then he raised his gaze to mine. And I knew in that instant, he'd been connected to Nuri when I'd shown him Raela's bright soul.

Anger rose, but just as swiftly died. In truth, I needed Nuri on my side if I was to have any hope of not only keeping Raela safe, but away from the forces that would come after her. In fact, given the shifters' rescue of the two of us, it was surprising Dream hadn't already sent her forces against this place.

"That's because we killed all those who were chasing you," Jonas said. "And because we know these mountains far better than any she might send here."

"That doesn't alter the fact that every moment we're here, we're putting your people in danger."

"Yes, but it's also a truth that if Dream succeeds in her quest, then my family and everyone else in these mountains will be fighting for survival as never before." He glanced down at medicot. Raela immediately gurgled and reached up to him with chubby fingers. A smile twitched the corners of his lips. "There is a belief amongst many shifter clans that in times of need, the souls of our mightiest warriors will be reborn into the young, so that they may lead the way out of great darkness. I see the truth of that in her."

"And Nuri?" I asked softly. Hopefully.

"Says she is far too young to guide us out of the current situation, and has no desire to see how much worse the future might be if this child *is* a reborn warrior."

My heart began to beat a whole lot faster, though I wasn't entirely sure if it was relief or trepidation. "Does that mean she supports my intention to raise Raela as my own?"

He glanced at me and raised an eyebrow. "Has she really any choice, given the rather deadly army you can raise against her?"

She was talking about the adult déchet soldiers who haunted the lower reaches of my bunker, and who had—rather surprisingly—acquiesced to my request for help when we'd gone into the heart of a vampire den to rescue five of the missing children.

"I hardly think she fears *them*," I said, voice dry. "She's an earth witch of great power, and can very easily force their souls on to whatever hell she desires long before they ever caused her or anyone else any harm."

Which was something she'd threatened to do on more than one occasion if I didn't help her quest to find the missing children—and her threat hadn't just been aimed at the adult déchet.

It was something that had made me extremely wary of her. While I respected Nuri—and even liked her—she very much reminded me of some of the shifter generals I'd been assigned to during the war. They'd often been so single-mindedly focused on one definitive outcome that they were blinded to the true cost of that action or to other, better means of achieving it.

"Even an earth witch of her status has their limits," Jonas said. "And she wishes you to know that your ghosts are no longer under any threat. Indeed, she says that Central may yet have need of their services."

I snorted. "Has she forgotten that those déchet were designed to kill shifters rather than protect them?"

"No, but Central is a racially mixed city." He shrugged. "But that is neither here nor there. Despite her serious reservations, she agrees with your desire to raise her. But for her safety, Raela cannot be taken back to the bunker until all this is over. That place is now too easy a target."

I frowned. "I don't like entrusting her safety to others. Not when it will draw evil to the door of this place."

"I agree." Jonas reached past Raela's grasping fingers and lightly tickled her belly. Her happy laughter filled the air and tugged a smile from my lips. "Which is why I'll make arrangements for Tala to take her to Jarren over in New Port. She can keep an eye on the babe, and he can keep them both safe."

Jarren was Jonas's grandson. I'd met him a couple of times now, and he was very much a younger version of Jonas. Not that Jonas looked, in any way, his age. The rift he'd gone through just after the war's end had frozen the aging process in him, although he was not in any way immortal. He could die, just as I could. It's just that it was a whole lot tougher to kill either of us.

My frown grew. "Isn't that simply shifting the danger from

one point to another? And why would Tala even agree to something like that, given she'd be leaving her life and her family here for who knows how long?"

"Jarren controls the New Port mercenaries, and believe me when I say that no one will dare cross him." The smile that twisted his lips was part pride, part amusement. "He is, in every way, a chip off the old block, in a way my sons and daughters never were."

"But what about Tala? We can't make any guarantee on how long she might have to be away."

"Tala is my great-grandniece and will do as I ask, as she—like most of my family—is aware of both what has happened to Penny and of the dangers we now face."

"Ah. Good." I glanced down at Raela. I hated the thought of parting with her, but at least it was only temporary and for the best. "Promise me, Jonas, that if I die, you'll find her a good home. Someone who will love rather than study her."

"I promise." He reached out and caught my hand again. "But nothing will. You and I made an agreement, remember, and I will not let you out of it so easily."

I grinned, as he'd no doubt intended. "Nor I you." I once again disentangled my fingers from his. Until the situation was settled with Dream, I could not allow myself to linger on the promise in his touch. The man's presence was distraction enough. "Was the geo-locator still in my pocket when you found me?"

He nodded as he moved around to the other side of the bed and sat down. "Central has sent a squad of rangers out to investigate the sand base, but Nuri has ordered no action be taken against whatever stands at the Longborne coordinates as yet."

My eyebrows rose. "Why? I would have thought it best to mount an attack ASAP, otherwise we're merely giving Dream time to mobilize her defenses."

"Yes, but she'd rather that than sending people in without knowledge of what they might be facing."

Confusion stirred. "Why would it be Nuri's decision rather than the House of Lords councilors?"

"They cannot decide on what she does not tell them," he said. "Remember, Dream is inhabiting the life of someone either in the government or on that council."

I frowned again. "Yes, but she's obviously given them the sand base's coordinates if the council has ordered a ranger squadron in to investigate."

"Because Dream would be well aware of that attack by now, so there is no harm in passing on such information. We both rather suspect that anything relating to Dream's plans or her experiments at that place would well and truly have disappeared by now."

"Only if those who didn't get out survived the mess I made of it." I hesitated. "That RTX is rather deadly when you use a few of them in close proximity."

"I did warn you they were powerful," he said, amused.

"Yes, but I hadn't expected them to be strong enough to practically destroy a base."

"I take it, then, that it was bad enough for an evacuation order to be given?"

"Yes, and if Dream follows the procedure of every other military base I've been in, then the rangers definitely won't find anything of note."

"We still have to investigate." He hesitated. "Nuri wants the two of us to check out the Longborne base."

"I figured that the minute you said she hadn't given the coords to anyone." My tone was dry. "I *am* surprised, however, that she's risking your presence on such a mission."

His expression hardened. "She had no other choice, given it might be a case of third time unlucky when it comes to you going into a base alone."

There was an undercurrent in his voice that had the ridiculously attracted part of me tripping along quite happily. "Meaning she had no choice because you gave her none?"

"Indeed. A good general does not take unnecessary risks with the people under his or her command unless there is no other option," he said. "And that is *not* the case here."

It hadn't been the case before, either, so what had changed? I doubted it was the tremulous threads of attraction, if only because he—like me—was determined to save this place and his people from Dream's mad machinations no matter what the personal cost.

Perhaps it was simply a matter of him still believing Nuri's earlier decree that if I didn't rescue the missing children, no one would. And those missing children were now intricately entwined in the greater mission to stop the vampires and the wraiths from gaining sunlight immunity.

"In that case, why is she only sending the two of us?"

A smile twisted his lips. "Because I can put my foot down, but only so far."

"Which surprises me given she gave way to your desire to keep Penny near despite her own—decidedly fierce—reservations."

"Reservations that ultimately proved correct." His expression was a mix of regret and anger—the latter aimed at himself more than anyone else. "If she is not in Longborne, I will hold you to your promise to investigate the rift into which she was taken."

"I know." And I couldn't help but hope that we'd find her at Longborne. I had a bad, *bad* feeling that going into that rift would be nothing short of stepping into a trap. "Has Nuri been able to uncover anything about Longborne itself?"

He shook his head. "She hasn't dared ask. Dream would be alert for any search or question regarding that place."

"So we're basically going in blind."

"Not exactly," he said. "The coordinates place it deep within the heart of the Algar Plains, which means it's not a military base, as none were ever built out that way—not even temporary ones."

I frowned. "Then what is Longborne?"

"The Algar region produces most of Central's fine wool and cotton. As far as we can ascertain, Longborne is, in fact, Warehouse Five. It apparently holds the cotton bales in climate-controlled conditions until they're sent to the mills for further processing."

I frowned. "I wouldn't think a warehouse would be a particularly safe place for a genetics lab to be situated."

"No, but old military bases in a usable condition are rather scarce these days." He thrust to his feet. "I'll go make arrangements and let you rest. Nuri wants us out of here by tonight, if you're feeling up to it."

"And still wants us out of here by then even if I'm not."

A smile twitched his lips again. "Indeed." He briefly placed his hand on mine. "Rest, Tiger. I'll be back in a couple of hours."

Shall I follow him? Bear asked, almost eagerly.

If you want to, I said, amused. *But I do trust him these days.*

Which was something I *never* thought I'd say about a ranger.

Then I will, Bear said, and zoomed after him.

He's such a boy, Cat said, in an almost motherly tone.

I laughed. It was sometimes hard to remember that she was actually six years younger than Bear. And while the mental age of all déchet had rarely matched their physical age, thanks to the use of growth accelerates, it often seemed—both then and now—that Cat was the more mature of the two.

"He's only had my company for over a hundred years, Cat. I think he's deserving of a little male time."

There is nothing wrong with your company, Cat said, rather indignantly. *And it's not like there're only girls in our bunker.*

"But he is the oldest of them." I glanced toward the door as a woman came in. She was wearing everyday clothes—light brown pants and an emerald, close-fitting top—rather than a white coat, but I was in no doubt that she was the doctor. And given her mottled black hair, regal nose, and the fact that her eyes were the same shade of vivid green as Jonas's, I also had no doubt that this was his great-grandniece, Tala.

She stopped and scanned the bed's readouts. "Everything is looking rather impressive given you were at death's door two days ago. How do you actually feel, though?"

"A little tired, but other than that, fine." I hesitated, and then said, "Has Jonas talked to you yet?"

Her gaze came to mine. "About going to New Port? Yes, he has."

There was nothing in her tone to indicate how she felt about the request. Or indeed, whether she was a willing participant in the scheme.

"If you have no desire—"

"I have no desire for this world to be plunged into another war, and yet we all know that's what comes." Her voice remained without inflection, but there was something in her eyes that spoke of anger and heartache. "The vampires grow bolder and the wraith attacks more frequent. Light is our one protection and if that fails us...." She grimaced. "So I will play my part in this drama and hope that, in doing so, the future we all fear does not eventuate."

"Thank you—"

"Duty doesn't require a thank-you." She glanced down at Raela, and the shadows of heartache pressed closer in her gaze. "But I cannot deny it'll be a pleasure to look after a little one again."

I bit back my instinctive question, as it didn't really take a genius to figure out what might lie behind that sadness. It was also obvious she had no desire to talk about it. "Please keep her safe. She means a lot to me."

Tala's smile flashed, though that heartache lingered. "As is natural." She stepped around Raela's crib and removed the IVs from my arm. "I've ordered a protein meal to be brought in to you, as well as some fresh clothes. I believe Jonas is intent on leaving at sunset."

"And you and Raela?"

"Will depart with the New Port shuttle in the morning."

I frowned, wondering if that was safe, even as I knew Jonas wouldn't approve any plan that would endanger either Tala's or Raela's life. She must have guessed what I was thinking, because she added, "I'm a regular visitor to New Port—I help out at the clinic over there a couple of times a month. No one will think it unusual."

"Oh, good."

She smiled and patted my arm. "Rest until your meal gets here. I suspect my great-uncle won't allow much of it once you leave this haven."

"Probably not," I agreed, amused.

She smiled, checked the readouts on Raela's medicot, and then gave me a nod and walked out. I adjusted the bed so that it supported my back in an upright position, and leaned back into its softness. I was neither sleepy nor tired, and I very much wanted to be doing anything other than simply lying here. There was a growing itch in the back of my mind suggesting I needed to get back to Central and the false life I'd created there—a life that involved being the lover of one Charles Fontaine. Until very recently he'd been the financial director at Winter Halo, and I'd initially hooked up with him in the hope of gaining information about the company. But he'd quit just before all the shit had gone down there in order to take up his family seat in the House of Lords, and as much as part of me might have wanted to end our relationship right there and then, I couldn't. Not when being his mistress might well provide our only chance of getting anywhere near Dream without raising suspicions.

And though he was little more than a means to an end—just another target in a very long line of them—I couldn't help but feel some regret over the situation. Charles was a very nice, if somewhat old-fashioned shifter, and he deserved more than the falsehoods I was feeding him.

I thrust the thought away in irritation. This was what I'd been designed to do, and at least this time, I was doing it by choice rather than order.

I reached sideways and carefully drew Raela from her cot. She giggled happily as I flicked aside the sheet and laid her on my chest. After squirming about for several minutes, she fell asleep.

I'm glad she's going to be living with us, Cat said.

"So am I," I replied softly, resting my hand protectively on Raela's back. "So am I."

There were no tears during our goodbye. Raela might be nothing more than a babe, but the old soul within her seemed to understand the necessity of our parting. I promised I'd be back for her as soon as possible, and followed Jonas from the room. I didn't look back. I very much suspected those nonexistent tears just might make an appearance in my eyes if I did.

Cat and Bear danced along happily to the quick sound of our footsteps as we made our way through the bright halls of this place. The shifter clans might be nomadic, but the more I saw of this medical center, the more it seemed to be a permanent installation. There was nothing temporary about the concrete walls or floors, and there was a heaviness to the air that spoke of an underground structure.

"That's because it is." Jonas cast a quick look my way. "There are three other such places situated across the breadth of these mountains. While every clan does have healers who travel with them, it's not practical to constantly move the more intensive medical facilities."

"So this facility is manned full-time?"

"Yes." He stopped at a door and ran his RFID chip across the sensor. The red light flashed to green and the door opened. It wasn't an exit, as I'd half expected, but rather a storeroom. "The clans all support the cost of running the four facilities and paying the medical staff. This particular one is currently running with a skeleton crew, as the clans have moved east until the summer solstice."

I followed him into the bright room. "I'm guessing it's no coincidence that we're here, then."

"Actually, it was, as this just happened to be the closest facility to where you were found."

He walked to the end of the room and disappeared around a corner. I waited, my gaze sweeping the rows of shelves. There was a fortune's worth of stock here—the clans certainly weren't miserly when it came to provisions for these centers.

Jonas reappeared, carrying a small pillow, a blanket, and what looked like a baby sling. I raised my eyebrows and he grinned. "Meet the new Raela."

He handed me the sling and, as I attached it, wrapped the small pillow in the blanket. "This isn't going to fool anyone for too long," I said, even as I tucked the wrapped pillow into the sling and then adjusted the sides so that it looked— at least at first glance—like there was indeed a baby sleeping inside.

"It only has to fool someone long enough for us to get into the waiting ATV and drive out of these mountains."

My eyebrows rose. "You think someone will be watching?"

"I'd rather err on the side of caution." He pressed his fingers against my spine and lightly guided me to the door. "If there *is*, then it's better they believe we've taken Raela with us. It'll take some of the heat off Tala tomorrow."

"If she hasn't got any children, though, suspicions will be raised regardless. And unless you've restricted entry into the hospital, it won't be hard to uncover Raela's presence here."

"Except she won't be here," he said. "Tala's taking her across to her sister's place as we speak. Meryn has eight of her own, and trust me when I say no one is ever going to notice one more amongst their number. They simply do not stay still long enough to count. Heaven help Jarren when they all hit his encampment."

I grinned. "I take it this won't be the first time they've all been there."

"No—although I think he and his people threw a celebration party when they left the last time." Amusement tinged Jonas's voice as he held open the next door and ushered me through. "Jarren's group are relatively young—there're only a couple of his people who have had children, and they're all rather well-behaved compared to Meryn's kids."

I chuckled softly. "They sound like my little ones."

"Even your little ones are staid by comparison." We went through another door and stepped into the twilight. The air was warm and the breeze filled with the scent of wild-flowers and eucalyptus. We were in what looked to be some sort of old crater. Rough red-stone walls reared upward on either side of us, and the circular courtyard was ringed with trees and bright blooms that nodded gently in the stirring breeze.

Several all-terrain vehicles were parked to the left of the courtyard, but Jonas guided me to the right, where an older woman waited beside a somewhat decrepit-looking vehicle. She gave me a polite nod before moving her gaze to Jonas. Her expression very much suggested they were more than old friends, and something odd stirred inside me.

I frowned and climbed into the vehicle, but Jonas stopped and kissed her. It was a cheek kiss, nothing more, and yet there was tenderness there.

"Thanks for the loan of the vehicle, Franki," he said. "I'll try and return this one in one piece."

"If you don't," she said, her voice holding a teasing note, "I'll expect a replacement or payment in kind."

He laughed, an oddly tender sound that agitated that odd feeling within. "Or both, if I know you."

"Indeed." She lightly slapped his arm. "Go, before I'm tempted to do something a woman my age should not."

He grinned, jumped inside the vehicle, and then claimed the driver seat. She slammed the door shut and then stepped back as he started up the ATV. As the vehicle rolled toward the crater's exit, I said, "Old lover?"

Thankfully, there was nothing but simple curiosity in my tone.

His smile flashed. "Some fifty-odd years ago now. We parted when she decided to have children."

I raised my eyebrows. "Why would that end your relationship? It's not like shifters are monogamous, is it?"

"Well no, but it was hardly fair for the other suitors to have to contend with someone who is a far superior offering."

I laughed. "And modest beside."

"Indeed." His smile faded slightly and he half shrugged. "In all honesty, our affair had run its course by then, and I was ready to move on."

Was that a subtle warning not to expect too much from him, or was I simply reading too much into his statement? I had no real idea—it wasn't as if I'd ever had to contend with these types of thoughts or emotions before. "How long were you together?"

"Ten years."

I blinked. "Seriously?"

He glanced at me, eyebrow raised. "You have to remember that while I might only look thirty or so thanks to the rift stopping the aging process, I was in fact over seventy at the time. Even the wildest of us are slowing down by then."

"So how many children do you actually have?"

"Five daughters, four sons, sixteen grandchildren and, I believe—as of this year—nine great-grandchildren."

I blinked again and did the math. "You must have started *very* young."

"Most shifters are sexually active by the age of sixteen—"

"Yes, but we were at war for five of those years, and yet you still had nine children by the time you hit thirty. Presuming you were too busy during the war to chase tail, that's one kid a year."

"I did say it was a very rare for me to lose a battle for a suitor's favor."

"I know, but—" I stopped and shook my head. "Wow."

He laughed. "Given shifters are fertile well into their seventies and eighties, imagine how many little Jonases there would now be in the world if the rift *hadn't* made me infertile. It's was probably a good thing, in retrospect."

I raised an eyebrow. "You can't mean that—"

"And *that* is where you are wrong." There was a sudden seriousness in his eyes that had my pulse doing that weird little skip again. "If not for that rift, I would not be here with you. I may regret many things that happened both during the war and after it, but I will never regret that."

"Thank you," I said, simply because I needed to say something and it was the only thing that came to mind.

"For what? Admitting a simple truth, even if it is one that was a long time coming?"

"No," I said softly. "For being willing to see not the monster but rather the person. For treating me with respect even when the very sight of me instinctively repulsed you."

"I was never repulsed by the sight of you, Tiger. Quite the opposite." Amusement twisted his lips. "It was a conundrum that caused a lot of sleepless nights, let me tell you."

And I couldn't be sorry about that. Not given it had led to this moment, and a future filled with bright possibilities.

If we survived the present, that was.

A comfortable silence fell between us as he guided the old ATV through the twists and turns of the rocky mountain road. It was only once the slope decreased and the tree line began to thicken again that I risked taking off the sling and tucking it behind my seat.

"Where are the Algar flatlands in comparison to our current position and Central?"

"Remember the road we were on when that rift caught up to us?"

"I'm not likely to be able to forget something like *that*."

"I guess not." Another of those warm smiles touched his lips. "If we'd taken the left fork that day rather than the right one that took us back to Central, and then traveled for another hour or so through an area known as the red sands desert, we'd have arrived at the plains."

"So, we've got a lot of traveling ahead of us?"

"It'll be an all-night run."

"Then I'll take my turn driving."

He frowned. "I hardly think that wise given you're—"

"Jonas, I've been lazing about for two days doing nothing. Trust me when I say that I need neither any more sleep nor further recovery time."

She gets irritable if she sleeps too much, Bear commented.

This is true, Cat said solemnly. *I wouldn't advise forcing any more on her*.

Jonas laughed, a merry sound that filled the cabin. I took a swipe at the energy of the two ghosts, but they ducked away, their giggles joining Jonas's and widening my own smile even further.

"I guess I should not ignore the advice of those who have known you longest," he said. "We'll work in three-hour shifts. Agreed?"

I nodded and settled into a more comfortable position in the seat. Silence fell between us again and the night rolled on without incident. I was at the control when dawn started spreading rose-colored fingers across the sky and the blip appeared on the radar.

I frowned and requested more information. The screen scrambled for a moment as the orientation shifted and magnified.

There wasn't one blip. There were three.

I swore softly and touched Jonas's shoulder. He woke instantly and sat upright. "Problem?"

I motioned to the radar. "Three of them."

He leaned forward and hit a couple of buttons. The screen scrambled once more before clearing. He studied the information on the screen for several seconds and then swore. "They're air scooters, from the look of it."

"Military?"

"Possibly." He glanced out the front window. There was nothing to see but miles and miles of nothingness. "Where are we?"

"About an hour away from the plains."

"Which puts us too far away from the old forest to get back there before our tail catches us." He scrubbed a hand across his jaw, the sound like sandpaper. "This puts a major crimp in our plans, given they'll surely have warned Longborne by now of our approach."

"Any idea where they could have come from? They couldn't have followed us from the Broken Mountains—the radar would have caught them long before now."

"They're probably from Central. It's the closest major city and the only one in the region that has military scooters."

"But why would Dream risk sending out either rangers or a

military unit after us? Especially when she could simply warn her forces at the warehouse to be ready for us."

"Something she's undoubtedly already done. And this is not the first time she's ordered rangers to chase us, remember." His voice was grim. "If she *is* on the Council of Lords rather than merely one of their advisors or a government worker, then few in the military would gainsay her."

It was still a very large risk, but maybe—given she'd now lost two of her three installations—she thought it worthwhile.

I glanced out the window to judge the amount of true darkness we had left—an easy task for someone with vampire in their blood. "How long will it be before they catch us?"

"Given their speed, about twenty-six minutes."

We had a good thirty-three minutes left before the dawn robbed me of the ability to shadow without a protective light screen and a whole lot of effort. "What sort of radar system have the scooters got in them?"

"The scooters are designed to quickly transport a small number of personnel from one place to another, and are therefore stripped to basics." He glanced at me. "Why?"

"Because if we're going to do something, we need to do it now, while we've still got the night on our side."

He raised an eyebrow. "You've got an idea?"

"That would depend on whether their radar systems are capable of seeing beyond the surface."

A slow smile touched his lips. "I like the way you think."

"Thanks. Shall we stop?"

"Indeed. Let's do this."

I stopped the ATV as he climbed out of the seat and moved to the back of the vehicle. The range of weapons he produced out of the storage bins had me smiling.

Nineteen minutes later, we were ready to rain hell down on our pursuers.

CHAPTER FIVE

WHAT'S HAPPENING UP THERE, Cat? I asked, as I struggled to keep my mouth clamped around the plastic breathing tube that was my one and only source of air right now.

It would have been a whole lot easier to simply shadow, as dawn was still at least eight minutes away, but we had no idea what might wait in Algar. Given it could take every bit of my vampiric shadowing skills to get us both into Warehouse Five, let alone back *out*, we'd decided to save my strength and go with an old-fashioned ambush instead.

They're doing a slow circle around the ATV, Cat said. *The jets are stirring the sand up, but they're not close enough to reveal either you or Jonas.*

Good.

Sand trickled past the collar of my shirt and itched at my skin. I resisted the urge to move, knowing it would only cause more sand to fall and possibly reveal my location. Burying ourselves in what amounted to a shallow grave close to the ATV had seemed like a good idea at the time, but six minutes of lying here with the weight of the earth pressing around me and the sand getting into unmentionable places was more than enough.

One of the vehicles has landed, Cat said.

The other two?

Hover.

Damn. We needed all three on the ground before we could move. It was the only hope we had of taking out all of our hunters without anyone either escaping or having the chance to warn Dream of the attack.

I continued to draw air from the short plastic tube, my body tense and muscles twitching with the desire for action.

The door opens on the one that has landed, Cat informed me. *Three men have gotten out.*

Are the other two crafts still in the air?

Yes.

I silently cursed. *Bear, can you go investigate the airborne scooters, and see if it's possible to disable them? Cat, can you check the landed one, and see how many men remain within?*

Already on it, Bear said.

Meaning Jonas had already asked him. I wasn't entirely sure how I felt about that, which was utterly ridiculous given we were a team.

In the grounded scooter, Cat said, *one soldier remains. Knocking him out would do for the moment, would it not?*

Indeed it would, I said, amused at the anticipation in her tone. *But wait until the other men are clear of the vehicle and there's no possibility of them realizing he's been attacked. Bear?*

I slipped in through a vent. There is a box of armaments secured at the rear of the vehicle. He paused. *The three who walked from the grounded scooter now approach Jonas's side of the ATV.*

Meaning we only had minutes, if that, to make this happen. *Jonas, I'm going to shadow and take out that third ATV. Bear, Cat, on my mark, move.*

Ghostly eagerness met my comment, and it was accompanied by a vague sense of agreement from Jonas.

I called to the gritty darkness of my underground hideaway, and wrapped it around me, inside and out. Then I pushed upwards, the sand falling like a waterfall both through and around me. It was going to itch like hell when I resumed flesh form.

Once above ground, I did a quick circle to locate the scooters—which were little more than cylindrical tubes with stubby wings—and then raced across to one uninhabited by a ghost. I approached the front of the vehicle warily and looked in through the front screens. Aside from the wash of light coming from both the radar and control screens, the cabin appeared to be relatively dark. Though there were eight seats within the craft, only four were occupied. Better odds, but I'd still have to be fast if I wanted to take them all out.

I located the air vent, took a deep breath—a useless action in this form, and one that was a definite hangover from flesh—and then said, *Right, going in. Hit them, people.*

The thought had no sooner formed than gunfire erupted. I surged through the vent and into the scooter's cabin. There were two people sitting in front of the control panels—one a sharp-faced woman who was obviously in charge given the rapid-fire orders she was giving—while the other two were unbuckling their harnesses, ready for action. The control board's blue-and-white light washed across some of my particles, making them sting and stir in reaction, but thankfully it wasn't strong enough to tear me back to full flesh. I partially reformed, silently drew my weapons, and then shot the two men at the rear of the vehicle before they even realized I was there. The driver was next. But as his brains splattered across the windshield, the commander spun and returned fire. One bullet grazed my arm and the other went straight through my particle chest—a killing shot had I been fully flesh.

I took her out, then reformed and dragged the driver's body away from the control panel. Once I'd landed the scooter, I cut the engine, opened the door, and went out into the ever-growing brightness of day.

Just as I did, the third scooter exploded into a huge ball of flame. I threw myself down, covering my head with my hands as bits of metal, glass, and Rhea only knew what else ricocheted through the air. Heat from the fireball briefly sizzled across my skin but just as quickly fled.

I pushed upright. *Bear? You okay?*

Yes. His energy spun around me, tired but filled with excitement. *We should explode more things. That was fun.*

A smile tugged my lips. *Cat? Everything okay with you?*

I knocked the driver out. He still breathes.

"Good," Jonas said, as he appeared from around the other side of the ATV. "Because I need to question him. How bad is that wound on your arm, Tiger?"

I glanced at it. The bullet had gone in and out, and the subsequent wound was as sore as hell. But nothing vital had been hit and the bleeding had already begun to ease. "It's nothing to worry about."

"And, as we so recently discovered, you'd say that even on the point of death." His tone was amused. "Let's go question Cat's prisoner."

I fell in step beside him. "Are these men from Central, do you think?"

"They could be, but they're not rangers, and the vehicles aren't military."

I frowned at the scooter we were approaching. "They *look* military."

"Yes, but I'd say they're decommissioned stock."

"Who else but the military would have use for them? They're not powerful enough for haulage, and they'd be useless as people movers given they can't carry more than eight. Besides, they were built for speed rather than comfort."

"Vehicles like these are often used in food production areas, especially in the livestock zones, where there's a need to do a daily check." He stepped onto the ramp and strode inside.

Cat's energy danced around us—a dangerous action given the metal bar she was still holding.

Jonas ducked without comment and pulled the driver off the control panel. There was a nasty-looking cut on the left side of his head and blood running down the side of his face and into his beard. His skin had a grayish tinge and his breathing was labored. He wasn't long for this world, I suspected.

Jonas glanced at the name inscribed on the man's uniform and then said in a commanding tone, "Grant, report. What happened here?"

The man groaned and tried to lift his head. It rolled back against the seat's headrest instead.

"Grant, this is an *order*. Report immediately."

"Ambush," he mumbled. "Unknown casualties."

"And the target?"

"Unknown."

"Can you make it back to base?"

"Need help."

"And you'll get it. But I need the coords, soldier."

He reeled off a set of numbers and Jonas glanced at me. "That's not Central. It's Carleen."

"None of the rifts there are large enough—" I stopped.

If Dream could create transportation rifts, why couldn't she alter their size to suit her needs? The one stationed over the bones of the Carleen ghosts was certainly growing, and while she couldn't risk using *that* one for vehicle transport given it was linked to the basement under Government House, that didn't mean she couldn't alter the others.

"Which means," he said, voice as flat as his expression, "they might have come from the same place Penny is now held."

"Penny isn't being held," I said gently. "She went there willingly."

And had stepped through *me* to do it.

She cannot be forgiven for that, Cat commented. *It was a betrayal.*

Yes, it was. And yet, I couldn't condemn her. Not when she'd let me live when she could have very easily done otherwise. Cat and Bear would have protected me with everything they had, but not even they could have won out against the sheer number of vampires who'd been in Chaos that night if Penny had ordered them to take my life.

And given her link with them—along with the fact she'd known they were about to attack Chaos and had warned no one—I very much suspected she was more than capable of controlling them.

Or soon would be.

Anguish briefly touched Jonas's expression, but was just as swiftly erased by the mask of emptiness. He returned his attention to the injured man. "That's too far, soldier. The closest medical facilities are at Warehouse Five—"

"Not authorized—"

"Call sign, soldier," Jonas snapped.

A groan escaped. "Echo three-two."

"Is there a transport entrance?"

"Never been there—" Grant's voice faded and his head dropped forward.

Jonas pressed to fingers against Grant's neck. "Unconscious, not dead."

"I take it you're planning to use this man as a means of getting close to the warehouse?"

"I can't think of another way of getting into that place easily —not without resorting to your skills. And, as we've already discussed, we may need those to get back out." He undid the driver's harness, then grabbed him under the arms and dragged him free of the seat. "You want to get our kit out of the ATV?"

"What are you going to do with it?"

"The ATV? Blow it up."

I raised my eyebrows. "Didn't you promise to bring it back in one piece?"

"I did," he said, rather cheerfully, "And not for one instant did Franki believe me. Which is why she demanded the replacement."

"Or payment in kind."

He glanced at me, and there was something in his eyes—a heat that spoke to not just to the part of me designed to attract and be attracted to shifters, but also the part that should *not* be there.

Heart. Emotion.

"However much affection I still hold for her, she is the past." His voice was soft. "I learned a long time ago to never look back, but rather chase the future. Especially when the possibilities on offer are worth chasing."

I half smiled. "Or not. You have no idea how staid I can really be."

"Which is all part of the exploration process." He placed Grant across the two rear seats and strapped him in. "Is there anyone left alive in the scooter you took out?"

"No."

"Good. I'll go over and strip the uniforms from the two who are the closest match to us, and meet you back here."

"How do you plan to blow the ATV up?"

"I scrounged another RTX brick from my kin—it's in our kit. Set it for ten minutes."

I nodded and headed out. He moved back to the control panel and, as I walked down the ramp, placed a mayday call. His voice was a close enough imitation of Grant's to make it believable.

Once I'd emptied the contents of the ATV's two storage bins into a couple of carryalls, I bent and stuck the RTX out of sight under the control panel—just in case someone happened by before the bomb went off—then grabbed everything else and walked back to the scooter. Jonas followed me in a few seconds later. His face was now not only covered with a whole lot more grime, but blood that wasn't his.

"Cover?" I asked.

He nodded and handed me a uniform. "This belongs to the commander. You'll probably have to roll up the sleeves until you shift shape, as she was a good deal taller than you."

I hadn't really taken all that much notice; aside from the fact both she and her men had been sitting, they'd also been nothing more than targets—which perhaps meant there was more déchet soldier in me than I'd ever dared admit.

Jonas turned around to give me some measure of privacy as we both changed. It really was ridiculous for someone like me to feel any sort of awkwardness in the presence of a man, but I guess this was the first time in all my long years I'd actually been more than *just* sexually interested in someone.

"Did Warehouse Five respond to the mayday call?" I rolled up my sleeves as I followed him to the front of the scooter and sat in the codriver seat.

He nodded as he punched buttons, first closing the door and then starting up the engines. As the red sand plumed around us, he said, "I think they must have sought permission from either Dream or from whatever base these scooters came from, as it took a few minutes to get approval."

"Even with permission, they're going to be suspicious of us and on high alert."

"Indeed. But I have a solution." He reached into his pocket and took out two bloody RFID chips held within separate plastic containers.

I raised my eyebrows. "They sort out the problem of me

getting into the facility, but you can't alter your appearance without help from Nuri's magic."

"No, but the man I took the chip from is roughly my coloring and height, and with all the grime, I should get a pass."

Our mission was in deep trouble if he didn't. "Do you know which one is which?"

"Of course." He shifted a grip slightly, revealing a small X marked on the top on one. "There should be enough false skin left from the kit you took into the sand base to cover us both."

I nodded and rose to get the kit. Once the scooter was off the ground and the coordinates punched in, he offered me his arm. I carefully located his RFID chip then placed the stolen one on top of it and sprayed on the false skin to hold it in place. I repeated the process with mine, then leaned back in the seat and glanced at the GPS. Thirteen minutes more until our destination.

"Did they give any indication which entrance we're being directed to?"

"It won't be the entrance the warehouse itself uses. It'd cause the sort of interest they're trying to avoid if an old military vehicle carrying a wounded soldier docked there."

"It will also make it impossible to have the sort of lockdown we'll probably face."

"If they don't place us under either a full watch or in a secure area, I'll be very surprised."

"Getting in is not going to be the problem—getting out will

be." I grimaced. "But I guess we can worry about *that* when we get to that point."

He glanced at me, eyebrow raised. "Did you approach all missions in such a haphazard manner?"

I half smiled. "It was hardly practical to plan anything in my previous line of work."

The amusement faded from his expression. "How many of your targets did you kill during the war?"

"How many did you?" I countered. "It was a war, Jonas. The only difference between you and I—aside from being on opposite sides—is the fact you had a choice in everything you did. I did not."

He was silent for a moment, then said, "I never really thought of it like that."

"Few did," I said. "The shifters have spent decades blaming the weapons for the atrocities they committed during the war when you should have focused your anger and hate on those who were *controlling* said weapons and pulling the trigger."

"All of which is true." A wry smile touched his lips. "But it would hardly have fostered goodwill between humans and shifters in the years afterward."

"No, but if people had taken a moment to *think* rather than react at the end of the war, you might now have a fighting force capable of standing up to the might of the Others."

And saved us from death in the process, Cat said.

"And *that* is something I really wish I had the capacity to change." Regret was evident in his tone. "But it was a decision the rangers were never consulted on."

"And one you would not have changed even if you had been," I countered.

"In truth, no. But I would have argued for a cleaner death." He glanced at me, expression grim. "Believe that, if nothing else."

I did believe, if only because he'd witnessed firsthand what Draccid could do when the gas had been used against his men during an attack against a human military base. However much he might have wanted revenge for both that situation and others, he would also have known there was a multitude of ordinary humans within our bunker—people who helped with day-to-day operations and kept the base running. He might have a deep, instinctive hatred for déchet, but he'd never been so blinded by it that he'd so wantonly and cruelly inflict such a death on those who were only doing their job.

Silence fell between us. As the minutes ticked by, a dark blot appeared on the horizon, growing even larger as we drew closer. It was a long building that was at least four stories high, and had a huge number five emblazoned on one section of its dark roof. It appeared to be made of the same metal as the curtain wall that protected Central, and I couldn't see any ground-level entrances. In fact, there didn't seem to be any entry points at all, which suggested they were either hidden or that we were approaching from the wrong angle.

It was unfortunate that our prisoner had never been inside the warehouse. He might be human, but given the restriction against killing them had apparently disappeared, I might have been able to use my seeking skills to pick up a sense of the layout so that we wouldn't be going in blind.

But, as usual, it looked like we'd have to do things the hard way.

"I'm not liking the look of that place," I said. "And I can't shake the growing sense that things will go very, very wrong inside."

"And I'm thinking you're right." He studied the building for a couple of minutes and then said, "I'll contact Nuri and see if we've anyone close enough to provide a diversion."

"I didn't think she wanted to risk any more people than necessary?"

"She doesn't, but she won't be pleased if we get in to that warehouse and can't get out."

"Any good commander knows that that's sometimes the price of gaining information."

"Yes, but in this case, she'll do whatever it takes to keep you alive." His gaze met mine. "The wind whispers of a future without hope if you are not part of the forthcoming battle."

My eyebrows rose. "So now I'm responsible for the fate of a world? When in Rhea did *that* happen?"

He shrugged. "The future is never static. It changes as events change."

"And the missing children?"

"She didn't mention them, so I presume her prediction hasn't altered."

"Marvelous." Not that I intended to stop searching even if their fate *had* altered. If the future was always changing, it meant there was always hope.

Jonas didn't reply, and the slight buzz of energy running across the back of my thoughts said that he was in contact with Nuri. I wasn't entirely sure what sort of diversion she could arrange at such short notice, but if it only distracted the guards within that building for a few minutes, it might very well mean the difference between getting out or not.

Living or not.

As the black building began to dominate the horizon, the radio came to life. "Vehicle approaching from the old Central Road, please identify yourself."

Jonas gave the call sign and then added, "We have an injured soldier on board and have received prior approval for approach and landing."

"Please hold position and wait for confirmation."

Jonas placed the scooter in hover mode and looked at me. "You'd better shift shape."

I climbed out of the seat and moved to the rear of the vehicle, well out of the sight of anyone who might be watching us through the front windows. I didn't want to expend too much energy on a full change, so I simply added a little to my height and then altered my face just enough so that at first glance it matched the commander's sharp features. Then I moved back.

Jonas's studied me for a second and then said, "That should pass. Ready?"

"As I can be." I hesitated, my gaze sweeping the rather ominous-looking building ahead. "But my wing-it approach to planning might not be the best mode of operation right now."

"It's not like we have another choice." Amusement touched his expression. "And between the two of us *and* our ghostly friends, I'm sure we'll figure out something."

There are grenades in the rear locker, Bear said, his tone hopeful. *I can blow more things up*.

And there's also another metal bar, Cat added. *It doesn't take much energy to whack heads*.

I laughed, as did Jonas. It was a warm, rich sound that filled the air and momentarily broke the gathering tension.

"Echo three-two," the metallic voice said. "Confirmation has been given. Please prepare vehicle for auto-guidance."

Jonas pushed a few buttons and then said, "Guidance is yours, control."

The scooter lurched slightly as the tractor beam latched on, and then slowly moved forward. Jonas rose and moved to the back of the scooter.

"We'd better conceal as many weapons as possible. I don't think we'll be allowed to carry within that building."

I rose and walked over to the second carryall. "And if they have body scanners in the building?"

"Then the game will be up regardless." His voice was blunt. "No amount of dirt and blood will hide the fact my DNA is very different to that of the RFID's owner."

"True." I took off my utilities belt, undid the coverall, and then strapped it back around my waist. After clipping on a number of handguns, a couple of knives, and the dart gun I'd used in the sand base, I did the coverall back up. The commander had been a much larger woman than me, so even though I now matched her height, the coverall remained loose enough that the belt and its cargo weren't immediately obvious.

I glanced out the front windshield and saw that we were now so close to the warehouse that I could see the heaving pitting that scarred the wall's black surface. That wasn't weather damage; it was war, which meant this place had been around far longer than I'd presumed.

As the vehicle turned and was lifted up the wall's steep side, I reached for another handgun and offered it, butt-first, to Jonas. "You need to shoot me."

He looked at the gun for a moment, and then at me, "Good idea. But it'd be best if we were both sporting wounds, otherwise we risk getting separated."

He took the gun, unclipped the safety, and then aimed the weapon's nose at the fleshy part of his left arm. The bullet ripped through both the uniform and his skin in short order before burying itself in the scooter's metal side not far from the door.

As blood began to soak his sleeve, he looked at me. "Ready?"

"Shoot me in the shoulder," I said, bracing myself against the pain that was about to hit.

"No."

"Jonas, I can heal—"

"Yes, but we can't risk you being incapacitated for even a few minutes."

"But a flesh wound might not get us—"

"I don't care. I'm not—"

I didn't let him finish. I simply grabbed the gun, flipped it around, and did it myself. It felt like a hammer had smashed through my shoulder and the force of it had me staggering back. I braced my good hand against the side of the scooter to steady myself, then closed my eyes and sucked in air as I battled the haze of red that momentarily threatened awareness.

"Rhea save me from stubborn women," Jonas muttered. A second later, he was gently pressing some sort of padding on both the front and the back of the wound.

"I'll be okay." I raised a hand and wiggled a couple of fingers. Needles of fire raced upward in response. "See? Still got full movement."

He made a disparaging sound. "Let's just hope that the ruse works, otherwise you've incapacitated yourself for nothing."

"It'll work." It had to. It might be the only real hope we had of getting into the true heart of the place.

The scooter stopped its upward movement and began to rotate again. Jonas reached into the medikit for the sealer, spraying the exit wound first. It ran out before more than a fine mist hit the entry wound.

"It's probably better that I'm bleeding when I get in there." I took the padding from him and held it against the wound with my good hand. "You'd better get back to the pilot seat."

He hesitated, seeming ready to say something, then half shrugged and went back to the driver seat.

I followed him over. Despite the pressure I was putting on the wound, blood seeped past my fingertips and soaked my coverall. I just hoped the pain was worth it—that it did, in fact, stop them noticing the ill fit of the uniform and the weapons it concealed.

A large section of the wall directly ahead of us had begun to slide to one side, revealing a brightly lit loading dock. Six well-armed soldiers lined either side of the small runway.

"They're not taking any chances," I murmured.

"I'd be more surprised if they *were*."

I sat down and scanned the area as the scooter was slowly drawn into the heart of the loading bay and parked at an angle to the left of the strip.

"Echo three-two, please lower the ramp and prepare for inspection," the metallic voice said.

Jonas glanced at me, eyebrow raised. "Ready?"

I nodded. He opened the door and then spun around in his seat. Three men flowed into the scooter before the ramp was fully down, their gazes doing a quick sweep before resting on us.

They didn't say anything. They just watched us, weapons raised and ready to use. After another minute or so, a fourth man appeared. He was holding a scanner rather than a gun.

"Present RFIDs, please," he said, his voice as deep as his body was wide.

"Commander Jenkins, at your service, sir." I rose and held out a blood-slicked arm. "I've a man who needs urgent medical care—"

"All in good time, Commander." He ran the scanner over my stolen chip and studied the screen for a minute. When the light flicked from red to green, he looked at Jonas. "Your turn."

Jonas held out his arm without comment. When the scanner beeped approval, he moved on to the driver Cat had attacked. Once the scanner had cleared our victim, the big man finally relaxed.

"Right, Commander, we've approval for you and you people to be taken to the med center for treatment."

"I believe Officer Grant might have a serious head injury—"

"And our facility is state-of-the-art. If for any reason we *can't* handle it, we'll certainly stabilize his condition and move him on to a larger center." He paused and glanced at his screen. "Headquarters wants a full report once the two of you have been cleared by the docs."

"Of course," I said, voice cool.

He nodded and glanced at the nearest soldier. "Escort the commander and Officer Wright to med center one. I've called an airbed for Officer Grant. He's to be taken immediately to trauma in med center two."

The armed man saluted and then glanced at us. "This way, if you please, Commander."

We followed without comment. As we walked down the ramp, a second soldier fell into step behind us. Our footsteps echoed almost forlornly across the loading bay's vastness. There were no other vehicles parked here and the only people evident were the remaining nine armed men. As we passed them, they turned as one and then spread out around the scooter. No one was getting in or out of that vehicle without going through them first.

There were three doors leading off the loading bay—two of them were large enough to allow vehicle access, but the third was smaller, and obviously meant solely for foot traffic. It was to this one we were led.

The door silently slid aside as we entered. I quickly scanned the door but couldn't see the telltale signs of inset scanning equipment. Relief stirred but didn't last. Just because this door didn't have it, didn't mean others wouldn't.

The corridor beyond was bright, white, and soulless, and it very much reminded me of every military corridor in every bunker I'd been in. But there were no doorways here, no windows for natural light, and certainly no signs to give an indication of where we might be headed.

I frowned and glanced at Jonas. *Keep calm*, his gaze seemed to say. Or maybe it was a distant echo of his thoughts. Either way, it made me smile. Trepidation might be stirring, but I certainly *wasn't* going to react without thought or reason.

You want us to investigate? Bear asked.

I hesitated and then said, *Yes, but keep together. If there's the slightest indication of anyone sensing your presence, get back to me ASAP.*

Unless there's a Nuri in this place, that's unlikely, Cat said, and then they both intoned, before I could say anything further, *but we promise to be careful.*

I smiled as they raced away, their laughter briefly gifting the cold air warmth.

Our footsteps echoed on. After another five minutes, Jonas said, "How much further, soldier? The commander is losing a lot of blood with all this movement."

"Three minutes," the man in front said, without looking at either of us.

Jonas grunted and flexed his fingers—the only sign of the tension I could feel in him.

We rounded a corner. A bank of four elevators lay directly ahead, each one guarded by two armed men. It was the first indication that this place was more than just a storage facility for cotton and wool bales. No matter how valuable a commodity either might be, eight men guarding access to lower storage levels was certainly overkill.

As we approached the first elevator, one of its guards stepped forward and wordlessly offered a scanner. Our guard ran his RFID chip across it and, a second later, the elevator door opened. We followed him in and, as the doors closed, our guide said, "Med center one."

The elevator swept us sideways rather than down, which was interesting. Maybe the laboratories we were seeking weren't underground, as we'd been expecting, but rather somewhere on the top level of this vast building.

The elevator came to a halt and the door opened. The soldier led the way down another bright, sterile corridor.

This one did at least have various doors leading off it. I scanned each one as we passed, but there was no indication of what might lie beyond them and no sound emanating from them. For all the physical security so evident in this warehouse, it seemed oddly empty and very quiet.

We finally approached a door with a simple red cross on it. The soldier stopped, scanned his chip and, as the door slid open, waved us inside. Neither he nor his silent partner followed us. Instead, they stationed themselves either side of the door. We weren't getting out without having to go through them first.

As the door closed behind us, a friendly voice said, "Jenkins and Wright, I'm presuming?"

I glanced around and spotted a stick of a man with a thick thatch of gray hair coming through a second doorway. He paused to thrust his palms under the sanitizer on the wall and then rubbed his hands together as he walked toward us.

"Security tells me you got into a spot of bother out in the Red Plains Desert," he continued. "Sorry to hear that, of course, but gunshot wounds are certainly more exciting to deal with than the usual crap we get in this med center."

"What sort of wounds are you usually dealing with?" Jonas stopped several feet away from me, his gaze doing a slow sweep of the room. Checking for security features, although at first glance, there didn't even appear to be cameras.

"Oh, the usual stuff for a warehouse like this—torn muscles and crushed limbs, mainly. You'd think people would be more careful around automated equipment, but no, they seemed to think automated means risk free."

Meaning either this doctor had no idea this place was anything more than just a warehouse, or he was a very good actor. I had a suspicion the answer wasn't the latter.

He motioned me to move my fingers from the padding. The bleeding had stopped quite a few minutes ago, so when he gently pulled the pad away, it tore the clot and started the bleeding again. He made a soft clucking sound. "In and out wound, from the look of it. Why didn't you seal the front rather than use padding?"

"Ran out of sealer," I said, aware that Jonas was now silently moving toward the second door. "How bad is it?"

"Have you full use of your hand?"

I nodded and wiggled my fingers.

"Then nothing vital was hit. But we'll put you on a medibed and see what that says." He paused and glanced around as Jonas opened the other door. "Hey, you can't go in there."

Jonas stopped in the doorway, preventing it from closing again. "I'm just looking for the bathroom facilities."

"They're over there." The doc somewhat irritably waved his hand to a small corridor behind and to the left of where we were standing. "That's my private quarters, soldier, and I'll ask you to come away."

Jonas gaze came to mine even as he obeyed. I knew then that, for whatever reason, we were alone in this place. "Sorry," he said evenly. "Meant no harm."

The doc grunted and returned his attention to me. "We'll get you over to the medibed and—"

The rest of the sentence died on his lips as Jonas knocked

him out and then caught him before he could hit the floor. He heaved the man over his shoulder, walked across to the nearest medibed, and dumped him into it.

I moved to the light screen and ordered the doc sedated and strapped down. "How long do you think we've got before those soldiers realize something is wrong?"

"How long is a piece of string?" Jonas retorted. Then he glanced at me and grimaced. "Sorry, just tense. This has been far too easy."

"It won't remain that way. It never does."

"That's comforting."

I smiled. "Were the doc's quarters in that room, as he said?"

"Yes. There appeared to be an unlocked light screen in there—he must have been on it when we came into the room."

"Fortunate."

"Yes."

He turned and walked back to the room. I shifted back to my own form and then followed, rotating my arm in an effort to ease the ache and keep it mobile. The bleeding had once again stopped—yet another indication that my healing abilities had been fast-tracked by the rift—but I couldn't afford any stiffness developing. Not with what was probably coming.

The doc's quarters were sparse even by my standards, consisting of little more than a single bunk, a locker, a small autocook, and the desk with the light screen. The screen had frozen on what looked to be the hairy butt of a man.

After a moment, I realized there were actually two men and that they were mid-coitus.

"He could have at least chosen a less graphic point to freeze on," Jonas muttered, and hit the pause button. The sound of approaching sexual gratification instantly filled the air. He pressed the mute button, then downsized the picture. "Right, let's see what this baby can tell us."

He opened the main drive and began flicking through the various sectors. I leaned my good shoulder against the wall and rolled up the sleeves on the now too-long coverall. From what I could see, there wasn't really a whole lot of information to be found.

After a moment, he grunted. "There's nothing but medical records on this thing. The doc hasn't got any access to get into the mainframe."

"That's not really surprising."

"No." Jonas thrust up from the chair. "I guess we're going to have to do this the hard way."

"It'd be best if we wait for Cat and Bear to return. They can provide a general layout and tell us where the bad stuff might be hiding."

"As long as they don't take too long. The countdown clock to discovery started ticking the minute we took out the doc."

He walked over to the doc's bunk and pressed a wall panel at the end of the bed. There was a soft click and then the panel opened to reveal a closet. Hanging inside were several lab coats and two small stacks of neatly folded clothing.

Jonas must have caught my surprise, because he glanced at

me, grin flashing. "This sort of setup is common in modern-day military accommodation."

"Pampered is what you lot are," I said with a smile. "We had to make do with a footlocker."

He chuckled softly as he pulled out two lab coats and handed one to me. "Not to one-up you or anything, but we rangers carried everything in backpacks."

"I guess lockers would have been impractical when you're trying to sneak up on enemy lines." I tucked the coat under my good arm, then unzipped the coverall and undid the belt. Once it was strapped back on the outside, I did the coverall back up and pulled on the lab coat.

"Not to mention awkward even when we weren't." His amusement faded. "Let's take out our guards and check the remainder of this floor while we're waiting for your ghosts to return."

I frowned. "There're no cameras here in the med room, but surely they'd have them in the corridors?"

"I didn't see any."

"Which doesn't mean they're not there."

"I know, but it's not like we have another choice."

That was certainly true. We walked out into the main room and across to the door. I stood on one side, Jonas the other. He glanced at me, eyebrow raised in question. I flexed my fingers and then nodded.

He punched the release button and, as the door slid open, we darted through as one, grabbed the turning guards, and thrust them together hard enough that the crack of heads was audible. It didn't knock either out but it dazed them enough that Jonas was quickly able to finish them off.

As he dragged the bodies inside, I walked over to the doc, pulled out a knife, and removed his RFID chip along with a good chunk of flesh. The medibed immediately sensed the new wound and instigated healing.

"That may not work outside flesh," Jonas commented.

"It might, given it's still connected to biomatter."

He nodded and cautiously moved out into the corridor. I scanned the ceiling but still couldn't see any sign of either cameras or other security measures. It was all rather puzzling. Even if this section was nothing more than part of the warehouse and the security here was as it had always been, why wouldn't they have implemented more measures when they'd taken it over as one of their bases of operation?

The doc's bloody RFID chip opened some doors but not others. The rooms it opened were a variety of storage areas, more medical facilities, and a number of bunk facilities. All of them were currently empty, and the odd feeling of disconnect grew. It was almost as if this area had all but been abandoned, but if that was the case, why did they have one of the warehouse's main treatment centers up here?

The rooms the chip didn't open, we ignored. Shooting the scanners would not only keep them in a locked position, but might well raise the sort of interest we were trying to avoid.

The corridor began a long sweep to the left, and Jonas slowed.

"What's wrong?" I said softly, tension immediately rising.

"There are guards up ahead."

"How many?"

"Four." He paused. "But they're not guarding another elevator foyer. I can't hear any movement up or down."

"The elevators might not be in use."

"Maybe." He paused and cocked his head to one side. I had no idea what he was listening to—I might have tiger DNA and my senses might be inherently sharper than most, but it still wasn't up to the acuteness of a full shifter's. "Two guards have just been dispatched to investigate the lack of response from the soldiers we killed."

"How long have we got?"

"Three minutes, if that, before they get here."

"That will give us time to get back to that last storeroom."

"Even hiding will only give us a few extra minutes." He spun around and headed back up the corridor. "We need to uncover what is being protected up ahead before our dead guards are discovered and the alarm sounds."

"The lab coats should at least give us a bit of leeway to approach without raising too much—" I stopped. Cat and Bear were racing toward us and they *weren't* happy.

What's wrong? I asked.

We found the labs, Bear said. *They're not underground. They're all on this level, behind the security doors at the end of this corridor.*

And? I said, when neither of them immediately continued.

And, Cat said, *there are children there. Seven of them.*

I blinked as the importance of that sank in. It could be nothing more than a coincidence, especially given I'd also found children at the sand base—children who'd been purchased rather than stolen. But if it wasn't....

If it wasn't, then we'd just stumbled upon *all* the remaining missing children.

CHAPTER SIX

"Is PENNY ONE OF THEM?" Jonas's question was soft. Urgent.

No, Bear said. *Sorry.*

Jonas's frustration surged, a sharp rush that briefly spiked through my mind before he got it under control. "It was a forlorn hope at best, and hardly one you need to apologize for, Bear."

"We *will* find her, Jonas." I placed a hand on his arm, offering sympathy even though I suspected he neither wanted nor needed it.

"I know." His voice was even, but the grimness in his gaze cut through me like ice. "Just as I know she might neither want help nor be capable of fleeing with us."

Personally, I doubted she *would* want to flee with us, if only because her actions at Chaos spoke volumes of where her loyalty now lay. "And if she doesn't want assistance or help? What will you do?"

"I don't know." He looked away. "I honestly don't know."

I squeezed his arm and then let my hand fall. And hoped, with everything I had, that he would not be forced to make a decision similar to the one I'd been faced with in the sand base. *Where are they being kept, Bear?*

In the secure bunkhouse at the far end of the corridor.

All seven are awake and aware, Cat added. *In fact, one of the boys spoke to us.*

I blinked as Jonas opened the storeroom door. *What did he say?*

He wanted to know who we were, Bear said. *And why we were there.*

What did you tell them?

That we were exploring, Cat said. *I think he thought we were real.*

I frowned. *Meaning he saw you as flesh and blood?*

I think so.

That was interesting if true, because even with my ability to both sense ghosts and communicate with them, I rarely saw my little ones as anything more than a shimmering sparkle. Only when they were playing in dust did they momentarily gain human shape.

And the other laboratories? I asked. *Anything—anyone —in them?*

Scientists. Bear hesitated. *And embryos.*

I briefly closed my eyes. I'd been hoping against hope that

we wouldn't find another creations lab in this place, but I guess it wasn't surprising that the evil trio had stretched their developments across all facilities. It made it easier to keep projects going if one or more of the labs got hit—which they certainly had.

There is no one in the intrauterine pods, Cat said. *And the cots and restraint cribs are also empty.*

Relief surged. That, at least, was going to make things a little easier. *What sort of security have the labs and the bunkroom got?*

Two guards remain at the door up ahead, which is scanner locked. There are five in the corridor behind that, positioned at regular intervals between the labs.

The bunkhouse is also scanner locked, and there is video monitoring, Cat added.

How far is the first guard from the main door? Jonas asked.

It took me a moment to realize he hadn't said that out loud. Obviously, the on and off nature of our communications were currently on—and it would certainly make things easier if it continued to be so, even though we could still communicate through the ghosts if it didn't.

He's not in the sightline of the door guards, Cat said. *But there's a body scanner in the door.*

Meaning no matter what we did now, the alarm would be raised the minute we went through it.

We stepped into the storeroom and let the door close again. "Best move behind the rear shelves," Jonas said. "Just in case they do a quick check of every room on their way to the med center."

They are close, Cat said. *Their guns are drawn.*

Jonas responded by drawing his. I shoved the bloody bit of flesh holding the RFID chip into the coat's pocket, then moved to the opposite end of the shelving and peered around. The door opened and a man stepped through. I pulled back, my breath catching in my throat as I waited, body tense, for any indication that they sensed our presence. Footsteps echoed as he moved cautiously into the room.

Should we knock them out? I asked.

Jonas didn't reply. I glanced over my shoulder and saw his frustrated expression.

He says it's a toss-up, Cat said. *Because alarms are going to be raised regardless once you both go through that door.*

All of which was going to make it even more difficult to get those kids out. And that, above everything else, had to be our priority right now. As the guard took another cautious step into the room, I said, *Cat, Bear, can you go see if there's another way out of this place? Perhaps check the roof, and see what's up there?*

They raced away. The guard paused and then retreated. The door closed again and silence fell. I cautiously peered around the shelving, but it was no trap. The room was empty. I sighed in relief and stepped out. Jonas joined me near the door.

"How do you want to play this?" I asked.

"As quietly as possible." He paused. "Is there enough light here to draw a shield around you?"

I nodded. "I could possibly include you within its confines."

"Have you done something like that before?"

"No, but I hadn't carried anyone with me in shadow until I did it with you in that bunker."

"*Not* an experience I want to repeat in any sort of hurry." He scrubbed a hand across his jaw. "You shield. I'll play it straight, and we'll see what happens."

I called the light to me. Once I was concealed behind its brightness, I cautiously stepped out into the corridor. The guards weren't visible, meaning they had to be investigating one of the other rooms.

We moved on, only slowing our pace once the corridor swept us out of the immediate sight of the two investigating guards. Even so, the tension in me didn't ease. It was something that wasn't likely to change in the near future—not when we're walking into a situation there might be no getting out of.

There was no darkness to hide in here. And while I more than likely could conceal Jonas behind the light shield, it was only a shield. A trick of the eye. It wouldn't allow me to rise above gunshots nor would the bullets go right through me without causing major trauma to my flesh—and his.

The corridor finally straightened and the guarded doorway came into view. A heavily armed man and woman stood either side of what looked to be more a double-width blast door than the sort of door you'd normally find in non-military buildings such as this. There was also what looked to be an updated version of the eye and blood scanners that were still in use in my old bunker on the wall behind the female guard.

And that meant if either our stolen RFID chip or the guards weren't authorized to go through that doorway, our rescue mission was dead in the water.

I tucked in behind Jonas, keeping him between those guards and me just in case one of them was alert enough to catch the soft shimmer of the shield.

The woman took a step forward and raised her gun. "Halt and identify yourself, Doctor."

"Medic Theodore Hasham," Jonas said easily. "I've been called into facility three."

The woman frowned. "We've not been notified, and that's highly unusual."

Jonas continued to head toward her. I moved across to the other guard, doing my best to move silently—a near impossibility on these floors. Thankfully, the guard was watching the known threat rather than the unknown.

"You know what control is like," Jonas said easily. "The left hand never knows what the right is doing."

"Nevertheless, I'll have to check." She paused and the sharp sound of a safety clicking off bit across the air. "Please come no closer, Doctor Hasham, or I *will* have to fire."

Go, came Jonas's whispered order.

I lunged forward, grabbed the guard, and smashed his face against the blast door. His nose shattered and blood flew, and he made an odd sound that was part surprise, part pain.

I repeated the blow, let him fall to the ground, and swung around. Jonas had disarmed the woman and had an arm wrapped around her throat.

"If you want to live, you'll obey every order." His tone was flat, emotionless, and all the more terrifying because of it. "Understood?"

The woman nodded, though she looked far from happy. But no matter how well she'd been trained, her skill set would never match his, even if they *had* been of equal size. He had the war and a hundred years of experience behind him. She did not.

He unclipped the comms from her ear and put it around his own. "What's your partner's call sign?"

"Seven-two."

It was little more than a gasp. Jonas hadn't eased his hold on her any.

"Can you open this door?"

She nodded.

"Is it possible to switch off the body scanner within the door?"

She hesitated. He tightened his grip, and while her breathing became even more of a struggle, her expression became angrier.

When he eased up again, she all but spat, "Yes, but neither of us have the appropriate code. And control's not likely to provide it. We haven't the clearance."

"The hard way it is then." Jonas shoved her forward. "Open the door."

She did so. As the blast doors slowly responded, he knocked the woman out and then glanced at me. I might have been wrapped in a light shield but his gaze came unerringly to mine.

"Drop the shield and save your energy. We're probably going to need it later." He drew a second gun. "Ready?"

"Yep. Let's do this."

As the light shield disintegrated around me, he went through the door. An alarm immediately sounded, the claxon sound sharp and loud in the silence of this place. I followed but swung on the other side to shoot both the scanner on the wall and the one in the door. If they worked along the same lines as the old blast doors in my bunker, then taking out the scanners would immediately kick in the secondary defense system, and the door would be sealed.

As sparks and smoke flew, a red light flashed and the door began to close again. Blast doors were notoriously hard to reopen, meaning we'd gained some respite from the additional forces that were undoubtedly on their way up. All we had to worry about now were the ones stationed on this side of the door.

I ran after Jonas, but we were barely halfway down the corridor when two men appeared. Jonas took one out; I took the other. We jumped over their bodies and ran on. From the other end of the corridor came the echoing sound of bootsteps—four more guards were approaching us.

Jonas slid to a stop, forcing me to do the same. "You want to try wrapping us both in that light shield?"

I held out my hand. Once he'd twined his fingers through mine, I reached for the light and dragged the power of it through me—and through him via our clasped hands—creating a shield faster than I'd ever done before. It made my head spin and my heart race, and for several seconds, it was only Jonas's fierce grip that kept me upright.

With the shield in place, we moved across to the other side of the corridor to wait.

The four guards soon came into view, the two on the far side of the corridor slightly ahead of the two on our side. Neither of us moved; we simply waited for them to come to us.

A hollow boom bit through the air. I glanced around and saw dust pluming from the walls either side of the blast door. They weren't making any attempt to get through it— they were instead trying to get *around* it. And that meant we once again had less time to get those children and get out of here.

Other side came Jonas's comment, then he squeezed my fingers and released my hand.

As the light shield shimmered and went down, I raised my guns and shot the two guards on the far side of the corridor while he took out the two closest. The poor souls didn't have a chance, but little sympathy stirred. They would have done exactly the same thing to us.

I reloaded my guns and followed Jonas. The booming

behind us grew stronger, and the nearby walls shook. We had minutes, if that, left.

Cat, Bear? I said, as the corridor straightened and revealed six doorways. *You got anything to report?*

They didn't immediately reply, but a few seconds later, Cat's energy whisked around me, her excitement making the air spark. *We found two air scooters and a hauler.*

"Are they being guarded?" Jonas asked, passing a door without bothering to stop and check it.

With time now at a premium, the children had to be our priority.

Yes, Cat said. *There are five men—two at the entrance onto the roof and one at the ramp of each vehicle.*

"I don't suppose any of them have drivers inside?" I asked.

No, Cat said.

Jonas glanced at me. "That's going to make things difficult. I can probably rewire the hauler if it's an older-style vehicle, but it'll take more time than I suspect we have."

"Have you heard anything from Nuri?"

"Yes, but they won't get here in time to be of any use."

"Then we've no choice but to make time."

Time for Nuri's forces to get closer, time for him to rewire the hauler.

"I'm not sure we have enough ammo to do that." His voice was grim. "Cat, what's our best way of getting up to the roof?"

There's an emergency exit opposite the room that holds the children, she said. *It's alarmed, so they'll know you're coming.*

"Not if I shadow, they won't," I said.

Jonas glanced at me. "How can you do that when there are absolutely no shadows in this place?"

My answering smile was flat and without humor. "With a whole lot of effort. But it's not as if we have much choice."

He hesitated, and then said, "I guess not."

We reached the end of the corridor and the two doors of interest. I dragged the doc's RFID chip out of my pocket and placed against the scanner guarding the door into the children's bunkhouse. Unsurprisingly, the red light flashed and the door remained firmly shut. I spun around and tried the exit door, but the result was the same.

I grimaced and dumped the bit of flesh to one side of the door. "Cat, do you want to go inside and see if you can convince—"

I stopped as the bunkhouse door slid open. Standing in front of it was a black-haired, black-skinned boy who had the most amazing eyes I'd ever seen. They were tri-color, but the colors weren't mixed. Instead, there were distinct rings of brown, blue, and silver. Though he looked to be no more than five or six, he very much reminded me of little Raela. There was a very old soul shining out of those eyes.

"Are you here to rescue us?" he asked.

It wasn't until that moment that I realized that unlike the

other children we'd rescued, his lips had not been sewn shut —and I couldn't help but wonder why not.

Jonas squatted in front of him and said, "Yes, we are, but there's no guarantee we'll be successful."

The child's gaze solemnly switched from him to me, and then returned. "We'll take that chance. But there are two problems."

I could feel Jonas's surprise and amusement. "Those being?"

"There are two who are too young to walk."

"They can be carried," Jonas said. "The other?"

"The other is that they're all not only control chipped, but it's attached to an incendiary device," I said before the child could. "Foot or heart?"

The kid's gaze came to mine. There was little emotion to be seen in either his expression or his strange eyes, and I had to wonder just what had been done to this kid—whether he'd not only been a victim of their drug regime but also perhaps some sort of physical alterations in the form of DNA or even brain manipulation. In some ways, he reminded me of the soldier déchet, though he was very obviously capable of thought and reason.

"Foot in six. Under the ribs in one."

"The latter being you?"

He nodded. "It cannot be removed here. There is no time."

No, there wasn't. Not if the noise coming from the other end of the corridor were any indication.

Jonas glanced at me. "None of the others we rescued had any sort of incendiary or control devices placed in them."

"They were placed in our bodies very recently," the boy said.

A crash echoed and dust drifted toward us. Jonas swore and then said, "Tiger, you take care of the guards up top. I'll remove the devices from the kids' feet and then bring them up. Cat, can you go down the corridor and let me know when the soldiers down there break through?"

As Cat sped off, I took a deep breath to gather my strength and then called the light to me once again. This time, however, I didn't just have to create a shield, but one that was thick enough to block out *all* light even as it continued to reflect everything around it.

And I had to do it quickly.

A storm of light and energy shimmered around me, sparking brightly as it grew thicker and denser, until the corridor had all but disappeared from my sight and darkness claimed the space in which I stood. I reached for that darkness, sucking it in, letting it surge through every part of me, ripping flesh and muscle and bone into nothing more than particles in seconds flat.

I would pay for that swiftness. But right now, I had work to do.

I drew in the shield until it was little more than a tightly wrapped bubble around my particles and then slipped under the door and up the stairwell. The topside door was both metal and scanner locked, but there was enough of a gap between the bottom of it and the concrete top step for me to slip through.

Bear? Where are you?

I rose on the other side of the door and paused just in front of the two guards. My body was beginning to pulse—a warning that my strength was slipping away faster than time. I moved farther away and shifted back to flesh. For several seconds lights danced in front of my eyes, and it was all I could do to stay upright. I gritted my teeth, ignored the pounding in my head, and kept a fierce grip on the light shield.

Next to the hauler, he said.

Do you think you can take out the guard there?

Of course.

His tone was indignant, and I smiled. *Good. Wait for my signal.*

I carefully unclipped the dart gun, moved closer to the first guard. He, like his friend, was wearing body armor and a full helmet, so I aimed for his thigh instead. The dart embedded deep into his flesh and he slapped at it, driving it deeper rather than dislodging it.

I fired at the second man—who almost instantly pulled it free and raised it to study. "What the fuck?"

"What?" the other man said.

"Some bastard just hit me with a dart!"

"Where the hell did they come from?" the first man exclaimed.

"I don't fucking know."

I crossed mental fingers that the dart had been in long enough to knock the second soldier out, and headed for the scooters and their guards.

"Control," the first man said, "There's some weird shit happening up here."

Which *wasn't* what I wanted to happen, but not a complete disaster given the stairwell was the only way—short of flight—on and off this rooftop.

Go, Bear. I swapped the dart gun for two machine pistols and raced toward the speeders. The guards heard my footsteps—it wasn't like the light shield muted sound—and even though their expressions were confused, they raised their guns and fired.

I immediately sucked in the darkness and thrust up into the air, and not a moment too soon. A deadly storm of metal shot through my particles and would have ripped me apart had I been flesh. I dropped down behind the two men, shed the shadows but not the light shield, and fired at the backs of their knees. As they went down, I ripped off their helmets and hit them. Hard.

Then I went back to check the two men near the door. One was down. The other I shot.

The hauler is now unguarded, Bear said.

Great work. Can you keep an eye on the two men near the scooters? If they show signs of becoming conscious, knock them out again.

With pleasure.

I finally released the light shield and had to thrust a hand against the metal exit door to keep upright. Everything was back to hurting and my heart raced so hard it felt like it was about to explode.

I sucked in air for several seconds, but it didn't seem to do much more than make my head spin harder. I swallowed heavily, then reached down, grabbed a guard, and hauled him up to the scanner.

The scanner's light flashed from red to green and the door slid open. I shoved the guard's body in front of it to prevent it closing again, and then grabbed the other man's arm and stumbled down the stairs, unceremoniously dragging him behind me.

I didn't have the energy to pick him up. I really didn't.

I'd barely opened the second door when Cat screamed, *They're in!*

Little bodies pushed through and began a hobbling run up the stairs. As the boy with the tri-colored eyes flew past, I said, "Take them to the biggest vehicle up there."

"Will do."

Jonas carried the final two—a girl and a boy. Both were unconscious.

"Go," I said, my voice little more than a scratch of sound. I hit the button and, as the door began to close, followed Jonas up the stairs.

Look out!

Cat's energy hit, shoving me to one side. The bullet that

would have gone straight through my gut gouged a thick hole in the concrete to my left instead.

I twisted around, raised both guns, and fired nonstop through the steadily decreasing gap. The low-ammo signal began to flash on both guns, but I didn't let up, not until the door had sealed. The scanner on the other side of the door beeped as someone punched in the code to open it, so I switched aim and blew up the control panel on *this* side.

They'd no doubt be able to force their way through in very short order, as it was nowhere near as solid as the main blast door, but even seconds might make the difference between escape and not.

I spun and raced back up the stairs. My head now ached so badly that the sunshine made my eyes water and seeing became difficult, though I wasn't entirely sure the latter could be blamed on the bright light.

Jonas says hurry, Cat said.

I pulled the guard out of the doorway, let the door shut, and then once again destroyed the control panel. After I'd stripped the guard of his weapons, I asked Cat to gather whatever she could carry from the other two, and then staggered toward the hauler. I barely made it up the ramp before I collapsed.

"Rhea help us," Jonas muttered, with a quick, concerned glance at me.

"Rhea has probably given us all the help we're going to get." I pushed backward on my butt until my spine rested against the hauler's wall. The children were all strapped in and hunkered down low in the seats, and I hoped with everything I had it was enough. Hoped that Dream *didn't* order the incendiary device placed under the boy's chest to be activated—that she valued their worth and whatever progress they represented over starting anew again.

Cat whisked in and dropped two machine rifles and a couple of handguns next to me.

"Well done, Cat." I reached for one of the machine rifles, checked the ammo clip was full, and then rested it across my knees.

Her pleasure spun around me, sharp and bright. But despite her high excitement, I could feel the tiredness in her. Carrying so much had taken a toll on her.

I glanced back to the stairwell door and saw a worm-like glow tracking up one edge of it. They weren't blowing this one open—they were simply cutting through it with a laser saw.

"Can this thing get into the air with the ramp down?" I asked.

"Yes." Jonas was still fiddling under the main control panel. "But it will slow us down."

"So will them taking out our engines," I bit back. "They're almost through the door. You need to get this thing in the air."

"Right. Done." He straightened. "Everyone, hang on—this is going to be rough."

I braced against the wall as best I could. As the engines came online and the big vehicle began to shudder and shake, I raised the machine rifle and sighted on the stairwell door.

The hauler lifted and slowly moved forward. The metal ramp scraped across the concrete, sending sparks and dust flying into the air. I ignored it and watched the glowing worm track through the last few inches of metal. A heartbeat later, the cut piece of metal was kicked out. I kept the gun sighted but didn't immediately unleash hell.

A black metal ball was tossed through the hole. It bounced several times on the concrete and then raced deceptively fast toward the lumbering hauler. It took me a moment to realize it was some sort of tracking explosive device.

I sighted and shot it. Three bullets missed. The fourth did not. With a giant whoosh, the thing exploded, and a huge blast of hot air and flame rushed at the hauler. I leaned away from the door, and let the heat of explosion sizzle across the lower half of my body. Cat's energy slapped at the smoldering material, dousing any potential threat of fire caused by the hot metal fragments that had hit me.

I sat upright again. Guards had poured onto the rooftop under the cover of the blast, and there was at least a dozen of them out there now, all of them wearing combat gear, all of them firing not at the hauler itself but her engines.

I cursed and returned fire, and though I hit multiple people, they were too well protected—and too well trained—to go down.

"Swing this thing around and protect our tail," I said. "We're not going to get out of here otherwise."

Jonas grunted in response, and as the lumbering vehicle

continued to lift and turn, I scrambled up and punched the ramp close button. Then I staggered over to the small port window, shattered the thick glass with a couple of shots, and continued firing at the men. When the ammo out light flashed, Cat threw me another gun.

Slowly but surely, we gained enough height to clear the roof. But the vehicle shuddered under multiple impacts and smoke began to taint the cabin air.

"Hang on," Jonas warned.

I gripped the edge of the shattered window just as he hit the booster. The hauler shot forward and my fingers slipped. Glass tore into my skin and blood dripped down the edge of the hauler.

One of the smaller children made an odd sound, and I glanced around to see his head rise above the seat and stare at me, a bright, needy light in his eyes.

Rhea help him... and us.

Before I could react in any way, the boy with the tricolor eyes placed a hand on his shoulder and simply said, "No."

The child blinked, and embarrassment stained his cheeks. He ducked his head away from me and slipped back down in the seat. The older boy's strange gaze met mine. "He has it under control. Mostly."

"Mostly is good." But the reality of mostly also meant he'd just swap one lab for another. Nuri might have accepted my desire to raise Raela, but she would not agree to my caring for any of *these* children. Not until we knew exactly what had been done to them.

And, if I was at all honest, neither my bunker nor I really had the facilities to look after them all. Even little Raela was going to be a stretch.

The hauler cleared the building's edge and continued to power forward. But these sorts of vehicles weren't designed for speed, and with smoke trailing from at least one engine, it was only a matter of time before we'd be forced to land.

I twisted around and peered out the shattered window. The men on the roof still fired at us, but we were now too far away for them to do any damage. A couple of them were running for the scooters, but these, like the ones that had chased us out in the desert, had no weapons.

But they didn't really need them. All they had to do was track our movements and report back until either the warehouse's operations center or even Dream herself could get armed vehicles into the air.

"Nuri's just given us orders to head for the southern edge of the forest," Jonas said. "We're to meet a surface transporter there."

"How far away is it?"

"Twenty minutes."

"I suspect that's nineteen minutes too far."

And not because of the smoking engine, but because the upper loading bay's door was beginning to slide open. I had no doubt that whatever vehicle came out of that bay would be fully capable of shooting us down.

"Is Nuri's diversion crew any closer?" I asked.

"Two minutes away."

That was cutting it close. The loading's bays door was almost fully open.

"Tell them to get ready for a fight."

Small black crafts swarmed out of the loading bay. It took me a moment to realize what they were and I closed my eyes, battling the instinctive rush of fear.

"What?" Jonas said immediately.

"They've sent remotes out."

"Where in Rhea's name did they get those? Only the military is supposed to have them."

"Dream obviously has some heavy-duty friends." And it wasn't like we hadn't come across bits of military equipment in the other bunkers we'd investigated.

But this was certainly the first time they'd been used on us.

"It seems an odd risk to take, though," I added. "Especially when they can simply flick the switch in—"

I paused, and glanced at the boy with the tricolor eyes. He smiled and said, "They called me Ten. I can't remember any other name."

"Ten is a damn number, not a name," Jonas said. "Even the déchet were given a name."

"Name *and* number," I corrected, with a smile at the boy. "But I rather like Ten. It's unique."

Jonas grunted. "Maybe we're far enough away from the warehouse that they can't blow it remotely."

I hoped so. These children deserved a chance at life after

everything they'd gone through. I just had to hope that Nuri would ensure the life they had in whatever facility they went into at least approached some sense of normality.

I glanced back and watched the black swarm briefly circle and then move as one toward us. "They've locked onto us."

"We really, *really*, need to find that bitch and stop her," Jonas muttered, as he tried to egg more speed out of the already maxed-out hauler.

I didn't say anything. I just watched the remotes getting closer and closer.

"Twenty seconds, if that," I intoned.

"Come on you bastard—*move!*"

Something silver shot past my window and a heartbeat later, the nearest remote exploded into a huge ball of flame. Two more went up in quick succession.

A shadow fell over the hauler—a shadow that very much resembled a gunship.

More remotes exploded, and a silly grin touched my lips.

Nuri's rescue party had just arrived.

CHAPTER SEVEN

JONAS LET out of huge whoop and eased the hauler's speed. As another gunship went over the top of our vehicle, he pressed a couple of buttons, then undid the restraints and rose from the seat.

"You," he said, voice severe as his gaze swept me, "need to sit down before you fall."

"Yeah."

I slid down the wall and leaned my head back. To say I felt like crap would be something of an understatement. And while my body could and would heal from the stress of holding particle form while maintaining a light shield, I wasn't entirely sure I had enough strength left to do so with any sort of speed. I needed sleep and I needed food, but I also needed to get back to Central as fast as possible. Now that the danger was over and we'd achieved what we'd initially set out to do—rescue all the missing children aside from Penny—that niggling feeling that Charles was looking for me was growing.

Jonas rummaged around the storage units and found the medical kit. Once he'd cleaned my cut fingers and sealed the wound, I said, "When we get to the rendezvous point, I need to leave immediately for Central."

He frowned. "You need to rest—"

"Charles is the only hope we have of infiltrating the House of Lords. We can't jeopardize that."

"Yes, but surely—" He paused, eyes narrowing slightly. After a moment, he added, "It would appear I'm outvoted. Nuri agrees with you."

I raised an eyebrow. "Your connection is strong enough that she can break into conversations uninvited?"

"Yes, although for the most part she respects our set boundaries."

"But not on occasions such as this," I guessed. "Where the mission overrides everything else."

"Yes. And in *that* respect, she very much reminds me of you. Neither of you seem aware that there *are* limits as to how far people should be pushed. That sometimes, the safety of one matters as much as the safety of many."

I placed a hand on his arm. "I'll be fine, Jonas."

"You won't be if you continue to push yourself." His voice held a note of anger. "I can feel your utter weariness, Tiger. It seeps through the link between us."

"That will have eased by the time I get to Central."

"Perhaps." He rose, forcing me to release him. "Rest up

while you can. I dare say you're not going to get much of it when you meet up with Charles."

My gaze jumped up at that, but his expression didn't give much away. "He's business, Jonas. Nothing more."

"I'm well aware of that. It was a simple statement of fact, nothing more, nothing less."

Amusement touched my lips. "Meaning I wouldn't be getting much rest if *you* were the one I was returning to?"

"Indeed. But my time will come, of that you should have no doubt."

The brief but decidedly heated flash of desire in his eyes made me even more determined to survive the battle that was coming.

I blinked. Battle? Dream would undoubtedly fight to the bitter end, but that thought seemed to imply there was a whole lot more headed our way.

I shivered and rubbed my arms, not really wanting to contemplate just how much "more" there might be. The only way I was going to get through the days to come without being overwhelmed by the enormity of the task still ahead was by proceeding one step—and one person—at a time

Whatever comes, Bear said, *we will be with you.*

Except when you go through a rift, Cat added, ever practical. *That we can't do. But if you call us when you arrive at the end point, we will hear.*

Which is what you should have done at the sand base, Bear added.

Watching our home and protecting the little ones is just as important as helping me, I reminded him gently. *Until we knew where that rift led, there was little point in calling either of you in.*

But you will call us in the future? Because you almost died in that place and we were too far away to guide your soul back to us.

I took a deep breath and slowly released it. I hadn't thought about that aspect of it, and given the last thing I wanted was to be separated from them on my death, I should have. *I promise. From now on, I'll call to you both.*

Good, they said together.

Jonas lightly touched my shoulder, drawing my attention back to him. "I'll wake you when we arrive at the rendezvous point. Until then, stop worrying. And stop chatting to the terrible twosome."

Cat and Bear giggled at that, and a smile tugged at his lips as he made his way back to the driver seat.

Of course, it was very easy for him to say don't worry and not so easy for me to do. Not when the seeker part of my psychic senses was randomly throwing nuggetty warnings my way, and refusing to clarify.

I closed my eyes and began the slow, steady breathing ritual that would sweep me into the healing trance. This time it was so deep that I had absolutely no awareness of what was going on around me. When Jonas touched my shoulder to wake me up, I jumped.

"We're here," he said, one eyebrow rising. "Nuri's arranged transport to take us across to the nearest rail station."

I scrubbed a hand across my eyes and pushed upright. Jonas caught my elbow to steady me. "Why the rail station? Wouldn't it be easier for us to simply drive there?"

"Dream will have people watching vehicles coming in and out of Central."

"If she had any brains, she'll be doing the same with the pods." I glanced around and noticed we were alone in the hauler. "Where are the children?"

"Already in the transporter."

"Damn. I wanted to say goodbye to Ten." I glanced past him and watched the clouds of dust spin past the ramp and briefly mask the trees. "Where are they being taken?"

"To the same place as the other kids."

I frowned. "Those kids deserve more than being stuck in another lab environment and studied like rats."

"Yes, but until we stop Dream, our priority has to be keeping them secure." He moved to one side and ushered me forward.

My frown deepened. "If it *is* a military installation they're being kept in, won't Dream be able to uncover it? Especially if she has taken over the identity of someone in the House of Lords."

Our footsteps echoed as we moved down the ramp. I glanced skyward and saw that the transporter carrying the children was already a distant speck. But there was a small ATV waiting to the right of our hauler—two men had exited from it and were walking toward us.

Jonas placed a hand against my spine and guided me toward

the ATV and the two men. "Trust me, she won't be able to force the information out of anyone, no matter who she targets."

It took me a moment to grasp the importance of the statement. I glanced up at him sharply. "That's why you won't tell me—just in case I get caught. You think I'll talk."

"With the right drugs, anyone can be made to talk. It's not personal, Tiger."

"Do *you* know the location?" I bit back.

"I did initially, but with my deepening involvement and the suspicions it has probably raised, Nuri has relocated them without telling me where."

"And you can't pluck it from her mind?"

"Her mind is a steel trap when it comes to hiding information she wants no one to know." His voice was dry. "And anyone who comes to arrest her would seriously be taking their lives in their hands at this point."

Because she wasn't only telepathic, but a powerful witch.

My annoyance died as swiftly as it had risen. "There surely can't be too many secure installations that Dream and the House of Lords don't know about."

"*That* is undoubtedly true."

Suggesting it wasn't a military installation but rather somewhere else. But I didn't ask the questions that continued to crowd my mind—he was right. I'd been caught twice now, and while I'd been able to escape each time, there was no guarantee my luck would hold if I were captured again.

In fact, I couldn't help but think that the odds were swinging further against me with every new encounter.

"Thanks for the timely rescue, Gus." Jonas held out his hand as the two men approached. "And sorry if we interrupted the games at the retirement home."

The older man laughed—a booming sound that tugged a smile to my lips—and grasped Jonas's hand. "They'd have to shoot me before they'd ever get me into one of those damn places. You're looking fucking younger every time I see you."

"No, you just keep getting older."

"That is indeed true." He gestured to the dark-skinned man standing beside him. "Do you know Keonne? He's Rai's kid."

"Nice to meet you," Jonas said. "Your dad was a good man."

"Thanks." Keonne's gaze came to mine. "And who is your lovely partner? Or are you intending to keep *that* information all to yourself?"

I smiled and stuck out my hand. "I'm Tiger."

"An unusual name for an unusual woman, I'm thinking," Keonne said.

"Enough with the flirting, young man." Gus sent a very amused smile my way, but it faded as he added, "Sherry will take you to as far as the Greenbelt refuel station. It's just a short walk from there to the rail station."

Jonas nodded. We'd both been at the refuel center fairly recently—it's where we'd procured the truck we'd used to rescue the two children who'd been taken to Winter Halo for more "processing."

"What are you going to do with the hauler?" I asked.

"Blow it up." Keonne raised the rucksack he was carrying. "With any luck, they'll think it went down with all aboard."

"At least until they get forensics here, anyway," Gus added. He slapped Jonas on the shoulder. "You two go. We'll take care of things here."

"Just be careful," Jonas said. "It's more than likely got a tracker fitted, so if someone isn't already on their way, they soon will be."

"Which is why we'll be setting the explosives and skedaddling." Gus nodded at me and moved on. Keonne gave me a half bow and a cheeky smile. "If you're ever up Pikes Peak way—"

"Flirt on your own time," Jonas said. "Right now, you have work to do."

Keonne laughed and walked after Gus. Jonas touched my spine and pressed me forward.

"I like those two. Have you known them long?"

"Not too much, I hope," he said, amused. "And half my life."

I squinted up at him. "Are they kin or mercenaries?"

"The latter, although they work within the Broken Mountains, serving as intermediaries between the various tribes and the main merc centers in both Central and New Port."

"Meaning they're brokers of sorts?"

A major part of Nuri's business, I'd discovered, was as a broker for the government. She negotiated deals and contracts—with a slice off the top for herself, of course—for goods and services that Central either could not find or would not contemplate for legal or safety reasons.

"Yes," Jonas said. "But for a smaller cut."

A dark-haired woman with wine-colored eyes glanced around as we entered the ATV. "Nice to see you again, Jonas. Now belt up so we can get this beast on the road."

"Sherry, this is Tiger," Jonas said, ushering me to a seat behind the other woman.

I was inordinately pleased that he sat beside me rather than move on to the co-driver seat.

"Nice to meet you, love." Sherry punched various buttons. As the door closed and the ATV's engines grumbled back to life, she added, "We've been told to get you onto the second-last string into Central, so we're pushing for time. There are some protein bars in the rear storage if you're hungry."

I was and, over the course of the sometimes-rough journey, demolished all but three of them. Those I left for Jonas.

We reached the refuel station just as the first threads of dusk were beginning to stain the sky. I peered over Sherry's shoulder and studied the sprawling complex. As the last refuel stop before Central City, this place had to cater not only to the many trucks and haulers heading in and out of Central, but also all those who were using the rail system. So there was not only a multitude of docking stations offering the different fuel options, but also a large eatery and what looked to be accommodation—something I hadn't noticed last time I was here. Nor had I noticed the brothel at the far end. I guess it wasn't all that surprising given the sex trade had been a respectable business for decades now and that for many, sex equaled relaxation. Of course, anyone setting up such a business had to follow strict guidelines regarding health and safety, and also had to pay their taxes in a timely manner.

It was odd, however, to find one outside the well-protected confines of a main city. But maybe the risk was factored into both the price charged and the money earned by those who worked there.

Sherry skirted the closest parking area and squeezed the ATV between two larger haulers. "Right," she said, as she shut everything down and opened the door. "I'm off for coffee. You two wait five minutes and then head over to the rail station. There's a camera behind the truck on our right, so keep your back to that and you'll be fine. Oh, and there's a change of clothing for you both in the side locker. Good luck."

"Thanks," Jonas said, but he was talking to her retreating back. He twisted around in the seat and flipped open the storage container. "There're a couple of coveralls, a kaftan, and a tunic in here—which one do you want?"

"Unless you've taken a sudden fancy for women's clothing, I'll take the tunic."

He handed it over then dragged out one of the coveralls for himself. The tunic was a pale pink rather than the silver gray of my other one, but it was similar in style—full-length and split to the thigh along one side to allow easier movement. The soft wool of the material enhanced rather than hid curves, and I knew from the many times I'd worn the same type of garment in the various camps I'd been assigned to during the war that they were not only extremely comfortable, but also sexy.

I once again made Jonas turn around and did a quick changeover. I also altered my features and changed my hair color to red so that anyone who'd seen me at the warehouse wouldn't recognize me. That I did it so quickly without experiencing undue dizziness or weakness was surprising. Or maybe it really wasn't, given these changes—or rather, improvements in my own natural abilities—were more than likely the result of being caught in that damn rift. There was no other logical reason for it to be happening. Not when I'd experienced neither physical nor psychic changes or enhancements in all my years of existence before then.

"Right," I said, "You may turn around now."

"I don't know why someone who was designed to seduce should be so damn modest when there's no one else here but us." His gaze skimmed me. "You need to wear those tunics more often. They do suit you."

My cheeks dimpled. "Thanks."

He glanced at the timer in the ATV's control panel. "The train will be here in ten minutes, so we'd best move. You go first. I'll follow a few seconds later."

I nodded and headed out. After a brief pause in the shadows of the large hauler, I headed for the rear of the ATV and turned left. The long rail platform was already filling with people, all of them waiting for the glowing, caterpillar-like pods that would transport them back to

Central after a long day of working in the various production zones that provided the city with the necessities of life.

I walked to the station without incident, and made my way to the midpoint section of the platform, where the crowd was the thickest. Jonas joined me a few minutes later and, as the string of pods silently pulled into the station, slipped his fingers through mine. I didn't know if it was to ensure we didn't get separated, and I didn't really care. I just enjoyed the warmth of his touch.

We made our way to the rear of the pod and sat down. A bell chimed and the doors closed. Within seconds we were leaving, the countryside blurring as the train picked up speed. Neither of us said anything, but the ghosts had fun, looking over everyone's shoulders and reporting back on what they were reading or eating. It was a somewhat amusing way to spend the hour it took us to get back to Central.

As the pod pulled into Central's station, I glanced at Jonas. "Are you heading back home?"

"Home" being the bunker we were currently sharing, not Chaos, where he lived with Nuri and two of her other mercs, Branna and Ela.

He nodded. "I'm supposed to be monitoring all the equipment there, remember."

The bunker had—up until very recently—been the site of a museum dedicated to not only preserving the last few bits of the day-to-day operational center of the Human Development Project, but also to emphasizing the evilness of gene manipulation and creating humanoids.

But Dream and her cohorts had blown much of it up in an effort to stop me accessing the place. In the process, the tunnels that were my main way in and out had collapsed, and one of them had taken half the hill with it. Central's engineers had consequently advised the Council to run a series of stability tests on the area before deciding on the viability of the museum. They were under the impression the southern exit had been part of an old sewer network that once ran under the area, and were worried that further collapses could endanger the whole hillside.

Nuri had been handed the task of finding someone willing to monitor the equipment twenty-four seven, and Jonas had stepped into the position not only to provide a quick and easy means of communication between me and Nuri, but to keep me out of Chaos and away from Branna.

If he comes after you again, Bear said, *I will hit first and ask questions later.*

A smile twitched my lips. I didn't normally approve of attacking someone without provocation, but in Branna's case, I was more than happy to make an exception.

I pushed up from the seat as the doors opened and people began to file out of the pod. "I'll return in the morning then."

Jonas nodded. "Just be careful, and remember what I said. Fontaine is first and foremost a government man, so don't give him any reason to suspect you."

"He's also a man in lust, and that often leads to a certain amount of blindness."

Jonas snorted softly. "*That* is a blanket statement and does not apply to us all."

"My experience suggests otherwise."

He raised an eyebrow but didn't argue. He simply pressed a hand against my spine and guided me out onto the platform. "I'll leave you here and head into the park. I don't want to be seen heading directly into the bunker, just in case it's still being watched."

I nodded. "Cat and Bear can keep you company."

"Oh good," he said, voice dry.

Is he being sarcastic? Cat asked. *Because it sounds like he is.*

Maybe just a little, I said. *Take care of him for me, and let me know if there's a problem.*

Will do, they said together.

I glanced at Jonas. "Don't let the vampires bite, Ranger."

He grinned. "Oh, they're quite welcome to try. I have a few new guns that need testing out."

I hesitated, tempted to step closer and kiss him goodbye. But that could lead to a whole lot more, and it was neither the time nor the place for such explorations. So I simply spun around and walked away—aware the whole time that he watched me.

Central City had two main defenses—the vast metal curtain wall that ran in a D-shape around the entire city, and the UV light towers that topped both the wall and every roof of every building within the city, providing its inhabitants with endless daylight. There were also only two ways to get in and out of the city—via the vast gatehouse here, and a matching gateway on the opposite side.

I was soon striding across the metal drawbridge that would be drawn up once the final string of pods arrived at the station. By the time full night arrived, the city would be locked down and no one would be able to enter or exit before the sun had fully risen again. The city might be bathed in eternal brightness, but if the lights failed, then the wall and the drawbridges were the city's only protection against the might of the vampires. Which, in reality, didn't mean much. Not when vampires could shadow and simply rise above the wall. It did, however, stop the Others, which meant that if the lights ever did go out, then at least there was one less horror to worry about.

The ends of the silver curtain that Central used in place of the more conventional portcullis gleamed brightly in the deepening gold of dusk, but the sensors fitted into the thick metal walls didn't react to my presence, though they would have had I been full vampire. It had taken ten years to completely rebuild Central after the war, and by then not only had all the HDP bases been destroyed, so had the entirety of the déchet population—aside from myself and Sal, as far as I was aware. As a result, they'd never built the possibility of DNA-mixed beings such as the déchet into their security systems, and I was extremely grateful for that. Feeding myself would have been far more problematic had I not been able to make regular raids into Central.

Central's internal layout consisted of a dozen roads; the outer roads were D-shaped like the wall itself, but the inner ones were full circles. Victory Street—the only street that ran from gatehouse to gatehouse through the heart of the city—intersected each of these roads, which also acted as delineation between the twelve districts within Central. Those near the wall were the poorer sections; the closer you got to Central's heart—where the main business district and government centers were situated, as well as the only green space available within the city—the more exclusive and richer the community.

I followed Victory Street—which was a spacious avenue that, despite the tall buildings lining either side of it, was still wide enough to allow real sunshine to bathe the street rather than just the UV light—until I came to one of the many pedestrian cross streets that ran between each of the main streets. They were little more than three-meter-wide canyons between the high-rise buildings, but like everything else in this city, they were bathed in eternal light. This one was empty, so I quickly drew a shield around my body and did a subtle shape shift, changing back to my natural silvery-white hair color but without the black stripes, and increasing both my height and breast size. The latter stretched the soft wool of the dress to its limits and probably revealed more than was decorous given I wasn't wearing either a bra or the clear under-breast shape-tapes—which were not only more comfortable than old-fashioned bras, but far more supportive without in any way restricting movement. But I doubted there'd be many men who'd actually complain about what might be on show. I knew Charles certainly wouldn't.

With the alterations made, I continued toward the apartment on Third Street that Nuri had procured for me as part of my Catherine—or Cat—persona. While apartments closer to the park were more prized—and therefore more expensive—even an apartment as close to the wall and drawbridge as this one was worth more than most of those living on Twelfth could ever hope to earn in their lifetime.

The building came into view. It was twenty floors high, but was sandwiched between two buildings and had little width. I ran my RFID chip across the scanner; after a moment, a green light flashed and the door opened.

The foyer beyond, like the building itself, was tiny but it was plushly decorated in gold and plum tones. I walked across to the elevator and, as I entered, a metallic voice asked for my floor number.

"Seven, please."

The doors closed and the elevator zoomed me up to my destination. I stepped out into the carpeted corridor. There were only two apartments here—one at the front of the building, and one at the back—which I guess wasn't surprising given the width of the place. The one I was using lay at the front.

I repeated the entry process and, when the door slid open, walked inside. The room beyond was a combination living and kitchen area. Despite the narrowness of the building, the entire place was bright and spacious—a feeling undoubtedly helped by the mezzanine level stopping well short of the double-height windows, which enabled light to flood the room. The entire space was white—a color that seemed to be favored amongst Central's elite—but there were some splashes of bright color in both the cushions that lined the L-shaped sofa and the sunset pictures that lined the wall.

I walked across to the circular chrome-and-glass stair tucked into the corner on my right and went up. There were two small bedrooms on the mezzanine level, as well as a small bathroom that somehow managed to fit a shower, basin, toilet, *and* a hipbath, the latter definitely a luxury only the elite could afford. I quickly stripped off and stepped under the spray, letting the water roll over my body to ease the lingering spots of soreness. The needle-fine jets were so hot the room would have steamed up if not for the efficient exhaust system that vented it up to the rooftop.

By the time I'd finished, dusk had given way to night, though that was something I knew thanks to my vampire genes. The quality of light streaming in through the windows certainly hadn't altered any.

The doorbell rang as I padded naked toward my bedroom. I paused, head tilted to one side as I listened. I couldn't hear any sound to suggest who it was, so I walked across to the nearby comm screen and pressed a button. Charles's countenance appeared, and his expression was an odd mix of frustration and annoyance.

I pressed the audio button and said, "Who is it?"

"Charles." His voice held a slight edge. "I'm sorry to call on you unexpectedly, but you weren't answering my messages and I was worried."

Worried I might have found another suitor, I suspected. Like the animal variety that had once roamed this world, a female cat shifter had the final say on who could and couldn't court her, and it was the males who had to strive for her attention and favor. In the camps, at least during the war, it wasn't unusual for women to have many children with different fathers, although those who were not nomadic did tend to stick to the same mate. It was a trait that had, at times, made my missions that much more difficult.

"Please, come in." I pressed the access button and, as the door opened, swung around and headed for the stairs.

"And I'm sorry to have worried you," I said as he walked in, "but I've been visiting an ill friend."

He paused to watch me come down the stairs and the annoyance in his expression gave way to desire. "I do so like it when you answer the door so divinely dressed."

"You caught me just getting out of the shower." I motioned to the small cabinet to one side of the autocook. "Would you like a drink?"

He hesitated and then nodded, his expression somewhat rueful. "I would like far more than just a drink, but it is hardly polite to ravish you senseless without at least paying lip service to the niceties expected of polite company."

"Indeed."

I followed him across the room, retrieved the whiskey bottle and a couple of glasses, and poured us both a drink. I took a sip and then leaned on the counter between us and said, "So am I now officially talking to a member of the House of Lords?"

"Yes." His gaze was on my breasts rather than my face. "I took the oath two days ago."

"Is that why you were trying to contact me?"

"Indeed." His expression was somewhat distracted, his gaze following the slight rise and fall of my breasts as I breathed.

"There's an inauguration ball on tomorrow night. I wanted you to come with me."

"Charles," I murmured, somewhat archly. "I will come for you anytime."

His gaze jumped to mine and then he laughed, a deep, warm sound that tugged a smile to my lips. "Good." He drained his whiskey and set the glass down on the counter. "Have we done proper justice to the niceties yet? Because my desire for you is so strong, it's taking all my control not to leap over this counter and ravish you here and now."

I downed my drink and placed the glass beside his. "Jumping over the counter is possibly not something a centenarian such as yourself should try."

"Ha! A challenge. Prepare to be molested very thoroughly, my good woman." He easily vaulted over the counter then lightly grabbed my arm and tugged me into his. "The thought of losing myself in your luscious body once again is all that has gotten me through the tedium of the last few days."

And with that, he kissed me. There was nothing tentative about this kiss, nothing measured or slow. It was heated and urgent, and spoke of the desire I could feel trembling through the body pressed hard against mine.

I wrapped my arms around his neck and returned his kiss. It might not have held the same sort of urgency or desire, but —unlike many of my targets in the past—I did in fact like Charles. And sex with him was at least pleasurable, which was more than could be said about many of those other targets.

After a while, he stepped back and stripped off, tossing his clothes onto the counter rather than neatly folding them as he usually did.

Then he picked me up, deposited me on the counter beside the untidy pile, and began to caress and tease me. For a man in a hurry, he did a damnably good job of making sure I was ready for him. But as his breathing got faster and the lust stinging the air so strong it was all I could smell and taste, he nudged my legs further apart and then thrust into me. From that moment on, there was little sound other than those of enjoyment. I didn't bother opening the door to my seeking skills, as I could feel the urgency throbbing through him and knew it wouldn't be long before he came.

Afterward, he rested his forehead against mine and said, "Sorry. I didn't mean for that to happen so quickly."

I laughed softly. "We have a whole night ahead of us. There's plenty of time for me."

"That," he said, slipping his hands under my rump and picking me up without withdrawing, "is very true. Shall we continue at a more leisurely pace in your bedroom?"

He didn't wait for me to answer. He simply carried me upstairs—a rather amazing feat that belied his age. The rest of the night did indeed continue at a slower pace, the long bouts of sex interspersed with soft talking and even some sleep. And though I did use my seeking skills to search through his memories, none of the people he'd dealt with over the last few days even slightly snagged my instincts. Certainly none of them resembled the woman we were chasing—which didn't really mean much when we were dealing with someone who could change their form at will.

It wasn't until we were eating breakfast the following morning that I broached the question of the ball. "What does it actually involve? I've never been invited to one before." I wrinkled my nose. "I'm not even sure I have something appropriate to wear."

He laughed. "Wear as little as possible, and you'll fit in just fine."

There was a teasing note in his voice that left me uncertain about believing him. "I'm being serious, Charles. I don't want to make you look bad."

He leaned forward and stole a quick kiss. "You won't. And I *am* being serious. I've attended a couple of recent balls in my father's place, and trust me, the brighter and gauzier the gown, the more fashionable the woman is considered."

"Are we talking about the same people who wear neck-to-ankle white tunics?"

He grinned. "Yes. The elite present a very different front to the world than they do in private."

"Huh." I grabbed another pancake off the pile and smothered it in cream and honey—two things I hadn't had in decades, and something I'd sorely miss once I got back to the bunker and my more basic autocooks. "What actually happens at these things?"

He shrugged. "A lot of talking, drinking, and eating. There's one section where I'm formally introduced and the family's seal is passed to me, but after that, just dancing and fun."

I raised my eyebrows at the anticipation in his voice. "What sort of fun?"

"The decadent kind." He pointed his fork at me, expression serious but a glint in his eyes. "I will remind you, however, that no matter who you might choose to play with, you're to come home with me."

Meaning the ball devolved into some sort of sexual free-for-all? That certainly wasn't something I'd been expecting. While male shifters didn't mind healthy competition for a female's attention, they did *not* like to share once they'd won it. Ménages à trois and orgies generally weren't something they participated in or even approved of.

Of course, over a hundred years had passed since I'd spent any time amongst shifter camps, so things certainly could have changed. And it wasn't as if I'd spent any time amongst Central's elite.

"I might," I teased, "if you promise to order me another of these most excellent breakfasts."

"Deal." He glanced at the time and sighed. "Time for me to go. I'll pick you up at eight this evening. Don't be late—or overdressed."

I followed him across to the door and tried not to let either relief or tiredness show in my expression as I kissed him goodbye. Jonas had been right—I wasn't fully recovered, and even though I had managed to catch some sleep last night, I needed a whole lot more.

But that wasn't on my immediate agenda. Not only did I have to head out to the bunker to both see my little ghosts and update Jonas, I also needed to buy something suitable to wear for tonight. The clothes Nuri had arranged for Catherine's use were rather exotic compared to my usual wardrobe of military garb, but I doubted they were—in any way—up to the standard Charles expected tonight.

I called to Cat and Bear and then went upstairs for a shower. They arrived just as I was getting dressed. As usual, they danced around me happily, but this time, their sheer exuberance made me feel old.

The little ones wanted us to tell you that they miss you, Cat said, when they finally calmed down. *But Jonas is managing to keep them amused.*

Meaning, I thought in amusement, he was probably being inundated twenty-four seven with their happy chatter and little pranks.

And Jonas said not to come back for a day or so, Bear added. *The museum is being watched.*

Unease stirred and my smile faded. "That's not exactly a new development."

In fact, we'd been working on that very assumption ever since he'd moved into the museum.

Yes, Cat said. *But yesterday Nuri was handed a hunt-and-kill order to contract out, and it was for someone fitting your description.*

The unease deepened to dread. "My actual description or one of my false identities?"

Both, she replied. *But not this one.*

I guess that was at least something. I wearily rubbed a hand across my eyes. While it was a rather logical step for Dream to take, it did mean the identity she'd stolen was someone with the contacts *and* the power to get such an order approved.

And it also meant I'd have to disappear behind a light shield whenever I wanted to go to the bunker and maintain *this* identity while I was within Central. And though I'd gone for months wearing a visage other than my own during the war, I knew from experience that the longer I was forced to maintain it, the more unsettling it became. It was almost as if my body started rejecting my altered form.

"That doesn't explain why Jonas wants me to keep away from the museum," I said. "He knows I can get there unseen."

Yes, but there's more. While Nuri refused to distribute the contract to interested parties, someone outside her network has accepted it. He paused. *And Branna has disappeared.*

It didn't take a mathematician to put those two things together and come up with a possible answer.

I should have hit him harder in Chaos, Bear added fiercely.

"It's never a good thing to kill without provocation, Bear." Even if I *had* done it, both in the past and more recently. But at least I *did* have a reason for my more recent kills.

I think Branna is an exception to that rule, he replied.

I smiled. While he often acted and sounded like the teenager he was, there were moments like this when he— and Cat for that matter—sounded so much older.

"I gather Nuri is attempting to find him?"

Yes, but Jonas said he's been working with the group for a long time, and he knows their contacts and methods well.

They do not expect him to be found for a few days, hence the warning to stay away. Cat's energy patted my arm. *We'll act as go-betweens until Branna is caught.*

"Good idea." I paused, and frowned. "But that still doesn't explain why I should stay away. Branna's not magic or psi sensitive. Like everyone else, he wouldn't see me if I was using a light shield."

No, but there are charms that warn a wearer if someone is using either magic or psychic powers, and charms that prevent the use of both personal magic and psi powers against the wearer. Four of Nuri's have gone missing.

"Personal magic? As opposed to what, exactly?"

Cat mentally shrugged. *He didn't explain it.*

Maybe because most people would be familiar with the term—and maybe because it was pretty self-explanatory. It could have simply meant spells directed at a particular person rather than greater spells, such as the rifts or the soupy-feeling shields that protected them. "Four?"

Two for him, two for someone else, they think.

The very last thing we needed was Dream getting her hands on charms like that... although as an earth witch of some power, it was rather odd that she hadn't already created such charms herself. Especially when she knew I was a face shifter and obviously using other identities.

Had the rift she, Winter, and Sal been caught in somehow erased some of her magical knowledge, just as it had erased much of Sal's memories of our time together during the war? Was she able to create the rifts, but do little else?

Or was it more a case of the rifts taking so much of her time and power that she simply didn't dare risk creating simpler magic?

I closed my eyes and took another of those deep breaths that didn't do a whole lot to calm the inner tension. In the end, the answers to any of those particular questions didn't really matter. Only the fact that Branna had probably accepted a kill order on me did.

"Can you ask Jonas to find out what the charms look like? And tell him I'm attending the inauguration ball with Charles tonight, so I'll need to know before then." I hesitated. "And ask him if Branna is aware of my Cat identity."

Because if he was, it would make going to the ball a whole lot more dangerous.

If he could get into the ball in the first place, that was. He might have accepted the kill order, but would he really go so far off the rails in his desperation to kill me that he'd forsake reason and be utterly willing to jeopardize the very future of our world by joining forces with Dream?

A large part of me wanted to give him the benefit of doubt— until I remembered the murderous gleam that entered his eyes whenever he was in my presence.

And if he *had* lost everything he valued in the war, as Nuri had suggested, then perhaps he figured he had nothing to lose—even if everyone else *did*.

Plus, why would he snatch four such charms if he wasn't working with someone else?

I'll go see Jonas now, Bear said.

"Thanks, Bear," I said, but I was talking to the air. He'd already disappeared.

I grabbed a coat from out of the wardrobe and then headed downstairs.

Are we going out? Cat said, excitement in her tone again.

"Yes, because I need to buy a dress for the ball tonight."

What's a ball?

It was such a simple question, but one that made me want to cry. It wasn't fair that my ghosts never had the chance to experience such things, either before or after their deaths. "It's a place where people wearing their prettiest clothes get together to eat, talk, and have fun."

Can we come with you?

I hesitated. If the ball was everything Charles had claimed, then I certainly didn't want them there. They might technically be over a hundred years old, but in some respects they were still very much the age at which they'd died—fourteen and eight respectively. While they were both well aware of what I'd done as a lure, in all the years since the war's end, I'd never let them accompany me whenever I went into Central seeking adult company for an evening. And I'd certainly refused to let them be present whenever I'd been with Sal or with Charles.

"We'll play it by ear," I said eventually. "If things get heated, then I'll ask you to leave."

I can't wait to see the dresses! Cat spun around me as I caught the elevator down to the ground floor. *You should get something very pretty.*

I smiled. "And you can help me pick it out."

She clapped her hands in delight. *You will look like a princess!*

My smile grew. While fairy tales hadn't exactly been part of a déchet's education, I'd spent the years since the war reading just about anything I could get my hands on, be it dry old manuals on how to fix the various bits of vital machinery within our bunker or the wide variety of fiction I'd found in the personal lockers and trunks. When I'd gotten through all that, I'd gone into Central and stolen some more. And when I'd discovered the fairy tales, I'd read them all out loud to my little ones. While ever-practical Cat liked her princesses to be no-nonsense and self-reliant, she'd always loved the scenes where they dressed up in pretty dresses and captured the prince's love. She was very much a romantic at heart, even if by design we déchet shouldn't even understand the concept.

I walked over to the nearest cross street and then up to Victory. While the shops and cafes in the outer ring of streets tended to be small, with their contents spilling out onto the pavement and filling the air with a riot of scents and color, the closer you got to Victory and the park that was Central's green heart, the more serene and orderly it became. Even those who'd ventured out so early moved with a superior sense of style and grace I could never match. And while the people who lived and worked in this sector didn't look anything alike physically, almost everyone was clad in either white or gray outfits, which lent to the over-whelming feeling of whitewashed uniformity. It certainly made the pale pink of my tunic seem bright by comparison.

I walked along the street until I discovered a boutique

displaying the sort of dresses Charles had described and, after a slight pause, walked in. An older woman clad in vivid orange immediately appeared from a rear room and greeted me warmly.

"And how may I help you this morning, madam?" she said.

I hesitated again, and looked at the surrounding extravagance of silk and gossamer. "I need a dress for the inaugural ball tonight."

Her face immediately lit up, and for the first time I wondered if I had enough credits on the RFID chip to pay for such a dress. Nuri had added extra to the initial five hundred, but I had no idea just how much.

"Please, come this way." She swept the curtain to one side and waved me through. This second room was all white-and-gold opulence, with mirrors on the wall and a plush but comfortable-looking chair to one side. Beside this was a small gold table that held fruit and a number of beverage options.

"If madam would sit, I'll pick out a number of designs for you." She paused, looking me up and down. Whether I came up to expectations I couldn't say, as her expression gave little away. "Would you like something to eat? A glass of champagne, perhaps?"

My smile felt somewhat tight as I perched on the edge of the chair. "No. Thank you."

She nodded and disappeared into the other room. Cat happily followed her, and proceeded to describe in a rather awed tone the various dresses that were being collected and placed onto a clothes rack.

The woman returned and the so-called fun began as she ushered me in and out of various material scraps. Bear returned in the midst of all this.

Jonas doesn't believe Branna knows about your Cat identity, but he is aware that you've infiltrated the elite's circle.

Which was almost as bad—unless, of course, Charles wasn't the only one there with a new woman on his arm. I carefully peeled off a flimsy piece of purple gossamer and said, *And the charms?*

Will look like the bracelets she used to change Jonas's appearance to that of a wrinkled old man, Bear said. *Only instead of strings they're made from interlaced wire, and will be either gold or silver, depending on whether they're magic or psi indicators, or a preventative measure against either.*

Which meant I just had to hope the elite were not into ostentatious displays of jewelry at such events, as that would make the task of spotting the charms all that much harder. I slipped another dress on and Cat sung her approval even as the woman made a sound of satisfaction. I glanced at one of the many mirrors. The dress was little more than a sleeveless sheath that clung to my curves as it fell to my knees. For the most part the silvery material was transparent, but there were four "modesty" lines of violet blue and rich jade sequined geometric patterns across my breasts, and a similar set that ran from my right hip to my left.

"Perfect," the woman said. "Just perfect."

It sparkles, Cat said. *All princess dresses should sparkle.*

I can't remember princess dresses showing a person's butt, Bear commented.

Have you not been paying attention? Cat said, in a tone that was mildly superior. *They* all *show her butt. It's the fashion.*

My lips twitched as I fought to restrain my amusement. "Are you sure it's not too revealing?" I turned around to study the aforementioned butt. The geometric patterns only covered the front of the dress, so I might as well have been wearing nothing for all the coverage this dress gave my back.

"It is, in fact, a little more demure than what has been popular this year," the woman commented. "But it does suit you."

"Then I'll take it."

The woman beamed as she quoted a price that could have kept me in supplies for the next six months. I swallowed my shock, ran the RFID chip across the scanner she produced, and held my breath as I waited for the payment to go through. Which, thankfully, it did.

Once I was dressed and my purchase carefully wrapped, I headed back to the apartment. *Can we investigate the area while you sleep?* Cat asked.

I nodded. "Just don't cause any trouble. And don't go too far."

We won't, they intoned.

As they raced away, giggling with excitement, I headed upstairs. In very little time, I was sleeping the sleep of the truly exhausted.

I woke just as the first traces of evening stained the skies high above Central's endless daylight. After stretching the kinks out of my body, I padded down the stairs to grab something to eat. Charles might have said there would be food available tonight, but I suspected I might not be able to eat all that much. That niggling sense of unease was growing, and my muscles were twitchy—tight. Neither sensation was all that strange, even if I hadn't felt them much since the war. Back then it had been caused by walking into an unknown and dangerous situation that could all too easily blow up in my face—and with Branna on the loose, that was a very real possibility tonight.

Once I'd finished my ham and cheese omelet, I reached out for my ghosts. Cat answered immediately, her happiness so fierce the air around her sparkled.

The women in this area are fascinating, she said. *They don't seem to do anything more than chat and eat. It's very strange.*

I smiled. "Where's Bear?"

Jonas called him. She paused. *But he's on his way back now.*

The niggling sense of unease sharpened abruptly. Bear appeared and said, *Jonas sent you this, and also wants you to remove the RFID chip from your left arm.*

A small silver vial appeared out of the center of his energy and dropped into my hands. I frowned and turned it over in my hands. "What is it?"

Sleeping potion, in case you need to escape Charles.

I raised my eyebrows. "Why would Jonas think I'd need to escape Charles?"

He didn't. Nuri did.

"Did she say why?"

No.

Typical. I placed the vial under the bench, out of immediate sight. "Why does he want me to remove the second RFID? Nuri rendered it inert, so it shouldn't register when I go through a scanner."

Normal scanners, no, but the Crystal Ballroom has full bioscanners on all entrances, and he said they'll pick it up.

Which *would* raise alarms, because while all citizens were required to have an RFID chip, no one was supposed to have two.

I started opening the kitchen drawers until I found a knife sharp enough to cut into my skin, but fine enough not to make too large a wound.

With it in hand, I walked up to the bathroom, sat cross-legged within the shower cubicle, and began the deep breathing exercises that would throw me into the healing trance. But I didn't slip all the way down—I just went far enough to control both the pain and the bleeding while maintaining enough awareness to guide the knife.

It was a rather weird sensation to cut deep into my skin but feel so very little. Blood welled sluggishly, and muscles parted as I dug down for the chip. Silver soon glimmered deep within the red; I flicked it out then imagined the bleeding stopping and the wound closing up. When both had happened, I pushed up out of the trance and glanced down at my arm. There was no evidence of the cut, not even a scar—just a solitary trickle of drying blood. The precision of my healing skills really *had* sharpened dramatically since Jonas and I had been caught in that rift. Usually there would have at least been a faint line.

I picked up the RFID chip, placed it and the knife outside the cubicle, and then stood.

Cat came racing in. *Charles is here.*

"What?" I glanced at the nearby comms unit and saw it was only seven. "He's early."

And cross, I think.

I swore softly as the unit's chime sounded.

"Catherine? It's Charles. I realize I'm early but—"

I pressed the audio button, cutting him off. "Is there a problem, Charles? It's not eight o'clock yet."

"I know, but there's been a last-minute format change and they've decided to do the inauguration process earlier. It's thrown the whole council into something of a tizz."

"I'm not ready just yet, but it shouldn't take long to be so." I buzzed open the door. "Come in and make yourself a drink."

I quickly hid the chip and the bloody knife, and then stepped into the shower. Charles appeared a few minutes later, a drink in hand. His nostrils flared slightly, and I realized with horror he'd caught the scent of blood. I shifted, drawing his gaze and attention. His hunger stirred, and that teasing, metallic scent seemed to have been forgotten.

"Do they often change the schedule like this without warning?" I asked, as the shower switched from clean to drying mode.

"No, but apparently the chancellor has been poorly of late. They've altered the program so she's not kept out of her sickbed too long."

I raised eyebrows, even as I wondered who the chancellor was and what she actually did. "Why get her out at all? Could a replacement not be found?"

"No." He grimaced. "It is a matter of tradition that the chancellor performs the ordaining ceremony and hands the family's crest to the heir, so that they can then place it in the wall of acknowledgment."

None of which made much sense to me. I brushed past him and went down to my bedroom. Charles followed, his hunger growing as I combed my short hair into order and then got dressed.

I walked across to the small wardrobe and paused, glancing at him. "Is footwear in or out at these things?"

"Out in the actual ballroom, but required until then." He drained the rest of the alcohol. "The streets are rather unclean, after all."

The streets were pristine in my opinion, but then we had been raised in very different environments.

I slipped on a pair of silvery sandals, grabbed a coat to cover my near nakedness until we got to the ballroom, and then smiled at Charles. "Right. Ready."

His gaze swept me and came up approving. "Perfection. I have transport waiting."

We headed out. Said transport was a two-person air taxi. The driver opened the door and ushered us inside then, once we were seated, climbed into the driver side. As the vehicle rose, I said, "Where exactly is the Crystal Ballroom located? I've heard of it, but never been there or talked to anyone who has."

"It's within the Government House complex."

"And everyone from the House of Lords is expected to go?"

"As well as anyone who is any position of power within governmental halls." He glanced at me sideways, his expression curious. "How can you not know any of this?"

I smiled, though it felt tight. Uneasy. "As I said, it's not as if I've ever had the good fortune of receiving an invitation to such an event before now."

"Yes, but the intricacies of the government and the House of Lords is something that is taught at primary level."

"Which was a long time ago for me, Charles." I placed a hand on his thigh and lightly brushed my fingertips across his groin. His cock responded instantly. "And it's very cruel of you to remind me of that."

He laughed softly then drew me in his arms and the matter of my education gap was quickly forgotten. As the taxi came to a halt, Charles released me. "Shall we continue this matter later?"

"Of course," I murmured, and looked past him.

We'd landed on a rooftop rather than in the street in front of

Government House as I'd expected, and there were dozens of other air taxis zipping in and out of the airspace around us. Men and women walked sedately toward an elevator tucked in one corner of the roof, a vivid parade of color and style. Lining either side of the carpeted walkway were at least a dozen armed guards. I climbed out of the taxi and glanced upward; two gunships hovered above us. They definitely weren't taking any chances when it came to security.

I slipped my coat over one arm then my other through Charles's. As we joined the queue walking toward the elevator and the scanner in front of it, I said, *Cat, Bear, do you want to start checking everyone, and see if you can find Nuri's missing charms?*

They immediately raced away. My stomach tightened as we drew near the bioscanner, and fear skittered, even though my RFID chip had been fully programmed for *this* identity.

"Shoes and coat in the tray, ma'am." The guard's voice was deferential but firm.

I obeyed, then walked through the scanner. Light swept my entire body and my RFID chip oddly tingled as its information was calibrated with the scanner results. No alarms sounded and the guard politely motioned for me to continue.

I collected my items and then stopped nearby to wait for Charles. The elevator took us down two floors and opened to utter opulence.

The Crystal Ballroom was well named. The room itself was a long, rather narrow expanse of white, with a stone floor that was shot with veins of silver and gold. Three rows of beautiful chandeliers ran the length of the entire room, filling the space with a glittering, almost surreal light. There were no windows; instead, vast mirrors lined every wall. They not only gave the room a feeling of space but also reflected the light and the riot of color that was its inhabitants.

A blue-clad figure appeared in front of us and bowed lightly. "Your coat and shoes please, madam and sir."

We handed them over. Charles placed his hand against my spine and guided me toward the stairs that led down to the ballroom proper. Another man waited here, and he was holding a thick golden staff with some sort of bird of prey atop of it. He hit it against the floor three times and then said, in a voice that echoed, "The Lord Charles Fontaine, first son of Jacob, heir to the seat of the Fontaines, and potential initiate to the House of Lords. Accompanying him is Catherine Lysandra."

It was the first time I'd heard the surname I'd been given, and it was one that meant "she who was freed." It made me wonder if Nuri was simply having some fun or trying to tell me something. The last surname she'd gifted me with—Zindella—had meant "man's defender."

"Potential initiate?" I said, as we made our way down the stairs under what felt like a million critical gazes.

"Every initiate is a potential until they are officially confirmed by the ceremony."

"Ah." I ran my gaze across the nearest cluster of people. The shop owner had been right when she'd said my outfit was demure compared to many. I'm not entirely sure why any of them had bothered getting dressed, because the bright gossamer scraps that probably cost a fortune hid absolutely nothing.

Charles guided me through the room, stopping at the various clusters of people to introduce me. I sipped wine and made polite conversation, but the tension in me was growing and I had no idea why. Certainly there'd been no one so far who even slightly tweaked the psychic part of my soul.

Cat and Bear returned, their excitement and wonder caressing my skin like electricity and making the small hairs on my arms stand on end.

I love balls! Cat said. *We should hold one of our own when all this is over.*

I'm not sure our bunker will ever be as pretty as this.

But we can pretend. She paused, and then added more somberly, *We have searched the entire room. No one here wears jewelry.*

Most are wearing even less than you, Bear added, something akin to bemusement in his voice. *It is very strange, even if it is the fashion.*

A smile twitched my lips. *I gather you also haven't spotted Branna?*

No, Cat said. *But we will keep looking.*

Remember he could be wearing a disguise, I said. *So if you feel an odd sort of energy hovering around someone, let me know.*

And be careful, they intoned as they raced away again.

We continued to make our way down the long room. While Charles had implied the ball was something of a sexual free-for-all, the behavior of everyone we met was reserved.

But maybe the veneer of politeness only cracked after the official part of the evening was done with.

As we approached another group of people, a silver-suited, dark-skinned gentleman turned around to face us. He had close-cropped hair, eyes as dark as his skin, and a nose that dominated his otherwise unremarkable features and rather reminded me of a bird's beak. Recognition stirred, but I couldn't immediately place him.

"Charles," he said, his voice pleasant and holding the faintest hint of warmth. "It's such a pleasure to see you again."

The two shook hands and then Charles said, "Catherine, I'd like you to meet my longtime friend and mentor, Julius Valkarie."

His name brought the memory to life. *This* was the man I'd used to sneak through the sensor and escape at Government House. Was it chance that he happened to be Charles's friend, or was Rhea playing games yet again?

I inclined my head politely. "It's a pleasure to meet you, my lord."

"Please, call me Julius, at least during this momentous occasion." His expression suggested I should consider it a great honor to be on such familiar terms with him. "I would love to introduce you to my lady, but I'm afraid she readies for the presentation."

"I heard she was poorly," Charles said. "Nothing too major, I hope?"

Julius shrugged. There was something in his expression that made me suspect he didn't really care. "She's been working all sorts of strange hours of late, so I daresay it's merely stress."

"Ah," Charles said. "The chancellor's job is not for the faint of heart."

A cool smile touched the other man's lips. "That is one attribution that can never be laid at her feet."

"Indeed." Charles glanced past Julius as a bell chimed lightly. "I'm being paged. Could I ask you to look after Catherine for me? She doesn't know anyone here, I'm afraid."

"I'm okay—"

"Of course you are," he cut in. "But it would make me feel better about abandoning you for the next hour."

The ceremony went for an hour? Rhea save me from boredom.... I forced a smile and dropped a kiss on his cheek. "Fine. I'll see you afterward."

As Charles left, Julius swung around and offered me his arm. "Come along, lovely Catherine, and we'll go find a comfortable position from which to view proceedings."

He escorted me down the room. At the far end, there was a raised platform and, on the wall behind it, six large gold-framed mirrors. In the middle of five were what I presumed were the crests representing each of the houses. The sixth was empty, and obviously waiting for Charles to place his family's crest within it.

To either side of this, inset from the main room, were several raised seating areas. Julius walked me up the steps of the one closest to the stage and guided me to a couple of plush golden chairs in the front row.

"So," he said as he elegantly crossed his legs. "How did you and Charles meet?"

"We ran into each other. Literally."

His gaze shot to mine, disbelief evident. "Truly?"

"Yes." I smiled. "How long have you and your lady been together?"

"A number of years now. Our arrangement—" He hesitated, an oddly calculating light touching his eyes. "—suits us."

Curiosity stirred—about him, and about his unnamed lady friend. I touched his arm lightly and unleashed my seeking skills. "I do hope tonight doesn't tax her strength and send her back to her sickbed."

Images began to flick through my mind. They were fragile things, but filled with desires and urges that were, I suspected, not the norm for those of the ruling houses—at least if Charles was anything to go by. Julius Valkarie liked to play with leashes and ropes, and he had a preference for boys who were very, *very* young. As young as Bear, had he been alive.

A shiver that was part disgust, part anger ran through me, and it took great control to keep my touch light on his arm when all I wanted to do was punch him.

"Are you cold?" he said, his expression a weird mix of cold amusement and concern.

"A little."

I dug deeper into his mind. Seeking information this way wasn't ideal—generally, when using touch rather than sex, it was better to have a specific question or item in mind rather than a more open slather, grab-everything approach. The latter often resulted in unwanted information—like his sexual preferences, and the fact that the only person he really cared about was Julius Valkarie. I narrowed my focus and attempted to find more about his partner. Fleeting images of a tall woman rose, but she had little more substance than one of my ghosts. It seemed she was the very last person he was thinking about right now.

"Would you like your coat retrieved?" he asked.

I pulled my hand away and resisted the urge to wipe the feel of him from my skin. I didn't care about his bisexuality or his fetishes, but I drew the line at anything involving children. "I'm sure another of these fine champagnes will warm me up."

As he motioned to one of the blue-clad figures, Cat's energy hit me, sizzling across my skin like fire. Something was *very* wrong.

More than just wrong, she said. *Branna just walked into the ballroom.*

Wasn't *that* just what we needed right now. But how in Rhea's name did Branna even get in? He wasn't an elite—he was both an outcast *and* a mercenary. At the very least, the fact that he lived in Chaos rather than Central should have set off a multitude of alarms.

Is he disguised? I leaned forward a little, trying not to be overly obvious about it, but the seating area was too far inset to give any vision of the raised foyer area.

No, Cat said. *He comes as himself. And he wears the charms.*

Which meant we needed to stop him before he got anywhere near me. *Is he just wearing the two?*

No, four.

So he hadn't yet managed to give a set to Dream—was that why he was here now? What other reason could there possibly be for him being at an event like this?

"What would madam like to drink," a polite voice said.

My gaze jumped up to the blue-suited man who stopped in front of me. "A champagne, please."

"Indeed." He plucked a fluted glass from the silver tray he was holding and handed it to me. "Would you like anything to eat?"

"No, thank you."

Another chime sounded, louder this time, and the babble of voices began to die down.

"Things finally begin," Julius said. "Though I do rather hate these formal bits of the evening."

"Except, of course," I murmured, "when the formal bits require your participation."

His gaze shot to mine, his surprise quickly dissolving to

amusement. "Indeed, you are right. And I begin to see why Charles is so enamored with you."

Branna is on the top of the steps, Cat said.

Can I push him down them? Bear said. *Please.*

"Charles is an eminently sensible man," I said to Julius, and then added silently, *You can't push him down the stairs. It would be too obviously an attack, and could well tell Dream we're here.*

He's walking down to the ballroom floor now, Bear said. *A waiter approaches with drinks—I could trip him up when he's near Branna, and steal the charms in the confusion.*

I hesitated. *Okay. But be careful. Cat, keep watch and warn Bear if anyone appears to be taking a little bit too much notice of Branna.*

Will do.

I took a sip of my drink as the lights dimmed a little and a small woman with blonde hair and a pinched expression walked onto the stage. In the sudden hush, the crash of metal and glass was extraordinarily loud.

"What was that?"

Even as I asked the question, I rose and walked to the platform's edge. At the back of the room, near the foyer stairs, stood Branna, his hair a gleaming mane of gold in the room's fading light. His white tunic was splashed with red wine and his expression was thunderous, but he didn't say anything as several blue-clad figures fussed around him.

"It would appear one of the waiters has been rather careless," Julius commented as he stopped beside me.

We have the charms, Cat said. *What do you want done with them?*

I hesitated. While it was logical to return them to either Jonas or Nuri, it was a very real possibility that sometime in the very near future I might need such charms myself. *Take them back to the apartment and hide them under the mattress.*

Okay.

As my two ghosts raced away, Branna suddenly felt his wrist and then spun around, glaring first at the floor and then at the people surrounding him. To say he was livid with fury would be something of an understatement—I could feel the heat of it even from where I stood.

"My, my, he does not look happy, does he?" Julius murmured. "I pity the fool waiter who ran into him. I suspect he will be out of work on the morrow."

"Accidents do happen."

"Not in the Crystal Ballroom, they don't."

After the small woman on the stage had formally welcomed everyone, a spotlight speared the shadows now crowding the platform, highlighting a curtained area to the right of the stage. I cast a final glance at Branna; he was on the move, his gaze never still, his nostrils flaring as he neared each cluster of people. Trying to find me via scent, I suspected, which meant he wasn't aware of my ability to change mine as easily as I could change my appearance.

I moved back to my seat and sat down. A curtain on one side of the stage was pushed aside and a tall, thin-faced blonde woman walked into the spotlight. Shock race through me, and it was all I could do to remain motionless.

Because *this* was the woman I'd chased through the rift in Carleen and into Government House.

Ciara Dream herself.

My fingers twitched as if desperate to reach for the weapons I didn't have. She walked toward the middle of the stage, the spotlight that tracked her movements highlighting her gauntness and the almost translucent quality of her skin. In fact, she was so pale that even from where I was sitting I could see the pulsing of her blood through the veins in her neck....

The thought died as my gaze narrowed. There wasn't an oddly shaped birthmark on her neck, and there should have been if this woman was indeed Dream.

Had she perhaps forgotten to add it when she'd last shifted shape?

No, I thought, as I studied her intently. While this woman was almost an exact replica of the form I'd witnessed Dream change into as she'd walked toward that rift, there *were* subtle differences. A broader nose, sharper chin, longer hands. But perhaps the biggest difference was the sheer lack of power emanating from her. The air around Dream had practically crackled, the force of it so strong—so corrupted and alien in its feel—that it had made every hair on my body stand on end.

But while this woman might not be Dream, it was pretty obvious she was closely related to the identity Dream had taken over. There could be no other reason for the similarities in appearance.

I leaned closer to Julius and whispered, "Is that your lady?"

"Yes." He glanced at me. "Why?"

"She looks familiar, although I do not believe we have ever met." I hesitated. "I do feel I should know her name."

He smiled, but there was speculation in his eyes. "Indeed you should, given she is the city's chancellor."

I smiled, even as tension stirred. "I've only recently returned to Central, and names were never my strong suit."

"And yet she has been in the position for many years and is well known beyond the walls of this city."

Meaning I'd just made a major mistake. I shrugged casually. "I apologize if my lapse offends you."

"It does not." He paused, his gaze returning to the woman on the stage. "Her name is Karlinda Stone."

Undoubtedly either Jonas or Nuri could tell me more about her—and, more particularly, if she had any siblings or not.

Charles walked onto the stage and was again introduced. He knelt in front of Karlinda, head bowed, as she proceeded to list the names of all those who'd held the position before him. I shifted slightly in my seat, my gaze searching the crowd, looking for a replica of the woman on the stage.

"Are you bored, Lady Catherine?"

I took a sip of champagne and then glanced at him. "Would you be offended if I said yes?"

He smiled. "No, indeed, as I suffer the same infliction. Tell me, what is it that you do?"

"I'm between positions at the moment, I'm afraid."

"But when you do work?"

I hesitated. "I'm a sexual massage therapist."

His laugh was soft, but it nevertheless ran across the silence. The woman on the stage glanced our way and frowned. As did Charles.

"I do not think your lady approves of such outbursts," I murmured.

"She doesn't approve of much at all. Her family are fundamentalists; in fact, it would be extremely amusing to introduce you to them."

I raised an eyebrow, even as my heart raced that little bit faster. An introduction was *exactly* what I wanted; if nothing else, it would be the quickest and easiest way to uncover if Dream really *was* impersonating someone from Karlinda's family. "And why would you wish to vex them so if you know beforehand they would not approve of my profession?"

"Because *I* do not approve of fundamentalists."

"And yet you have a relationship with one."

His smile flashed, but there was cold amusement in his eyes and perhaps even a touch of disdain. Not for me, but rather for Karlinda. "Because, as I said, it suits us both."

A statement that made me wonder what—given Julius's bisexuality and preferences for young men—she was getting out of the situation. I didn't know much of anything about the fundamentalist movement, but the very nature of the word suggested a belief system that went back to basics—and surely that also meant sex. It was doubtful she'd be into leash and rope play—unless, of course, that was what he meant by a beneficial relationship. Perhaps their relationship was a cover for darker desires.

I watched the ceremony for several more—exceedingly long —minutes, and then switched my gaze to the two guards standing on either side of Charles and the chancellor. Both were armed and watchful, their gazes constantly roaming the room, looking for any sign of trouble or danger. Yet there was something about the man closest to Karlinda that stirred my instincts, though I had no idea why. And if said instincts had any idea, they were frustratingly mute.

Movement caught my eye and I glanced around to see Branna step into view. He paused, his gaze sweeping first the people immediately around him and then the seating area. I took a sip of champagne and schooled my features into an expression of bored disdain. His gaze went right past me, then recognition stirred and he looked back. Not at me. At Julius.

He began to make his way toward us.

Which suggested he knew Julius. But did that, in turn, mean the man sitting so elegantly by my side was the reason for the kill order? And that he was working with Dream?

How else would someone like Branna—who was, for all intents and purposes, an outcast, and as such would never have been invited into middle society let alone the upper echelon—come to be in a place like this?

He walked up the steps and strode toward us, every movement vibrating with the anger I'd so often sensed in him. It was an anger that had come from the war, a fury that stemmed from the loss of everyone he cared about, and one that had become so inflamed the minute he'd learned I was déchet that it seemed he'd been claimed by an unreasoning form of insanity.

He stopped in front of Julius and knelt down. He didn't even glance at me, though his closeness had my skin twitching. "Forgive the intrusion, my lord, but I was wondering if you know where Hedda Lang might be. She was supposed to meet me here, but I cannot find her."

Julius sniffed—a disdainful sound if ever I'd heard one. "I have no idea where that woman is, nor do I care. And you are in my line of sight, young man."

Branna made a low sound that rather reminded me of a growl, but did nothing more than nod and move away.

I watched him for several seconds and then glanced at Julius. "Such impertinence."

"Indeed," he drawled. "But the fault is not his but rather Hedda's. She should not have given him clearance to come to this event."

My stomach clenched, even if my expression remained cool and calm. "So you do know him?"

"Not really." He shrugged. "I merely dealt with the formalities finalizing the contract he accepted."

Oh *shit*. I drank more champagne. "What sort of contract? He does not look the type who would be looking for menial work. He looks too mean for that."

Julius chuckled. "Indeed, he does. And it was a simple hunt order for an escaped felon. Nothing serious."

There was nothing serious about a hunt order? Rhea help me.... I shifted a little closer and let my arm touch his. It wasn't the best type of contact for seeking, but I couldn't do anything more without being obvious. "I do hope you're not forced to deal with fellows such as he on a daily basis. That would be... unpleasant."

"Indeed," he replied, even as my psi skills snagged a title— Minister in charge of Home Defense. "But fortunately, I merely sign the paperwork. It is Hedda and her people who handle the day-to-day operations of our department."

Meaning Hedda Lang was his second-in-command? That would certainly explain all the military and government equipment and boxes we'd uncovered in the various bunkers we'd raided. As his second, few would bother questioning her orders—especially if Julius didn't particularly pay too much attention to what he was signing.

"Why would Hedda invite such a man to an event like this?"

Branna was now on the far side of the room—I could see the top of his golden hair as he prowled along the edges of the room.

"Rhea only knows," he said. "She's sometimes a strange woman."

If this Hedda was indeed Dream, then that was something of an understatement.

I glanced toward the platform and saw that the ceremony appeared to be coming to its conclusion. A blue-clad woman was carrying a velvet cushion to Karlinda. On it sat a metallic crest similar in style to the ones already inset into the mirrors on the rear wall.

Cat whisked back into the room. *The bracelets are hidden in the apartment.*

Where's Bear?

Watching Branna, she said.

I leaned forward and glanced to the right. Branna appeared to be heading back toward the elevator foyer. Perhaps he'd given up on trying to find Hedda.

If he leaves this room, can you both follow him? We need to know where he's hiding out if we're to have any hope of dealing with him.

Will do, Bear said.

Cat's energy kissed my cheek. *I do not like the feel of the man beside you. Be careful.*

It's usually me who's saying that, I said, amused.

She giggled. *I know. It rubs off.*

She left, leaving me alone with the man she disliked. I returned my attention to the platform and watched the remainder of the ceremony. Once Charles had placed his family's crest into the empty mirror, polite applause rolled around the room.

"Is that it?" I asked.

"The official part of the evening, yes." He rose and offered me his hand. "And now the fun begins."

I hesitated, and then placed my hand in his. And got a weird flash of... not darkness, but rather emptiness.

I frowned, unsure what it meant, but he released my hand before I could delve any further, and led the way off the platform. As I followed, music began to play, the beat heavy and languid.

Charles helped Karlinda down the stairs and kept a hand under her elbow as they walked toward us. The older woman was more than a little unsteady on her feet and there were deep shadows under her eyes. She really wasn't well.

Charles released her into Julius's care and then wrapped an arm around my waist and kissed me soundly. When he finally released me, he said, "Karlinda, this is Catherine, the woman I was talking about."

She held out a rather limp-looking hand. "It is a pleasure to meet you."

I clasped her fingers lightly, and couldn't quite control the gasp that escaped as a multitude of images hammered into my mind. Images of pain, blood, and darkness, of skin being pierced, and of a weakness that rose as life was drained.

"Are you all right?" Charles asked, concern in his tone.

I nodded, unable to do anything more, my throat dry and my thoughts skipping along as fast as my pulse. Despite the confusing rush of images that continue to batter my senses, one thing was abundantly clear.

Karlinda Stone wasn't sick.

She was being drained by a vampire.

CHAPTER EIGHT

But how was something like that even possible?

No vampire could survive in Central—not when the light towers bathed every single part of the city, permanently erasing the shadows and therefore any chance of a vampire ever stepping foot on her streets. Dream and her partners might have succeeded in giving the vampires who'd recently attacked Chaos some form of immunity to both firelight and normal light, but ultraviolet had still turned them to ash.

I needed to talk to Jonas and Nuri—and fast.

But that was next to impossible given where I was and who I was with. This was Charles's night, and I couldn't leave without eyebrows being raised—especially if Dream *was* Hedda. She might not be here, but her boss was, and it was very likely that—even if he weren't knowingly a part of plans—she'd ask him about the evening. I couldn't risk doing anything that would throw her suspicion my way.

"Julius," Karlinda said, "I'm afraid the ceremony has, as you feared, taken too much out of me. Would you mind greatly if I go home?"

"Of course not." A cool, unsurprised smile touched his lips. "Do you wish me to accompany you?"

"Of course not." She glanced at Charles and me. "You must both come to dinner tomorrow night."

"I wouldn't want to tax your strength—" Charles began, but Karlinda cut him off with a wave of her hand.

"You won't. Consider it an apology for walking out on your party tonight."

Charles inclined his head. "Then it would be my honor."

She nodded and, without a backward glance, left the three of us. My gaze followed her, and my feet itched to do the same. I half considered asking either Cat or Bear to follow her, but it was far more important right now to uncover where Branna was rather than who—or what—was feeding on Karlinda.

"I'll see you tomorrow, Charles," Julius said, anticipation in his voice. "I'm off to pursue satisfaction."

"Indeed," Charles agreed, and caught my hand. "Shall we dance, my dear?"

He didn't wait for an answer. He simply led me deep into the heart of the slow-moving throng and then pulled me so close that every movement, be it breath or excitement, was felt. As the night wore on, and alcohol was consumed, the dancing dissolved into a whole lot more. While I avoided having sex with anyone other than Charles, there was no real joy in the act. Not when all I wanted to do was get out of the place, and away from these people.

It was close to three by the time I persuaded a somewhat drunken Charles to leave. The air taxi deposited us at my building and I all but carried Charles into my apartment.

"A nightcap," he announced grandly. "We both need a nightcap."

A smile twitched my lips. "You need to lie down, Charles, before you fall down."

"I will only do so if you are with me." He somehow planted a somewhat awkward kiss on my cheek. "My need for you has not dimmed despite the pleasures of the night—"

"So I see," I replied. "Do you think you can make it up the stairs alone? I'll make us a nightcap."

"Indeed I can," he said, and dutifully staggered toward the stairs.

I watched, ready to spring into action should he look ready to topple, but he reached the landing without incident and disappeared into the bedroom. I poured two whiskeys, placed the sleeping draught into one, and mentally hoped it was fast-acting as I followed Charles up the stairs. He was sitting upright on top of the blankets rather than under them, and looked altogether too awake despite his drunken state.

"A vision in sheer blue and jade visits me." He patted his thighs. "And she brings a nightcap."

"Technically, you're visiting me, Charles, not the other way around." I sat astride his lap and handed him the glass. "To the newest Lord. May he rule with a hard but fair hand."

He chuckled softly and touched his glass against mine. "The hard bit will be no problem with you in my life."

"Evidently," I said, amused. Certainly the alcohol hadn't diminished either his ardor or his capabilities. "Do you know what is wrong with Karlinda?"

He raised an eyebrow. "I would rather not talk—"

"Humor me," I murmured, and gently slid up and down against the thickness of him, "and I might just humor you."

"Ha! Saucy wench." He downed his drink in one gulp, placed the glass aside, then caught my hips and held me still as he slipped inside. "Karlinda's strength has been on the decline for several years, but it has gotten much worse over the past few weeks."

"Can they not find the reason?"

"From the little Julius has said, she has a low blood count and is iron deficient, but they do not know its cause."

It was possible that both problems were related to her being a vampire's meal ticket, but I'd never known *any* vampire to assert such self-control. Their usual mode of operation involved a feeding frenzy that left their victims little more than bloody bones.

My body began to rock in time to Charles's gentle movements. I drained my whiskey and placed the glass on the table beside his. "And what of Julius? If they are constant companions, why would he not have caught the illness?"

"Because they do not live together, even though they are an

acknowledged couple." His grip on my hips tightened. "I hope you don't have designs on the man, because that would rather aggrieve me."

"Oh, I don't know," I teased. "There is a fierceness about him—a danger—that many would find attractive."

"If it's fierceness you want, my dear, then it's fierceness you shall get."

With that, he slipped down the bed and artfully shifted positions so that I was on my back. From there on in, he allowed no more talking and gave no quarter until both of us were satiated.

Only then did he finally fall asleep.

I carefully slipped out of his arms, grabbed a tunic from the cupboard, and then padded into the shower to wash the smell of sweat and sex from my skin. The last thing I wanted was to be seeing Jonas stinking of Charles. Once dressed, I quickly left.

Central was a city of never-ending light, and the everyday rhythm of life had evolved to cater for that. Many businesses were open twenty-four seven, and though the streets were far from crowded, there were still plenty of people out and about.

I made my way through the streets until I reached a cross street that led to Twelfth and—once it was empty—called the light to me and disappeared behind its shield. On Twelfth, I made my way to the top of the nearest building and continued to climb upwards via various rooftops, until I could go no further and there was only the rusting heaviness of the metal curtain wall between me and the night-clad world beyond.

I took a deep breath to gather my strength, and then thickened the walls of the shield until the brightness within disappeared and there were only shadows. I shifted to particle form and leaped upwards. A heated ache instantly throbbed across my body, but I ignored it. There was no other way to get out of Central at this time of night.

I flew over the top of the wall's wide walkway and plummeted down the other side. As the brightness of the UV towers began to fade, the light shield unraveled, until there was nothing between the night and me. It should have eased the ache in my head. It didn't.

I cursed softly and arrowed toward the bunker. The entrance door had been closed against the darkness, but even as I approached, it opened. No light spilled out to warm the night; Jonas had obviously turned it off in preparation for my arrival.

I dropped down and regained human form, but weakness washed through me and sent me stumbling forward. Jonas caught me before I could fall. He didn't ask if I was okay— he really didn't need to, given the connection we now shared. He simply helped me inside, shut the door, and then escorted me across to a chair and sat me down.

"You're taking one hell of a risk coming here." His voice held none of the anger and concern that washed from his mind to mine.

"I know, but I used that drug you sent and Charles is out cold—"

"I wasn't worried about Charles, but rather whoever is watching this place." He stalked across to the autocook sitting next to the old brick tower that still held the solar panels powering a good portion of the equipment in the underground levels. Long before this level had become a museum, it had been a heavily fortified base for day-to-day operations. But there was little left of the equipment that had survived both the war and the subsequent cleanout of all things déchet, nor was there anything to indicate the museum it had then become. Everything had either been destroyed or removed after Dream and her people had set off the bombs in an effort to contain me underground.

"Look, I'm sorry, but Cat and Bear are following Branna and I have information I needed to get to you and Nuri."

"Why the hell didn't you tell us you'd found Branna? We could have—" The rest of his sentence was lost to a cacophony of happy noise as all the little ones swept into the room. I didn't bother trying to calm them down—it had been a few days since I'd seen them, and I missed them as much as they'd missed me.

I waited until their excited chatter and their tingly kisses began to ease off, and then said, "I hope you haven't been annoying Jonas too much."

"Aside from all the noise," Jonas commented dryly, "they've been good company."

This set off another round of chatter and giggles. Jonas rolled his eyes and walked back with what looked like a mug of green swill and a plate piled high with meat, eggs, and bread.

He sat down opposite and slid both across the table. "Eat,

then we'll talk. Your chatty little ones might have calmed down by then."

Which only set them off again. I plucked a knife and fork from the nearby container and hoed into the food. I had to admit, I felt a lot better by the time I'd demolished it.

Jonas pushed the so-far ignored mug of green muck a little closer. It was an herbal drink favored by shifters for its energy-boosting properties, but I was not a fan. It rather tasted like fouled swamp water.

He waited until I'd drunk the damn stuff and then said, "So, Branna?"

I crossed my arms and grimly updated him on not only everything that had gone on over the last twenty-four hours, but everything I suspected.

By the time I'd finished, his expression echoed mine. "I would like to think that Julius Valkarie is not involved in Dream's schemes, but who knows how far the tendrils of her evil has spread."

"You know him?" I asked, surprised.

"Know of him, more precisely. He is, as Minister for Home Defense, the commander and chief of the ranger division, and a good one at that."

"I got the impression he left the day-to-day operations to his staff."

Jonas hesitated. "He never used to, but it's been a while since I resigned from the ranger division. Things could have changed." He pursed his lips for a moment, his expression thoughtful. "If Hedda is in fact Dream, then that might also explain the chancellor's current state of ill health."

"How so?"

"Hedda is Karlinda's younger sister."

"But she's not—" I stopped. Sal had told me that Winter was a rare vampire survivor and that he'd been the force behind the push to give vampires light immunity. But they were *all* survivors of a rift that had mashed their DNA together, and while Sal had never shown any hunger for blood, that didn't mean the other two had similarly skipped the need. And the vampires in the bunker I'd raided had not only mistaken me for someone else, but had called me mistress. Not master. *Mistress.*

If Dream *was* feeding off the people closest to her Hedda Lang persona, then she'd been doing it for some time, given Karlinda's gradual descent into frailty. But how the hell was she getting away with it without someone catching on?

"Why would anyone catch on?" Jonas asked, obviously following my thoughts. "They were taking multiple blood samples at Winter Halo with no one being the wiser. It would be very easy for Dream—in her Hedda disguise—to take the same sort of approach with her so-called sister."

"Yes, but surely someone would have connected the dots and have realized the weakness and anemia got worse after every sisterly visit?"

"Why would they? Hedda isn't a registered survivor of a vamp attack and she shows no outward signs of vampirism." He grimaced. "And, unfortunately, not even Nuri can make a move on her without concrete proof. All we have so far is suspicion."

"It's far more than a mere suspicion."

"Yes, but we still cannot act against her without proof. She is both too well regarded *and* well guarded for any action against her to succeed."

"You don't have to get close—any long-range rifle would take care of the problem nicely."

A smile touched his lips. "Except that Dream is a body shifter like yourself, and unless we get close, we can't be absolutely positive it's not the real Hedda Lang we're shooting."

That was, rather annoyingly, all too true. "What does the chancellor actually do? Is it an official or ceremonial position?"

"Historically, the chancellor was the chairman of the governing body of the universities board, but after the war it became a position within the House of Lords itself. He or she is responsible for overseeing the running of the house, and is called on to vote if there is a tie on a piece of legislation." He frowned. "Why?"

I leaned back in the chair and rubbed a hand across my eyes. "Karlinda invited Charles and me to dinner tomorrow night, so I figured I'd better be aware of what she actually does. It's possible Hedda will be there. If she *is*, then I might be able to act against—"

"No," he said immediately. "Hedda Lang, as divisional second, is never without protection. It would be nothing short of suicide to even contemplate carrying a weapon into Karlinda's premises, let alone trying to use it."

"So I'm simply to sit there and do nothing?"

"I'd rather you not sit there at all," he said. "Even without the bracelets Branna stole, she's still an earth witch of some power. She might well sense that you are more than you seem, just as Nuri did."

"Nuri had the advantage of a psychic connection with Penny and knew from the outset that I was lying."

His expression clouded over further at the mention of his niece's name. I knew why without even asking.

"Jonas—"

"I cannot let it be," he said, his expression suddenly fierce. "And I will *not* give up on her. Not until I know, with absolute certainty, that there is no hope."

"I know, but—"

"You, of all people, should understand why," he continued. "You went against reason and put your life on the line to rescue a child injected with wraith pathogens simply because you believed she had a chance—that she deserved the opportunity and the time to prove she was not the sum of what they'd done to her. How can you expect me *not* to offer my own flesh and blood that same chance?"

Because there *was* a difference, I wanted to say. But was that really true? Penny might have fled with the vampires, but she'd also let me live, and surely that meant something. After all, Dream had ordered the vampires to kill me on several occasions now, and Penny was no doubt well aware of that fact. And that, in turn, meant that somewhere deep inside, the child that was Jonas's niece still survived.

"But the longer she remains in their hands," he said softly, "the less chance there is of that remnant remaining. It needs to be done, if not today, then in the next couple of days."

"To echo your earlier words, we're taking one *hell* of a risk if we go out today."

"No more than the one you took to come here," he said.

"And Nuri? What would she say to this sudden change of plans?"

He didn't immediately answer, and the soft buzz at the back of my thoughts told me why—he was checking with her. A slight smile tugged his lips. "She agrees it's a fool's mission. But she also said that if we're going to do it, it has to be done now, because there will be no other chance."

I took a deep breath and released it slowly. I'd only come here with the intention of updating him and Nuri, but given Charles was knocked out for a good part of the coming day, there was no real reason why I *couldn't* investigate the rift Penny had disappeared into.

I scrubbed a hand across my eyes and then met his gaze grimly. "I will not go into that rift without a means of being tracked or indeed rescued. I've barely escaped from three of their facilities now. I fear I will not escape a fourth."

"All that can be arranged." He reached across the table and caught my hands in his. His fingers were calloused and oh so warm, and oddly made me feel safer than I'd ever felt in my entire life.

"For the first time in *my* long life," he continued, "I'm excited about the future and what it might bring. I don't want to lose that feeling, Tiger. And I would, if I lost you."

His words had an odd sort of tightness forming in my chest. I wasn't exactly sure what it was, but it felt heavy and wonderful all at the same time. "But we barely know each other. We don't even know if this thing between us—"

"Is real?" he cut in, amused. "It definitely *is* if it's managed to turn around the opinion of this world-weary, déchet-hating ranger."

I took a somewhat shuddery breath and released it slowly. "Wherever I end up, it's likely to be a trap. It might take an army to break me out, and not even Nuri, with all her contacts, will be able to rustle up such a force."

"Sometimes the best force to use is no force at all."

"Being enigmatic is doing nothing to ease my fears."

He smiled. "I know, but it's better you don't know details in the event you're captured. You just have to trust me."

I did trust him. I just didn't trust the fact that Dream hadn't already countered whatever they were planning to do. "You do realize that we lures are immune to all manner of drugs? They'll find it hard to get any information out of me."

"Hard doesn't mean impossible, Tiger. You were affected by that drug in Winter Halo, remember."

It wasn't like I could forget it. Even though the drug had done nothing more than cloud my senses and mind, it had still been something of a shock that there were now drugs my immunity couldn't handle. Although, given time, my natural healing abilities would chase any drug, no matter how deadly, from my system. It was the reason I'd survived being all but melted by the Draccid gas, after all.

But would I have that time if I were caught again? If Dream had issued a kill order within Central, why wouldn't she order the exact same thing everywhere else?

A rubbed my arms against the growing chill within. "How soon can you be ready to move?"

"Within the hour." He smiled, but it failed to lift the concern swirling through me. "Why don't you catch some sleep while I get everything in motion. My sleeping pack is over near the tower."

"Thanks." I pushed up and walked across. Once the pack was unrolled and the air mattress inflated, I climbed in. And went to sleep with the wild, rich scent of cat filling every breath and the happy chatter of the ghosts washing through my mind.

It wasn't Jonas who woke me—it was Cat, and her energy was filled with uncertainty.

"Is everything okay?" I climbed out of the sleeping roll and hastily tugged down my tunic. Jonas's quick amusement told me he hadn't missed the movement but he didn't say anything. Which was good, because how could I explain the ease with which I walked around naked in front of strangers, and yet was so totally reticent to do so in front of him? Except, perhaps, as a reluctance to tease the one person who actually meant something to me.

Branna went into Deseo, she said. *He did not come out.*

Deseo was the brothel on Twelfth Street that Sal had not only once owned, but one that held a false rift sitting in its basement. "You've checked the entire building?"

Yes. He's not there, but Bear still watches the exit.

I glanced across at Jonas. "Meaning he might have left via the rift that exits into Carleen. Do you think he suspects the rift they took Penny into might be my next point of attack?"

"It's possible, given he knows I'll be pushing for you to follow Penny through it." He hesitated. "The bigger question is, how did he even see the Deseo rift, let alone enter it? I can't do either, and I now share your DNA."

"Perhaps Dream reprogrammed the rift to allow him passage." And perhaps he had one of those eye things the sand base's people used to see them.

Jonas hesitated, his gaze briefly distracted. "Nuri says she doubts that's possible given everyone who is capable of using them has vampire in them."

"But if he didn't go through the rift, where the hell is he? He can't just disappear."

"No." He paused again. "Nuri's going to send Ela into Deseo to scan the owners and guards. Branna can't have gotten into a locked basement without someone either seeing him or giving him access."

Ela was not only a mercenary, but also a telepath of some power. She'd been sent into Deseo when I'd first discovered the rift there, but as far as I was aware, hadn't uncovered anything. I very much suspected that, other than confirming

Branna's presence there, it would probably be the result once again.

"What if Branna comes back and sees her?"

Jonas's smile was grim. "Simple—she'll kill him."

I didn't think there'd be *anything* simple about that particular task.

What do you want Bear and me to do? Cat said.

I hesitated, but given my earlier promise, it was better if they were here, where it was relatively safe, to wait for that call.

Bear, come back, I said, and then returned my gaze to Jonas. "Is everything ready to go?"

He nodded. "I'm meeting Nuri and a crew of mercenaries in the old forest. Once you're through the rift and we pick up the signal, we'll move."

"And the tracker?"

He held up a hand. Between two of his fingers was what looked to be a rather long white pill.

"I'm gathering I have to swallow that, because it sure as hell is going to be obvious if you stick it in my arm or even my foot."

He smiled. "Unlike most trackers, this one is made of a substance that can't be picked up by scanners."

I frowned as I plucked the pill from his fingers and studied it. "What about bioscanners?"

"The newer ones might."

"So it could be a problem if it's still in my system for tonight's dinner with Karlinda."

"No, because private residences rarely have bioscanners installed. They're too expensive."

"Ah, good." I grabbed some water and quickly swallowed the thing. It felt like I was swallowing plastic. "What about a comms device? If something happens this time, I want to be able to contact you."

"I have an ear-mic ready, but you'd better kit up before we place that on." He paused, amusement tugging at the corners of his lips. "I asked your little ones to bring up some clothes from your bunker. They rather cleverly brought up weapons, as well."

They giggled and danced around with pleasure at the compliment. Jonas shook his head and handed me the neatly folded combat pants and a camouflage shirt. They'd obviously retrieved them direct from the old stores because the machines that washed my clothes no longer pressed them.

I arched an eyebrow and, with a snort of amusement, Jonas turned around so I could change. The little ones then handed me two smaller guns, a machine rifle, ammo for them both, and my knife. Jonas attached the ear-mic, his scent filling my nostrils and stirring desires that could not be acted upon. Not yet.

"Do you know how to use one of these?" His voice held the slightest hint of huskiness.

"Yes. It automatically activates if someone contacts me, but I have to press it to reply."

"Make sure you keep us posted." He stepped back, giving me space I wasn't entirely sure I wanted. "I want to know when you're at the rift, when you're through, what you find. We need to know what to expect if we need to come in and rescue you."

"Will do, though I don't expect—" I stopped as Bear reappeared.

Sorry for losing Branna, he said. *I looked everywhere, but there are no exits out of that place aside from the one we were watching and that rift.*

"It was hardly your fault," Jonas said, before I could. "I don't think either Nuri or I would have done any better."

I should have hit him harder when we were in Chaos, Bear said somewhat gloomily. *It would have meant fewer problems.*

"None of us were to know that he'd be so filled with hatred he'd side with Dream," I said.

"And I'm not entirely sure he *is* doing that," Jonas said. "He undoubtedly wants you dead, but I doubt he knows Hedda is actually Dream. I think he's merely accepted the contract, and that's as far as his involvement goes."

"Except that he disappeared from Deseo, and as Bear pointed out, that rift was the only way he could have done so without them seeing him."

"Also true." Jonas hesitated, and half shrugged. "I just find it hard to believe he'd betray us in such a manner."

"Except I don't think he sees it as a betrayal. I think he sees it as a service—he's ridding the world of a monstrosity that should not exist."

"Possibly. Discovering your existence after losing most of his kin in the war... I think it has unhinged him."

"You lost people in the war, Jonas. You're not unhinged."

"Some would refute that statement."

Branna didn't head immediately to Deseo after leaving the ball, Bear commented. *He met with a woman at a cafe on Tenth.*

"A woman who resembled the chancellor, by chance?" Jonas asked.

No, Cat said. *She was dark-skinned and had green eyes.*

"The same woman who watched Rath Winter slap me around via a comms unit?" I asked.

Yes, Bear said. *That one.*

Jonas swore and scrubbed a hand across his jaw. "Did you by chance hear what they were saying?"

No, Cat said. *We didn't want to get too close, in case she sensed us. But she gave him a small bag.*

"A bag?" I said. "What type of bag?"

A small leather one, Bear said. *It didn't look like a gun. It was the wrong shape.*

"Given he met her before he went through the rift, maybe it was a means to pass through it."

"Maybe." Jonas walked across to the door, his anger and

frustration evident in every stride. "Either way, you'd better be careful when you're in Carleen."

We could come with you, Cat said. *And keep watch.*

I hesitated, and then shook my head. There was a chance—however minor—that the item Dream had handed Branna wasn't a device to slip through the rift, but rather some sort of weapon capable of dealing with ghosts. After the events in Winter Halo, she had to have guessed I had help that was not of flesh and blood. It was better that they kept out of the way for the time being—presuming, of course, Branna had ended up in Carleen when he'd gone through that rift. For all we knew, Dream had reprogrammed it to take him somewhere else.

But what if he attacks you? Bear asked, concern evident.

"Then I'll kill him."

Good, they both intoned.

Once I'd again said goodbye to the little ones, I walked toward the now open door. Dawn was spreading plumes of pink across the sky and the air held an electricity that spoke of an oncoming storm.

"What is the range of the tracker?" I asked, as I stopped beside Jonas.

"Extremely long, hence the size of the thing." He touched my back briefly. "Don't worry. We won't leave you stranded out there. Not this time."

"Good."

And with that, I left.

The day was still too new for either the drawbridge to be down or the pods at the station to be powering up, but I nevertheless made my way swiftly across both City Road and the rail platforms, and into the park beyond. This place had always been a green barrier between the city and Carleen, but these days it was a silent place, devoid of any life. The vampires—who lived in what remained of the underground sewage and utilities systems—guaranteed that.

It took an hour to reach Carleen's southern border. I stopped on the edge of the clearing that separated the park from the broken city ahead. Though Carleen was now little more than a vine-covered mass of rusting metal and disinte-grating concrete, it had once been home to over twenty thousand people, most of them families. Unfortunately, it was still home to many of those people, as the evacuation order had been issued far too late. Even then, many of the people who'd died here had done so in the one place they thought they'd be safe—the massive bomb shelters under the city's main plaza.

The only scents riding the strengthening breeze were that of decay and neglect, and I could see no movement beyond the wall other than the occasional bit of bright plastic being chased along by the wind. I couldn't even feel the presence of the ghosts, but that wasn't surprising given they'd recently relocated to the other side of the city. They hadn't done so willingly—they'd been forced into it by the false rift that was now, in their words, staining their bones with its corruption.

I hesitated a bit longer, unsure as to why, then pushed on. After leaping onto a low section of wall, I stopped again, taking in the ruptured remnants of buildings and—farther to my left—the remains of what once had been a main road through the city. It was littered with building rubble, weeds, and trees that had been twisted into odd shapes thanks to the eddying magic of the rifts. Those eddying bits of plastic added spots of bright color to many darker corners, but this place remained eerily shadowed. And while a pall of darkness had hung over this city ever since its destruction, it now felt deeper.

Darker.

The false rifts—and the magic Dream used to create them—was corrupting not only the bones of those who had died here, but the entire city.

I jumped down from the wall and made my way through the luminous splashes of alien moss and the broken remnants of life and buildings until I reached the main road that sloped up to the main plaza. I was barely halfway up it when the faint but foul caress of alien energy touched my skin. I stopped abruptly, knowing immediately what it was but unable to believe Dream's shield had grown to such an extent that it now covered half the hill. I reached out with one hand, just to be sure, and a jagged whip of light instantly appeared, snapping toward me with a speed and strength that was frightening. I leaped back, but even so, the very tip of it hit my arm and raised a welt not unlike that of a burn.

I cursed and moved off the road, picking my way through the both the rubble and the moss that was beginning to take over the entire area. While the moss had been present in Carleen for as long as the rifts, ever since Dream had created the false rift that now dominated much of this hill, its spread rate had all but doubled. Maybe it was feeding off the energy coming from her rift—an energy that felt almost as alien as the moss itself.

But the bigger question was, why would Dream want a rift so large? It was now more than double the size of the ones they'd used in Winter Halo to transport trucks and was, in fact, as big as some of the old battle cruisers I'd seen in the war. I had no idea if such machines still existed, but even if they did, surely Dream could not acquire one without alarms being raised.

Unless, of course, the size of the rift had nothing to do with transporting machines across this world, but rather transporting them *to* this world.

Cold dread stepped through my body and I shivered. Perhaps Dream's plans had evolved since the deaths of her partners. Perhaps she and the wraiths were now planning an all-out war, and this hideous rift was their starting point.

I pressed the ear-mic and said, "Jonas, can you hear me?"

"Yes," he immediately said. "Is there a problem?"

"Yes and no. You know that rift Nuri investigated—the one hovering over the bones of Carleen's dead?"

"Yes."

"The shield protecting it has grown massively, and it also rather weirdly seems to be feeding the alien moss. Nuri needs to find a way to either stop it from growing any further or destroy it."

That's presuming she *could* do either, of course. It was always possible that this rift had grown so strong it had not only taken on a life of its own but was now beyond any chance of destruction.

"I'll pass the info on, but she won't be able to do anything immediately."

"Okay," I said, and signed off again.

I was nearly back at the old curtain wall before I found a way around the rift's girth. I picked my way through the thin strip of land between the two, trying to avoid both the acidy moss and the whips of energy trying to grab me. My arm still burned even though the first whip had barely touched me, and the skin remained red and puckered. Given the wound was neither very serious nor deep, the healing process should have at least kicked in by now and eased the pain.

Unless, of course, a wound caused by such unnatural magic was beyond even my rift-enhanced healing capability.

It was ten minutes before the foul caress of the rift's energy began to fade, and by that time I was on the other side of the plaza. The desolation here was almost complete—beyond the remnants of the road, there was just dust, weeds, and the occasional splash of the luminescent moss. I had no sense of the ghosts, though they should have been here somewhere. Had Dream gotten rid of them? As an earth witch, she had that power.

Concrete and metal dust puffed up with every step until I was surrounded by a cloud of fine gray soot that not only announced my presence, but made breathing difficult. If Branna was here, he would see me coming.

If being the operative word. I still had no sense of him, but then, he was soldier trained and I was not. It was totally possible I'd never see him—not until it was too late.

Once again the desire to call to my ghosts stirred, and once again I resisted. I just didn't like the feel of this place—or the fact that the Carleen ghosts seemed to have disappeared. If something here had so frightened them that they hadn't even appeared to remonstrate my lack of progress in freeing their bones from the rift's taint, I simply couldn't risk bringing either Cat or Bear here.

As I neared the bottom of the hill, foul energy began to lash my skin, though it had none of the power of the rift at the top. Up ahead, to the right of the road, was an odd, circular patch of darkness in an area that was nothing but sunshine and dust. That darkness wasn't the rift itself, but rather the wall of gelatinous shadows that protected it.

I paused, waited until my accompanying cloud had been swept away by the wind, and then drew in a deep breath. There was nothing to suggest I wasn't alone in this place. And yet... the more I stared at the rift, the more I was sure I was walking straight into the arms of a trap.

I should just turn around and walk out of this place. It would be the sane and sensible thing to do. But I'd already broken one promise, even if for a very good reason. I didn't want to break another—especially when, in reality, one was linked to the other.

Penny might yet be saved. The chances might be remote, but while the slightest speck of hope remained, I could not ignore it. For Jonas's sake, if nothing else.

I unclipped a gun and held it at the ready as I strode toward the shadows that protected the rift. The minute I stepped into them, they thickened, becoming a real and very solid presence that pressed down upon me like a ton of weight. Every step forward was an effort, and all too soon my leg muscles were quivering and I was gasping for air.

Then, with little warning, the shadows lifted, and I was stumbling forward in an effort to catch my balance.

I barely had when I realized I was not alone in this place.

Before I had the chance to see who or what it was—before I could even raise my gun in an effort to defend myself—something hit my shoulder, spun me around, and left me kneeling on the ground in a whole world of pain.

CHAPTER NINE

For several, all too vital seconds, I simply couldn't move. It was all I could do to keep breathing. My left shoulder had become a raging inferno and the sheer heat of it had my entire body shaking and sweating.

The stirring dust told me my attacker approached. I drew in a breath, tasting within it the sharp, dry scent of grass and sand.

Rhea help me... Branna.

Here, in the one place neither my ghosts nor Jonas could help me. And *that* was undoubtedly deliberate.

I closed my eyes for a moment and fought for calm. I could survive this. I *would* survive this.

Though I remained hunched over, I forced my head up. He walked toward me casually, a gun in one hand and some sort of oblong-shaped device in the other. His expression was one of grim satisfaction.

"What in Rhea are you doing, Branna?" My voice was little

more than a harsh scrape of sound. "Dream wants to give our world to the wraiths and vampires—surely even you can't want that?"

"Of course I don't." He stopped just beyond my reach—but not that of the gun I'd somehow managed to keep hold of as I went down. It was the reason I remained hunched over—I didn't want him to see it.

But as much as I wanted to shoot him—as much as I wanted to see him broken, bloody, and very, *very* dead—it wouldn't be the wisest move right now. Aside from the fact that the pain pulsing from my wound would hamper my speed, he was far too wary—far too watchful—right now. He would be on me long before I could pull the trigger.

"Your death," he continued evenly, "has nothing to do with any of that. It's a simple business transaction. Nothing more, nothing less."

I snorted, but the slight movement sent new waves of pain crashing across my body. Sweat broke out across my forehead and dribbled down my spine. Fear bloomed.

Something was *very* wrong.

I'd been shot many times before, but never had a wound affected me like this. It was almost as if my flesh was reacting to the bullet lodged in my shoulder... so what had he shot me with? Not an ordinary bullet, that was for sure, and it couldn't be silver. I might have shifter genes, but my skin didn't react to its touch. Not like this, anyway.

"Ah," Branna said. "You begin to understand your predicament."

"You're the one in a predicament," I growled. "Hedda Lang is Dream, Branna. She's using you—using your hatred—"

"No," he cut in. "You've got all ass-about. I'm using *her*—"

"To betray our whole damn *world*," I said, without really thinking, "because you're so blinded by hatred—"

"You are an *abomination*," he growled, the fires of insanity briefly flaring in his eyes. "One who has no right to live when all who were decent and good died at your hands—"

"It was a *war*," I responded heatedly. Desperately. And then sucked in a breath and tried to calm down. Going down that path was pointless, because Branna was never going to see beyond his memories and madness. Not when it came to me, anyway. "Do you actually think Dream will let you live after you've fulfilled the contract and killed me?"

"Oh, I'm not so foolish as to trust any government official, given the amount of times I've seen outside contractors disappear. It's part of the reason why I hung around with Nuri for so long—thanks to her connections, she was safe from such actions."

"If you think she'll in any way protect you after this—"

"I'm well aware that she won't, which is why I'll disappear the minute you're dead." He paused, and that fierce light in his eyes faded. It made me feel no safer, however. "And now that you've rescued those children, I can do so with a clear conscience."

"How in Rhea can your conscience *ever* be clear knowing you're working for the woman who was responsible for destroying those children's lives? The same woman who wants to annihilate humanity?"

"I have every faith that Nuri will find a way to stop her." He shrugged. "And it's not like she predicted that you were—in any way—vital in doing that."

It was so rationally said, and yet so very insane. "No matter where you go, Branna, Nuri and Jonas *will* find you, and they'll most certainly kill you."

"Oh, they can try," he said, unperturbed. "But I know their network far too well to ever be caught by it."

"So what the hell are you waiting for?" I tightened my grip on the gun and tried to do the same with the pain. "Why don't you just kill me and be done with it?"

"Because I want to watch you suffer. I want you to feel the agony and utter uselessness that I did when your kind erased my entire clan. And when I finally see fear rather than defiance in your eyes, only then will I kill you."

"Don't hold your breath waiting for *that* to happen."

Even as I said it, I whipped out the gun and fired. He was fast—faster by far than me—and the bullets smashed into his right knee and his left shin rather than his black heart. The rest missed completely, disappearing into the gelatinous shadows.

But Branna was at least down, and cursing, his knee and his leg a bloody, broken mess. It gave me time. Time to gather strength; time to get the damn bullet out of my shoulder. I switched the gun to my left hand, but my fingers were numb and unresponsive, and simply wouldn't grip it.

Fear surged anew. I let the weapon drop, unclipped my knife, and with my eyes on Branna, I plunged the blade into my shot shoulder. The wave of new pain that hit was so fierce that for a moment I feared I was going to black out, but I fought the sensation with everything I had.

Branna rolled onto his stomach and pushed upright. Thankfully, the gun he'd been holding lay between us. Part of my brain was screaming at me to pick up my weapon and fire every last bullet into his traitorous flesh, to take him out before he could reach that gun and finish what he'd started. But the other part was just as fiercely warning I needed to remove the thing in my shoulder before it killed me.

And that prospect was frighteningly close. The waves of heated agony washing from the epicenter of my shoulder were increasing in strength and volume, and I had a bad, *bad* feeling I only had minutes left.

I dropped the knife and dug my fingers into the wound. A scream escaped and sweat poured down my face, stinging my eyes and blurring my vision. I gritted my teeth and pushed my fingers deeper into my flesh, until I felt something solid. Simply touching it sent another wave of cold sweat and agony crashing though me—how in Rhea was I ever going to move it?

A grunt of pain had my gaze leaping upwards. Branna had begun to drag himself toward his gun. Why he wasn't shifting shape to heal himself I couldn't say. All shifter's cells had a set point—an optimum level of health and strength that they always reverted back to—which meant the only wounds they couldn't heal by moving from one form to another was silver.

But perhaps he didn't want to waste the few minutes it would take. Perhaps he simply wanted to kill me while I was still incapacitated.

Energy and determination surged. I bit down on my lip, using one pain to counter the other, then gripped the bullet with two fingers and pulled it out.

It wasn't metal. It was *wood*.

Like most déchet, I'd been warned both before *and* during the war that my vampire genes might make me vulnerable to wood. But I'd never had such a weapon used against me, not during the war and certainly not after it. The shifters obviously *hadn't* been aware of the inbuilt design fault, or they would have used wood against us.

The fact that Branna had shot me with such a bullet could only mean one thing—Dream had been a part of the déchet program. There was no other way she could have known about the vulnerability.

I dropped the bullet to the ground and tried to force my body upright. I didn't succeed. My head swam, pain pulsed through me, and my vision shifted in and out of focus. But if I collapsed now, Branna would win.

I forced bloody fingers to pick up the gun and then shot him. Not once, not twice, but four times. I put one bullet through each forearm, waited until he collapsed onto his face, and then shot out each shoulder. Blood sprayed and he roared, but it was a sound of fury and frustration rather than pain.

I felt no satisfaction. I barely felt relief.

Despite the fact it would have undoubtedly been safer to

simply kill him outright, I needed to question him. But there was some deeper, darker part of me that also wanted him to suffer.

I crawled forward and knocked his weapon well away from us both. He might be broken but I wasn't about to take any chances.

But the effort of moving had taken what little strength I had left and the buzzing in my thoughts—the desire to just let go and slip away—was so damn strong that I actually *did* close my eyes. I quickly forced them open again and sucked in several deep breaths, fighting for control over both my body and the pain. When the latter had eased just a little, I called to the healing trance and slipped just far enough into it to keep awareness.

Animals were at their most dangerous when cornered, and Branna would not be the exception.

He watched me, emanating a rage that was so raw, so deep and furious, that it burned across my skin like flame.

"Tell me about the black woman you met at the café on Tenth," I said. "The one who handed you a small leather bag."

Surprise briefly lifted the anger and hatred from his expression. "I'd rather *die* than give someone like you any sort of information."

"That woman," I ground out, "was Dream in her true form. If we can find her, we can put a stop to her mad schemes, Branna. Surely even you cannot want to live in a world that is controlled by the wraiths and the vampires."

"It will *never* come to that."

"Nuri believes otherwise."

He hawked and spat. The globule landed on the top of my thigh and began to dribble down the side of my leg. I didn't yet have the strength to do anything more than let it.

It said all that needed to be said.

"You will die in this place of darkness and creeping evil," I continued. "And until Nuri sends your soul on to whatever particular hell awaits traitors such as yourself, it will be a daily reminder of the unthinking, ungiving hatred that has led you to betray not only our world, but those you once called friends."

His body finally began to shift—shimmer—as he reached for his alternate form in a last ditch attempt to keep on fighting.

I raised the gun and shot him a final time. As his head disintegrated and his brains sprayed the ground around him, my strength finally fled and I fell backward.

I was unconscious before I hit the ground.

I had no idea how long I remained that way. The sun was high in the sky by the time I woke, but I had no idea if it was the same day or the next. While I doubted it was the latter, having never been shot with wooden bullets before now I had no idea how long it took for such a wound to heal.

I breathed deep, smelled death and corruption, and opened my eyes. Branna's broken body had slipped into rigor mortis, and the blood on his clothes and skin had dried. All of which meant I'd been out for at least four hours.

I glanced down at my shoulder and carefully touched the wound. It was sore—damn sore—and the wound was still red and angry looking. I gingerly raised my elbow and moved it around. The shoulder twinged but I otherwise had full movement.

Yet again I'd been lucky—if it had taken me any longer to remove the wooden bullet, I might have lost use of my arm.

I retrieved my weapons then pushed upright and walked over to Branna. For several minutes I simply stood there, staring at the man who'd been a flesh and blood representation of the hatred, fear, and utter intolerance that had become such a major player in the war. It might have started with a land grab but it had devolved into so much more.

It said a lot about Jonas's character that—despite having as many reasons to hate me—he'd managed to see beyond it all while Branna never could.

Jonas. Both he and the ghosts would be worried by my silence. I took in a deep breath and then raised a hand and activated the earpiece.

"What in Rhea has been happening?" he immediately said. "It's been six hours since—"

"Branna happened," I cut in. "He was waiting within the rift's shield and damn near killed me."

"Why didn't you contact me immediately?"

"Because between taking care of Branna, being in a deep state of unconsciousness, and trying *not* to die, I was too damn busy."

Jonas swore. "You'd better come back. We can do this another—"

"Leaving now only gives Dream the chance to either move this rift or to set another trap," I said. "We can't risk either."

"You can't afford to blow your Catherine identity, either, and you will if you fail to show up tonight."

"I've still got at least six hours. That gives me time."

"Not much, given the rifts drain so much from you."

"Jonas, I'll be fine."

He made a sound that was pure frustration. "Contact me again when you get on the other side of that thing—and *that* is an order."

"I will, but *not* because you order it."

"Fine," he growled, and then the line went dead.

I knelt, rolled Branna over, and quickly patted him down. The small leather bag Bear had mentioned was tucked into his left pocket, but it was empty. There was little else to be found. If he'd intended to run after killing me, then he was doing so with little in the way of provisions.

I reloaded my gun and then glanced around for the thing he'd been holding in his other hand when he'd shot me. After a moment, I spotted it near the edge of the rift and walked across. The rift started to spin on its axis as I neared, and bands of jagged energy began to spit and strike its dark surface. The closer I got, the faster the rift spun, the more volatile those bands became. The force of them slashed at my body, leaving my arms and legs littered with bloody streaks. They would grab me if I got too much closer.

I snagged the oblong-shaped device and then jumped back

quickly as the lightning came uncomfortably close to wrapping itself around my arm.

The rift's movements eased once I moved away again. I frowned down at the device, turning it over in my hands, trying to figure out what it was. It wasn't a weapon—there was no trigger, barrel, or clip. It also didn't appear to be any sort of communications unit. It was just a heavy, black metal brick.

So why was Branna carrying it? It obviously had some use, otherwise, why would he have gripped it with such determination?

I glanced back at the rift and realized its surface was the same greasy black as the brick. Were the two connected? Was this device the reason Branna had been able to traverse the rift without the hideous side effects that always affected me?

I guess there was only one way to find out.

With a deep breath that did little to steady my nerves or the sick sensation of dread, I once again walked toward the rift.

The minute I was close enough, two bands of energy once again snaked out, capturing both my wrists and ankles. Though their touch still felt like fire, it didn't burn into my skin as it had on previous occasions. Even the ferocity with which I was dragged into the rift was muted. As its darkness enclosed me, its energy charged through me, tearing me apart atom by atom, until there was nothing left of my body but specs and memories. But there was also little in the way of pain this time, just the endless darkness and the odd sensation of movement. Then that movement ceased and I was slowly but carefully put back together. The whips holding me disintegrated and I was pushed out of the darkness and into the light.

Sunlight, not artificial.

I blinked and looked around. I'd landed in a forest, not another military bunker, as I'd half expected. I couldn't immediately see any buildings or even any indication of life, but there was a vibration running through the ground under my feet and the air was tainted with the thick smell of rot and death.

And that meant there was a vampire nest somewhere near.

I rubbed a hand across gritty eyes and swore softly. This day was just getting better and better. A nest was the last thing I wanted to tackle alone, especially when I wasn't overly equipped with either weapons or ammo. I'd barely survived the last time I'd entered one, and I'd had all those things and more.

But the sun was still high in the sky, so if there was a nest in the area, the vampires would at least be comatose—and they needed to be, given I had to get past them to uncover if they were in any way connected to Dream.

I raised a hand to press the ear-mic and said, "Landed. Will update more when I discover where."

"Be careful."

"Always."

I turned it off before he could reply to *that* particular statement, and then made good on my promise to call for Cat and Bear. Once I'd shoved the black brick into Branna's leather pouch and put it into a pocket, I checked which direction the foul scent seemed to be coming from and walked that way.

The wind pushed me along, its touch cold and filled with the promise of rain. I glanced up, but the canopy was so thick in this section of the wood that even the sunlight struggled to get through—and the beams that did were tinged with green. At least if it did rain, I'd have some protection.

I continued to follow the well-worn path up a steepening incline. Eventually, it plateaued, and the trees gave way to sunshine with a suddenness that made me blink.

Below me lay a city.

Or rather, the broken remains of one.

It ringed the hill on which I stood, and—like Carleen—had obviously been bombed into oblivion during the war. There were small sections of metal curtain wall defiantly standing tall, but for the most part it was a melted, twisted mess. What remained of the rest of the city was laid out in a grid pattern, but the buildings themselves were little more than piles of concrete and metal bones.

There was no obvious place for vampires to hide but this city, like old Central and Carleen, would have had a vast network of underground systems in place to service its occupants' needs. That's where they'd be.

I walked on, but the path ended abruptly and the ground gave way to a steep cliff. I carefully peered over the edge and saw not only the piles of dirt, rock, and tree roots at the bottom of it, but also several exposed and broken pipes that stuck out like stiff fingers from the cliff face.

There was a sewer system running under the hill, and the

stench coming from it.... I gagged and stepped back. There had to be a lot of vampires under the hill for their smell to be *this* strong from such a distance.

I pressed the ear-mic and said, "Jonas, you there?"

"Not only here, but on the move. We're about half an hour out from your location."

"Which is?"

"Fairhaven."

"That's not a place I'm familiar with."

"It was one of Central's satellite cities," he replied. "And had been purely residential."

Meaning there'd been no military installations near it, I suspected. That he hadn't said it suggested there were people with him who hadn't been fully informed about the situation.

"Have you spotted Penny?" he continued. "Or located the building in which she's being kept?"

"Not exactly." I hesitated. "There's a large nest of vampires here though."

He didn't say anything. He didn't need to. Even without the link between us being active, I knew him well enough to know he'd be angry—at himself as much as at the situation. He'd sworn long ago to protect his niece and, like me, he kept on failing.

"I found a couple of places the vampires could be using to access the underground system," I continued, "but Penny wouldn't be able to use any of them."

Because unlike either the vampires or even possibly Dream, she couldn't take on a shadow form. But even as that thought crossed my mind, doubt stirred. In truth, we couldn't be so sure of that now. Not after everything that had been done to her.

"Right," he said. "Find that access point, but don't go in until we get there."

"Jonas, they're going to feel the pulse of your blood the minute you enter the system—"

"Yes, but we need to be outside, armed and ready, in case you either find Penny or get caught."

"Does that mean you have UV lights with you?"

"Indeed we have." His reply was grim. "I wasn't about to take any chances given it was vampires who snatched her."

They hadn't snatched her—she'd answered their call and followed them into the park, where she was transferred into an ATV that had subsequently disappeared into one of Carleen's false rifts.

Cat and Bear appeared and spun around, at once excited to be somewhere new and more than a little uneasy about the vampires being so close.

"I'll let you know if we find anything."

"Are Cat and Bear there?"

"They just arrived."

"Good."

The line went dead. I swung around and studied the trees.

There had to be another entrance here somewhere—one that I'd missed on the way up—and it would be logical to have it somewhere close to the rift.

Except the track I'd followed up here was little more than a footpath, and if Dream was using the rift to move supplies and even test subjects back and forth, then she needed something wide enough to cater for vehicle use. Even the smallest ATV wouldn't be able to traverse this one.

I glanced down at the city again and studied the roads, looking for one that might have once swept up this hill. After a moment, I found a likely candidate and moved off the path to follow the edge of the cliff around. Cat and Bear roamed ahead, checking every nook and cranny, even though it was unlikely the entrance into the main nest would be in any way hidden.

The farther along the cliff we got, the worse the stench got, and *that* at least meant we were heading in the right direction.

There are bones up ahead, Cat said. *They are piled up strangely.*

Do they resemble a humanoid figure? I asked, remembering the macabre homage to humanity I'd found in the other nest.

One does, Bear said. *But others resemble animals.*

Probably the ones they fed on—though if there were many animals left in this place after almost a hundred years of vampires hunting them, I'd be very surprised.

The edge of the cliff swept to the left and the remains of a bitumen road appeared. I followed it into the trees and soon came to an intersection of four roads. The road I was on continued ahead, the one to the left disappeared back into the trees and was—if the indentations on the road's surface was anything to go by—the one used by the ATVs. I swung right.

Found the nest entrance, Bear said. *It lies near the base of the hill and to the right of the road you're on.*

Is it a large sewer entrance?

Big enough to allow ATV entry. Cat paused. *There's one inside but it's empty. Do you want us to investigate further?*

No. Wait for me to get there.

Will do.

The ear-mic buzzed and then Jonas said, "We're ten minutes out."

I pressed the receiver. "Cat and Bear have found the entrance. I'll send them over to guide you once you arrive."

"No need—you swallowed a tracker, remember?"

I hadn't remembered, but maybe that was because I was just so used to it being the ghosts and me against the world. It was a rather weird—but also very gratifying—realization that *that* was no longer the case. Not only would Raela join our little family once all this mess was over, but very possibly Jonas—*if* things worked out between us.

I rather thought they would. Or at least I hoped they would.

"Right," I said. "See you soon."

As I continued down the hill, fat blobs of rain began to

splatter around me. I glanced up. While there were still patches of blue, a thick strip of heavy gray hung directly above this section of the city. I was about to get drowned.

I broke into a run in an effort to beat the oncoming storm, but just as I hit the bottom of the hill, the clouds opened up and the rain pelted down. I was soaked through in an instant.

It's dry in the outlet tunnel, Cat said helpfully.

And warm, Bear added.

That's really not helping right now. My voice was dry and their giggles ran through my mind, bright and happy.

I stepped off the road and followed the sense of their energy through the scrub. Up ahead, visible through the smattering of trees, was another cliff face, though this one was semicircular in shape. Drifts of rubble and dirt appeared, and the nearby trees bore the scars of that long-ago landslip. But there was a clearly defined—and very wide—path weaving its way through it all. I eventually reached the base of that cliff and a clearing that was a sort of forecourt to the sewerage entrance.

There were indeed bones here—mounds and mounds of them. Some had simply been discarded into drifting piles, but most had been used to form effigies of the vampires' food sources. The one representing humanity stood on the left side of the road in the center of the clearing, and it was definitely the biggest, but on the right side there were numerous other piles that vaguely resembled various animals. There were also bloodied bits of flesh and internal organs in various states of decay scattered around the base of each of these, which were undoubtedly offerings to ensure more success in hunting. I had no idea if those organs were human or animal, just as I had no real idea where this city was in relation to the nearest human population or even Central. But it was possible that—like the nest that lay in the sewerage remains near Central—these vamps were using their sick and dying as an additional protein source. They tended not to be overly fussy about things like that.

The sewer outlet itself was a big, semicircular opening in the middle of the scarred and pitted cliff face. There were remnants of red brick in amongst the cleared pile of rubble on the left edge of it, and a couple of fingers of black metal that might have been the original entrance's grate to the right.

I continued to follow the well-defined path and did my best to ignore the stench rolling out of the opening ahead. Neither the wind nor the pelting rain did anything to alleviate the almost thick solidity of it, and it was everything I could do to ignore the growing urge to just turn around and run.

It was an urge that rose more from knowing what awaited inside that sewer than the smell.

I stopped just inside the entrance. Water ran from my clothes in a dozen different rivers, but even though I was wet right through, there was no chance of being cold.

Bear was right. This place was *warm*.

That was extremely unusual for vampire nests, as they tended to prefer a cooler clime. The heat—along with that odd vibration I'd felt near the rift—all but confirmed there was more than just a nest here.

I stripped off and wrung out as much water from my clothes as I could, but getting back into them was damned unpleasant. I shifted from one foot to the other, my impatience growing. Time was something we didn't have a whole lot of right now; if Jonas didn't get here soon, I was going on without him.

Just as well I'm here then, isn't it? His thoughts slipped easily into my mind, his mental tones warm and amused.

I swung around and saw him striding toward me. There were at least a dozen men and women behind him, all of them well armed and bearing heavy backpacks. They were all also wearing wet-weather gear, so they were a whole lot drier than me.

Thanks for the warning, guys, I grumbled to my ghosts.

Sorry, they both said at the same time, *we were watching the tunnel, not the clearing.*

Which, considering it was the direction any danger would come from, was perfectly reasonable. "There's something other than a nest of vamps in this place," I said, as Jonas and his people came to a halt.

All of them were regarding the sewer entrance and the smell wafting out of it with varying degrees of horror and distaste—even Jonas, who knew exactly what to expect within the stinking tunnels of this place.

"My guess is it's a generator," Jonas said.

I frowned. "It would have to be a pretty powerful one if we're feeling it at the top of the hill."

"Or it's old and not well maintained. Given whatever

complex it's supplying power to is sitting on a vampire nest, I'd imagine getting people out to fix the thing would be rather hard." He glanced at the woman standing just behind him, and she immediately stepped forward and held out a backpack. He passed it on to me. "It contains grenades, more ammo for your weapons, and a halo light."

What's a halo light? I asked silently, not wanting to ask the question aloud when it was obviously something I should have known.

A small but extremely powerful UV light disk that clips onto your belt. When activated, it creates a halo of light around your entire body. The rangers have been trialing them for the last couple of weeks.

And just how did you get hold of them? I asked, amused. *A little mercenary thievery, perhaps?*

We do have to keep up to date with the latest in weaponry, otherwise we'd very easily lose our standing amongst mercenary ranks.

And obviously *that* would be a bad thing. I hitched the pack over my shoulder then added aloud, "If I find her, I'll contact you."

He nodded. "Be careful. And keep the ear-mic open when possible so I can hear what is going on.

"When possible" meaning when I was in human form, not vampire.

I nodded and, with Cat and Bear by my side, turned and headed deeper into the sewer drain—though in this section at least, there was very little of the old structure left. The widened walls had been braced with steel and concrete, and the ground underfoot was concrete rather than brick. An open drain ran down the middle, and if the increasing water level was any indication, at least some storm water outlets remained in working order deeper in the mountain.

We reached a semicircular junction. An old ATV and several air transports sat here, but I couldn't see any security measures. There certainly weren't any guards.

Which was odd. Granted, this place was a vampire den, but there still should have been other protections if Dream had established some sort of center here. Especially given we'd now taken out all three of their laboratories.

I opened the backpack, found a small silver disk that looked like a button more than any sort of light, and clipped it to my belt. After I'd hooked several more ammo clips onto the various hooks on my belt and pants, I swung the backpack on and then walked past the vehicles. There were three tunnels leading off this main area; I paused again, studying them with a frown. The stench coming from the left tunnel was so thick it was almost liquid, and that suggested the den was down there. The middle tunnel seemed to slope upward rather than down, meaning there might be another exit point up that way—perhaps one that was closer to the rift. The tunnel on the right was where the vibrations seemed to be coming from.

It made sense to go that way. No matter how in tune Penny might now be to the vampires, surely she wouldn't want to be near them on a permanent basis. And given Dream had been so desperate for her retrieval that she risked sending her semi-light-immune vamps into Chaos—and thereby outing their existence—she surely wouldn't tempt fate by keeping a successful but still all too human test subject in such close proximity with them.

I switched over to particle form and moved into the left tunnel. There was no concrete propping up this section of the sewer, and it certainly wasn't wide enough to drive a truck through. Water dripped from the upper sections of the old brick arch and slime hung in drooping ropes of thick green. I avoided both as best I could, but the occasional drop still splashed through my particles, making me shiver even though I shouldn't have felt the cold in this form. But I *could* feel fear, and there was plenty of that gathering as we moved deeper and deeper into the mountainside.

Somewhere up ahead, a light flickered. It was a pale yellow glow in a world that was otherwise black, and trepidation stirred. It rather looked like flame thanks to the way it was flickering on and off, but no firelight I knew was capable of directing such a powerful beam of light directly upward.

I slowed, and then stopped. I had no immediate sense of vampires, so I shifted back to human form and studied that single, solitary light.

Do you want me to investigate? Bear asked.

I hesitated and then shook my head. *I don't like the feel of it.*

All the more reason for me to investigate, he said, quite reasonably.

You may be right, but I'd rather you both keep close.

I unhooked a couple of guns and walked on. That flickering light grew closer but no warmer. I reached up and switched the ear-mic on. It was far better to do so now, when I had the time, because Rhea only knew what was about to happen.

But I was pretty sure it wouldn't be a vampire attack, even if that would undoubtedly happen before we got out of this place.

If we got out of this place.

My footsteps echoed across the heavy darkness, a sound accompanied by the steady drip of water. Several foul droplets hit the back of my neck and dribbled down my spine, but I wasn't entirely sure the shiver that followed was due to their coldness.

As I drew closer to that light, it became obvious there was a small figure standing near it. *That* figure wasn't a vampire, but it also wasn't human. It was someone who—like me— stood somewhere in between.

Penny, the ghosts said, even as the same thought ran through my mind.

I stopped again, but the force of whatever machinery they were running was now so strong that my body shuddered under its force and my feet were slowly being inched forward against my will. The sheer strength of those vibra- tions was undoubtedly the reason for the flickering light—it was, as I suspected, a flashlight, but it was lashed to the top of a rather unsteady rod of metal.

Penny stood in what looked to be a small sewer junction. There were tunnels to her left and her right, but no indica- tion where either of them led. From the little I could see of it, the left one lacked the grime and the hanging strings of green, which suggested it was used more often. Whether that was by the vampires or someone else, I had no idea.

She was alone in the junction, but there were vampires near. I could smell them. Hear them.

But did Jonas know she was here?

They could communicate telepathically, but I had no true idea just how strong that link was. The last thing we needed right now was him rushing into what could possibly be a trap.

Cat, I said. *Can you go back and tell Jonas not to move into this place until I give the word? There's something very wrong with this whole situation.*

Done, she said, and zipped away.

And me? Bear asked.

For now, stay with me. I'll need you as backup if this all goes to hell. And it would, of that I had no doubt.

Penny was obviously well aware of my presence, but she didn't say anything. She simply watched me. Though there was little life in her expression, I doubted it was due to drugs or any other method of control. That same remoteness had been evident in Chaos, before she'd knocked me out and run to the vampires.

I drew in a deep breath and then stepped into the junction. No reaction from her, and no attack from the nearby vampires.

Or anyone—any*thing*—else, for that matter.

But that didn't mean there wouldn't be.

I stopped again. A gentle breeze brushed my face and teased the ends of my hair, its touch cooler—fresher—than anything I'd smelled so far in this wretched place. It also had a slightly metallic and recycled smell—something I was very familiar with given the air in my own bunkers often had that same problem when the purifiers were playing up. Vampires didn't need either ventilation or fresh air, so who else was using this place?

I took another step forward. Neither Penny nor the vampires I couldn't see moved.

Sweat started trickling down my spine. I wondered what would happen if I simply grabbed her and ran... but even as that thought crossed my mind, she said, "Don't."

Shock crashed through me, followed swiftly by a deepening feeling of dread. She'd known what I was thinking—but how? Penny wasn't telepathic—her ability to hear both her uncle's and Nuri's thoughts had come from the rift they'd all be caught in.

I took another step and swiped at the sweat dribbling down the side of my face. It wasn't the heat of this place, because with the breeze washing past my skin, it was quite pleasant—or as pleasant as a sewer filled with vampires was ever likely to get. It was fear. Of the situation, and of what this little girl—who was almost as old as me—might unleash. Not so much on me, but rather the man who would move mountains to protect her—to save her.

"What's going on, Penny? What are you doing here?"

"You should not have come after me." Her voice, like her face, held little in the way of emotion. And yet there was an odd sadness in her eyes. "Neither of you should have come after me."

It was no surprise she knew Jonas was here given their connection, but the question was, did the vamps? The nest as a whole should be well asleep, but the ones in the nearby corridors certainly weren't. I could hear their restlessness; could feel the growing tide of hunger and anger. They wanted to attack. They wanted to rent and tear and feed. Was Penny restraining them? Or was it something—or someone—else?

Was Dream here?

"No," Penny intoned softly. "But she is aware you have come here."

"Because you told her?"

"No, although it is my place to do so. It was the vampires who contacted her."

Her place.... Two simple words that sent another chill through me. She really did see herself as part of the den.

"Why would they do that? She wasn't vampire-born, so why would they obey her orders?"

"She is the mistress," Penny said. "They have been waiting for her arrival for a very long time."

Meaning they saw her as some sort of goddess? This situation was getting stranger and stranger. "Does that mean she makes her way here as we speak?"

If it did, then I was going to grab Penny and get the hell out of this place, even of that action brought the whole damn den on top of us. As much as I wanted to end Dream's madness, Penny was our priority.

"There is no need for her to come here," she replied. "She will simply retrieve your remains and have them stored until a new lab has been set up."

That will not happen, Bear said. *If you die, Cat and I will get your body out of this place.*

Thanks, Bear. To Penny, I added, "You don't belong here. You're not one of them, no matter how much the drugs in your body are making you believe otherwise."

Though my voice was as soft as hers, it echoed loudly across the black silence. In the right-hand tunnel, the vampires' stirrings got louder and the sense of their hunger grew.

Jonas is ignoring your order, Cat said. *He will be with you in a few minutes.*

Which was both frustrating and unsurprising. He'd gone against all common sense—against even Nuri's advice and fears—to keep Penny in Chaos and as close as practical to him. There was no way he'd leave a confrontation such as this to a second party.

"I do not belong in Chaos or Central, either," she said. "I never really did."

"You belong with your family and friends—"

"My family is dead," she broke in. "I do not know those who would call me kin these days."

"You have Jonas—"

"Jonas will die in this place, as will you. There is no escape."

A statement I had every intention of disproving. But the mere fact she could say something like that without even the barest flicker of regret chilled me to the core.

"What *is* this place, Penny?" I asked. "What do they do here?"

"Here?" she said, vaguely waving a hand. "Nothing."

Was the vagueness deliberate, or did she really not know what I meant? And if it were the latter, why not? She was neither young nor dumb.

"I meant this place as a whole. What does Dream keep here other than vampires? What does she do?"

"It is little more than a storage facility," came the remote reply.

Mere storage facilities didn't vibrate like this place was. "Storage for what?"

"Weapons, equipment, ammunition." She shrugged lightly. "Everything that is needed for a war."

"And is that what Dream intends—a war?"

"I don't know her plans or desires," Penny said. "I cannot hear her thoughts."

"And yet you heard mine?" And if she could read my mind, did that mean Dream would also be able to?

But surely if *that* had been the case, it would have applied to both Sal and Winter, given they all shared the same DNA.

Penny smiled, but it contained little in the way of warmth

and her eyes remained remote. "Because we both now share a connection to Jonas."

Relief surged. At least if I did unknowingly run into Dream in some incarnation other than her Hedda Lang one, my thoughts wouldn't give the game away. "And the vampires?"

"Their blood runs through my veins, as it runs through yours and hers. While it merely enables you to hear them, it has made me a part of the greater mind."

Greater mind? Did that mean vampires were capable of some sort of shared consciousness? I seriously hoped not. Up until now, the various vampire nests had been operating independently, but if Dream had somehow tapped into that shared consciousness and could make them to act as one, we would be in serious trouble.

"Why is Dream part of that consciousness and yet I'm not?"

Penny shrugged. "I do not know."

There was too damn much that she—and we—didn't know, I thought grimly. "Then how did she become mistress? Surely only someone vampire-born could become the mistress?"

"Again, I do not know," Penny replied. "It is not my place to question these things."

"What does the greater mind tell you?"

"Many things, but not that."

Of course not, I thought, frustrated. "Then why are the vampires in this place? There is nothing left for them to feed on, and no human outposts nearby."

A strange smile touched her pale lips. "The vampires have always been here. But soon, they will be everywhere. Even in Central."

Her matter-of-fact tone had alarm stirring. "And how does Dream plan to achieve this? We've destroyed her bases and disrupted her research."

"Disrupted, not completely destroyed. Bases and research labs can be rebuilt."

I eyed Penny for a moment, seeing the certainty in her, the conviction. There was something else going on, something we weren't seeing. Something that could yet kill us all. "Yes, but that will take years to do, and we'll find her long before she can achieve either."

"While that is indeed possible, it *doesn't* negate the truth of my statement. The vampires will soon control Central."

"The attack on Chaos was proof enough that while there are vampires who have gained *some* immunity, there's still a long way to go before they gain full protection. Central is bathed in UV lighting day and night, Penny. The minute they breach the wall, they *will* die."

"But what if the lights no longer worked?"

For several seconds, I could only stare at her. Then fear crashed through me and realization dawned. We'd been so damn focused on finding the children and shutting down the labs that we'd never considered the possibility of a plan B.

"Are you saying that's what Dream intends? To shut down the lights?" I couldn't quite keep the urgency and fear from my voice. Because if that *was* what Dream intended, then

Nuri needed to tell the authorities and have her apprehended immediately—even if we didn't yet have absolute proof that Dream and Hedda were indeed the same person.

"I don't know her plans," Penny said. "I only know what the vampires tell me—what has filled their dreams in the long hours of the day these past few months."

Vampires dreamed? That was a concept I did *not* want to contemplate. And yet if the last few months had taught me anything, it was that they were not the unthinking beasts I'd always thought them to be.

Footsteps began to echo across the silence. Running steps, oddly desperate.

Jonas.

"And what do they base these dreams on, Penny, if they have not been promised such a thing?"

"I do not know." Though she must have heard the noise Jonas was making, Penny made no acknowledgment. Nor did she look concerned. "I have only been a part of the greater mind these last few weeks."

"Can you ask the greater mind what they base their information on, Penny?"

The vampires are on the move, Bear commented. *They are coming up from the den to cut off our retreat.*

Warn us if they look ready to attack.

"Why would I do that?" Penny asked.

"Because you're not a vampire." I took another step forward, even though I was certain the minute I made any attempt to snatch her, the vampires drawing ever closer would attack. "You're not one of them, no matter what Dream has done to you. You're one of us—a shifter."

"Except my heart no longer beats for the sunlight. More and more, the night is my mistress, just as it is theirs. And the hunger—it grows." She hesitated and glanced past me as Jonas stepped into the junction. "Hello, Uncle."

He stopped beside me. Though he wasn't touching me, I could feel the tension in him—the fear. It washed in waves across my skin and through my mind, and it made my heart ache for him.

"Penny, you can't stay here," he said. "You must fight them —fight what they have done to you."

"I would be more worried about what the vampires intend to do to you." He might have been nothing to her for all the emotion she was showing. "You knew this was a trap. Tiger warned you of it, many times. And yet you still came."

His fists clenched—the only outward sign of the strength it was taking not to grab her and run. But he, like me, feared that doing so would unleash the vampires.

If we were to get out of this place in one piece, she had to come with us willingly. And even then, I suspected, survival was not guaranteed.

"I came because you are family," he said flatly. "I will not leave you here, Penny. I cannot."

"The vampires will attack the minute you move against me. There are too many of them for you to beat."

"You and Dream misjudge our strength and determination," he growled back.

She studied him for a moment, and then said, "And what good do you think it would do if you could get me out of here? This darkness in me grows by the day, and there is nothing you or anyone else can do to stop that. I will endanger everything else you hold dear, Uncle, and we both know it."

"What has been done can be undone," he said. "We will find a way to save you."

Just for an instant, tears glimmered in her eyes. And there was something else—a spark of sudden awareness and fear—that suggested the grip of whatever thrall she was under had briefly broken.

"If your desire *is* to save me," she said, with just the smallest hint of desperation. "Then there is only one thing you can do."

His shock coursed through my mind and added depth to my own. And yet, I knew in my heart it was nothing but the truth, however unpalatable. If the drugs and pathogens injected into her had already altered her chemistry and perhaps even DNA to the point that she now felt more comfortable with darkness and vampires than light, shifters, and humanity, there was a very big chance it could not now be reversed. That it would continue to change her until she reached the end point—whatever that end point was, be it as a vampire or the means through which the vampires gained immunity. In either scenario, the child Jonas had spent over a hundred years protecting would no longer exist.

I wanted to reach out, to offer him both comfort and under-standing, but I very much suspected he'd rebuff both right now.

"No." The denial exploded out of him.

"If you really want to save me, then it is the only way." The desperation was stronger in her voice. "You will still die in this place, but at least I will be free of the darkness."

The vampires flood into this tunnel, Bear warned. *They will be on you in minutes.*

I swore and looked at Jonas. If he'd heard Bear's warning, there was no sign of it.

"No," he repeated. But it was softer, and filled with anguish.

"You *must*," she said. "Please, I—"

Whatever else she was going to say died on her lips, right alongside the spark of awareness. Her body straightened fractionally and the remoteness returned. "Your death approaches, Uncle. Do not say you weren't—"

She never finished the sentence.

Jonas raised his gun and shot her.

CHAPTER TEN

THE VAMPIRES SCREAMED IN FURY, and the force of their approach became so fierce it was a foul wind that ran before them, promising our deaths even as it battered our bodies.

"Turn on your halo light," Jonas snapped. "And run."

"There *is* nowhere to run," I bit back, even as I obeyed.

He scooped up Penny's limp body and then raced toward the left tunnel. Vampires flooded out of the right one, their desperation such that they flung themselves at him, undeterred by the halo's light or the ash of their comrades that rained all around them.

Bear screamed a warning. I slid to a stop, swung around, and unleashed a rain of metal at the thick mass that poured out of the exit tunnel. Some vampires went down while others flashed to particle form to avoid being hit. As had happened in Chaos, there was no pausing to tear at their fallen comrades; their hunger for flesh and blood might be so fierce that it had become a physical force, but the flesh they wanted was *ours*.

"Tiger, move it!"

I turned and raced after him. The vampires chased us, their noise deafening in the confines of the smaller tunnel. Every vampire who got close was killed either by the halo's UV light or by bullets. The junction and the tunnel soon became thick with the dead, and the air heavy with their ash, but it didn't stop them.

The walls of the left tunnel were again brick rather than concrete, and the air washing down from up ahead was much, *much* warmer than it had been in the other tunnels. That strange vibration was growing ever stronger, and there was a constant rain of grime coming from the ceiling. It certainly wasn't the ventilation system causing this shaking. No system, however strong or out of sync it might be, would affect the earth as badly as this.

But it wasn't just the shaking now—it was the noise. A weird crunching, grinding noise.

I ducked my head sideways as a vampire's talon arced toward my face. It hit as ash but nevertheless was a reminder of the fate that waited if these lights failed.

"Jonas," I yelled, firing at the vampire who appeared between us before leaping over his cindering body, "have you any damn idea where we're going?"

"We need to find out what Dream is storing here," he replied. "Especially if she does have plans to kill Central's lights."

"I can send the ghosts—"

"Yes, but they can't act against whatever is up ahead."

I wasn't entirely sure we'd be able to, either—especially if there was no way out of whatever lay ahead other than the tunnel we were now in. No matter what sort of weapons Jonas and his crew might have brought with them, there were simply too many vampires in this place. And the halo lights wouldn't last forever.

"Ours might not," he replied, obviously hearing the thought, "but we've a good crew behind us, and the equipment they carry will."

"Yeah, but a dozen people will not win out against an entire den, no matter how damn good they are."

"They don't have to erase the entire den. They just have to stop any more vampires accessing the tunnels out of here."

Which still left us dealing with the hundreds—if not thousands—who'd already poured into the exit tunnel.

Up ahead, light began to burn—bright, fierce light. UV light. But did it represent safety or yet another trap?

Cat, Bear, can you investigate what's up ahead?

It was better to know than not, even if the reality of the situation was that we had no real choice but to charge into whatever waited. Because the vibrations were getting stronger, the vampires' attacks more desperate, and the air so thick with ash and brick dust it felt like every breath was filled with death and decay.

One of my guns clicked over to empty. I didn't stop to reload it; I simply hooked it back onto my belt, reached for another, and kept on firing.

The UV light was now strong enough to start peeling away

the darkness, but the vampires remained undeterred. One after the other they threw themselves at us, until the sheer amount of ash raining down on us became a physical weight, and our steps inevitably slowed.

A metal grate came into sight; it covered the entire width of the tunnel, and while there *was* a gate, it was closed and locked. Jonas barely paused—he simply unloaded shot after shot into the lock until it disintegrated and then kicked it open and ran on.

"Bear? Cat?" I yelled, as I followed Jonas through. "What the hell is happening? What are we running into?"

A big cavern that's being used as both a store and living quarters, Cat replied. *There are four people here, but they sleep.*

There's also another tunnel—a big one, with string lighting rather than UV, Bear added. *Do you want us to investigate it?*

If they were using simple string lighting in that tunnel, then vampires obviously weren't a problem—and that, in turn, was a hopeful sign that maybe there *was* another way in and out of this place. *For now, just keep an eye on it and let us know if there's any movement. Cat, keep an eye on the sleepers and tell us if all the noise we're making wakes them.*

The vampires poured through the gate after us, but the UV light was now so fierce that they quickly became nothing more than a wave of ash and fury. I breathed through clenched teeth in an effort to filter some of their muck from my lungs, and shook the weight of it from my shoulders.

Ten more strides and we were in the heart of that lifesaving brightness. But this was no sewer junction—it was a cavern. A vast, open, but far from empty cavern. The UV lights were sitting in what appeared to a sort of antechamber, and were both freestanding and hanging on sturdy chains from the ceiling high above. They formed a wide semicircle around the tunnel's entrance, and the lights on the floor immediately in front of it were well protected against any sort of missile the vampires might have used against them. Beyond the lights were boxes of various shapes and sizes stacked on top of each other, and which formed wooden and plastic skyscrapers that reached for the ceiling. Some of them were marked with government stamps, some of them not. The evil trio had obviously been stocking this place for years, if not decades.

I slid to a stop beside Jonas, the harsh rasp of my breathing making little impact against that odd, masticating sound that ran in time with the vibrations under our feet. It very much sounded like something was eating the rock and earth —and *that* had trepidation stirring.

There were no signs of guards in this area, no perimeter alarm, and absolutely nothing to indicate *any* sort of secondary protection had been installed in the immediate area.

"Maybe the evil trio thought the vampires were enough," Jonas said. He shifted the position of Penny's body and then added, in a voice that was bleak, "And maybe the trap still awaits ahead. Shall we move on?"

I nodded and cautiously led the way through the UV towers and into the nearest canyon walkway. The boxes on either side were braced by metal and wire, which was undoubtedly necessary given the vibrations were strong enough that the various stacks would probably have collapsed into the walkway without it.

The canyon soon gave away to another open area. This one contained various bits of machinery, big and small, as well as a long series of interconnected buildings. The tunnel opening Bear had mentioned was to the left, and not only was it massive, but looked to be man-made rather than natural.

Cat, where are the sleepers?

End building to your right, she replied. *They show no signs of waking.*

Anyone else about?

No.

Bear?

There's movement in the tunnel, but it's not coming this way, he replied. *And there's no scanners or anything in place around the entrance.*

"If those four people can sleep through gunfire *and* all the racket that's coming from the tunnel, then they surely won't be woken by any noise we make." I glanced at Jonas. "But I still think it's rather strange that there doesn't appear to be any form of security other than the vampires."

"It might just be a case of not needing anything else." His gaze was on the tunnel and he didn't look happy. "Fairhaven is the furthest away of Central's old satellite cities, and the only one that has no human occupation near it."

"There's not exactly an abundance of people hanging about

Carleen, and surely it would be an easier point from which to launch an attack."

"Yes, but discovery is also more likely given its proximity to Central. And now that there are human habitats near both Greenfields and Indara—thanks to the farmland reclamation projects happening there—they're also risky places to build a military force. Especially a vampire one." His gaze came to mine. "I think we need to investigate what's happening in there, though I rather suspect what we're going to find is tunneling."

Penny's warning—that vampires would soon be in Central —echoed ominously through my brain. "Why would they even consider tunneling as an option if Fairhaven is so far away from Central? That makes no sense."

"Neither does the desire to hand our world over to the wraiths and vampires, but that's nevertheless what they're attempting." He walked across to a short stack of boxes, carefully placed Penny's body on top, and then rotated his shoulders. Just for an instant, I saw the glimmer of tears, but they didn't fall. He might be grieving for his niece, but he wasn't about to give in to emotion. Not yet. Not until he had the time to do so properly. "I think it's a matter of them covering all bases."

"Yes, but even if they succeed in tunneling right underneath Central without anyone noticing—and seriously, with the vibrations the machinery causes, how likely is that?—it still won't help them." I waved a hand at the lights hanging high above us. "There're still the UVs, and surely not even Dream, no matter who she's impersonating, could—"

I broke off as he held up a hand and then touched his earpiece. "What's up, Maz?"

I couldn't hear the conversation, so obviously my ear-mic was running on a different frequency. But his expression told me what I needed to know—his people were under attack.

"Okay," he said eventually. "Set up a ring of UVs outside the main entrance to keep them in, and then retreat to the transports. We'll find another way out of this place and then contact you for retrieval."

"They all okay?" I said when he'd finished.

He nodded. "The vamps took out two of the UV lights they were installing and hit them pretty hard, but they've only suffered a few minor casualties. The same can't be said of the vamps."

Good. The fewer vampires we had to contend with if we were forced back into those damn tunnels, the better. "What makes you think there's a second exit out of this place?"

"Because if the noise and vibrations *are* coming from a tunnel borer, then there have to be some means of dealing with the waste—and there's nothing to indicate it's being redistributed through this cavern." He picked up Penny again, and again I saw that brief silver sheen. "Let's go."

"Wouldn't it be better if I use my seeker skills on the sleepers and get some layout information first?"

He hesitated. "Aside from the fact there's no guarantee your skills will get that information, I suspect it would be better not to linger here any longer than necessary. Dream would have been informed of the attack by now, and reinforcements are undoubtedly on the way."

"And the sleepers? Shouldn't we do something about them?"

"I think it's better we uncover just how far the tunnel has gotten. If they wake, we'll deal with them."

"Cat can cover our retreat, then."

He nodded and moved forward. Cat whisked around me briefly before moving to a rearguard position. The closer we got to the tunnel's entrance the bigger it appeared, until it all but consumed the gaze. The air washing past us was not only heavy with heat, dust, and moisture, but also machinery fumes. But there was no underlying hint of vampire and that, at least, was good news.

We kept close to the tunnel's left edge as we moved deeper inside. Two strings of lights ran down either side, and the curved walls were smooth and black. Despite the growing intensity of the vibrations running through the earth, no dust rained down on us. Unlike the walls in the other tunnels, these ones seemed immune to movement.

The shadows got thicker the deeper we moved into the tunnel. The string lights were little more than a guide and didn't really lift the deeper darkness of this place. But the dust and moisture content steadily increased, until every breath was filled with wet grit. We'd choke on the damn stuff if we didn't do something about it soon.

"Jonas, wait."

I swung off my backpack and then stripped off my shirt. The lightweight material had been designed to wick water away from the skin no matter what the conditions, and while the outside was wet with sweat, the inner layer—the one close to my body—was not. I cut two thick strips out of the shirt, tied one around my mouth and nose, and then did the same to Jonas.

"Good idea," he said, "although I'm not entirely sure having your scent so constantly in my nostrils is the right move right now."

I smiled. "Better my scent than the vampires'."

"A truth I will never deny."

We continued, but the tunnel showed no signs of revealing its secrets and I had no idea how much time was passing. I had to hope it wasn't the hours it seemed, because I really *did* have to get back to Central and Charles.

The noise of the borer gradually grew in intensity, but there was little evidence of the waste that should have been present. The huge tunnel began to gently curve around and, up ahead, light glowed. Figures and machines moved within that lit area

Jonas slowed but didn't stop. "Bear, can you go see what's going on up there?"

He immediately raced off and, a few seconds later, said, *There are trucks and a conveyor belt. They are autonomous, but there are four men who appear to be supervising.*

Can you follow the conveyor and see where it leads? I asked, and then glanced at Jonas. "I wonder when the shift changeover is?"

The question was barely out of my mouth when Cat said, *A truck is moving toward you.*

Are the four men who were sleeping inside it?

She paused, and then said, *Yes.*

How far away is it?

Only a few minutes.

I pulled off my pack and gave it to Jonas. "I'll go deal with the truck."

"Be careful."

"Careful is second nature for someone like me."

My tone was dry, but his responding smile held more concern than amusement. I shifted to particle form and swept back up the tunnel, keeping high to avoid getting caught in the lights of the approaching vehicle.

It was an old-school troop carrier—the type with an enclosed metal cabin but a simple canvas covering over the rear cargo area. I swept over the top of it and then dropped down. There were three men inside.

Cat, can you keep an eye on the driver? If he suspects anything or tries to contact the people ahead, knock him out.

Inside and waiting, she said, rather enthusiastically.

Which made me suspect that even if the driver didn't react, Cat would still deal with him. I swept under the canvas and hovered above the three men. Two were sitting on the right bench and one on the left. All three were armed. I flexed particle fingers, trying to ease tension but not really succeeding. Then I reclaimed flesh form and dropped into the middle of the three, punching one in the face with all the force I could muster then sweeping around with a booted foot at the second. Even as he fell sideways with a grunt of pain, the third man reacted. He was fast—but not quite fast enough. I shot him in the head just as his gun cleared its holster.

The truck slewed to the right, throwing me sideways onto the man I'd knocked down but not out. He wrapped an arm around my neck, his grip viselike, and slipped something cold and hard into my side with the other. *Knife*, some part of my brain said, even as pain surged and the heat of blood began to soak my undershirt. I twisted my arm around and fired the gun. His grip immediately went slack, and I pushed away from him, pressing one hand against my side as I swung around and fired several more shots. Then I repeated the process with the man whose face I'd smashed. He might have been unconscious but I was in no mood for mercy.

The truck straightened abruptly. *I'm now in control*, Cat said.

And the driver?

Fell out.

Amusement ran through me. *Are you okay steering for a couple of seconds while I take care of him?*

Of course.

It was indignantly said and my amusement grew. I shifted back to particle form and raced back up the tunnel. The driver was groggily attempting to get back to his feet. I reformed the hand holding the gun and shot him. There was no silencer on the gun, but even in the vast space of this tunnel, the gunshot made little impact against the greater noise coming from the borer up ahead.

I went back to the truck and, once I'd reclaimed flesh, took over from Cat. The bleeding from the knife wound had slowed but not entirely stopped. Thankfully, the truck had been set to semiauto, so I really had to do nothing more strenuous than steer.

The vehicle headlights soon picked out Jonas standing close to the guide lights. I slowed to a crawl but didn't stop. While the noise of the tunnel borer might have covered the gunshots, we were now within sight of the area ahead, and there might just be someone there alert enough to become suspicious. The very last thing we needed was another alarm being raised—although in truth, it didn't really matter anymore. Dream would presumably have tried to contact Penny or have checked in with her vampires by now, and would surely be aware that we'd reached the safety of UV-protected tunnel. The trap we both still feared might not be waiting here, but rather on the surface the minute we appeared.

Jonas is onboard, Cat said. As I allowed the truck to gain speed again, she added, *He said to slow again just before you're about to go into the cavern so he can jump out, and then increase speed. He'll take out the four men in the cavern while their attention is on you.*

Can you ask him why he's communicating through you rather than directly with me?

She paused. *He said he keeps forgetting he can do that.*

And, he added directly, *when I do, it's often to find you in pain and bleeding—like now.*

I'm fine—

Tell that to someone who doesn't know better, he bit back. *Slow down now.*

I returned my attention to where we were going and saw that we'd almost reached the cavern. I braked gently, gave Jonas time to clamber out, and then hit the accelerator and drove into the open area. One thing was immediately clear —this was no storage area but rather a full-blown work site. There was a constant stream of trucks moving in and out of the tunnel directly ahead, all of them obviously automated given none were equipped with cabins. The conveyer belt was on the right side of the cavern, and was a massive metal thing that was at least four meters wide and had to be responsible for at least *some* of the vibrations we were feeling. The belt disappeared up into the mountain and ran at a high enough speed that much of the debris bounced around wildly—only the sloping sides of the supports kept much of it on the belt. Beyond the conveyor were a series of buildings that I presumed were shelters for the men and the monitoring equipment.

To the right of the other tunnel entrance was a row of what looked like drill bits for the borer and, given the sheer size and weight of the things, they obviously didn't bring them here through the vampire tunnels. And that meant there had to be another entrance.

The truck's appearance didn't immediately gain the attention of the four people standing in the various areas of the cavern, but when I kept on going, that quickly changed. I directed the truck toward the next tunnel, and then switched it over to full auto and doubled its speed. The truck gathered momentum as it rolled on, neatly avoiding the various loaders as it moved into the tunnel's mouth. I slid the driver window down and, when the shadows had closed in enough that I was able to take particle form, swept out of the cabin and back into the rear of the vehicle. I shifted shape again, picked up Penny's body, and then reclaimed the shadows.

Carrying another person in particle form was never an easy thing to do, even when at full strength, and pain instantly began to throb through me. I ignored it and raced back up the tunnel as fast as I dared, but I'd barely reached the bright cavern when my strength gave out. I twisted around as I fell, not wanting to use Penny as a buffer between the ground and me even though she was dead, and hit hard. For several seconds I could barely breathe, and there were a multitude of stars dancing in front of my eyes.

Feet appeared in my line of vision. I somehow found the strength to roll away from Penny and grab my gun, but thankfully, it was Jonas rather than one of the guards.

"Seriously," he said. "Could you not simply have stopped the truck to retrieve Penny? It would have been a whole lot easier."

"Easy isn't something I apparently do." I pushed upright. "Besides, I'm hoping the truck will gather enough speed to incapacitate the borer if it happens to hit it."

He swung his pack around, dug out a medical kit, and then offered me a spray-on sealer. "That knife wound has opened up."

I tugged up my blood-soaked undershirt, sprayed the stuff on, and then tossed the empty can away. The sealer stung like blazes but that was better than losing any more blood. My head was spinning enough as it was.

I finally reached the top of the conveyor, Bear said. *It leads outside.*

If it had taken him all this time to hit the end of it, then we were far deeper underground than I'd initially presumed. *Does it dump its cargo in the forest or within the city?*

Neither, though I can see the wall's remnants in the distance. It appears to be an abandoned, open pit mine.

Any guards or security evident? Jonas asked.

No, but there are automatic trucks distributing the soil waste. Bear paused. *There's dust rising in the distance—I think vehicles are approaching.*

"What's the bet that's Dream's people?" Jonas walked over to Penny and picked her up. "We'd better get out of here, and fast."

"The only way to do that is to ride the conveyor," I said, "and that could get dangerous given the amount of rock and soil that'll be following us up. It'll crush us at the other end if we don't move out of its way fast enough."

"Yes, but we've no other choice."

That was true. I followed him across the room. The conveyor soared above the two of us, rattling and shaking as it transported the continuing dumps of rubble upward into darkness. There wasn't even the faintest glimmer of sunlight visible—the quarry and freedom were still a very

long way away. I swept my gaze around the nearby buildings and constructs, and spotted a walkway that arched over
the entire width of the belt. "That's probably our best jump-
ing-on point."

Jonas nodded and led the way across. We climbed the three-
story staircase then stepped out onto the platform. There
were no railings to hold on to, and the whole thing swayed
rather alarmingly. I stopped in the middle and looked down.
The belt raced past, its speed scary. If either of us survived
this, it was going to be a miracle.

"I have no intention of dying on this thing," Jonas said.
"And *every* intention of making it to Central, not only to
give Penny a decent burial, but to stop the bitch responsible
for all this."

I had the very same intention, but that didn't make the
thought of jumping off this platform onto that conveyor any
less daunting. I swallowed heavily and glanced at the pairs
of trucks delivering the waste in almost rhythmic sequence.
After a moment, I realized there was a couple of seconds
break between each load as the pairs maneuvered in and out
of position—and that brief moment gave us an empty belt to
jump onto.

"On my mark," I said, watching the trucks and the conveyer
belt through narrowed eyes. "Go—"

We jumped as one. I hit the belt upright and in the
middle of two rubble loads but both the incline and the
speed of the thing had me stumbling backward. I crashed
into the pile of rock and dirt and then threw myself
forward to avoid several bouncing rocks. One hit my calf
hard enough to bruise, but the other missed. I'd barely

pushed up onto my hands and knees when a wave of pain hit me.

It wasn't mine. It was Jonas's.

I quickly swung around. He was lying on the other side of the belt, face ashen and teeth gritted as he tried to realign a leg that was twisted up behind him. Even in the growing darkness I could see the gleam of bone. I swore and scrambled over to him, dodging the rocks and dirt that were bouncing back from the pile of rubble in front of us.

"You need to straighten it." His words were little more than a wheeze of agony. "I can't shift to heal until you do."

I moved into position and then met his gaze. Sweat poured down his face and his eyes were ablaze with pain. "Ready?"

He took a deep breath and then nodded grimly. I gripped his ankle and carefully realigned his leg, trying to ensure there was no further damage to either the blood vessels or nerves in his leg.

He made no sound, but I nevertheless felt his pain. It was a tidal wave that crashed across my senses, and was so damn fierce I couldn't help but shudder under its impact.

His breath hissed in and out, and entire body quivered. How he was even conscious I had no idea.

"Right," he said, his voice hoarse. "Step back."

I shuffled back, keeping my center of balance low to counter the conveyor's incline. As his body began to shift from human to panther form, I glanced past him, suddenly wondering where Penny's body was. After a few seconds, I spotted her—she'd obviously been flung forward when Jonas hit the belt—on top of the pile of debris behind us, her body constantly under attack from the various bits of rock being bounced into the air. I scrambled over and dragged her back down. It was enough that she was dead; she didn't deserve to be pulverized as well.

Jonas was in the process of switching back to human form, his bones knitting and leg healing even as I watched. "Fuck," he said when he was able, "that *hurt*."

I sat down in front of him and gently pulled the torn edges of his pants apart. All that remained was a thick red scar, and even that was now beginning to fade. But I was well aware the toll that sort of healing took on a body.

I touched his shoulder lightly and said, "Rest. I'll wake you when we near the end of this thing."

That he didn't even bother to argue spoke not only of his weakness but also the wound's severity. I'd witnessed shifters heal bullet wounds, gut shots, and broken bones during the wars, and knew that the more severe the wound, the longer it took to regain physical strength. Jonas could be out of action for anything up to twenty-four hours.

I turned around to keep an eye on the rubble bouncing all around us, and, with Cat's help, batted away the various bits that threatened to hit us. The belt rolled endlessly on into the gloom, and time was something that slipped by without acknowledgment. There was no glimmer of sunlight up ahead, nothing to indicate we were anywhere near approaching the end of this thing.

But the air was growing sharper—cleaner—and a breeze was now running gentle fingers through my sweat-dried hair.

Whether I could see it or not, we were getting close to the quarry outlet.

"Cat, can you race ahead and see how far away we are?" As she obeyed, I added, *Bear, what's happening out there?*

Five vehicles went past the quarry and have landed on the hill above us. There are twenty soldiers, all armed.

Is Dream there?

There are nine women amongst their number, but they do not feel like Winter or even Sal did.

Meaning her presence was unlikely. I guess that was no surprise—why would she take such a risk when it was easier to send her people...? I frowned and said, *What sort of uniforms are they wearing? Is it along the lines of what the mercenaries in Chaos wear, or more military in design?*

He paused. *There's one military, the others are mercenary. The military man seems to be in charge.*

Instinct stirred, and while I wasn't sure why, I also wasn't about to ignore it. *Are you able to get a close look at him?*

Bear hesitated and then said, *He's a thick-set man, brown hair and eyes, and a scar under his left eye.*

Which was an exact description of the man who'd been guarding Karlinda at Charles's confirmation ceremony—the one who'd stirred my instincts for unknown reasons.

He was obviously one of Dream's people and surely had to know her identity in Central, be it Hedda or someone else. And that meant he was someone we needed to talk to.

Cat returned. *About three hundred meters ahead, the*

conveyer belt flattens out. A half a kilometer after that, it drops down into a rubble pile.

Thanks. Bear, are any of those men keeping an eye on the conveyor's dump point?

No, they've moved down the hill. He paused. *There's an entrance there.*

One big enough to allow truck entry, I'm guessing?

Yes.

Let me know if any of them do head back to the quarry.

I twisted around and touched Jonas on the shoulder. He woke and quickly glanced around. "Everything okay?"

I half smiled. "I should be asking you that, given you're the one who shattered his leg, not me."

He grunted and sat up. "It's healed, and I'm okay. What's the sitrep?"

Once I'd updated him, he said, "I agree we need to talk to him, but I suspect that group has a shoot first, ask questions later policy."

"More than likely, but you've people here, and I'm betting they're every bit as good as the mercenaries he has."

"Undoubtedly." He motioned past me. "But attacking them means yet another delay, and we're losing light fast."

I swung around. The conveyor had started to flatten out and, up ahead, visible through a rough-cut gap, was a sky streaked with pink and yellow. I wasn't going to make it make to Central in time to meet with Charles, no matter what I did. I swore and scrubbed a hand across my eyes. "I don't suppose Nuri would be able to get a message to Charles? Tell him I'm sick or something?"

He didn't answer, but his distracted expression told me he was already relaying the message. After a few minutes, he said, "She's on to it, but she said it would be best if you got back to the apartment as soon as you can, because he's the type to come checking."

"So I've discovered." I eyed the drop-off point that was approaching way too fast, and then pushed upright. "Cat, how far is the drop?"

A couple of tree heights, at least.

Which meant about a hundred feet. I glanced at Jonas. "That sort of drop may or may not be survivable, but the ton of waste that'll be following us over the edge definitely isn't."

"No, but we don't have to jump." He bent and picked up Penny's body. "There're walkways on either side of the conveyer up ahead."

"There are?" I glanced back and saw what he meant. The conveyor's sloped sides flattened out as it neared the fall point, providing a three-foot wide strip of stationary metal either side of the belt. Calling it a walkway was something of a misnomer given the rubble spillage, but it at least wasn't moving and it was certainly better than risking a hundred-foot drop. "Stepping off is going to take coordination—and I'd appreciate it if you didn't break a leg this time."

Amusement glittered briefly in his bright eyes. "If you insist—"

"And I do. Your ass is too heavy to carry far—and I say that from experience."

"Then I won't." He gave me a severe look that was somewhat spoiled by the smile twitching his lips. "Please ensure you offer me the same courtesy."

"Deal."

He moved over to the other side of the belt. I walked back to the rubble pile behind us to gain some room then—just before my section of the conveyor hit the flattening edge—ran forward and leaped high.

I hit the platform and stumbled forward several feet before finding my balance and coming to a stop. I glanced quickly across the belt and saw that Jonas not only still held Penny, but was also upright and uninjured. Relief stirred, but we were hardly out of the woods yet. Or out of the tunnel, as the case may be.

Bear, any movement up there?

Two soldiers are stationed either side of the gateway into the mountain, but the rest have gone inside.

Jonas? I asked silently. *How are we going to handle this?*

We aren't doing anything, he replied evenly. *You need to get back to Central, remember.*

Yes, but—

But nothing, he said. *We can't afford to blow your Cat identity now that we're so close to pinning down Dream.*

He was right—I knew that—but it was nevertheless frustrating when I really wanted to be there when that soldier was questioned. If he had the answers we needed—if he could point us to Dream in whatever guise she might currently be using—it would save me the trouble of going back.

But if he didn't, then I'd risked blowing my identity for nothing.

You can use one of the transporters to take—

No, I cut in. *Branna was using a device that allowed him to move through the false rift without harm. I used it to get here, and I can do so going back. It didn't take the toll on my body that previous crossings did.*

And unless Dream had discovered Branna's remains, she'd hopefully think it was him using it rather than me.

Good, Jonas said. *But be careful, both when you're using that rift and when you're in Central. Dream will suspect you're impersonating someone within either the ranks of the House of Lords or the councilors, given what happened to Branna at the inauguration ball.*

I know. I glanced ahead and saw that the fading remnants of daylight had been swept away by the night. *Cat, Bear, stay here with Jonas and help out. I'll call you once I'm back in Central and rested.*

And be careful, they both intoned solemnly, their mental tones an almost exact replica of mine. It was a solemnity that didn't last, because they quickly giggled at their own cheekiness.

I grinned and became shadow. Though the quarry itself was heavily shadowed, there were multiple beams of light cutting through the night at its base—some of them belonged to the automated loaders endlessly shifting the rubble from the pile to the trucks, while others belonged to the vehicles that sped each load away to whatever location had been programmed into them.

I rose up the quarry's face and paused again at the top, trying to get my bearings. After a moment, I spotted several broken fingers of metal reaching skyward and realized they were the remnants of Fairhaven's curtain wall.

It didn't take me long to reach them. The entrance to the vampire's den was easy enough to spot—the fierce glow of the UV lights Jonas's people had set up not only lit the den's entrance and the sky, but provided an umbrella of light for a good portion of the nearby forest and the hillside above it.

I eventually reached the intersection. Once again I paused, but the night was still and there was no indication that anyone was nearby. Not that I really expected much move-ment, but given Dream appeared to be at least one step ahead of us right now, I wasn't about to take a chance.

I moved on, and the burn of dark energy began to caress my particles. I dropped down to ground level and shifted back to human form. The foul caress of that energy instantly got worse, and my skin jumped and twitched in response. I swept my gaze across the immediate area and soon found the gelatinous patch that was the rift's protective barrier.

I dug Branna's black brick out of my pocket and gripped it tightly as I walked into the barrier. This time, there was little in the way of resistance. The shadow still had a high viscosity, but it slid around me rather than pushing against me. In very quick order, I was through the barrier and striding toward the rift's oily blackness. The whips of lightning quickly latched on to my arms and legs and dragged me forward, but once again there was little in the way of pain. The journey through the rift was similarly free, and I was deposited on the other side in the same condition in which I'd entered. Exhaustion might still pound through every fiber, but its cause wasn't due to anything the rift had done. The brick, it seemed, really did help.

I walked past Branna's body and then hesitated. While I wanted nothing more than to see him rot in this place, it didn't make tactical sense to leave him here. The vampires might have told Dream I'd entered their den, but Penny hadn't confirmed it. There was a chance—a very, very *slight* chance, given she seemed to have no awareness of all the times I'd used the rifts—that with both the brick and the rifts being born out of her magic, she'd be aware when one was used to go through the other. It was also very slightly possible that she'd think Branna had used the brick to chase me into the rift, and that he'd come back out after I'd gone into the den itself. But for that to remain a viable possibility, I couldn't leave his body here.

I swore, walked back, and awkwardly hauled him over my shoulders. My legs immediately buckled under his weight. I forced them to lock until I was steady and then, with one hand bracing his body to stop him from slipping, and the other gripping the black brick, I went through the gelatinous barrier.

Once on the other side, I paused again. Where in the hell was I going to dump him?

We can take care of that, if you wish, someone said from behind me.

I jumped sideways, stumbled over a rock, and dumped Branna's body onto the ground in an effort to keep balance. Then I grabbed a gun with my free hand and swung around. There was no one behind me.

No one but ghosts.

Sorry to have startled you, the tall, wispy figure in front of me continued. *I didn't mean to.*

His low tones were rich and pleasant, and recognition stirred. It was Blaine, the man who appeared to be in charge of Carleen's ghosts.

But why could I hear him so clearly?

I might have an innate ability to hear the whisperings of the dead, but Carleen had been a *human* city, and that had always put the dead here beyond both my seeker and communication skills. Lures might have escaped most of the DNA interventions and restrictions that had been placed on our soldier brethren, but our creators had certainly ensured we could not read their very human thoughts. Every other time I'd communicated with these ghosts, I'd done so through a link with Cat. Her DNA was almost pure tabby, and that meant she was not only a great tracker but highly tuned to all things supernatural. These ghosts had always been little more than wisps and energy to me, but for her, they were fully fleshed beings.

But maybe this sudden clarity was once again a result of the rift Jonas and I had been caught in—maybe the alterations that allowed me to communicate directly with my own ghosts were now allowing me to hear these ones.

Whatever the reason, it was something of a blessing.

Communicating through Cat was not only unwieldy but also very dangerous—for me rather than her, given the drain such a deep link put on my life force.

"How did you know I'd be able to hear you, given Cat's not here?" I asked.

He shrugged, and it was only then that I realized he was no longer a mere wisp of energy, but gradually attaining a full —if still ghostly—form.

There is something different about the energy you're emitting, he replied. *It's more like that of your little ghost, so I thought it worthwhile to try. You looked as if you needed help.*

"And I very much do." I hesitated, watching as more ghosts drifted closer. The anger I'd sensed in them every other time I'd come into Carleen remained, but a thick thread of fear and horror now ran through it. "What's happened?"

The witch met with the wraiths, he said. *Here, on our soil.*

I swore. I'd been hoping that Samuel Cohen—the cloaked figure I'd been tracking before the wraiths had chased me back through the graveyard outside these walls—had been the only one of the three capable of communicating with the Others. But I guess that was always a forlorn hope given their shared DNA. "How long ago was this?"

Three days ago.

So not long after I'd killed Cohen and all but destroyed their Winter Halo operation. "Did you hear what they said?"

We dared not get too close to the witch, because she has acted against us in the past, he replied. *But we know they plan to wage war against Central, and every other human habitation. That cannot be allowed to happen, no matter what the cost to us. The wraiths, and the witch, must be stopped.*

I frowned. "I know the witch can banish you from this place, but what threat are the wraiths?"

Of themselves they are not. It is the rifts through which they move that are.

My confusion deepened. "But those rifts have been here for more than a century now—why would they suddenly be a threat?"

It is not those *rifts of which we speak,* he said. *But rather the one that now dominates the central plaza—*

"But that's a *false* rift," I cut in, even as fear surged. The last thing we needed was the wraiths having a direct path into the heart of the city. "It leads into Government House; it is *not* linked to whatever realm the wraiths emerge from."

Perhaps the witch can tune it to be either. She has been present whenever the wraiths have emerged from it.

I swore and scrubbed a hand across my eyes. "That still doesn't explain why the plaza rift is a threat to you. Is it the staining?"

Yes, because it not only stains our bones, it disintegrates them. When our bones are gone, our spirits are banished to who knows what hell. He paused, and sorrow washed across his thin face. *It takes the young ones first—we have already lost five.*

Damn it, why was it always the littlest ones who paid the

deepest price? "I'm really sorry, but we *are* trying to stop the spread of that rift—"

You won't succeed, he cut in. *The only way to destroy the rift is to kill the woman who created it.*

I frowned. "What makes you think the false rifts are linked to her life?"

Redda says it is so, and she was once also a powerful witch. He turned and beckoned to someone. A matronly figure moved forward, but her form wasn't as solid as either Blaine's or many of the others, suggesting she was an older ghost—perhaps even one who'd died long before the final bomb had destroyed the city.

It is true. Her voice was faint but kindly. *I've seen the witch Nuri here several times, but she is not strong enough to stay or remove the magic of the rifts now. No one is.*

"But what makes you think its existence is linked to the woman who created it?"

Because she used her blood in the spell. Only when she no longer takes breath will the power of her blood within that spell fade. Until then, the rifts will remain.

"You saw her create them?" I asked.

Yes.

"Would you be willing to tell Nuri what you saw?" Surely once Nuri knew what sort of spell had been used—and what exactly had gone into it—she stood a better chance of being able to destroy the rifts?

Yes, the woman said. *But it will not help. Your only hope— our only hope—is for you to destroy its creator.*

"Then destroy her we will." All we had to do was find her—and that wasn't proving to be easy. I glanced back at Blaine. "We believe we might have uncovered the witch's identity, but we're still a long way from stopping her."

He didn't say "try harder" as I half expected him to. Instead, he waved a hand at Branna. *We shall hide this one beyond the walls, in the deep pits of the madman's graveyard. He deserves nothing less after his treachery.*

The madman's graveyard? Was that the one outside the walls? The ghosts there hadn't seemed particularly crazy, but it wasn't like I'd had the capacity—or, in the end, the time—to talk to any of them at the time.

Blaine nodded and made another motion. Half a dozen ghosts moved forward—some more "real" than others—and, after picking up Branna's body, quickly whisked him away.

We cannot help you fight against those who would destroy Central, Blaine continued, *because we are bound by our deaths to Carleen and cannot move too far beyond its walls. Nor can we fight the witch or the wraiths.*

I frowned again, unsure why he would make such a statement when I hadn't asked for either of them. I opened my mouth to say as much, but stopped when he raised a hand.

But we can act against the vampires who pass through our city, and immobilize the vehicles that move in and out of the false rifts. It may not stop either, but it will at least decimate the vampires' numbers and force the witch and her people to find other avenues for their vehicles.

If they were capable of such actions, why in Rhea hadn't they acted before now?

But the answer was, in reality, pretty obvious. Up until now, the situation hadn't really affected them. Just as had happened during the war, the inhabitants of this place had shielded themselves from the realities of the conflict until it had arrived right on their doorsteps—and by then, it was altogether too late to act.

I really hoped history wasn't about to repeat itself.

"Anything you can do to hamper their movements will be appreciated."

There was little point in saying anything else. These ghosts might be a little late in realizing the enormity of the situation, but at least they *had* realized, and were now willing to help—and at the possible cost of banishment. And if they were successful, they might just give us something very vital —something we desperately needed.

Time.

Time to find Dream, time to stop her.

We will do what we can, he replied.

I nodded and left. It didn't take me long to make my way to the nearest break in the wall, but the only way to shorten the time it would take to get through the park that divided Carleen and Central was to become shadow. But I was running ever closer to the edge of exhaustion, and I still had to get into the city unseen.

But that inner voice was now telling me I didn't have a whole lot of time left—that I needed to get into the city as fast as possible.

Frustratingly, she once again refused to say why.

Which left me with little other choice but to take my alternate form and race through the night and the trees. A cool breeze rustled the leaves and played through my particles, but it didn't do a lot to ease the gathering tide of weariness. I ignored it; there was little else I could do.

The city's vast metal wall soon came into sight. I spun upwards, gathering speed. As the light from the UVs began to unravel the shadows and shift me back to flesh form, I made a final lunge for the top of the wall. My fingers latched onto the edge and, after several huge gulps of air, I reached for the light, wrapped it around my body, and then hauled myself up onto the top of the wall. Where I lay on my back, staring up at stars that weren't visible thanks to the brightness of the UVs, waiting for the wash of weakness to again ease.

I needed time—time to heal, time to sleep—but that nagging inner voice was still insisting I wasn't about to get either in the immediate future.

I seriously hoped my inner voice was wrong.

I quickly made the minor changes necessary to alter my natural form to Catherine's, and then pushed upright. After a quick look around to orient myself, I padded along the wall until I found a rooftop where the drop wasn't steep. I repeated the process, leaping from one rooftop to another, until I found a means of climbing down to the ground. From there, I made my way through the various streets and pedestrian access lanes until I was near my temporary apartment on Third.

But I'd barely entered the street when I spotted two people coming in the other direction.

Two people I knew.

The first was Charles, and he did not look happy.

The second was the chancellor.

And then I saw something else.

The latter was surrounded by a halo of energy—a force so angry it hissed and spat at the air like striking snakes. It was surprising Charles appeared unaware of its presence given he walked right next to her.

That force alone told me this *wasn't* Karlinda Stone. That it was, in fact, Hedda Lang.

Or, as we knew her, Ciara Dream.

CHAPTER ELEVEN

I IMMEDIATELY REACHED for a gun but even as I did, she raised a hand and something hit me—a force so powerful it pushed me off-balance and started tearing at my shield. Pain ripped through my brain and the shield that hid me began to flicker and disintegrate. I pushed the last of my strength into it and raised the gun again.

Or, at least, I tried to.

But my arms were now locked to my sides, my fingers were becoming numb, and that numbness was spreading all too swiftly up my limbs and across my chest. Every breath was becoming a struggle; if I stayed here, I'd die.

This bitch wasn't going to win, and she certainly *wasn't* going to kill me. Not that easily.

I spun around and lunged for the walkway, hoping against hope that putting a building between us would break the grip of her magic. It didn't. The creeping numbness continued to move upward and my lungs started to burn as breathing became more and more of a struggle.

Distance—the only hope I had now was distance.

I ran on desperately, my head spinning and my lungs burning. A dozen more steps and the tendril of her magic finally snapped. The abruptness sent me staggering forward, but this time, I wasn't able to stop the fall. I went down hard, skinning my palms in the process.

I gulped in air then pushed upright and ran on. Dream would be after me, of that I had no doubt. I couldn't be found by her—not in this condition, and certainly not when I now knew just how dangerous her magic could be.

I *did* have the means of combating it—the very same charms Branna had stolen from Nuri—but they were tucked under the mattress inside the apartment. Right now, they might as well have been on the moon.

I found a cross street, raced down it, and then turned right into Fourth Street. The light shield gave out as I did so and a woman did a quick step sideways to avoid me. Her curses drifted after me, but were thankfully lost to the noise of several airbikes going past. Unless Dream had super hearing, she wouldn't have caught it.

I ran toward the curtain wall end of the Fourth Street until I was close to where it intersected with Victory, and then paused, leaning against the wall of the building, my breath a harsh rasp and my body a quivering, aching mess.

Several people gave me disparaging looks, but none of them said anything. After a minute or so, a woman strode to the door of the nearby doorway and brushed her RFID chip across the scanner. As the door opened, I moved up behind her, pressed my gun against her spine, and said, "Don't make a sound and keep on walking. If you do anything else, I'll shoot you. Understand?"

She made a small sound in the back of her throat, but kept on walking. Thankfully, there was no one in the foyer and the elevator was already open and waiting.

"What floor do you live on?" I asked.

"Nine."

The elevator immediately responded, and we were soon moving upward at a rapid rate. When the doors again opened, I directed her out into the corridor and then stopped. "Where is the fire escape?"

"To the left." Her reply was little more than a squeak.

"And your apartment?"

"Right."

The stink of her fear increased. No doubt she was imagining all sorts of horror endings, and part of me hated that I was frightening her so much. But this really *was* a case of life and death, and right now compassion was a luxury I couldn't afford.

"Can you access the fire escape?"

She nodded. I pushed her left and we strode down the curving hallway. A green-and-white exit sign soon came into view, but even as we approached, the door opposite opened and a tall man stepped out.

"Meagan," he said, but his welcoming smile quickly faded as he took in the situation. "What the fuck is going on?"

I raised the gun and pointed it at him. "Step back into your apartment and lock the damn door."

He immediately did so. I stopped the woman in front of the scanner and told her to open the door. Once she'd obeyed, I said, "Now run back to your apartment as fast as you can."

She glanced over her shoulder, her expression a mix of disbelief, hope, and even more horror. I realized then she was afraid I was going to shoot her in the back.

"I'm not going to kill you," I said. "I just want to get onto the roof. So go."

She did so, almost reluctantly at first, and then faster. As she disappeared around the corridor's sweeping curve, I stepped inside the stairwell, shot out the scanner, and then ran up toward the rooftop as fast as I could. Which in all truth wasn't that fast.

I didn't immediately exit, though. Instead, I cracked open the door and scanned the nearby area. The rooftop was a maze of light towers, solar panels, the various bits of comms equipment that sprouted like weeds on every rooftop in the city, and aircon units. Thankfully, there was no indication that anyone was up here.

I opened the door a little wider and studied the curtain wall. Fourth Street was still a long way from it, but I had no intention of either trying to reach it or going over it. Not tonight anyway.

There was no alarm sounding, and the casual manner in which the guards strolled along the top of the wall suggested they hadn't yet received any advice to be on guard.

I stepped out onto the rooftop and moved across to the street side of the building, using all the paraphernalia on the roof to hide behind. I had no doubt that both Meagan and the man I'd threatened were currently in the process of contacting corps. I needed to get out of this area, but I also needed them to believe that I'd jumped from this building to the one directly opposite. They might not believe it for long, but by then, the scent trail should have gone cold.

I grabbed my knife, made a small cut on my left palm, and smeared some blood across the parapet. It was a dangerous ploy given a sample could be taken and tested, and while that alone wouldn't reveal my déchet origins, it would nevertheless unveil a number of inconsistencies when compared to the information on my—or rather, Catherine's —RFID chip. And as second-in-command of Home Defense, it would be easy enough for Hedda Lang to access that information. But I was right out of other options. The wound healed almost as soon as I'd finished. Despite the weariness throbbing through me, my body still had some reserves left. Either that, or I was recharging far faster than I ever had.

I hoped it was the latter, because I was in serious need of that sort of luck right now.

I took a deep breath and then reached for the light shield again. It flickered and pulsed around me, coming into being almost reluctantly, but eventually did solidify. Once all light had been cut out, I became shadow.

It was never going to last long, but it didn't really need to. I made my way back to the rooftop of my building, found the exhaust vent outlet, and then slipped down into it. Finding my apartment took three tries, and I'd barely made it inside when my strength gave out and I crashed to the floor of the shower. The water immediately came on full force, and my resulting groan was one of both pleasure and pain. The hot water soothed the aches, but the jets were so strong that even through my clothes it stung my abused body. I didn't move for too many vital seconds but eventually pushed myself upright and stripped off so I could wash away the rest of the blood, grime, and sweat. Once I was dry, I gathered my clothes and hid them—along with most of my weapons—in the rear of the other bedroom's wardrobe. A quick look at the intercom in the hall revealed it was empty. It was damn lucky I'd encountered them in the street rather than here, in the apartment building. Dream might suspect my Catherine persona, but she would have had proof positive if they'd been standing at my door as I'd come out of the elevator.

But the fact she wasn't here now didn't mean she soon wouldn't be.

Which meant I not only needed to protect myself from her magic but heal as fast as possible. In my current condition, a three-year-old could probably beat me senseless.

I walked into my bedroom and retrieved two of the charms Cat and Bear had hidden, and slipped them over my hands. Energy briefly stirred the small hairs on my arms, and I hoped it meant they were both active. I'd be in serious trouble if they weren't.

I then shoved a gun between the mattress and the wall, where it could be easily retrieved but not so easily discovered, and started climbing into bed—only to stop again. I had no idea if Dream would recognize what the charms were, but I didn't dare take that chance. I walked across to the wardrobe, picked out a semi sheer, long-sleeved night-gown with cuffs wide enough to conceal the charms, and slipped it on. Once under the sheets, I made doubly sure I could reach the gun easily enough, then closed my eyes and dropped into a deep healing state.

I was woken, who knew how many hours later, by a hand on my shoulder, lightly shaking me.

My groan was real rather than feigned—being so abruptly pulled out of the deep healing state always resulted in several minutes of confusion and sluggishness.

The hand shoved me again, a little more viciously this time. I slipped one hand under my pillow in readiness to grab the gun even as I stirred and forced heavy-feeling eyes open.

There were two men in the room. One I knew, the other I didn't.

And the latter was not only armed but had the sight aimed squarely at my head. At such a close distance, a weapon that powerful would not only blow my brains apart, but take out much of the wall behind me.

"Charles, what are you doing here?"

My voice was little more than a croak. That alone told me I hadn't been under anywhere near long enough.

"I was worried—"

"I sent you a note," I cut in, my voice holding an edge of annoyance. "Didn't you get it?"

Something flickered in his eyes, but I wasn't entirely sure if it was remorse or annoyance. "Yes, but I heard there was an escaped felon in the area, and I wanted to check that you were okay."

"How would an escaped felon get into a building as secure as this?" That edge was stronger and it *wasn't* feigned. "And how did *you* get in here?"

"You have to understand—"

"Understand what?" I raised my tone and forcing an edge of fury into it. "That you broke into *my* apartment with an armed guard? One who *still* has a gun aimed at me?"

He had the grace to at least look uncomfortable. "Yes, sorry, but Officer Richmond is under strict instructions to remain vigilant until otherwise notified—"

"Notified by whom?" I sat upright. I had no sense that there was anyone other than these two men in the apartment, and it would appear rather odd if I remained lying down in such circumstances. I could still reach the gun easily enough if I needed to. "Really, Charles, it's rather obvious there's no one here but the three of us. Or do you think *I'm* the escaped felon?"

"No, no, of course not," he said quickly. "But you didn't respond when we pressed the urgent call button, so we deemed it prudent to come in and check."

"And by what right have you done such a thing?" I flicked the sheet off and rose. I didn't bother controlling my anger, and the force of it was such that he took a rapid step backward. "We might be sexually involved, Charles, but there's *no* commitment between us, and you certainly have no authority over *any* of my actions. So unless you and your weapon-bearing friend have the appropriate invasion order, a complaint *will* be lodged."

I stalked past him. The soldier at the door stood to one side but didn't relax his guard any. I continued to the stairs and headed down. Thankfully, both Charles and the guard followed. Obviously, the latter's orders had been to keep an eye on my movements rather than search the apartment.

Charles followed me across to the kitchen. "Come on now, there's no need for that. I only acted out of concern—"

"Does that mean you haven't got an invasion order?"

"He doesn't need one," a new voice said. "Not when I was with him and gave the go-ahead."

My gut clenched. Though the voice belonged to Karlinda, the foul energy now stinging the air belonged wholly to Dream. I cursed the lack of foresight that had me standing here without a weapon within reaching distance, and swung around to face her.

She strode toward me easily, the chancellor's frail outer shell so at odds with the force of energy rolling off her. It felt like thousands of tiny gnats were nipping at my skin, and it was all I could do to remain still and not react in *any* way.

"I wasn't aware it was within the chancellor's power to issue such orders," I replied coolly.

"Generally, it isn't."

She stopped on the other side of the kitchen counter and motioned toward my hands. Only it wasn't a simple indicator of what she wanted, but rather an unleashing of power—something I knew only because the charm on my left wrist began to burn. The fact I wasn't once again battling to breathe meant Nuri's magic was effectively countering Dream's.

Now I just had to hope that my earlier guess was true—that a major part of her physical and magical strength was being sucked away by the rifts, which in turn meant she wasn't capable of sensing either of the charms.

And if the quick flick of confusion that ran across her expression was anything to go by, she couldn't.

She frowned and then said imperiously, "Show me your palms."

"What? Why?" I feigned confusion even as my heart began to beat a little faster. While I was aware the scrapes had healed, I had no idea if the skin was still pink or not.

"Show me your palms," she repeated, voice flat and holding an edge. "Immediately."

"Karlinda, is all this really—" Charles began, only to stop when she cast him a steely look.

"Why?" I said, even as I held out my hands, palms up. The skin wasn't pink, but I batted down the quick stab of relief. I wasn't out of the woods just yet. She grabbed my hand and quickly ran her fingers across not only the newer skin but also the old. Looking for callouses, I realized, because the woman I was pretending to be certainly wouldn't have them.

Thankfully, my skin was baby smooth. It might have been a long ago since I'd been a lure in enemy encampments, but both the training and the instinct for self-preservation was very, very ingrained, even when it came to such a tiny detail. My strength level had to be very, *very* low for it to be otherwise.

But while my hands had healed without scarring, I couldn't be so sure that the same could be said about the rest of my wounds—especially the one caused by Branna's wooden bullet.

Dream released me, and it took every ounce of control to not wipe away the feel of her touch on my nightdress.

"You didn't answer my question, Chancellor," I said. "Why did you want to look at my hands?"

I was well aware of the why—she'd found the spot where her magic had snapped and I'd scraped my hands open on the sidewalk. But it was an obvious question to ask, and it would be damn dangerous to do anything other than the obvious right now. Especially when the soldier hadn't yet relaxed his stance.

She waved a hand, but this time it was a mere gesture rather than an indication of another spell being aimed my way. "It was merely a precaution."

"As the man with the gun still aimed at my face is a precaution?" I bit back. "I don't like what you're implying, Chancellor—"

"Please," she said. "Mistakes do occasionally happen in the quest to make this city safe, and this is obviously one of them. I sincerely apologize for the stress we have caused you."

Her apology was many things, but it certainly *wasn't* sincere. But I bit down on my instinctive reply and watched as she nodded at the guard. He immediately spun around and walked out. It didn't make feel any safer. In fact, it had quite the opposite effect, if only because her suspicion still spun around me, as sharp as her energy.

"I shall leave you and Charles to talk over—"

"No, you won't," I said calmly. "You can take dear Charles with you. I have no desire to be in his presence right now."

"Catherine, please," he said. "My actions were born out of a desire to see you safe—"

"That does not excuse you all breaking into my apartment and treating me like a common criminal," I said. "So you can see yourself out of here, and I might—*might*—consider talking to you tomorrow, once I have calmed down."

He didn't look happy, but he nevertheless turned and walked toward the door. I followed; a quick glance at the scanner showed that it hadn't been damaged in any way. They'd obviously used some sort of override key to get in.

I nevertheless asked, "Am I still able to lock my door? Or does whatever method you used to get in mean I now have to seek out someone to repair it?"

Dream glanced over her shoulder. Though her expression gave away little, her eyes glittered with suspicion. I may have been unaffected by her magic and passed the touch test, but she still wasn't convinced about my identity. And *that* meant she'd be keeping a close eye on my movements from here on in.

"The door wasn't broken," she said, but didn't bother explaining why. She continued down the hall into the waiting elevator.

Charles paused and said, "I'll ring tomorrow, then?"

"You can certainly try."

With that, I hit the door release to cut off any reply he might have made. Then I took a deep breath and leaned my forehead against the door. Damn, that was altogether *too* close.

But I wasn't out of the woods yet. Not when Dream was so suspicious of me.

I took another deep breath and called Cat and Bear. I couldn't make any untoward moves for the next twenty-four hours at least, but Nuri and Jonas needed to know that Dream was impersonating the chancellor on either a full-time or part-time basis. And while she was here in that guise, where was the real chancellor? Was she dead, or merely knocked out?

And did *that* mean Jonas was also right—that Dream was impersonating Hedda Lang only part of the time? But how could a situation like that even work on any sort of long-term basis?

I scrubbed a hand across my eyes. There were so many damn questions, and in reality, we were still no closer to getting those answers or stopping the bitch.

My two ghosts appeared. They buzzed around me, their excitement levels high, both of them speaking at the same time and so fast that I had no idea what they were actually saying.

I waited until they'd calmed down, and then said, "I'll get you to repeat all that because I didn't even catch half of it."

Their giggles followed me as I walked across to the autocook to grab a coffee. It appeared almost instantly, and was so hot it steamed. Even so, it didn't do a lot to chase away the tiredness that still rode me. I punched in an order for a steak and vegetables, and, once I was propped up on a seat, said, "Right, tell me again what happened when I left?"

Jonas and his people reentered the vampires' cavern, Bear said. *There was a big fight and lots of gunfire.*

"Did anyone get hurt?"

One of Jonas's people was killed, two were hurt, Cat said. *But most of the opposition died.*

"Including the man in charge—the one with the scar under his eye?"

He was injured but died not long after Jonas started interviewing him, Bear said.

"From his injuries?"

No, from a poison capsule, Jonas said. He was very annoyed.

I could imagine. "Are they on their way back?"

Jonas is, along with the injured. The rest remain to guard the facility.

"He surely can't expect eight or so mercenaries to be able to hold such a vast complex."

No, Bear said. *Nuri gathers a larger force, but Jonas said it is difficult given they cannot yet involve the corps or anyone official.*

Because they weren't sure how far Dream's evil tentacles reached. "What are they doing about the tunnel borer?"

They shut it down and locked away the men who were controlling it, Cat said. *As near as they can figure, it was only fifty or so kilometers outside of Central.*

Meaning they'd come close—so damn close—to achieving their goal. And while we were now safe from a tunneled attack, it really didn't mean anything. If Dream *did* have a plan B that involved the lights, then everything we'd achieved up until now would be for naught. We needed to uncover how far the tendrils of her evil had spread, and we needed to do it fast if we wanted to save this city.

"Did the soldier mention anything about Central's lights?"

Jonas never had the chance to ask.

"Damn." I grabbed my steak out of the autocook and dug out some cutlery from a nearby drawer. "Was he able to get anything at all from him?"

Little more than his name and rank.

Which was no damn help at all. I concentrated on demolishing my meal and then, once I was done, said, "Bear, I need you to go back to Jonas and tell him Dream was here in the guise of the chancellor, but I don't know if this was a one-off event or if she's doing it more often. Tell him I wasn't in a position to act against her, and that I think she suspects who I am."

If that is so, Bear said, mental tone concerned, *it might be best to leave.*

"I can't, because there's not enough time left to set up a new identity or to get someone else inside." Besides I knew— better than anyone—just how difficult it could be to track a body shifter. After all, I'd escaped dangerous situations more than a couple of times by altering my form and my scent to that of another.

But the strength and presence of mind required to pull off multiple changes over such a long period of time was finite —even for someone who'd been designed to do just that— and Dream certainly hadn't been. Sooner or later, she *would* trip up. We just had to be sure we were near enough to take advantage of it.

And to do that, I had to remain near Charles.

What about me? Cat said, as Bear raced away.

"I need you to keep watch. I have to rest and recover, but I don't trust that Dream or her people won't come busting in here again."

I didn't actually think she would—not tonight, anyway. She was more likely to have my every move watched instead, but in this particular case, it was better to be safe than sorry.

No one will get near this place, Cat assured me. *Not without me seeing them.*

"Thanks, Cat." I drained the last of my coffee, then dumped everything in the auto wash and headed back upstairs. I was asleep almost as soon as my head hit the pillow, and this time nothing and no one disturbed me.

I woke to insistent buzzing. I blinked, trying to place the noise and not having much success.

"Cat? Bear? Everything all right out there?"

They both whisked in, neither of them in any way alarmed, which in turn had me relaxing. Whatever the noise was, it obviously *wasn't* any sort of threat.

The comms unit buzzes, Bear said. *Charles's face appears on it. He looks increasingly unhappy.*

"How often has he rung?"

This is the fifth time this morning, Cat said.

He seems very determined to talk to you, Bear added.

"That he does."

Are you going to talk to him or continue to ignore him? Cat asked curiously.

"I'll talk to him, but not immediately."

In fact, I needed to do a whole lot more than talk, if only because I needed to know what had gone on between him and Dream when they'd both left the apartment. I just couldn't be seen forgiving him too easily. That would only confirm Dream's suspicions about me.

I slipped out of bed and padded into the bathroom to check the state of my various wounds. For the most part they'd healed without leaving a mark, but—as I feared—the entry point for the wooden bullet was a somewhat puckered mess. I narrowed my gaze, imagined it smoothed out, and reached for the shifting magic. My shoulder tingled, and the flesh instantly began to rearrange and to some extent smooth out, but the scar still remained visible. It might be little more than a white blob, but that would be enough to stir Charles's curiosity, given how intimately he now knew Catherine's body.

I tried to erase the mark a second time, but once again failed. It seemed I was stuck with it.

The incessant buzzing stopped. I took a shower, got dressed, and then headed down to grab something to eat. I'd barely finished my omelet when the nearby comms unit came alive and Charles's face once again appeared. This time, I answered.

"Charles," I greeted, voice cool. "What can I do for you?"

"I ring to beg forgiveness for my invasion of your privacy." Though his tone was contrite, there was an odd gleam in his eyes. It was both regretful and angry, which was rather odd. But maybe he simply didn't like being forced into making an apology. Many of the shifters I'd encountered in the past had been like that—they saw it as an affront to their pride, for some weird reason. "Though it came from a place of genuine concern, I can understand why you were so angry."

"I woke up to a gun being pointed at my face," I replied evenly. "That's not exactly something anyone wants to experience in their own home, Charles."

"I know, but Karlinda insisted she accompany me and I couldn't refuse." He paused, and half shrugged. "I have let her know how unacceptable the whole situation was. If you wish to lodge a formal complaint, I will not gainsay you."

"That is very kind of you."

My tone was sarcastic, but his expression suggested he didn't catch it. "Can I take you out to dinner as an apology?"

I hesitated. While the need to catch Dream and put a final end to her machinations was a pulse growing ever stronger, there was also a deepening urge for caution. The suicide of the soldier Jonas had been questioning suggested Dream's net was not only wide, but also very loyal, and we needed to find and destroy all its tentacles just as much as we needed to stop the woman who controlled it. Because some of those tentacles *had* to be working within the power grid—why else would Penny have mentioned the lights going down if Dream hadn't found some means of making it happen?

Nuri—or rather, her kin, given she was still considered an outcast in this city and, as such, had limitations on what she could and couldn't do—might be working to expose all of Dream's agents, but they needed time.

And that, I feared, was the one thing none of us really had.

Still... only fools rushed in, as the old saying went.

"You can," I replied. "But not tonight. I'm still very upset at you, Charles, and would not be pleasant company, I'm afraid."

Frustration and anger momentarily flitted across his face before he got it under control, and instinct stirred. Had Dream asked him to give me a more thorough examination? It was a distinct possibility, especially given Jonas's earlier warning that Charles was, above all else, a government man. He had no idea Dream had usurped the chancellor's identity, and he'd admitted that he did not have the power—or, I suspected, the will—to go against her.

If *that* was the case, then I'd have to keep my wits about me, and simply use my seeking skills via touch rather than anything deeper. I couldn't completely erase the scar in my shoulder, and Dream would undoubtedly know its cause.

"Tomorrow then," he said, tone conciliatory despite the frustrated gleam in his eyes. "Shall we meet at Zendigah's at, say, seven?"

Zendigah's was an upmarket restaurant on Second, and a favorite of Charles's. It was also well frequented, which at least offered some protection against anything untoward happening while we there.

"That would be lovely," I said coolly. "I'll see you then."

I signed off and then walked across to the large windows. Light and sunshine caressed my skin with warmth but did little to erase the chill gathering around me. Trouble was coming. I could feel it with every psychic piece of me, and there wasn't a whole lot I could do to avoid it. Indeed, the annoying inner voice suggested, avoiding it was possibly the worst thing I could do.

I rubbed my arms and studied the street below. There were plenty of men and women going about their business, and none of them snagged at my senses. But I had no doubt that there would be watchers down there somewhere. I'd given Dream plenty of time to put them in place.

"Let's go for a walk." I headed out the door and strode toward the elevator.

Where are we going? Bear asked. *The market again?*

A smile tugged at my lips. The last time we'd gone there, they'd spent their time chasing each other through the many higgledy-piggledy rows of textiles, meats, and produce, and had ended up upsetting an entire cart, sending oranges rolling everywhere.

"I'm not sure someone of Catherine's stature would visit such a place. But we might head down to Seven Sins and grab a macaroon." Or two. I might as well make use of the credits while I still had them.

Macaroon? Cat said. *What's that?*

I hesitated, wondering how to describe something my ghost had never seen let alone eaten. "It's similar to a sweet biscuit, only it's thin and crunchy on the outside, softer than a cloud on the inside, and the absolutely most delicious thing I've ever tasted."

Sounds interesting, Bear said, though his mental tones were uncertain.

But that wasn't really surprising, given that sweet things and déchet weren't always compatible. Our taste buds tended to lean toward the bitter end of the scale—a result, no doubt, of the fact that there'd been nothing resembling sweets or desserts offered to déchet in the military bunkers, and they'd certainly been in scarce supply in most of the shifter camps I'd been sent to during the war.

I wish there was a way I could share the experience with you both, I said silently, as I stepped out onto the street. *Because they do taste amazing.*

Could we link? Cat said. *It lets us share sight—maybe it might now let us share taste.*

I paused on the step and glanced around, feigning uncertainty as to which way to go, when I was in fact looking for anyone appearing overly interested in my appearance. There didn't appear to be, but I guessed Dream—in her Hedda Lang guise—did have the entire corps division under her control. They weren't likely to make such a simple mistake.

We can try. I headed left. *Could you both keep watch, and see if you can spot someone following me?*

They buzzed around me excitedly and then whisked away. I rather suspected everyone who had the temerity to be walking in the same direction for more than a dozen steps would now be getting a ghostly once-over.

I unhurriedly made my way through the various crosswalks, and after fifteen minutes Cat said, *We've found him.*

Well done, both of you. What does he look like?

Mean, Bear said. *He's got black hair, a big nose, and small lips. He's dressed in a white tunic like everyone else, but he has an earpiece.*

Suggesting he was reporting my every move to someone. *Keep an eye on him. If he makes a move toward me, or if anyone else joins him, let me know.*

Will do.

I continued winding my way through the streets. I'd barely reached Sixth when Cat said, *Jonas is near, though he wears a disguise.*

I resisted the urge to look over my shoulder and kept on meandering. *What does he want?*

She hesitated. *He needs to talk to you.*

Tell him I'm being followed.

He says he's aware of that. We told him where you're going, and he said he'd see you there.

I frowned. *That could be dangerous given I'm being tailed.*

He said he won't sit at the same table or acknowledge you in any way.

Okay then. I paused. *And my follower? Where's he currently?*

He's looking into a shop's front window six back from your current position, but on the other side of the road.

I again resisted the urge to look as I swung into the walkway that led to Seventh. I came out half a block down from Seven Sins, and not far away from the building where Nadel Keller—the man I'd initially intended targeting to get information on Winter Halo—had drawn his last breath. Dream didn't muck about when it came to loose ends, even one as remote as Keller.

Seven Sins came into sight. I paused just inside the entrance, my gaze sweeping the small but pleasant front room. The place wasn't crowded, and there were only three tables occupied—one by a couple, one by two women sharing a platter of sweets, and, at the back of the room, a gray-haired, craggy-faced man of indeterminate age.

Jonas, in disguise.

I walked over to one of the tables near the window and sat down. A waitress immediately walked over; once I'd placed my order and scanned my RFID chip to pay for it, I crossed my arms and leaned against the table, staring out the window as I said, *Is there a problem or is this just an update?*

The latter, mostly.

Mostly? A smile teased my lips. *Does that mean you were desperate to see me?*

If I were to say yes, how would you respond? Amusement ran through his mental tone.

I wouldn't be averse to hearing it, though I rather suspect it's more a case of needing to pass information, and not wanting to keep using the ghosts as go-betweens.

That would also be true, though it doesn't mute the strength of the original intention. His amusement faded. *Nuri's kin have managed to install recording equipment in the chancellor's quarters—*

How the hell did they manage that? I cut in. *Isn't she guarded twenty-four seven?*

Yes, but Nuri isn't the only earth-capable witch within her family, and they have... various ways of getting what they want. Although none of them hold her power or experience.

Naturally, given none of them had survived a rift *and* had their life span extended and abilities sharpened. *When did this happen?*

Because if it was *before* last night, then they might just have captured either Hedda Lang or Dream herself taking on Karlinda's form.

It was operational by last night, but I can't say at exactly what time, he replied. *And we won't be able to access the recording until at least tomorrow evening.*

I frowned. *Access it? Does that mean it's not wirelessly connected?*

It does indeed, he said. *We had to go old-school, because all transmissions in and out of Government House, the House of Lords, and the homes of all officials are monitored twenty-four seven.*

Wouldn't that be problematic when it comes to deal making or information that requires the highest security?

Yes, he said, *but there are devices and codes in place that can be employed in such situations. We know them, but can't use them given this is an unapproved operation.*

Because if they did, they'd alert the very person they were trying to entrap. *And Hedda Lang? Are you trying a similar tactic within her office?*

No—we're working on something else.

The waitress returned with my coffee and macaroons. I gave her a smile of thanks, and then said, *You'll have to excuse me for a second—I promised Cat and Bear we could try linking so they can understand how good these things taste.*

Seriously? The amusement was back.

Yes. Sweets like this weren't offered to déchet, Jonas. We got what our bodies needed for growth, nothing more and nothing less.

After getting to know your little ones, I find that a rather sad fact.

Indeed it was. *Cat, you first.*

As she whipped through me to create the deeper-level connection that we'd used before the rift, I concentrated on trying to reverse the polarity of it—or at least equalize it. She pulled free, but the connection remained sharp. Not only could I see through her eyes, but—if her gasp was anything to go by—she could now see through mine. I bit into the macaroon. It was every bit as good as the first time I'd tasted it.

That's lovely, Cat said, awe in her mental tones. *And unlike anything I've ever tasted.*

An ache was beginning to stir behind my eyes; a warning the deep-level link was starting to drain my strength. *Cat, you need to disconnect and give Bear a go.*

She immediately did so, and a second bite had him echoing her words. He didn't linger either, but the ache remained when he broke the connection. I rather suspected that, given their silence, it had also drawn heavily on their own strength.

Let's not do that too often, I said.

No, they agreed, mental tones weary.

But at least we have something interesting to share with the little ones, Bear added.

I raised my eyebrows. *Meaning everything you did with Jonas wasn't?*

That's business, Cat said, sounding all grown-up. *Very different.*

I snorted softly, finished the rest of the macaroon, and then picked up my coffee, holding the mug between my hands as I continued to stare out the window. There was a dark-haired man five doors down who seemed to be spending a very long time contemplating whatever lay inside the bakery's window. My watcher, I suspected.

Has Nuri managed to find enough mercenaries to guard the vampire base and its tunnel? I asked.

Yes, because we're pulling people from every operation we can, and we're also installing battery-operated UVs across every entrance and in the tunnel. His tone was grim. *We're hoping it's enough to stop any vampire or wraith attempt to regain control of the area.*

If Dream is Hedda Lang, could she order a corps assault?

She can, but she'd first have to gain House approval, and then Julius Valkarie would have to sign off on it.

So we have time?

But not much.

Trepidation stirred. *Don't tell me Nuri's had another of her future insights.*

We've three days, he said, mental tone flat. *If we haven't stopped Dream by then, it's all going to go to hell in a handbasket.*

As declarations of doom went, it was right up there with her statement that if I didn't find the missing children, no one would. Of course, in the end it had been a combination of Jonas and me that had found them, and I really hoped this one could be similarly sidetracked.

Because we were now battling more than just the mad desires of three people. We were fighting for the safety of our city, if not our world.

Did she say how?

I bit into the second macaroon, but the heavenly sweetness suddenly tasted bitter. It seemed fear could kill taste buds quicker than anything else.

It involves the lights, just as Penny warned, he said, *which is why we're currently using every resource we have within the government and without to check the identities of everyone who has access to the grid. But again, it'll take time.*

Especially when identities are easily enough faked.

I could feel his smile through our link, though it held little in the way of warmth or amusement. *Having used them ourselves for many a decade, we're more than capable of spotting a dummy identity when we come across it.*

What do you want me to do, given Dream is having me followed and obviously suspects my Catherine identity?

He hesitated. *We need you to maintain cover. While she's relegating her attention and her forces to ensnare you, she's not paying attention to what else is going on.*

And if she does ensnare me? I asked. *Or worse, simply decides to get rid of me?*

She won't kill you, he replied. *Not immediately, anyway.*

I frowned. *Why not? It makes far more sense for her to simply get rid of me. While I'm still alive, I'm capable of causing her problems.*

Yes, but you are now also involved with Charles. The Fontaines have been a powerful force within the House for years, and she cannot afford to have him offside at a time when her plans are nearing fruition. She will need to have concrete evidence against you—or at least against Catherine —before she can act.

The need for evidence was why she was having me

followed, obviously. But that wouldn't be the end of it, and it was those unknown plans that were worrying me.

Charles has said he can't gainsay the chancellor, I said. *Why would it be any different when it comes to Hedda Lang?*

Because one controls the House of Lords, he said, *and the other is merely a government official, no matter the fact that she is second-in-charge of the Department of Home Defense.*

There's one rather large problem in that particular statement, though, I said. *Dream is assuming Karlinda's identity. What's to stop her from ordering me killed?*

The fact that she can't—not without the order first going through the House for approval.

Which didn't mean she couldn't convince Charles I was up to no good and have him do something about it. But even as that thought crossed my mind, I discounted it. Charles was, at his core, a kind-hearted, old-fashioned gentleman who believed in doing what was right by Central. Dream might have talked him into breaking into my home, and she might be able to convince him to interrogate me or check out the lumps and scars on my body in greater detail, but he would go no further. He wouldn't kill—at least not without reason and, even then, not without proof. It just wasn't in his nature.

I finished my coffee and put the cup down. The dark-haired man who'd been inspecting the bakery for an overly long time was nowhere in sight. I doubted he'd be too far away, however—unless, of course, someone else had taken his place. Dream knew what I was, and would suspect I'd be more likely to spot a tail than the average person.

I'm meeting Charles for dinner tomorrow night, I said. *But I'm not risking going back to his apartment to read him more thoroughly. Nuri's not the only one getting bad vibes about the whole situation.*

If you do think Charles will betray you—

It's no greater a risk now that it has ever been, I replied, even as I crossed mental fingers to void the lie. *You were the one who warned me that he's a government man, after all.*

Yes, but—

You've already said Dream won't outright kill me, I cut in, *and anything else I'll escape from.*

And if she can't, Bear and Cat intoned, *we'll all help her, won't we?*

Once again I felt Jonas's smile, and this time it warmed places deep inside. *Indeed we will.*

I finished off the remainder of the second macaroon and then rose. *If there's nothing else, I'd better leave. Lingering might raise too many suspicions.*

Be careful in Charles's company tomorrow night.

I glanced his way as I moved away from the table and gave him a smile. *And you make sure you keep me updated, or I shall ask the little ones to harass your ass.*

His answering smile was quick and bright, and even though he wasn't wearing his own countenance, still sent my pulse rate skittering. *It's impossible for them to do any more than they currently are.*

Are you sleeping?

He paused. *Yes.*

Then they can do more.

His laughter ran across my thoughts and tugged a wider smile to my lips.

Then perhaps we should agree to share the company of Cat and Bear, so that messages can be relayed in good time.

A good plan, I said, and walked out.

I hesitated, looking right and left, and didn't spot my tail. Either he was watching from inside one of the nearby retail stores or he had indeed swapped over with someone else.

I took my time making my way back to the apartment, and then did nothing more for the remainder of the evening but rest and eat. After everything that had happened over the last week or so, it was a rather nice interval.

And one that instinct said I'd better enjoy.

At six the following evening I got ready for my date with Charles. I decided to dress more conservatively than usual —the tunic I chose was loose rather than figure-hugging, and the side split only went as far as my knee—in order to send an indirect message that he wasn't to expect anything of a sexual nature this evening.

Shall we accompany you? Cat asked as I gathered a shawl to ward off the evening's chill from my shoulders.

I hesitated and then shook my head. "Keep an eye on the apartment, just in case anything untoward happens."

I didn't really expect it to, but it was always possible that Dream would use my time away to do a thorough search. I'd hidden my uniform and guns as best I could, but a decent scanner would undoubtedly uncover the latter.

I headed out. The evening air was even colder than I expected, and a light drizzle was falling. I pulled the shawl over my head and shoulders, and kept to the building side of the sidewalk, using the various awnings and overhangs as added protection.

Zendigah's was a small three-story building situated on the corner of Second and a cross street into First, and its interior was as shadowed as any of these places ever got. A large hearth dominated the small front room, and the fire belted out so much heat I started sweating almost as soon as I entered. There were a number of leather sofas and high-backed chairs scattered around the room, and all of them were occupied. I knew without looking that Charles wasn't here—his preference was for a table on the top floor.

A waiter made his way toward me and gave me a welcoming smile. "A pleasure to see you again, Catherine. Lord Charles Fontaine awaits at your usual table. If you'd please follow me, I'll take you up there immediately."

"Excellent. Thank you."

We made our way through the small room and up a rather steep set of wooden stairs. The second level held six well-spaced tables, all of which were occupied, and another fire-place belting out heat. As we went up to the next level, I had to hope the heat wasn't repeated; otherwise, the pinpricks of sweat dotting my skin might become a flood.

Thankfully, it *was* marginally cooler up on the final floor of the building, as the flames in the hearth had been allowed to die down. Like the level below, the end wall here was entirely glass, and it gave a direct view down the cross street and into the park. Charles's table—the one he always got, no matter how busy the place—held the prime spot for that view.

He rose as we approached. "Catherine," he said, his voice holding a very slight edge that I couldn't quite place. "It's lovely to see you again."

I gave the waiter a smile of thanks as he held out my chair, and, once seated, I said rather formally, "A feeling that's mutual, I assure you."

"Would you like a drink before you order, madam?" the waiter said.

I hesitated, and then said, "What would you recommend?"

"A predinner aperitif such as champagne, perhaps?"

"That would be lovely, thank you."

He nodded and disappeared. I crossed my arms and leaned back into the chair. "So how have you been, Charles?"

He smiled. "A little out of sorts, I must admit. The events of the last few days have been... unexpected."

"A statement I certainly agree with." And one that had my instincts stirring, although I wasn't entirely sure why.

"Yes."

He paused as the waiter returned and poured a small amount of champagne into my glass. Once I tasted it and nodded my approval, the waiter topped it up and disappeared again.

"Please believe I had no control over the events that unfolded," Charles added. "And I certainly had no intention of frightening you in any way."

"That I can accept," I said. "But was the gun in my face truly necessary?"

"Of course not, and I told Karlinda as much."

I raised an eyebrow. "And her response?"

He grimaced. "She rather crossly reminded me that I was the one who'd insisted on being accompanied by an armed guard."

"But isn't she, as chancellor, always accompanied by a guard whenever she is out?"

"Indeed, but she is not someone who likes being placed in an awkward position, and that is exactly what happened." He picked up his wine and took a drink. "I'm not in her good books at the moment, I fear."

"Does that really matter? You're a member of the House now; what possible sway can she have over you?"

"None," he said. "But it's nevertheless a bad idea to put her offside. She holds the balance of power, remember, and if any legislation I bring to the floor is locked, she's the one who will have final say on whether it's passed or not."

"Ah," I said. "I didn't realize."

He raised an eyebrow, speculation flaring briefly in his eyes. "I still find it very surprising that you cannot remember the intricacies of the government and the House of Lords when it is something that is taught at a primary level."

I forced a casual smile. "It is not as if I've had any reason to remember such things over the course of my life, Charles. I am a sexual masseuse, remember, and the politics and problems I deal with on a daily basis are very different to those faced in the House of Lords."

He laughed softly. "I guess *that* is totally true."

A statement that oddly sounded as if he *didn't* believe me—or, perhaps, didn't believe my other statements. I drank some champagne, my wariness increasing. "I do hope you haven't permanently fractured your relationship with her. As angry as I am, it was never my intention to cause harm to your professional standing."

"If there's one thing I've learned from my father, it's that all rifts can be healed. Are you ready to order?" he added.

When I nodded, the waiter silently appeared. Once we'd both placed our order—beef Wellington along with a full-bodied red wine—Charles leaned forward and said, "Let's discuss something else. What have you done since I saw you?"

I told him, and the conversation rolled on from there. But that uneasy flicker remained alight inside me, a flame no doubt fed by the odd tension that seemed to be emanating from him. Normally I would have written it off as tension born of sexual frustration, but this felt darker—angrier—than that.

After we'd consumed our main meal and sweets, he reached across the table and caught my hand in his. "Is it too much to ask that you come back to my place for a nightcap?"

I wrapped my fingers around his and unleashed my seeking

skills. All I was after was information on Dream, in either her Karlinda disguise or her Hedda Lang one, but Charles's thoughts were annoyingly vague, and the fragments I caught appeared to be centered only on one thing—sex. Which was not unexpected; Charles might seriously like me, but he liked our sexual encounters even more.

And yet those fragments didn't explain the dark edge still evident in both the energy rolling off him and in some of his movements. He was restless, angry, and neither of those could be placed at the feet of sexual frustration.

"Just a nightcap," he added. "With no expectations of anything more."

I hesitated, uncertain which way to go. While instinct was warning it would be dangerous to go back, it wasn't saying why, and I still very much believed that Charles himself wasn't a threat. And maybe if we were in his home rather than in a very public place, he'd relax enough that I could get the information I needed about Dream without resorting to anything more than touch.

"A nightcap, yes," I said softly. "But I'm not staying the night, Charles."

He sighed and pulled his hand from mine. "I guess that is to be expected."

We lingered for coffee and then went back to his apartment. He lived in a family-owned building situated two blocks down from Zendigah's, right behind the area on First Street that held most governmental buildings. Regulations restricted construction height to a maximum of twenty levels on both First and Second Streets, and his building was one of the tallest. He scanned us in and then escorted me to the elevator. It, like the building itself, was glass fronted and, as we got higher, offered amazing views over the parkland. Once we'd reached the twentieth floor, Charles again placed a hand against my spine and guided me to the right. The tension in him, if anything, had increased, and trepidation stirred. But it was too late now to back out of the situation—not without stirring the kind of suspicion I was trying to avoid. While I might not have seen my follower, I had no doubt he was still out there.

The sensor beeped as we approached and the door opened. The room beyond was one vast white space, with walls of glass on two sides that provided spectacular views over both Government House and the park. The furniture was either white leather or glass, and there wasn't much else in the way of color aside from the gleaming metal of the autocook and kitchen appliances.

I paused to shake the drizzle from my shawl and then hang it up, but Charles moved across to the drinks cabinet. He met me near the plush L-shaped sofa and offered me one of the two balloon glasses he was holding.

"Here's to overcoming the challenges that come with any relationship," he said, "and to successfully moving on."

A smile touched my lips as I clinked my glass lightly against his. "Here's to hoping that you do not consider a gun in the face a normal progression in your relationships."

He laughed softly. "That is not what I meant, and you know it."

"Indeed." I took a sip of the cognac then licked my lips in appreciation. He watched the movement almost avidly, and again, uncertainty stirred. At any other time, I would have simply marked it down as sexual interest, but the gleam in his eyes owed as much to curiosity as attraction, and that was decidedly odd. It wasn't like he'd never seen me drink cognac before— My stomach suddenly dropped.

What if he'd put something in it?

What if Dream, in her Karlinda disguise, had convinced or even forced Charles to drug me so that she could interrogate me further? As a lure, I'd been made somewhat immune to every known drug at the time of my creation, but newer drugs *could* affect me, as I'd discovered when I'd gone undercover in Winter Halo.

I trusted Charles, I really did, but I couldn't ignore the possibility that his sense of duty had forced him to take a step he otherwise wouldn't.

"Shall we sit?" he asked, waving one hand toward the plush sofa.

I nodded and did so, but when he moved toward one of the chairs, I laughed and patted the cushion next to me. "I'm not that mad, Charles."

He smiled and sat beside me, his thigh pressing lightly against mine. Unfortunately, the fact that we were both fully clothed prevented my seeking skill from getting anything more than vague flashes, and they really didn't tell me anything other than the fact he was frustrated. Whether that meant sexually or otherwise, I couldn't say.

I put the cognac on the table then lightly placed a hand on top of his. But the flashes remained vague, and that was decidedly strange. Charles had always been something of an open book, so why couldn't I read him now?

Had Dream given him a charm to counter my seeking skills?

It was possible, but if she *had*, then it was something that was more concealable than the ones around my wrists, given the short sleeves and open neckline of his shirt. Nor could I sense the flicker of foulness that seemed so much a part of her power. But maybe the magic within a charm was simply too small to register. Or perhaps the fact I was wearing Nuri's charms was not only protecting me, but also preventing me from sensing other magic.

"I'm sorry you had to cut short your dinner with Karlinda," I said. "I imagine such an invitation is a rare one to receive, even though you and Julius are friends."

"Invitations have been few and far between since her illness," he agreed, "but there will be other times."

"What do the medics say about her illness? Why haven't they traced its source if she's been ill for so long?"

He shrugged, a movement that brushed his shoulders against mine. Desire didn't stir; it had no hope against the rising tide of trepidation. The longer I stayed here, instinct said, the greater the danger. But yet if I left now it would not only be out of character, but also suspicious to both Charles and Dream. I had to continue playing the game until it became absolutely necessary to do otherwise.

And it wasn't as if this was the first dangerous situation I'd ever been placed in. My life during the war had always been a balancing act in which one wrong word or deed could have spelled the end—and very nearly had on more than one occasion.

"The ceremony was the first time I'd seen Julius in a while.

He didn't share details on her condition, and I didn't think it polite to ask." He placed his drink down on the table and then shifted to face me. "May I kiss you, Catherine?"

"Indeed you can."

He immediately gathered me in his arms and did so. As kisses went, it was an ardent, urgent, but oddly desperate thing, and once again it was concern that stirred more than desire. Even weirder was the fact that despite this more intimate connection, I still wasn't picking up anything other than vague smudges from his thoughts. He was definitely wearing some sort of charm.

And that meant, whether I wanted to believe it or not, he was here under Dream's orders, even if *he* believed the request had come from Karlinda.

I eventually pulled away and then reached for a cognac—his, not mine. He smiled, picked up the other glass, and then clicked it lightly against mine. "To a desire that has not banked for either of us."

I smiled and took a drink. He downed his quickly then pushed to his feet. "Another?"

"Yes, thank you." I drank the remainder and handed him the glass. If my drink *had* been spiked, then it would soon become apparent given how quickly he'd consumed it. He walked across the room, refilled the glasses, and then returned. If he'd slipped something into the drink the first time, he certainly hadn't tried it the second. He handed me the drink and sat back down.

I took a sip and then we kissed again, no less urgently on his part and still with that odd edge of desperation.

For the next few minutes there was no sound, but this time, when we parted, an odd buzzing seemed to fill my ears, and my head was starting to spin. For one insane second, I thought it was lack of air, but then the reality hit.

My drink hadn't been drugged. His *had*.

Once again Dream had been one step ahead.

"Oh, Charles," I said, as he plucked the glass from my nonresistant fingertips and placed it back on the table. "You have no idea what you've just done."

The disorientation was getting worse, and my breath was a now short, sharp pant of air. Whatever he'd given me, it was obviously a newer drug, not an older one. I took as deep a breath as I could in an effort to drop into a semitrance state, and reached for the healing magic to chase the drug from my system.

Only I couldn't.

It wasn't there. Or rather, it was, but I was unable to reach what was a vital part of my DNA.

Whatever I'd been given had basically placed a chemical wall between my psychic gifts and me.

"I've done what I had to do." His voice was flat and yet held twin edges of anger and sorrow. "If you are innocent of the crimes Karlinda has leveled against you, then I ask forgiveness. But if you are not—"

He didn't finish the sentence. He didn't need to.

I licked my lips and tried to ignore the roaring that was sounding louder in my brain. "Charles, Karlinda is not who you think she is. You have to believe me—you *have* to trust me—"

"I cannot," he cut in. "Not when you threatened the lives of two people and have used your position as my lover to rob countless of my friends."

Confusion ran through me. "In Rhea's name, *none* of that is true—"

"I saw the security tapes," he cut in fiercely. "You held a gun to that woman's spine and threatened to *kill* her."

Meaning there *had* been security cameras in that corridor even if I hadn't seen them. "Yes, but not for the reasons you think. Charles, you have to listen—"

"No, I don't." He thrust to his feet, his movement filled with repressed anger and his eyes blazing. "You are not what you seem and this—you and I—is nothing more than a sham."

I opened my mouth to deny it, but no sound came out. In growing panic, I reached for Cat and Bear, not sure what they'd be able to do but not wanting to be alone.

But the mental lines were dead. Our connection had been severed right along with every other psychic skill.

I swore and tried to get up, tried to fight him and escape, but my flesh was unresponsive. The last thing I saw before unconsciousness took me was not Charles's back as he opened the door, but rather Karlinda's victorious expression as she stepped into the room.

Dream had finally ensnared me.

CHAPTER TWELVE

WAKING WAS PAINFUL.

My head felt like it was full of roaches trying to claw their way out, and my body was on fire. Sweat poured from my forehead, dripped from my spine, and appeared to be creating an ever-increasing pool underneath me. Pain was a sledgehammer that crashed through every sensory outlet, and it felt like my head was about to explode.

It was a feeling I was familiar with, as I'd suffered the exact same symptoms when Branna had darted me with *Iruakandji* the day I'd first entered Nuri's bar with Penny and an injured Jonas. It was a drug that had been developed in the latter part of the war by the HDP, and one that had been rarely used. While it *had* killed shifters with great alacrity, it had proven unviable in real-time usage. Not only had it been extremely costly to make, but it was also very deadly to déchet, no matter how little shifter they had. Even we lures had not been immune to its effects, although for the most part, it didn't actually kill us. It just put us through many hours of hell.

But the *Iruakandji* was not the worst of it, because there were heavy weights on my wrists and my ankles, and a fierce heat burning against my skin. My *naked* skin, if the cold feel of the concrete against my shoulders and butt was anything to go by.

I forced my eyes open, desperate to see where I was. It was a concrete box little more than six by six with no windows and no obvious air system, although there had to be something here, given I wasn't suffocating. The bright lights weren't UV, which was rather surprising, but they were uncomfortably warm and hurt my eyes.

Even so, I could see the cameras. My movements were being monitored.

The door was solid metal, and it was inset into the doorframe, meaning it was sliding and, as such, left no space between the door and the frame. And that meant that even if I could draw a light-blocking shield around me and then become shadow, I would not be able to escape this place.

Jonas said it's better not to escape, Cat said softly. Wearily. *They intend to use this development to bring down Dream.*

It was all I could do not to snap my head around in her direction. I hadn't even sensed they were near—obviously, whatever drug Charles had given me still lingered in my system.

Are you two okay? You sound weary.

Yes, they both said. *But it was a long night.*

I pushed up into a sitting position—an action that not only sent the roaches into a fever pitch and had sweat dripping down the side of my face, but also had the chains on my wrists snapping tight. Those chains were solid silver and would have burned the hell out of me if I'd been, as my RFID chip said, a full shifter. I wasn't, so they did little more than warm my skin.

Of course, it also told my jailers that my RFID chip had been tampered with.

I shifted my butt backwards until my spine was pressed against the wall and then hugged my knees to my chest in an effort to keep upright. It was a position that pulled the chains on both my ankles and wrists tight, but I didn't care. The roaches now seemed intent on eating my brain and the pain was unlike anything I'd ever experienced before. They'd obviously upped the dosage this time. I closed my eyes and breathed in slowly—deeply—until the sensation faded enough to think. Speak.

What happened while I was out of it?

They gave you a truth drug when you started showing signs of awareness. Exhaustion ran through Bear's mental tone. *Hedda Lang was here, interrogating you.*

And? I asked, my heart suddenly somewhere in the middle of my throat.

She got nothing about any of us, Cat replied. *Not the bunker, not who we are—who you really are—and nothing about Nuri, Jonas, or anyone else. We made sure of it.*

A mix of astonishment and pride at their initiative ran through me. *How did you manage that against someone like Dream?*

You know how we created the deeper connection that allowed us to taste the macaroon? Bear said. *We did that, but instead of sharing taste, we were able to curtail what you said.*

Oh Rhea, no *wonder* they were so damn tired! *If I could hug you two without making those watching the cameras suspicious, I would. But it was a damn big risk to take with Dream in the room. If she'd sensed you—*

But she couldn't, Cat said. *This room is shielded against psychic and magical intrusion. It restricts her.*

If that's the case, why is it not stopping me from conversing with you?

Because we three are one, Cat said. *It was only the drugs that stopped you hearing us earlier.*

So where are we?

In specialized holding cells under the Ministry of Home Defense building, Bear said. *You have been here for two days.*

Two days? That wasn't good, given Nuri's three days until hell breaks out declaration. If she was right, then that event would happen tonight.

Yes, Bear said. *Dawn has only just risen.*

Sunrise was something I would normally feel, so whatever they were using to block psychic abilities was also affecting my vampire soul.

What are Nuri and Jonas currently doing?

Working on getting you out of here, Cat said. *But more than that, we do not know. Jonas wanted us here, keeping you safe.*

He was decidedly angry when we all lost contact with you so abruptly, Bear added.

That, Cat said, in a superior sort of tone, *wasn't anger but rather fear. Trust me, I can sense these things.*

A smile twitched my lips, and I quickly ducked my head so that the cameras didn't pick it up. And noticed in doing so that I was no longer wearing Nuri's charms. I guess that was no surprise. I dare say I'd also been internally examined to ensure I'd had no devices and micro-armaments hidden.

Did they give you any idea at all just how they intended to free me?

No, they just said to trust them, even when all seems dire.

I did trust them, even if the statement didn't overly imbue much confidence. *I'm going to try and drop into the healing state. Can you wake me if anyone approaches? But stay in the cell—you both need to rest and regain your strength as well.*

As their yeses ran through my thoughts, I closed my eyes and started the deep-breathing exercise that would drop me down into the healing state. It wasn't easy. In fact, for several minutes it felt like I was swimming through a sea of thick, gelatinous muck—one that rather reminded me of the shielding barriers around the rifts. Maybe Dream had added her own barriers to what was already present.

But as with the rifts, I eventually did push through, and relief stirred as the healing began. Because if I could push through the restrictions to heal, then I could probably do the same when it came to my other skills.

Time passed, though I had little awareness of it given the deepness of the trance.

But as full awareness began to return, I heard the cell door retract. I didn't open my eyes, but flared my nostrils, drawing in a deeper breath to sort through the various scents. The overwhelming stench of my own body hit me first, but underneath that was a scent I was all too familiar with.

It wasn't Hedda or even Karlinda, as I'd been expecting, but rather Charles. And he was angry—at me, at himself, and at the entire situation.

The door slid shut behind him, and for several minutes, silence reigned. But I could feel his gaze on me. Feel his increasing anger and flare of disgust.

"I know you're awake," he said abruptly. "They're monitoring your movements and life signs in the control center."

It was only at that moment I realized I was still wearing Catherine's shape rather than my own. Obviously, despite being knocked out and drugged, I hadn't reached the point of exhaustion. Instinct, and perhaps even Cat and Bear's deep connection with me, had helped me maintain form, and thereby the identity lie.

I didn't move, didn't look up, and didn't bother to reply. Everything that needed to be said had been said. I wasn't even truly mad with him, because from his point of view, with the information he'd been given, he'd done exactly what duty and any clear-thinking individual might have done. And, when it came down to it, I *had* been using him. In that, he'd been very correct.

But I *was* annoyed at him. Annoyed that he hadn't given me the benefit of the doubt—that he hadn't even offered me the chance to explain.

"Your trial starts at three this afternoon," he continued. "It is the last order of business for the day."

I couldn't help wondering if that was Dream's doing. Couldn't help wondering if the lateness of the hour was part of her schemes, and part of the doom Nuri saw rising.

"I have insisted that you be given the chance to bathe before then. However great your crime, it is not right for you to be treated this way."

I remained silent. He was the reason I was in this place, and I had no intention of making anything easy on him—especially when I suspected his reasons for being here came from a vague sense of uneasiness and guilt.

"They did a search of your apartment," he said. "They found the guns and the old uniform."

Again, I refused to respond.

He dragged in a ragged-sounding breath. "For Rhea's sake, Catherine, talk to me!"

I finally opened my eyes and looked at him "Why? What difference does it make? You've already made up your mind about me, so what else needs to be said?"

He scrubbed a hand through his hair. "I don't know. I just —" He stopped and shrugged. "I'd hoped there was a good reason for your actions, but I guess in the end it doesn't really matter, does it?"

"It matters, Charles, more than you can *ever* imagine," I

replied, battling to keep my voice even. "Just not for the reasons you think. And when this is all over, kindly remember that never once did you give me the benefit of the doubt. You believed everything they said about me, even if it contradicted everything you knew about me."

He frowned. "I'm not sure I—"

"No, you wouldn't," I cut in. "But you will, and soon. Are you going to be at the trial?"

He hesitated, confusion flickering briefly through his expression. "Yes, because I'm a witness."

Of course he was. Aside from that video, the clothes and the guns they'd found in my apartment, they had little other real evidence against me. It was the fake evidence and the trumped-up charges that were worrying me, though. Dream —in whatever incarnation she might be wearing—would ask for the death penalty, and if current laws followed laws of old, then evidence against me had to be pretty serious for that to even be considered.

"Thank you for coming to see me, and I would indeed appreciate the chance to freshen up should it happen. But do not expect anything more than that out of me. *Ever*." I paused, and grabbed hold of the anger that had come pouring out at that last word. "I hope you have a long and fruitful life, Charles, without too many regrets."

He frowned, but obviously recognized a dismissal when he heard one. With a sharp nod, he spun around and walked out. The hallway beyond, I noted, was as fiercely bright as this cell. There were also two guards standing opposite my door—both heavily armed—but the bigger threat was the cameras themselves. I dare not wrap a light shield around me and become shadow to escape—not in this cell and certainly *not* when I was taken upstairs for the trial. To do either would be to reveal myself as déchet, and that was something I refused to do. If death was declared my fate, then I'd go down fighting, but I would die in human form and without the tag of monster to follow me into the afterlife.

No matter what does happen, Bear said, *we will fight by your side.*

I know. And I love you both for it, but I don't want either of you to save my life at the cost of your own. I paused, and then added, *If this is to be my end, then I need you both to guide my soul back to the little ones. We cannot leave them alone.*

No, they agreed. *Already they are scared, even though we have told them all is well and that you will be back soon.*

I closed my eyes and tried to ignore the ache that ran through my soul. But one way or another, I would soon be back to them, especially if I believed Nuri's proclamation

And I did.

More time passed. Eventually, the door opened again and three men stepped into the room. None of them said a word, and only one of them was armed. One of the unarmed men stepped forward, placed a metal collar around my neck, and then handed the long chain to the other unarmed man. The cuffs on my wrists and ankles were then unlocked and I was gruffly told to rise.

I did so. Pain slithered down my legs, but it came more from them being locked in one position for so long rather than any lingering damage from the various wounds I'd received recently.

The man holding the end of my chain turned and walked out, forcing me to follow. One of the armed guards in the overly bright corridor preceded us; the rest followed.

We reached the end of the long, somewhat soulless corridor and went through another door that bristled with all sorts of scanning equipment. No alarms sounded, so obviously both the guns and my DNA had already been taken into account.

It was a thought that had fear stirring anew. *Did they take blood samples when I was under?*

Yes, Bear said. *Several vials of it. They also took saliva samples.*

Meaning pretending to be anything *other* than what I really was might now be useless. When the results of the two were combined, the presence of several déchet markers in my DNA would be revealed. With that sort of information, Dream could make a viable case for my immediate destruction.

We marched down another long corridor—this one lined with doors on either side—and then reached a sort of antechamber. It was again solid concrete and circular in shape, with a seating area on the left side and six shower-heads on the right. As bathing facilities went, it was as basic as you could get, but I wasn't about to complain. Not when I smelled so bad it was turning even *my* stomach.

The guard motioned me toward the nearest shower. I stepped underneath it, and a mix of heated water and air instantly began to blast me. I raised my arms, turning one way and then the other—or as much as the leash would allow—to wash the grime away. After no more than a couple of minutes, the water stopped and, once the air jets had dried the remaining droplets from my skin, I was handed some clothes—a loose pair of pants that tied at the waist, a shirt, and a pair of boots.

Once I'd dressed, I was led out into another corridor—this one shorter—and then into a waiting elevator. One of the guards scanned his RFID chip, the elevator doors closed, and we were quickly whisked upward.

We entered another antechamber, but this one bristled with light panels, cameras, mobile autosentry guns, *and* armed guards. Dream wasn't taking any chances on my escaping this time.

A set of heavy, intricately carved metal doors dominated the wall directly opposite the elevator; from beyond it came a single voice, but I couldn't make out what he was saying.

Do you want me to scout the situation in the next room? Bear said.

I hesitated. *It might be better not to. If Dream senses your presence, she might just raise a spell to either displace you or to stop you from interfering.*

Or worse.

She'll sense our presence anyway, Cat said. *Because you're not going in there alone.*

A smile tugged at my lips before I could control it. *I know, and I wasn't about to suggest that anyway. I'm hoping all her attention will be on me, so if you keep close to the roof, it's possible she won't sense you.*

I was escorted to the doors and then told to stop. I flexed my fingers, trying to ease some of the tension flowing through me, but that slight movement had the sentry guns on either side of the door coming to life and their barrels swinging around to face me.

I froze and, after another minute, they went dark again. Even so, it was a timely reminder not to make any untoward movement once I was in the chamber beyond.

I reached instead for the light. While I had no intention of creating a shield, I needed to know if my ability to do so remained hampered. Once again my efforts were met by the gelatinous soup. I swore internally and pushed down into it. After a few moments, I felt the caresses of energy across my skin and the air briefly sparkled. I immediately released it and reached instead for the vampire part of my soul. Shadows stirred in response, but the brightness of the surrounding lights prevented it from doing any more than that.

I nevertheless felt like rejoicing. I might not want to use either ability unless it was an absolute last resort, but at least I *could* if it became necessary.

The voice coming from the other room stopped and locks tumbled as the huge doors in front of me began to open. Once there was a four-foot gap—the width required for the two sentry guns to get through, I suspected—they stopped. The guard holding my chain walked forward. I had no choice but to follow.

The vast hall beyond was a mix of white stone, gold, and

rich woods. Huge arched windows lined either side, and long flags bearing the various coats of arms of the House's lords hung from the ceiling, providing a rich spectrum of color to the otherwise cold space. At the far end of the room stood a raised platform, and in center of this was an ornate gold speaker's dais. To the right there was a large, plush-looking chair, and on the left six plainer ones. Below and to the right of the platform was what looked like a silver bird-cage. On the other side was a doorway that appeared every bit as solid and as intricately carved as the one I'd just passed through.

Three stepped rows of padded seating lined either side of the room, but only three-quarters of the seats were taken. I scanned the many faces but I couldn't see Karlinda, Hedda, or even Julius. I did spot Charles. He had a front seat view near the dais.

The soft murmur of conversation disappeared as we entered, and in the heavy silence I was led down the center of the room. The three-foot-wide matting under our feet deadened the sound of our footsteps, and the accompanying sentry guns were as silent as my ghosts as they rolled along either side of us.

The guard holding my chain walked across to the cage and directed me to step inside. Once I had, he wound up the chain, locked it onto the frame of the cage with a U-bolt, and then closed the door. The auto-sentry guns positioned themselves on either side of the cage.

I really hoped Nuri and Jonas did have a plan, because I wasn't getting out of this with any sort of ease.

A woman stepped up to the dais and proceeded to read out

a long list of crimes—real and imagined. I paid them no heed and scanned the area instead, wondering where Dream was.

Karlinda watches proceedings in a small room behind the dais, Bear said. *But she does not feel like Dream feels.*

Meaning it was more than likely the *real* chancellor. *And Hedda Lang?*

She waits outside the main doors with five other people, Cat said. *And she* does *feel like Dream.*

Is she armed?

No.

Which at least meant that if Jonas and Nuri's rescue plan went wrong, Dream couldn't simply turn around and shoot me. Of course, she didn't actually have to. As Hedda Lang, she could order either the autosentries or the many guards around the room to do it. And it wasn't like I could escape the gunfire. I might be able to reach my psychic talents, but it would take far too much time to break through the soup. Bullets would rip me to shreds long before I could draw a strong enough shield around my body to cut the light and become shadow.

Who are the other five people with her?

I don't know, Cat said. *There are three men and two women.*

Two of their number would undoubtedly be the couple I'd threatened to get onto the rooftop. Charles had said he'd seen the videos, but maybe this court also required direct evidence. I had no idea who the other three were—but, given the continuing assortment of trumped-up charges, they were obviously meant to be additional witnesses.

When the reading of my crimes had finally come to an end, Karlinda appeared on the platform and moved to the solitary chair. Once she was seated, she said, in a voice that was surprisingly strong given her frail appearance, "Let the proceedings begin."

"Who gives evidence to prove these crimes?" the speaker immediately asked.

The doors opened and six people stepped into the room. One was indeed Dream in her Hedda guise, although the foul feel of her energy was severely muted by whatever spells or charms were being used to protect this room and the people within it. The fact I could feel that much gave me greater hope that those same restrictions were increasingly unable—for whatever reason—to curtail my abilities. The two people I'd threatened were indeed in the group, but the remaining three were strangers. All six stepped onto the platform and said, "We do."

There was a scuff of noise to my left as Charles stood up. "As do I."

He made his way from the seating area to the platform, his gaze studiously on the platform and the speaker rather than me. But he was well aware that I watched him, if the increasing stain of red on his neck and cheeks were anything to go by.

"Prosecutor, please present your case and question your witnesses," the speaker said, and then stepped away from the dais.

What followed was a long and rather tedious session designed purely to add weight to my supposed guilt. I had no idea how much time actually passed; the light coming in through the windows was as intense as ever, but the vampire part of my soul whispered dusk was close.

As was whatever doom Nuri had foreseen.

Once the five people and Charles had been questioned, the speaker said, "Is there anyone here who wishes to act on behalf of the accused, and cross-examine the witnesses?"

I half hoped Jonas or Nuri would appear to do just that, but it didn't happen. I curbed my frustration, tried to ignore the ever-increasing feeling that time was running out, and said, "I would like to act on my own behalf."

A murmur ran through the room; the speaker waited for it to die down and then said, "That is not allowed. You must find a champion or remain silent."

"Then this court makes a mockery of justice."

Another murmur ran across the room, but this time it was edged with surprise and perhaps a hint of anger—both undoubtedly due to the mere thought of *anyone* daring question the integrity of the process.

"Guards," the speaker said. "If she speaks again out of turn, gag her."

So much for the integrity of the process, but I guess with Dream basically in charge of the Department of Home Defense, the likelihood of true justice happening had always been minute.

The speaker dismissed the witnesses, and once Charles had resumed his position, finally called Hedda Lang onto the witness stand. Metal glittered on her wrist as she stepped forward, and it took me a moment to realize what it was. She was wearing one of Nuri's charms—the one that protected her from the attacks of both a magical and psi nature. It obviously didn't curtail the nature of the spells that protected this room, but it *would* make it damnably difficult for Nuri to attack her magically if and when both she and Jonas got here. Of course, Nuri might also be curtailed by the room's spell work.

Hedda presented all her so-called evidence of my crimes, including the video Charles had mentioned, and another of the search of my apartment that had resulted in finding the guns and my old uniform.

When she'd finished, the prosecutor said, "And what sentence are you asking this court to approve for these crimes?"

Dream looked directly at me, and said, with more venom than even Branna had flung my way, "Death."

Another murmur ran around the room. Karlinda raised a hand before the speaker could intervene, and silence instantly fell.

"The crimes, as grievous as they are, do not warrant such a sentence, Director Lang. Unless you can provide this court with more evidence, the penalty of death cannot be requested or applied."

Hedda's answering smile was a cold and evil thing that chilled the very core of my being.

"If the court so wishes, I ask that Doctor Jason Harding be called onto the witness stand."

My heart began beating a whole lot faster. I very much suspected what was now coming, and I feared it. Feared the response of both the people *and* the machines around me.

A call immediately went out and, after a few minutes, a small, bald man appeared. He looked ill at ease with all the attention suddenly on him, but nevertheless strode to the platform without faltering. Once there, he took Hedda's position on the witness stand and, when the prosecutor asked for his professional qualifications, said, "I'm the director of the Bernstein Laboratories."

"And your connection to this case?"

He glanced at me and my heart sunk. I'd seen that look before—it was the same sort of expression the scientists in the HDP creations labs got when the latest bonding experiment proved successful. In the professor's eyes, I wasn't a flesh and blood being, but rather a sum of DNA that needed to be taken apart and very carefully examined.

"Doctor?" the prosecutor prompted.

"Ah, yes, sorry," he said. "We were asked to process and report back on some DNA samples by Director Lang."

"And is that not outside of normal procedure?" the prosecutor said. "Home Security has its own crime labs, after all."

"Yes, but there were irregularities in the DNA sample they could not explain, so they asked us to investigate further."

"And this DNA—did it belong to anyone in this room."

"It was marked as belonging to Catherine Lysandra."

The prosecutor unnecessarily motioned to me. "And what conclusion did you come to?"

"That her DNA is something that has not been seen since the war," he said. "It tells us she is neither human nor shifter. That she is, in fact, déchet."

Rhea help me, I thought, and closed my eyes, waiting for the hail of bullets that would end my life. The energy of my two ghosts buzzed around me, ready to protect me though not even they could prevent every single gun in this room from firing, let alone protect me from the subsequent rain of metal.

But there were no gunshots, just a chaotic tumble of noise that was both disbelief and fear.

"Enough!" Karlinda's voice rang out clearly over the pandemonium and silence again fell. "That is *clearly* impossible, Doctor. All remaining déchet were rounded up and erased in the aftermath of the war. It is simply unthinkable that any could have escaped that net."

"And yet the results of our tests cannot be argued with," the doctor said. "I can bring in as many of our technicians as you desire, but the test result will remain the same. Her genome sequencing is unlike anything we've seen, and it matches the very few HDP records that *do* remain."

"Are you, beyond a doubt, certain of this?"

"As certain as we ever can be given the majority of the department's documents were destroyed alongside the déchet."

"This is the reason I ask for the death penalty," Hedda said. "It's not because of the crimes she stands accused of here today, but because she is an unwanted—and very dangerous —leftover of a bygone era. The sentence of death was given a long time ago; it is up to this court to apply it."

"If Catherine Lysandra is to be given a death sentence for having unusual sequencing," a new and very familiar voice declared. "Then perhaps you'd better sentence me to that same fate."

Relief washed through me and I briefly closed my eyes.

Jonas.

Finally.

He strode through the doors in full ranger uniform and didn't even glance my way. But I nevertheless felt the rush of both his anger and his concern. It chased away some of the fear that had settled deep inside me, even though I was far from out of the woods—or the cage—just yet.

"By whose permission do you barge into the middle of this hearing and make such a statement?" the prosecutor said. "You have no right—"

"He has every right," another voice said. "As he is here under my protection *and* command."

My gaze snapped past Jonas. Julius Valkarie stepped into the room, flanked by four heavily armed guards. His gaze settled on mine briefly, and there wasn't a scrap of fear or loathing to be seen.

Jonas, I said, *what in Rhea is going on?*

I promised to rescue you. He stopped in front of the platform and bowed to Karlinda. *And I never break a promise.*

Of that I'm glad, but how did you draw Julius into it?

That was the easy part, he replied. *And the fun has only just begun.*

As long as your version of fun doesn't involve gunfire, because I'm standing here trussed tighter than a boar ready for cooking, and under the watchful metal eyes of two autosentries.

Julius has sent his men into the control room. The sentries will soon be deactivated, and the chain clamp released.

Dream will have loyalists scattered amongst the guards in this room. If she feels threatened, she will order them to shoot, and escape in the confusion.

Oh, I have no doubt she will try both, but trust me when I say escape is not an option for her today. This room is completely sealed.

Aside from the open door, you mean.

There're a hundred men lining that corridor, and full magic shields enabled. She won't get past them, no matter what she tries.

I hoped he was right. But the day was getting older and Nuri's deadline was drawing closer, and I had a bad, *bad* feeling that even if we killed Dream right now, her plans would remain in play and cause chaos to the people and the city we both cared about.

The prosecutor cleared his voice and then said, "Chief Director Valkarie, to what do we owe this honor?"

"I'm here to see justice done. Right now, I don't believe that to be so."

Two of the guards accompanying him stopped either side of him. A third moved to the steps closest to the door, and the fourth man moved across to my side of the platform. Their guns, I was relieved to see, were not aimed at me, but rather held in a "ready" position that was semi-aimed at the stage.

Dream didn't seem to notice—or, if she did, she didn't think anything of it. Though her expression was one of annoyance, there was no indication that she thought this anything more than a minor blip in her plans.

"Director," she said. "I don't understand the reason for your presence here. You yourself signed the approval for both this trial and the DNA tests, and the authenticity of the results—both from our labs *and* from Bernstein's—have been verified."

"Indeed they have," Julius replied evenly. "It's the conclusion—that Catherine Lysandra is in fact a surviving remnant of an atrocity long thought erased—that I'm calling into question."

"And what evidence do you give to back these claims?" the prosecutor said. "Because your word is not enough I'm afraid, Chief Director."

"I would hope not," he replied coolly, and motioned someone near the door to come forward.

A dark-haired, brown-skinned man climbed the steps and walked across the platform to the witness stand.

"Introduce yourself," Julius said.

The man cleared his throat, and with a somewhat apologetic look at Professor Harding said, "My name is Doctor Karl Wainsworth, and I'm also a director at Bernstein's."

"And why are you here today?"

"I was asked to run tests on a blood sample by yourself, Chief Director."

"And where did this sample come from?"

"From the ex-ranger standing beside you, sir."

"And you're absolutely sure of this?" Julius said. "You can positively guarantee that the sample was not tampered with in any way?"

"Yes, because I took both the blood and DNA samples myself."

As murmurs ran through the room, the U-bolt holding my chains in place snapped open. A heartbeat later, the red light that indicated the cage was locked flicked across to green. The collar remained in place, but at least I could now move if I needed to.

Good, Jonas said, obviously catching my thoughts. *Because you will need to get out of that cage fast. The shit is about to hit the proverbial fan.*

I don't suppose you care to illuminate me on how?

And spoil the surprise?

I snorted softly and flexed my fingers—and then froze, waiting for the autosentries to react. They didn't, but their deactivation failed to make me feel any safer. Not when so many armed guards remained in the room; not when we had no idea just how many of them might be loyal to Dream or the woman they knew as Hedda Lang.

"And what did your results reveal?"

"That the ranger has a mix of genes that has not been seen since the war." Wainsworth glanced across at his fellow doctor. "If we apply the same principles to my samples as to the one Doctor Harding investigated, then despite the fact that Ranger Galloway had an illustrious career during the war *and* was heavily involved in the cleanup and rebuilding process *after* it, he is also a déchet."

And by what piece of magic did you arrange that bit of nonsense? I asked.

His amusement ran through my mind, as warm as the sun on a bright summer day. *In case you've forgotten, we were in a rift together. There's no other trickery—magical or otherwise—needed. The results are fact, not fiction.*

Another murmur ran across the room. My gaze flicked to Dream. Her expression was anything but happy, but I wasn't getting any sense that she was overly worried by the current turn of events—probably because even if Wainsworth's testimony took the prospect of my being a dreaded déchet off the table, she still had me for all the other crimes.

"And what do you believe is the reason behind these abnormal readouts?"

"I believe the cause is the same one that led to Ranger Galloway being outcast—he is a declared rift survivor."

Dream snorted. "There's no record of Galloway being caught in a rift with a vampire."

"There's no such record for *any* survivor," Julius stated. "As you should be well aware, Hedda. Nor is there any requirement either these days *or* back then for survivors to declare such information."

"Be *that* as it may," Dream said. "There is also no record of Catherine Lysandra being a rift survivor."

"No, because many still fear the specter of being outcast, as it remains in law even if it is no longer applied."

Dream drew in a breath and released it slowly. "None of which alters the depth of her other crimes. I demand her sentence be deportation to the Higain penal settlement."

Where I would, undoubtedly, meet with an untimely end. At least I would if she had her way.

"*You* cannot demand anything," Julius said. "Please bring in my second witness."

Get ready to move, Tiger. Cat, Bear, make sure that guard on the left side of her cage doesn't get the chance to fire.

With pleasure, they intoned grimly.

As inconspicuously as I could, I removed the chain from the U-bolt. Several links clinked against each other and the guard on my right glanced my way. I ignored him, my gaze on the door, as if waiting like everyone else for Julius's next witness to be revealed.

When he was no longer looking at me, I switched the chain to my left hand and placed my right on the door. It moved fractionally but thankfully made no sound. Tension ran through me, and I barely restrained the desire to just get the hell out of the cage.

Footsteps began to echo in the hallway beyond—one set strong, the other less so. My gaze switched to Dream. There was just the slightest flicker of unease running through her expression, but she didn't look ready to run.

"You cannot keep bringing in witnesses without previous approval of the court, Chief of Home Securities or not." Her voice held just the slightest hint of rebuke. "This is an unwarranted action and the speaker should—"

"I cleared my actions with the chancellor before this trial began," he replied equally. "And she is the only authority in this court that I have to answer to."

Dream spun around. "Is this true? What game is being played here?"

"No game but justice," Karlinda replied. Though her back was to me, I didn't need to see her face to envisage her contempt. It was very evident in those four words.

"I wish to lodge an official protest—"

"So noted," Karlinda replied calmly. "Now please remain quiet until the next witness arrives."

Dream's gaze narrowed but she swung away from the chancellor and returned her attention to the door. But the first people through were guards. They walked up to the dais and silently moved around it, until it was completely surrounded. Three then moved up the stairs and stood either side of Karlinda.

The murmuring got louder, Dream's unease stronger.

Her fingers were flexing and the foul caress of magic began to stain the air.

She's gathering her magic, I warned Jonas.

She won't be able to do much, he said. *Not with the spells around this room.*

Are you sure of that?

Nuri is.

The footsteps drew ever closer, until, without any sort of fanfare, Nuri stepped into the room.

And with her was Hedda Lang.

She was pale, gaunt, and so unsteady on her feet that she continued to lean on Nuri, but it was unmistakably her.

"Now what game do you play?" Dream snapped, even as her fingers began to move faster. The threads of foulness were gathering around their tips, gradually forming a pulsating ball not dissimilar in feel and look to the shields that protected her rifts.

"No game," Julius replied, as half the guards surrounding the platform turned and raised their guns, covering Dream as much as protecting Karlinda and the speaker. "Although I, the Department of Home Security, and even Karlinda herself, have certainly been the targets of a most heinous one."

"I don't like what you're implying, Chief Director," she said, as her fingers stilled. "I have given the department nothing but the utmost loyalty for the majority of my life, even at the cost of my own personal life. I will not have you besmirch my reputation by bringing this wretched *look-alike—*"

"I am no look-alike," Lang said, as she and Nuri stopped beside Julius, "and I'm willing to take whatever tests are necessary to prove it. Are you, dear impersonator?"

Dream's eyes narrowed, and the ink-like foulness she'd gathered to her fingertips began quivering, as if it was about to be launched.

Jonas, warn Nuri Dream has gathered what I presume is some sort of energy weapon to her fingertips.

"Usurping my life and keeping me prisoner is one thing," Lang continued. "But you also attempted the same on my sister, and for *that* I cannot forgive you."

"This is insanity itself!" Dream's voice held an edge. "Chief, I demand you provide whatever proof you might have for believing this charlatan, or stand aside and let this court proceed."

"As you wish," Julius said. "Control, play the tape."

A light screen shimmered into existence. On it was a rather luxurious bed; in that bed was Karlinda. For several seconds there was no sound other than Karlinda's soft snores. Then somewhere beyond the camera's range came the sound of a door swishing open, and then Hedda Lang appeared on screen. She walked across the bed and for several seconds simply stared down at the woman who was her sister. Then she drew a syringe out of her pocket, gently pulled Karlinda's right arm from under the sheets, and withdrew blood—blood she subsequently squirted into her mouth.

A riot of denials erupted. Dream didn't move, didn't twitch. Her face was hard and her eyes narrowed. She was ready to move—to react—and yet still she waited.

I had a growing suspicion that we really shouldn't.

Jonas—

We cannot move on her yet, he said. *There is protocol to be followed, even when the crimes are as heinous as hers.*

That protocol might just allow the bitch to escape.

That protocol gave us the time to save your life and gather the necessary evidence against her. His voice was grim. *She won't escape, I promise you that.*

I didn't reply. I didn't even dare twitch. Because Dream's gaze was now on me, and there was an oddly gloating glint in her eyes. She might be about to go down, but she wasn't about to do so without taking me with her.

And *that* meant whatever she planned, it was more than just gunfire. Given how many soldiers Julius had bought into the room, the minute *any* of her people made a move toward their weapons, they'd quickly be dealt with.

Which meant it had to be something *other* than the sphere clinging to her fingertips. I had no idea what she intended with do with the thing, but given it felt similar to the rift shields, it most likely was some sort of barrier—though whether it was meant to protect her or do something else, I couldn't say. But she was well aware that I could pass through the rift barriers unchecked, so I doubted it would be used against me.

No, there had to be something else here. Something that had been planted well before this court had come into session.

Cat, I said abruptly, *do you want to check the area? Look for any sort of hidden weaponry. Look under chairs, nooks, and things like that.*

Done.

As she raced away, I dropped my gaze to the cage's floor. There didn't seem to be anything out of the ordinary, and if she'd had something along the lines of a detonation plate installed, I surely would have heard the soft click of it being armed as I'd stepped into the cage.

I glanced briefly at the light screen. Dream was still holding Karlinda's hand, but her form was now changing—shifting— to that of the woman still lying on the bed.

Movement caught my attention. I looked quickly back at Dream, but she remained in the exact same position.

But the foul ball was no longer wrapped around her fingers.

I swore softly and quickly looked around, trying to find the thing. After a moment, I caught its faint trail—it was tumbling through the air, heading straight toward the still open doors of the control room.

Jonas— I stopped abruptly as a soft click caught my attention. Nothing else immediately happened, but that creeping sense of doom became a flood.

Out of sheer instinct, I pushed through the soup restraining my powers and then started gathering threads of light to me. I didn't immediately weave the shield but rather held them at the ready.

The foul ball hit the doors into the control room and then spread, a canker that clung weblike to the metal. No one else seemed to notice, but even as I thought that, I saw Nuri's head snap around and her gaze narrow.

Energy stirred, its feel bright and clean, and the foul net began to quiver. It did not fall, however.

Another soft beep caught my attention.

Frowning, I studied the cage again and then looked up. Nothing. So where was that damn sound coming from?

I returned my gaze to Dream. She had one hand in her pocket and she was very obviously holding something. For several seconds we simply stared at each other—her eyes glinting with triumph while my gut churned with ever-increasing fear.

Then she silently mouthed, *Goodbye.*

At the same time, Cat screamed, *Bomb!*

I cast the shield around me, called to the shadows within my soul, and then threw myself out of the cage. But even as I did, a huge eruption of heated air clubbed me, battering me sideways and then sending me tumbling head over heels. I crashed into the corner of the dais near the rear wall, and was battered by a tidal wave of wood and metal and bloody bits of flesh. My head rang and the various parts of my body that hadn't quite shifted pulsed with pain. Warmth flowed down my leg and neck, but it didn't matter. I'd survived the blast.

Given the number of body parts around me, so many others hadn't.

I released the light shield, regained full flesh form, and then pushed up onto my hands and knees. I couldn't immediately see anything more than a blur of smoke. After a moment I realized why, and scrubbed a hand across my eyes to clear the blood clinging to my eyelashes.

And saw utter devastation.

The bomb must have been planted under the seating nearest my cage. The guards and the lords who'd been sitting there were nothing more than raw remnants barely resembling anything human, but the main force of the blast had been directed at me rather than them, and those who'd been seated farther away were bloody but alive. And being herded out the building—Charles amongst them.

Jonas? I said urgently. *Are you okay?*

Yes. His reply was a little groggy, but fierce relief shot through me. *As are Julius, Nuri, and Karlinda.*

And Dream?

But even as I asked that question, I heard footsteps and looked up. Dream was on the move, but she wasn't running away. She was coming straight at *me*.

And she was armed with a wooden stake.

With a scream that was all madness and anger, she launched off the stage, the stake held high and ready to use as she arrowed toward me.

I thrust away from her and then spun around, lashing out with one leg. She landed with catlike surety and twisted away from the blow, and in that moment, I saw a glint of metal in her other hand. I swore and launched at her, grabbing at her, but she was faster than a lizard and, in one smooth movement, dodged, raised the gun, and fired.

But just as she did, Bear hit her and knocked her sideways. The bullet that would have blasted my face apart tore instead into the wall three feet away. As she stumbled and fell, the weapon went flying. Bear chased after it.

Cat, grab that stake, I said, even as I hit the ground and rolled back up to my feet.

Dream was down, but she was twisting and cursing as she battled the unseen force that was Cat for the control of the stake. And then she started speaking, and though I didn't understand the words, I felt the rise of energy and Cat's squeal of surprise. I quickly stepped forward and stomped as hard as I could down onto Dream's stomach.

Her breath left in a sudden wheeze and the force of the spell died. Cat ripped the stake from Dream's grip and Bear, who now held the gun, hovered several feet away. Given the anger emanating from both ghosts, Dream only had to twitch the wrong way for that gun to be fired.

Cat handed me the stake. I sat astride Dream's stomach and placed my knees on her arms to hold them still. She bucked and heaved, trying to dislodge me, but I held on tight. When that didn't work, she began mouthing words that were undoubtedly the beginnings of another spell. As the threads of foul energy began to weave around me, I raised the stake high and thrust it into her shoulder. As much as I wanted to plunge it into her black heart, it would have killed her far too quickly.

But like me, she had vampire genes, though hers had come from a rift rather than scientific modification.

Like me, she would burn. Burn as fiercely as if she were standing in the fires of hell itself. And it wouldn't end, not until the stake was removed, and I had no intention of doing that.

The pain was obviously so fierce that she could no longer hold an alternate image. Her body rippled and pulsated with a savageness I knew from experience would—under any other circumstance—be both excruciating and draining, and the black-skinned, green-eyed woman I'd glimpsed only twice soon appeared.

Her eyes were little more than slits, her face pale with shock and agony, and she was beginning to stink of sweat and fear. But all I could feel was her fury.

"You think you've won?" Her words were little more than vicious pants of air. "You have won *nothing*."

"Which is why you're now dying slowly rather than receiving a clean death," I replied evenly. "Tell me what you've done—what plans you have in place regarding the UV lights—and I'll end your life now rather than delighting in watching you suffer."

She hawked and spat. Bear batted the globule away before it got anywhere near me.

"You'll get nothing from me." Her breathing was faster, her words more difficult to hear, and her body temperature was increasing so rapidly my thighs were heating up. "And my pain is nothing compared to the utter desolation and despair that will soon overtake this city."

"It's impossible to totally erase light from this city," I said. "Even if you manage to bring the grid down, there are backup generators and battery-sourced units all across the city."

Her sudden smile had a chill running down my spine. "Keep thinking that, déchet. It will make the inevitability of both your death and that of this city so much sweeter."

Footsteps approached. I reached across, grabbed the gun

from Bear, and twisted around. Jonas raised an eyebrow at me and held up his hands—as did Julius. Neither of them had escaped unharmed—their clothes were torn and bloody, Jonas was limping and had a chunk out of his thigh, and Julius had a cut across his forehead and blood dripping from a roughly bandaged hand that was missing two fingers. But they were at least up and mobile. There were so many behind them who were not.

"I do hope," Julius said, "that it is not your intention to shoot us given our rather timely rescue of yourself."

"Sorry." I lowered the weapon. "I thought it might have been her people approaching."

"I rather think her people would have simply shot you." Julius squatted beside Dream, studying her as one might an interesting bug. "What madness has taken hold that you would risk this city's safety?"

Dream's breathing was now loud gasps for air, her body was shaking, her clothes drenched with sweat, and the fire caused by the stake so fierce her skin was beginning to glow an eerie yellow-orange. But she nevertheless dredged up the strength to say, "Madness? No. It's revenge. Revenge for everything your people did against mine."

"It was a *war*," he said. "Atrocities happened on both sides."

Which were the very same words I'd once said to Jonas. I could feel his gaze on me and looked up with a smile. He echoed it, but there was a tension in him, one that suggested he, like me, knew there was far more to come. That the destruction would not end with Dream's death.

"We've shut down your labs, and destroyed all the

pathogens and mutations you were developing," he said. "Your vampires will never now gain light immunity—"

"Maybe not in this generation, maybe not even in the next, but it will come." Her voice was little more than a harsh croak now, but it nevertheless resonated with satisfaction. "They have been given the basic framework. It will spread and grow, and then humanity and shifters alike will no longer dominate the landscape."

"But you're *human*, so why—" I hesitated as my seeking skills whispered her secrets to me. "You *were* a part of the HDP team."

Her gaze jumped back to mine and something cold—very alien—stirred in her eyes. "I ceased being human—ceased being Ciara Dream—the minute our paths crossed a vampire and a wraith in that rift."

Julius sucked in a breath. Obviously, Jonas and Nuri hadn't gotten around to telling him that particular part of the story. "You cannot have had dealings with the wraiths—that is *impossible*!"

"As impossible as déchet still being alive today," she agreed, and began to laugh.

Only her laughter gained a high note of keening that spoke of fear and grief, and then it became a whole lot more. It was almost, I thought with a chill, a call to arms. But who was she rallying? All her forces were surely either dead or captured....

She started to convulse. I thrust up and stepped away from her; her keening grew until the sound went beyond human ears—possibly even beyond shifter's ears—but not beyond mine.

But why— The thought stalled. I had *vampire* in me. This wasn't the crying of a dying woman in pain—she was mustering the vampires.

My gaze shot to the blown-out, broken remnants of the arched windows. Even though UV lights burned any hint of the oncoming night from the sky, they had no effect on my inner timer.

Dusk was settling across the sky high above us. Though the vampires might not yet dare to venture from the safety of their underground haunts, they would nevertheless hear the cry of their mistress. Not audibly, because I doubted Dream's keening, however high-pitched and powerful, could reach that far across the night.

But it didn't need to.

She was a part of the greater hive mind.

Her keening would echo through the entire population— not just through the den nearest to Central, but all of them.

And they would answer her call en masse.

Even as that thought crossed my mind, the lights went out.

CHAPTER THIRTEEN

THERE WAS a brief moment of shocked silence, and then a thick wave of confusion and terror hit the air. In the many years since the war, Central's citizens had never faced darkness. And while this room was a long way from the true ink of night, it didn't matter. Most of them were blind even in shadowed light.

Jonas wasn't. And, thanks to both my vampire and tiger genes, neither was I.

If the surety with which Julius grabbed the gun out of my hand was anything to go by, he could also see. He shot Dream through the forehead, ending both her suffering *and* her rallying cry.

"Why the fuck haven't the backup gens kicked in?" Jonas said. "I thought you said you'd secured both the grid and the backup systems?"

"We did," Julius bit back. "But obviously *not* securely enough."

A heartbeat later, a siren started. Jonas swore and glanced at me. "That's the gate closure signal. There must still be people out in the rail yards."

"They're dead people if they don't hurry up and get inside."

"If the entire city has lost its lights, neither the drawbridge nor the wall will stop the vamps."

I knew that better than anyone—the same way I'd gotten into the city countless times at night would be the very method the vampires used. Only this time, the towers would not be alight to stop them.

Julius touched his ear-mic, and after a moment, said, "Thank Rhea for that—at least we've not been left totally defenseless."

Jonas and I shared a glance. Obviously, though this room—and the entire area around government house, if the twilight beyond the shattered windows were anything to go by—had lost light, some of the UV towers remained operational.

There was yet hope that the destruction Nuri envisaged might not yet happen.

"Order an immediate evacuation to the north side of the city," Julius continued. "And that includes all units manning the southern end's wall and the gates. Push them back to the lit areas and set up a new defense line."

"Chief, you can't simply abandon—"

"Ninety-five percent of the population has little to no night vision, Galloway," Julius snapped back. "We have night vision glasses, but they're useless against vampires in shadow form. I'd rather protect who and what we can and get the grid back online ASAP than waste lives fighting what will amount to a black tide we *can't even see*. If the attack in Chaos taught us one thing, it's that humanity has little hope against the vampires when they act to one purpose. And if the wraiths come with them—"

Rhea help us all.

He didn't say those words, but it was what we were all thinking.

"I don't think the wraiths will be a problem," I said, even as I crossed mental fingers. "I don't think they're quite ready to attack just yet."

"I hope you're right," Julius said. "Because the last thing we need are those bastards causing even greater chaos."

Because the wraiths would attack both structure *and* people, whereas the vampires at least only went after life.

"The Others will not be our problem." Nuri stopped on the edge of the dais and stared down at us. "But the only true hope this city has is to get the grid back online. It's not just the local nest Dream called into action—it was all of them."

Jonas stared at Nuri, his gaze narrowed and tension emanating from him. "You have a plan."

"I do."

Her voice was as flat as her expression. Even the halo of her power was tamped down. It almost seemed as if she didn't want to waste the tiniest fraction of energy on any sort of emotional or metaphysical display.

"And I'm gathering it does not involve me."

"It does not."

"I won't—"

"Be of any use up on that wall—"

"I'm a *soldier*," he bit back. "And I have full night vision. I belong on that wall, fighting to protect this city."

"You will *die* on that wall," she snapped. "You might be able to see at night, but you cannot see or sense vampires in shadow. You would be dead in a matter of minutes—"

"As we all will if we keep standing here arguing about it—"

"Not us all, Jonas. Not if we're sensible." She paused. "And is death what you *really* want, after possibly finding the one thing you have long searched for?"

His fists clenched and anger practically leached from every pore in his body. For one instant, he didn't say anything and he didn't move.

Then he looked at me.

And I knew in that instant I was his "possibly."

I didn't know what to say—there were so many emotions tumbling through me, many of them so very new and so very precious. And yet I didn't have the time to think about them, let alone savor them. Night was but minutes away. We had to move.

"I will *not* leave you to fight alone—"

"But I won't be alone," I said. "I'll rally the ghosts again."

"No. It's too great a—"

"It's the city's *only* hope," I cut in, "and you *know* it."

"What I know," he growled, "is that I will *not* leave you and a goddamn bunch of *ghosts* up there alone to fight for this city."

"Ghosts?" Julius said. "What nonsense is this?"

"Catherine is a witch," Nuri said equably. "Only her power is the ability to call those who haunt this world."

"And what dead...." He paused, and an odd sort of dread spread across his expression. "Are we talking déchet who died in the bunker?"

"Yes," Nuri said.

"Is that not dangerous?"

"Yes," I replied.

"*Too* damn dangerous," Jonas said, glaring at me. "I will not allow—"

"You," I said gently, but with a steel that came from too many years of having no control over my own actions, "have no say over what I can and can't do. Not now, not ever. I'm *done* with all that."

He scrubbed a hand across his eyes. *I did not mean—*

I know. I gently touched his arm, and then returned my gaze to Julius. "I've done it once before, when we went into the den that lives in the remnants of the old city's sewage and storm water systems. It was the only reason we were able to get those children out."

"Then do it." Julius glanced at Jonas. "Galloway, I need you to lead engineering into the southern power station—"

"You cannot order me to do anything, *sir*—"

"Jonas," Nuri said coldly. "This fight has moved beyond the grip of mere mortals—it belongs to those of us who are ultimately far more."

"Meaning one woman and a handful of ghosts? That hardly seems fair odds against what comes."

"It is not one woman, but two," Nuri said. "It's time I called to the earth to protect her people. Play your part, Jonas, and allow *us* to play ours."

"Besides," I added softly. "We only have to hold for as long as it takes to get the lights back online. The faster that is done, the greater our odds of survival."

He didn't say anything for several long seconds. He simply stared at Nuri before switching his gaze to me. "Fine. But you survive, no matter *what*. Is that clear?"

I crossed my arms across my chest, although all I wanted to do was to grab him. Hold him. "I will."

He nodded and glanced at Julius. "Is the team being assembled?"

"As we speak. This way."

Julius nodded at Nuri and me, and walked away. Jonas followed, every step echoing with anger and frustration. I glanced at Nuri. "Will he be okay?"

"If he's sensible," she said. "But I'm not entirely sure he's capable of that right now. How fast can you get me to the wall?"

I smiled, though it held little in the way of amusement. "Are you sure you're ready to be transported as matter?"

"It's not like I have any other choice," she replied. "I'm not exactly built for speed, and the vampires are rising as we speak."

Bear, I said, as I walked toward the dais. *Can you go with Jonas? Keep him safe for me?*

And me? Cat said, as Bear chased after Jonas.

I took a deep breath and released it slowly. *I need you to go to Carleen and ask the ghosts to make sure no vampires get through their city. But be careful, Cat, please.*

I will, she said simply, and raced away.

It made me feel altogether too alone. I walked up to Nuri and, once she'd slipped a long, thin backpack over one shoulder, wrapped my arms around her ample body and called to the shadows. Energy surged in response, tearing through me and into Nuri, breaking the two of us down to particles between one heartbeat and another. Feeling her in and around me—separate and yet not—was a very weird, and very *different* experience. And it was in that moment I realized Nuri was far more than a mere human capable of magic. She was the earth personified—she was the richness that gave life, and the quakes that could tear it apart. She held the strength of mountains and the gentleness of the gossamer grass that crawled across the highest peaks. She was human—and yet not. Because of the earth. Because of the power it imbued her with.

And for the first time since the lights had gone dark, I actually felt a sense of hope.

I rose from the platform and shot through the nearest window—it was the quickest way out of the building and into the streets. It was strange to see the veil of darkness drawn around this portion of the city—strange and scary. Central's wide streets were packed with people running toward the southern end, and though many held torches or other kinds of portable lights, they seemed a puny defense against the gathering weight of night. There were buildings dotted randomly throughout the dark streets where lights did twinkle—places that obviously had emergency generators or battery storage in situ that hadn't been affected by the general shutdown. But there was no such light coming from the streets closest to the walls—for the people there it was a daily struggle just to survive. Emergency lighting was not something they could ever have afforded, and it was those sections of the city that would be hit first.

I glanced over my shoulder as I moved forward. The demarcation line between light and dark seemed to be close to Sixth Street, where it intersected with Victory. Every light, every tower, on every building—even the towers lining the curtain wall—beyond that point were ablaze, which at least meant there was a place of safety for Central's residents. There would be no such refuge for those in Chaos. The upper levels might have some access to UV lighting, but for the most part, the ramshackle nature of the place offered little in the way of protection. But then, those who lived there were well aware of the dangers. The most recent attack might have been the most devastating, but it certainly hadn't been the first.

But perhaps they would escape the initial onslaught. Perhaps Dream's rallying call would draw the vampires directly here, to the one place they'd been unable to access since the city's rise from the aftermath of the war.

I followed the straight line of Victory Street, arrowing as fast as I could for the gates. The curtain wall loomed, the tarnished silver of her metal seeming to glow against the gathering shadows. Though the UV towers were no longer ablaze, they still shed a bloody light. It didn't reach down to the wall and wouldn't stop the vampires, but it would at least restrict the air space in which they could move.

Not that *that* would make much difference when half the city lay in darkness.

We drew closer; the drawbridge was up, meaning the soldiers who'd guarded it had hand-cranked it into place before obeying orders and leaving. There was also a ribbon of white following the gentle inner curve of the wall and, after a moment, I realized what it was—light tubing. Obviously, it had its own backup power source, and as such had escaped the destruction of the main grid. It was a shame Central's leaders hadn't similarly separated the wall's UV towers from the main grid and backup gens—but then, who would ever have thought that such treachery could come from one of Central's own?

I swooped up the wall's steep metal side and then came to a halt on top of the wall. Once we were two again, Nuri strode to the edge and looked down. "They come," she said softly. "I can feel the vibration of them through the steel."

I didn't ask how that was possible because it didn't really matter. I flexed my fingers and said, "What's the plan?"

She glanced at me. "Gather your ghosts. I will endeavor to raise a fire wall."

I didn't bother asking what that was, either—I'd find out soon enough. I leaped off the wall, became shadow, and raced across the darkening rail yards and its silent pods to the now destroyed southern exit that had led into my bunker. I might not be able to use it, even in matter form, thanks to the explosion and the compact nature of the rubble that now filled the tunnel, but the déchet soldiers who haunted the lower levels of the bunker wouldn't be similarly restricted.

I followed the sunken line of the trench to the point where it would have entered the old nursery that had become something of an antechamber for the South Siding exit, and then regained form. With little time to waste, I knelt and placed a hand on the ground. I had no idea if it would actually help summon the ghosts, but it couldn't hurt. This was the first time I was contacting them directly—the last time I'd rallied them, I'd done so through Cat. But if I could communicate directly and easily with Carleen's ghosts— who were human—I saw no reason why I could not do so with the déchet soldiers.

I closed my eyes and silently said, with as much force as I could muster, *Déchet soldiers, I need your help again.*

For several seconds there was no response, and then a thick wave of energy began to rise from the earth all around me. A heartbeat later, a sharp voice said, *What is it you ask of us now?*

"Central City has fallen into darkness. I need your help to help protect it from the vampires."

Rising to rescue children is one thing, but why should we now help those who did nothing to save us?

"You cannot hold those who live today accountable for the atrocities of the past—"

Perhaps not. The speaker stepped into view. Death had caught him midchange and he was now forever locked into a form that was a mix of human and bear. He also didn't appear to have his thought and emotional centers medically neutered, which meant he was one of the luckier ones who'd been *chemically* restrained, the effectiveness of which would have disappeared on his death. *But they never saw it as an atrocity, never believed there was anything wrong with erasing our entire population. Has that opinion changed in the time since?*

"No, but allowing *them* to be erased only repeats the mistakes of the past, and makes you no better than them."

A ghost of a smile touched his lips. *And what if we are not?*

"You would not have answered when I called if that were so." I hesitated, and glanced toward the city. A rippling, shimmering curtain of green, browns, pink, and blue was forming above the wall. It wasn't like any sort of light shield I'd ever seen before, but it was nevertheless beautiful. Whether it would be enough to stop the vampires, I had no idea.

And they were so close the stink of them was beginning to stain the air.

"I need an answer, and quickly," I said. "Will you once again follow me into battle?"

A murmur rose all around us; there was so many of them

here that the air shimmered and sparked with a force every bit as powerful as the one over the curtain wall. The bear-man smiled. *Is it not in the end what we were designed for?*

"Then let's go."

I claimed shadow form again and led the charge back to Central. The shimmering multihued curtain grew stronger as I neared the top of the wall, and as I went through, it tore the shadows from me and forced me back to human form.

I stumbled for several steps, then caught my balance and turned around. And saw that it wasn't one shimmering wall, but rather two.

Nuri stood at the rear of the gatehouse. Her face was pale, but her eyes were filled with a light as bright as the rainbow of color that now surrounded us.

"The first barrier of earth fire will force them from shadow, just as it did you." She unslung the pack and handed it to me. "The second forms a thick cap over the darkened parts of the city, and will stop them from entering."

I quickly opened the pack; in it were four long and very deadly looking wooden knives. I drew them out, slung two across my back, and gripped the others. They felt well-made and well-balanced in my hands.

"I know from personal experience just how painful wood embedded into flesh can be," I said, "But will a mere cut be enough to incapacitate them?"

"Yes." She handed me a halo light. "Have your ghosts fan out along the wall. They do not need to kill—they just need to keep throwing the vampires back through the first barrier. Every time the vamps go through it, it will weaken them."

"And you and I?"

"Will be their main target." Her voice was grim. "I cannot fight. I dare not even move, as it's going to take all my strength and concentration to maintain the earth fire barriers. It will be up to you to keep them away from me."

I frowned. "Then why don't you stand on the other side of the second shield?"

"Because I cannot. I must be between the two to maintain them."

"That's rather inconvenient."

A smile ghosted her lips but failed to lift the seriousness from her eyes. "Yes. And while the halo light *will* stop them, it will not stop their ash from falling."

"And if enough of that falls, it could smother the halo's light."

"Yes."

I took a deep breath and released it slowly. "Okay then."

Her smile grew, but it remained a pale imitation of its usual self. "Good luck."

"We're going to need it."

"Indeed." She paused. "They are here."

And with those two words hovering in the air, they hit us.

It was hell itself, broken loose.

Wave after wave poured through the first shield, a seething mass of claws and fury that hit me so fast and so forcefully that, halo light or not, it pushed me back several feet. I swore, braced against the impact of them, and started swinging the long knives. There was no finesse in my blows. There didn't need to be—the wooden blades sliced through the skin of the vampires with the ease of metal, spraying blood and fire through the air. The vampires screamed and went down, their bodies writhing and burning. But both their screams and their bodies were quickly crushed as the vampires behind simply ran over the top of them.

I kept swinging, the blades a blur. Every impact shuddered up my arms, and the black dust of vampire remains rained around me, covering my clothes and staining my skin. Every breath became thick with ash, until it felt like I was going to choke.

They did not stop coming.

No matter how fast I was, no matter how many I sliced and diced, no matter many hit the halo light and became ash, there was simply an endless wall of them.

And the noise—their screeches of fury and pain sliced through the air, the din so loud it had to be echoing right across the city. Nuri's fire walls rippled and swirled every time a vampire hit them, and the smell of sweat and desperation began to taint the air. Not from the vampires.

From her.

She might be powering the shield through earth magic, but she was the connection between the two. And it was taking a toll.

There was nothing I could do for her. Nothing except keep her as free from the vampires as I could.

But it was getting harder.

At least the lines of ghosts to my left and right were standing firm. They tossed the vampires back over the wall time and time again, often in waves as thick as the wall itself.

But, as with Nuri, it was beginning to take a toll. While all ghosts *could* interact with our world, every time they did, it drained them—perhaps even to the point of oblivion.

What the hell were they doing down in Central? Why weren't the lights on yet?

They're working on it, Jonas said, mental tones distant.

Tell them to work faster. These bastards aren't going to stop.

I know. Just hold on.

I didn't get the chance to reply; something crashed into me and sent me flying. I hit the ground with a grunt and, just for a second, the halo light shimmered and died. Vampires piled on top of me, smothering me, biting and tearing at my skin with claws and teeth. The long knives were useless for close work, and I screamed in fury, bucking and kicking in an effort to be free of them. Then the halo light came back online, and the weight that had been pinning me down evaporated into ash. I took a shuddery breath and scrambled upright. Pain twinged down my side, and there was a multitude of cuts on my arms and legs—some deep, some not. The blood pouring from them stung the air and stirred the vampires into a deeper frenzy.

I battled my way back to Nuri, and swung the knives around in fast, circular motions, trying to discourage the vampires who were continuing to fling themselves at her.

The stench of ash and burning flesh was so thick—so caustic—that my stomach churned, and a layer of ankle-deep cindered flesh now smothered the wall's metal base.

And still they came at us.

Many of the ghosts were now beginning fade—even though they kept forcing the vampires back through the fire wall, vampires were getting past them now and flinging themselves at the secondary wall. It torched them as easily and as thoroughly as the halo lights and the UVs, but they didn't seem to care.

And with every hit, the pulsing in the earth fire became more evident—more desperate—and it was a desperation that echoed through Nuri.

Like the ghosts, her strength was fading.

One of my knives hit something solid and stopped dead, and the shock of it reverberated up my arm. Half the blade sheared off and went spinning into the night. I swore, slipped the broken half onto my belt, unslung another, and kept on fighting.

But something glittered near my feet—something that oddly looked like metal. I risked a look. It *was* metal—some sort of pole that had been torn from Rhea only knew where.

The vampires were starting to arm themselves.

Air whistled, and I ducked instinctively. A metal rod swept over my head, missing by inches. I lunged forward, stabbing the vampire through the heart and then spun around to cut off the head of another.

And in that moment, saw Nuri fall.

"No!" I screamed, and ran toward her. Vampires threw themselves between us, piling on top of the other, desperately trying to impede my progress while others tried to smother the protective halo of light. Their ash spun around me, thick and cloying, filling every breath with their foulness. I cut and stabbed and slashed my way through them all, and then knelt in front of Nuri. She lay on her side, her face white and etched with pain, one hand clutching the bar now buried in her stomach. Blood poured from the wound, staining her skirts with a swiftness that spoke of death.

"Get me upright," she panted, eyes still blazing with fury and determination. "I need to be upright."

"No, you need to remain still, and *we* need to stop that bleeding."

Both our halo shields shuddered under the sheer mass of vampires hitting us, and the rain of ash was now so thick the air was almost unbreathable.

"If you don't get me up, this city falls," she bit back. "So fucking do it, soldier, and *now*!"

I swore but did as she asked and hauled her upright as carefully as I could. She hissed and cursed, and cried out in agony, but there was determination there too, and it was as strong as the blood now pulsing over her fingertips.

"I'll be all right," she said. "Just make sure they don't hit me like that again."

"Nuri—"

"I can use the earth magic to halt the flow of blood," she said. "So get up and fight the bastards, before their ash suffocates us both."

"And you call *me* stubborn," I growled.

"I'll call you a whole lot more if you don't do what you're damn well *told*."

I couldn't help grinning, despite the situation. "You sound just like a mom scolding her child."

"If I'd *had* a child, I'd like to think she would have been as fierce and as strong as you." She touched a bloody hand to my face, and I knew that despite everything she might have threatened, she, at least, had never seen me as a monster. "Now go."

I turned away and kept on fighting. I kept close, though, trying to protect her as much as I could. But it wasn't just vampires I was battling now, but a range of missiles from rocks to metal and Rhea only knew what else. The halo light might protect me from the vampires, but it was no help against projectiles, and as many as I batted away, more got through.

Then a large rock appeared out of nowhere. I dropped my knives and thrust out my hands, although I wasn't entirely sure whether I intended to catch it or simply push it aside. Such was the speed at which it was traveling that something snapped in my left wrist and pain bloomed like fire. I nevertheless deflected the rock, not just enough to miss me, but also Nuri. It bounced two feet to her left, continued through the earth fire, and dropped down into Central.

It was only then I realized the earth fire was beginning to fade.

I half spun, only to get hit side-on by something thick and solid. I reeled away, gasping in pain as ribs buckled and cracked. Breathing was suddenly hard and my head spun. I blinked away sweat and tears, and saw a black mass coming straight at me—a mass that was a tumbling, screaming clump of claws, teeth, and fury. I raised my weapons—only to remember I no longer held them. I swore and reached back for my last long knife, but the mass hit me and sent me stumbling backward again.

A heartbeat later, the halo light went out.

I swore, caught my balance, and then ran, with every ounce of strength I had left, at the writhing mass that was now running at Nuri. But I didn't attack it—I leaped *over* it. Claws grabbed at me, tore at me, and I hit the ground in a stumbling run and somehow made it to Nuri. I stepped into the circle of her light, and straddled her back as she hunched over the pole still embedded in her gut, her body shaking and the stain of her life pouring from the wound to the metal floor of the wall, growing ever wider.

I drew the broken knife from my belt and slashed left and right, cutting limbs and faces and bodies. It made no difference. No matter how many I killed, they just kept on coming, an endless tide from which there was no escape and no respite.

Many of the ghosts had now faded completely. Just as many still fought on, but there were ever-increasing gaps along the line, and the vampires obviously sensed that the firewall preventing them from entering the city was close to collapse, because they were throwing themselves at it with growing intensity.

And every hit, every blow, reverberated through Nuri's body and tugged ever more strongly at her fading strength.

I kept on fighting. But my arms were aching, my body bruised and bleeding, and my vision was beginning to fade in and out. If they didn't get the damn UVs on soon, all this would have been for naught.

On and on and *on* it went.

Nuri was shuddering, her breathing so harsh it filled the air with her pain. Inevitably, the first earth fire wall fractured, its brightness fading as it floated away in long, wispy lengths.

The wall at our back—the one that protected Central—was close to doing the same.

As was her halo light. It was pulsing and losing strength.

"Hang on, Nuri," I shouted. "You have to hang—"

A vampire reached through the fading circle of light, hooked its claws into my arm, and yanked me sideways, away from her, away from the light. I was flung like meat into the air, and vampires leaped after me, desperately slashing at my body. I hit the ground on my back but somehow thrust upright, only to be sent sprawling again as a vampire threw himself at me. I somehow shoved the shattered knife between us and impaled him. With a huge whoosh, his body erupted into flames, setting my clothes alight in the process. I screamed, tossed him aside, and reached desperately for the vampire half of my soul.

But even as the change started, something whistled through the air and light exploded around us. The vampires screamed and died. Then a hand grabbed mine, hauled me upright, and ripped the burning clothes from my body.

Jonas.

And he *hadn't* come alone.

There were men everywhere. Men *and* light.

Because even as more bombs went off, the lights in the city came back online, one street after another, until the darkness was banished. The UV towers lining the walls began to glow, but their light was not so instant.

It didn't matter.

The vampires were running.

Reaction set in, and I began shaking so badly I could barely stand. Jonas took off his coat and carefully wrapped it around my shoulders. I hugged it closer, licked my lips, and somehow said, "Nuri—"

"I know." He kissed me quickly—fiercely—and then released me and ran over to her.

I didn't move. I couldn't. All I could do was cry as I watched Jonas kneel down beside her, and touch her shoulder with a gentleness that spoke of how much he cared.

Light began to rise from her body, a light that reminded me of shields that had protected the city.

But it wasn't earth energy.

It was her soul.

I didn't say anything. I couldn't.

For several seconds, neither did she.

Then she smiled, and it was as if the sun had just come out from behind the clouds. *Do not grieve for me, Tiger. It was my time, and there was nothing you could have done to alter my fate.*

I don't agree—

Because you have never believed in giving up—and that is the reason I can leave without regret, because Central now has you to look after her. She hesitated, and glanced down at the man still holding her body. *As has he.*

And with that, she moved on.

Jonas dropped his head and howled in anguish.

Central was safe.

Jonas and I were alive.

But Nuri was no more.

EPILOGUE

Two days later, I once again stood in front of the dais in the Hall of the Lords. Though much of the bomb damage had been cleared, the gracefully arched windows were still boarded up, and there were many seats empty—evidence of the destruction Dream had wrought.

Both Karlinda and Julius stood on the dais in full formal regalia, but this was not a trial, and I was not alone.

Jonas stood beside me.

Cat and Bear hovered either side of us.

While no one in this room would be aware of their presence, they'd played a major part in bringing down Sal, Cohen, and Dream, and they deserved to be here at this ceremony.

"This city owes the two of you a debt that can never truly be repaid," Julius was saying, "You've saved this city not only from a heinous plan to use our children as guinea pigs to gift both the wraiths and vampires light immunity, but also from an attack the likes of which has not been seen in over a hundred years."

He paused as a smattering of polite applause ran around the room. A smile touched my lips. We may have saved them, but Rhea forbid they show too much emotion in this place of rule and tradition.

Applauding is generally frowned upon. Jonas glanced my way, his green eyes glinting brightly in the warm light filling the room. *So it's as overt as you'll ever get here.*

"Jonas Galloway," Julius continued, "in appreciation for your actions, your status as outcast has been struck from the records. You are—and will forever be—a full citizen of Central City, with all rights as a retired general restored."

Jonas bowed. "Thank you."

Julius's gaze switched to me. "Catherine Lysandra, your deep involvement in rescuing the missing children, in exposing those who would have brought this city to its knees —even at the possible cost of your own freedom and life— and in calling forth those who have long been vilified by this city to protect the very same city, has created a debt I doubt we can ever fully repay. So I ask you to name your price, and we shall endeavor to match it."

I glanced uncertainly at Jonas. *Is he serious?*

Very, he replied. *So what is the one the thing you have always wanted, Tiger?*

"Home," I said out loud.

A place for me and for my ghosts—somewhere where we no longer had to fear discovery. A place where we would *always* be safe.

A hint of a smile touched Julius's lips. "I think we'll need a bit more information than that."

My heart raced and my fists were clenched. Hope and excitement surged, but I also feared to unleash them too fully. Feared that the one thing I really wanted was the one thing they would not risk.

I licked my lips and said, "If you are truly serious, then what I desire is the old HDP museum and the grounds around it."

Julius's eyebrows rose. "But that is outside Central's walls, and considered unstable ground besides."

"I'm aware of that, my lord."

"It is also, by your own statement, haunted by the ghosts of the déchet who died there," Karlinda said, a touch of horror in her voice. "I could think of nothing more... unsettling."

"Those ghosts will not harm me," I replied evenly. "But they will visit hell on any vampire who dares step foot in that place."

Julius shared a glance at Karlinda, who simply nodded.

"Are you sure we cannot offer you something more befitting your station?" he said. "An apartment in the mid-districts, perhaps?"

I shook my head. "The museum and the surrounding land is payment enough, and all I desire."

"So be it then." His gaze moved past me. "Lord Renison, please ensure the transfer documents are processed as a matter of urgency."

I blinked against the sudden sting of tears.

I had a home. *We* had a home. A place where I could live with my ghosts and raise Raela in complete and utter safety.

For ever and ever? My two ghosts said together. *It can never be taken away from us?*

Never, ever.

They danced in excitement, their joy so fierce that, for just a second, the air around us sparkled.

"And Nuri?" Jonas asked softly.

"Will be posthumously returned to full citizen status, and her name restored to the halls of her ancestors."

"And she will be given a full state burial," Karlinda added, "as befitting someone of her station and her courage."

Jonas nodded. "Again, thank you."

"Lords, ladies," Julius said. "Please offer your thanks to these two courageous people."

And with a more robust round of polite applause, the ceremony ended. Each lord and lady then stepped up to personally thank us; inevitably, Charles's turn came around.

"I will forever regret that my lack of trust almost caused this great city to fall," he said. "Can you ever forgive me?"

"You did what you thought was right, Charles," I replied

evenly. "I can forgive that, now that the danger has passed and we are all safe."

"Ah." His quick smile was edged with a sadness that told me he'd caught what I *hadn't* said. "I will miss you."

I placed a hand on his arm. "I enjoyed our time together. Please believe that."

"I do." He leaned forward, kissed my cheek lightly, and moved away.

I would not, I knew, ever see him again.

Once the remainder of the lords had thanked us, we were escorted out of the House and into Government House, where we were again officially thanked.

It was close to five by the time we were free. Dusk was still an hour away, but there was already a steady flow of people coming in through the gates—the attack was still too raw a memory for anyone to risk being caught on the platform near dusk.

"So, what happens next?" I asked, as we made our way toward the gate.

"That depends," Jonas replied evenly.

I raised an eyebrow. "Meaning what, Ranger?"

"Meaning," he said, "I would very much like permission to move into that run-down bunker of yours and help you restore it to some sort of order."

"Would you now?" I kept my tone light. "And why would you want to do something like that?"

"Because I have grown somewhat fond of your ghosts, and have found myself missing them these last couple of days."

"So it's just the ghosts you've missed? Because I'm sure I can arrange for Cat and Bear to visit you on a daily basis—"

He laughed, caught my hand, and tugged me into his arms. "Damn it, Tiger, you know it's not just the ghosts. I've missed *you*. I missed *being* with you. I want to explore what lies between us, and I want to help you raise little Raela."

I didn't immediately reply. I just stared into his eyes, seeing in those green depths an echo of all the emotions that were tumbling through me.

Emotions my creators had thought me incapable of.

"I believe I could agree to something like that," I said softly.

"I'm glad," he said, and kissed me.

It was both a promise and a commitment, and it made my blood race and my heart sing.

This man—this ranger—was mine.

"Shall we go home?" he said eventually, and offered me his hand.

I smiled and twined my fingers through his as the two ghosts raced ahead of us.

Ever since I'd been created, all I'd ever wanted was to be accepted for who and what I was.

I had that now. Central City would no longer be a place I had to sneak into. I could come and go as I pleased, whenever I pleased, even if the identity by which I was now known was not truly my own.

But I also had something far more precious—for the first time ever, I had a home.

I had someone who cared and—between the ghosts and little Raela—a family of my own.

For the first time ever, I *belonged*.